# TWO FLAGS
## IN THE
# WILDERNESS

### GREG YOCHERER

## HERITAGE BOOKS, INC.

Published 2002 by

HERITAGE BOOKS, INC.
1540E Pointer Ridge Place, Bowie, Maryland 20716
1-800-398-7709
www.heritagebooks.com

ISBN 0-7884-2143-3

A Complete Catalog Listing Hundreds of Titles
On History, Genealogy, and Americana
Available Free Upon Request

## AUTHOR'S NOTE

Long ago, Professor Harry Brown of Michigan State University required the students in his undergraduate History of the American West class to read Francis Parkman's *Montcalm and Wolfe*. I don't know what effect that book had on my classmates, but from the moment I read it, I've been hooked on the history of the French colonization of North America.

While many of Parkman's historical interpretations have been revised over time, no one has ever surpassed his ability to paint indelible word pictures in the minds of his readers. From *Pioneers of France in the New World*:

> The French dominion is a memory of the past; and when we evoke its departed shades, they rise upon us from their graves in strange, romantic guise. Again their ghostly camp-fires seem to burn, and the fitful light is cast around on lord and vassal and black-robed priest, mingled with wild forms of savage warriors, knit in close fellowship on the same stern errand. A boundless vision grows upon us; an untamed continent; vast wastes of forest verdure; mountains silent in primeval sleep; river, lake and glimmering pool; wilderness oceans mingling with the sky. Such was the domain which France conquered for Civilization.

The years passed and I studied the works of many fine historians who wrote about New France. My interest level never diminished, and I developed a desire to impart my enthusiasm to others. I decided that my vehicle would be historical fiction, but wasn't sure about the exact setting for my story until I read *The Fox Wars* by R. David Edmunds and Joseph L. Peyser. The dramatic possibilities inherent in this heroic, but at the same time tragic episode, immediately attracted me. The end result may not capture the full potential of the subject, but it is the best I could do.

In order to make the book accessible to readers who do not specialize in the Eighteenth Century, I have used modern names for many geographic features. Hopefully, this device will not lessen the enjoyment of readers who are familiar with La Belle Riviere and the Riviere au Boeuf.

I want to acknowledge the invaluable assistance provided by Roxanne Carlson, my editor at Heritage Books. Her recommendations, particularly concerning dialogue revisions, were sorely needed and much appreciated. My regular contact at the publisher, Corinne Will, provided encouragement and responded to my questions with dispatch. Doretta Olsen filled in the numerous gaps in my knowledge of Word Perfect. Chris Pappas did a great job on the maps and the cover illustration. Finally, the staff of Fort Ticonderoga and the attendees of the annual War College of the Seven Years War at that site have invariably been generous with their insights.


Greg Yocherer
Streamwood, Illinois
April, 2002

For my family, who have always been there
when I needed them.

# MAPS

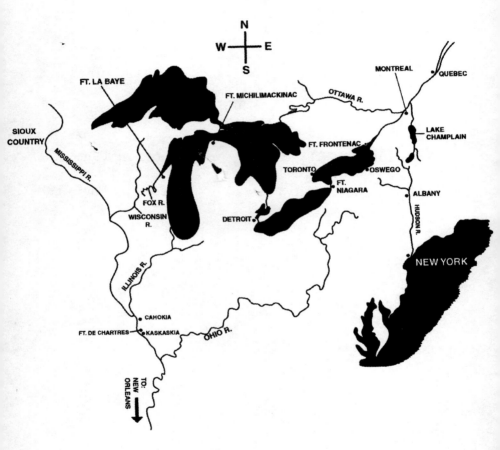

## CHAPTER 1
May, 1731


Jean Baptiste's muscles ached. It was a month since they had left Michilimackinac, but he was still not used to paddling ten or more hours each day. He had to admit that progress was much easier than it had been when they first left Green Bay. Battling upstream on the lower Fox River had been exhausting work, especially when rapids or obstructions in the river made portages necessary. At those points, the canoes would be landed and all the merchandise off-loaded. The canoes, along with the barrels, bundles and boxes of trade goods and supplies would be carried around the rough or blocked stretch of water. The vessels would then be launched again, the goods reloaded and the paddling would continue until another trouble spot was encountered; then the entire process would be repeated. The distance from Green Bay to the Lake of the Winnebagos was only fifteen leagues, but this short trip had required a full week to complete.

On the upper Fox, the French party still traveled upstream, but the current was much slower, meaning distances could be covered with much less exertion.

Then, a few days ago, they had portaged from the upper Fox, which flowed northeast to Green Bay, to the Wisconsin River, which flowed southwest to the Mississippi. Now moving with the current, the canoes sped downstream, past high bluffs and numerous wooded islands. The weather as well as the current proved cooperative; the sun blazed through crisp, clear air, and everyone's spirits were high.

Today promised to be different. The chill in the air this morning added to Jean Baptiste's stiffness. The weather was still unusually cool, an hour after they had broken camp and resumed their journey. The lad was glad he had decided to wear his gray-white capote over his blue veste. His blue woolen fatigue cap, complete with tassel and the anchor symbol of the marines, added another element of warmth, though he knew his soiled and travel worn uniform would never pass one of Sergeant Fournier's inspections. A heavy mist hung over the river, but even the cool, damp conditions could not depress his spirits. In a few hours they would reach the mighty Mississippi! Only seventeen years old, Jean Baptiste Joubert, Sieur de St. Croix, a cadet in the Compagnies franches de la Marine was still excited about experiencing his first great military adventure.

His older brother Maurice, a lieutenant, was in charge of the expedition. At twenty-six, Maurice was a veteran of eleven years service in the marines, the regular troops stationed at the scattered outposts of New France. A dedicated soldier, he fancied himself to be a ladies' man. Usually thought handsome, with the scar from an old Mascouten arrow wound giving his face desired dash, he normally dressed in a well tailored off-white and blue marine uniform while on leave, his golden gorget of rank buffed to a high shine.

Having a greater appreciation of the hazardous nature of the present assignment, Maurice was somewhat less euphoric than his young brother at the moment. Due to the manpower shortage at their post on the Straits of Mackinac, only three enlisted men and Jean Baptiste could be spared from the garrison.  With this small force he was to lead and protect a convoy of canoes carrying trade goods and supplies needed to re-establish the profitable commerce with the Sioux, commerce which had been badly disrupted by the recent war between the French and the Fox tribe.  The French had been victorious and the power of the Fox broken, at least temporarily.  However, roaming bands of Fox warriors were still a threat along the Fox-Wisconsin waterway, and Maurice knew better than to underestimate them.  He had fought them on a number of occasions, and they had always proven not only brave but unusually determined adversaries.

The lieutenant's party was less than a day's journey from the Mississippi. Although they would again have to travel upstream once the great river was reached, he would feel more at ease. When they headed north on the Mississippi toward Sioux country, they would be leaving Fox territory and would paddle along the west bank, making a surprise attack from Fox lands to the east more difficult.

Maurice was proud of his young brother. The lad had been in the service less than two years, but had learned quickly and well under the guidance of old Sergeant Fournier.  His swift progress as a cadet, or officer candidate, had been noted by both the previous post commandant, Captain Dubuisson, and the present one, Captain Montigny. Both of these elderly gentlemen had long and distinguished military careers in New France, Montigny having received the coveted Cross of the Order of St. Louis nearly twenty years ago, and both seemed to feel that Jean Baptiste would develop into an effective marine officer. The boy was adept at the manual of arms, woodcraft and small unit exercises. Perhaps best of all, he was able to develop a warm rapport with the Indians living in the vicinity of the fort, particularly the Ottawas. His marksmanship was average at best, but hopefully would improve in time. Considering their father's influence and the boy's real merit, Maurice felt certain that Jean Baptiste would attain an ensign's commission within a year or two.

The lieutenant was in the lead canoe with Jean Baptiste and a fusilier named Arbut. Two large canoes were next, carrying the bulk of the supplies and manned by six paddlers each. Most of these men were traders or *voyageurs* with years of experience in the woods. They were led by a jolly rascal named Etienne Dufort, who had a reputation that scandalized the Jesuits, but who nonetheless was held to be a cool head in a tight situation. The only man with no wilderness experience was the clerk, Rene La Pointe, who would be in charge of business activity at the Sioux post. Despite a rather delicate appearance, he had learned rapidly on the journey, handled his paddle with some skill, and seemed to be enjoying himself. Finally, the other two fusiliers, Leveau and Murat, formed the rear guard in a small canoe like Maurice's.

"Close up! Leveau, Murat – Get that canoe in front of you moving! No gaps in the line – No stragglers." The lieutenant wanted to get to the Mississippi as quickly as possible, leaving this area where he felt so vulnerable.

They coasted along the north shore of an large, heavily wooded island in the river. The island split the stream into two relatively narrow channels. They had not used the south channel because from a distance, they had seen a number of fallen trees blocking the way. Maurice sensed that something was not right, and alerted the men by raising his paddle straight over his head. Their scout, an Ottawa named The Turtle, had left camp an hour before them, proceeding on foot along the north bank of the river in order to warn the canoes of possible danger. Normally, The Turtle would leave a sign for them on shore at a place like this, letting them know that the way was clear and also instructing them which channel to take. Maurice could locate no marker from the scout.

"Make sure your weapons are handy," he told his young brother, who was seated directly behind him in the canoe. "Something is wrong. The Turtle should have left a sign for us here. Dufort! Move up close to us and have your muskets ready."

Jean Baptiste heard a noise to his left and looked toward the island. Suddenly, something dropped from high in one of the tall trees near the island's shore. Its crashing through the branches alerted the French, but the object did not reach the water. A rope tied around its middle arrested its fall when it was still ten feet above the river. The other end of the rope had been tied to a stout branch, and the bound object bounced up and down several times, accompanied by falling leaves and broken branches, before twisting slowly at the end of the rope.

It was The Turtle. At least the corpse was wearing leggings and a shirt that Jean Baptiste recognized as those of the Ottawa scout. He had been scalped and his face mutilated. A lance had been driven completely through his body and left there. The men of the convoy were momentarily frozen by this horrific sight. Suddenly, Jean Baptiste heard a splash behind him, along with the shouts of several men. He turned in time to see an enormous Indian, his entire body painted red and black, bald except for a red crest of hair running front to back, explode from the water and overturn the canoe containing the rear guard marines. The warrior had swum underwater from the north bank of the river, the diversion caused by the sudden appearance of The Turtle having directed the Frenchmen's attention the opposite way. The young cadet fired quickly, but missed. In a moment, the giant Fox had stabbed Murat in the chest, and then grappled with Leveau.

A ragged volley of shots and arrows struck the convoy as Jean Baptiste watched the struggle in the water, while at the same time pulling a pistol from his belt. Maurice shot the warrior who had dropped The Turtle's body from the tree, then Jean Baptiste heard his brother grunt. Turning from the struggle in the water, the youngster saw that an arrow had gone through Maurice's upper arm. As he reached to help his brother, from the corner of his eye he saw something approach underwater. The warrior emerged from the depths like a giant sturgeon leaping, intending to overturn this canoe as well. The boy had a quick impression of a snarling countenance, the entire head painted black except for a white mask around the eyes. With no time for thought, The boy fired into the Indian's face, blowing much of the back of his head away. The Fox's look changed to one of surprise as he sank back into the river.

Maurice had been hit again, this time a musket

ball in his side. He yelled to the others "Get downstream as quick as you can! Don't stay here and fight. They've had time to prepare this spot, and we don't know their numbers. Keep moving! Keep moving!"

The fusilier Arbut, paddling in the rear of Maurice's vessel, needed no further urging. Although not a big man, fear multiplied his strength, and the canoe shot forward. Dufort dispatched the giant warrior at the rear of the convoy with a musket shot, but three more Foxes had swum to the scene and captured Leveau. The three were using the marine as a shield as they waded toward the island.

Jean Baptiste had reloaded his musket and debated whether to shoot Leveau. He had little time to consider the matter, but decided not to, leaving the man to his captors' dubious mercy. Maurice was losing consciousness, probably from blood loss. The young cadet had to act. He hoped he remembered what Maurice and Sergeant Fournier had taught. From the number of shots fired at them, the boy knew the enemy party was fairly numerous. In addition to The Turtle and the three marine casualties, he could see that at least five men in the two large canoes had been hit. They had to break away. Above all, the trade goods, which included muskets, shot and powder, had to be kept out of the hands of their attackers.

"Dufort!" he yelled. "Get your men moving!"

"What about Leveau?" asked the portly trader.

"We have to leave him. We'll all be dead or prisoners if we don't get out of here."

Kiala watched the three remaining canoes disappear down river. The ambush had not gone well.

Something had alerted the French commander just before the trap was sprung, and they had recovered very quickly from the shock of seeing their dead scout. As a result, two of Kiala's men were dead, and a third had injuries that would probably prove fatal. Though his remaining warriors, eight in number, had wanted to pursue the French, he recalled them. Their enemy had been hurt, but was now fully alert. Additional Fox casualties were simply unacceptable. In the past year, the Fox had suffered disastrous losses at the hands of the French and the many pro-French tribes. Not only warriors, but also hundreds of women and children had died. Many others had been captured and now lived among enemies such as the Illinois and the Potawatomi. The surviving core of warriors had to be maintained and hopefully strengthened through alliance with formerly friendly tribes, such as the Mascoutens, the Kickapoos and the Sacs. Wisaka had not smiled on his people this day. The Fox desperately needed the supplies and weapons carried in those canoes. Kiala had thought that if the marines in the two small canoes were quickly put out of action, the two large canoes would be his at little cost. It had not worked out that way, not this time.

"Kiala." The war leader was aroused from his thoughts by the voice of Beaver Tail, one of the warriors who was angry because they had not pursued the French. "What shall we do with this prisoner?"

Leveau had not been seriously injured, but he was terrified. He had been a marine since the spring of 1726, joining the service in his native Normandy and subsequently assigned to duty in New France. He had participated in two campaigns against the Fox, and knew the fate that frequently awaited captives. Leveau had no knowledge of the Fox tongue however, and so was ignorant of what was being said.

Kiala realized that his men were bitterly disappointed that the two supply canoes had escaped. They had expected many scalps, and so far, had only two. Beaver Tail and the others were also in a rage over their losses. Kiala knew that these men would not continue to follow him if his leadership resulted in failure. Although he would have preferred to save the prisoner until they returned to camp so that the whole village could enjoy the sport, he decided to placate his disgruntled followers.

"Because time was short, we had no opportunity to test the courage of the Ottawa. We have time now. We will stay here until Elk Horn dies or shows signs of recovery. Meanwhile, let us burn the Frenchman, giving him a chance to prove he is a man."

This decision was greeted with enthusiasm. Several warriors selected a young tree, cut it down, trimmed it, sharpened one end of the trunk, and buried the sharpened end deep in the middle of a space cleared of underbrush. Kindling was gathered and spread around the base of the trunk. Leveau began to realize what was coming and suddenly envied the quick demise of his friend Murat. He struggled against the ropes that bound him, but to no avail.

When darkness fell, the torture began. Kiala did not participate, instead withdrawing down river along the bank a short distance where he could contemplate his next move. The screams of the marine echoed through the woods all night, until toward dawn, his soul fled at last.

The survivors of the convoy were relieved at their

escape, but wondered if their deliverance was only temporary. Two of the voyageurs had been killed outright. Four of the others were wounded, two of them seriously. Before noon they abandoned and sunk the remaining small scout canoe in order to consolidate their depleted manpower on the larger vessels carrying the supplies. As their gear and the semi-conscious Maurice were transferred from the small canoe, Jean Baptiste and Dufort had time to talk.

"How are your wounded?" the young cadet asked.

"Antoine is bad. The ball got a lung. I think the other three will pull through, but only one of them will be any use with a paddle now. That leaves only nine of us to handle these canoes, eight if we don't count the injured man. How is your brother?"

"He is bad too. Arbut has some experience tending the injured, but he says more skill than he possesses is needed. We got the arrow out of his arm, but the ball in his side worries me."

At nightfall, they reached the Mississippi and had a decision to make. Dufort opened the conversation as the two canoes floated side by side, the paddlers smoking their pipes during a rest period.

"I'd suggest that we consider going south on the big river instead of north to Sioux country. We hardly have enough men to make headway against the current, we are not in condition to fight off another attack, and if we are attacked again and lose, all this powder and shot will fall into those bastards' hands. Besides, at Cahokia, your brother could get the medical attention he needs. So could Antoine and the others."

"I hate to abandon our mission, but I think you're right. During lucid moments, Maurice says not to worry about him, but Arbut thinks his condition is very serious. I won't lose him."

Dufort added, "We need to tell our people in the Illinois Country that the Fox are on the prowl again. In the past, those settlements and the nearby Illinois villages have been favorite targets."

The cadet changed the subject. "What was La Pointe shooting back there? It sounded like artillery going off."

"He has two large bore pistols that he carries at all times. I don't know what he loads them with, and I doubt he hit anyone, but the noise alone had to be worth something."

"By the way, you and all your men did well at the ambush. That was a nice shot you made on the giant."

"You did fine yourself youngster. I imagine that pistol ball gave raccoon face a hell of a headache, though I doubt it lasted too long."

With that Etienne roared with laughter, and his men joined in, even the wounded ones. Antoine laughed hard enough to start his wound bleeding again, and for a time they thought it was his finish. The convoy crossed the Mississippi and camped on the west bank, about fifteen leagues from the scene of the fight. They kept a three man guard all night.

Jean Baptiste could not sleep. The events of the day kept running through his mind. The body of The Turtle, Maurice's injuries, the death of "Raccoon Face," abandoning Leveau. Quitting the mission might blight his career before it was fairly started, but his concern for his brother plus the other considerations discussed persuaded him that heading south was the right decision. He got up to check the guards, inquired how one of them who had been lightly wounded was feeling, then headed off a short distance into the woods where he could be alone. Suddenly, his body began to tremble, he dropped to his knees and became violently ill.

## CHAPTER 2

Six days later the two canoes neared Cahokia, northernmost of the French settlements in the Illinois Country. The wounded voyageur Antoine did not get that far. Two days earlier, he succumbed to his wound and they buried him on the west bank of the Mississippi. Today, a bright, very warm and humid day, the little party spied a single canoe approaching from the south as they glided with the current. The small canoe, containing two occupants, angled toward the east shore as they approached. Dufort bellowed in the Cahokia dialect that they were French and therefore friends. The small canoe changed direction again and cautiously approached.

The canoe contained two warriors, a Cahokia and a Kaskaskia, two of the tribes of the Illinois confederation. The Cahokia was the younger of the two; his companion was not only older, but substantially overweight and rather dissolute in appearance. Each wore only a breechcloth and moccasins. The Cahokia wore his hair in a scalplock with a single hawk feather dangling in back. The Kaskaskia's hair was long, hung in a greasy mass to his shoulders, and was held in place with a red bandana. They asked Dufort if he had brandy.

He passed them a jug and asked if they would accompany the French to Cahokia. Dufort knew the way, but with liberal applications of strong drink, he thought he might learn something useful concerning the situation in the French settlements. The two Indians looked greedily at the piles of trade goods in the canoes and eagerly agreed to accompany the French.

Two hours later, they reached the landing at Cahokia, which was shielded by the Island of the Holy Family. This island had been formed by a small channel of the great river, and separated the town from the main body of the Mississippi. Little information was obtained from their new companions, other than the news that little brandy was available in the settlements at the moment. They had soon drunk themselves into semi-consciousness, and barely made it to the landing before passing out. The town was a short distance from the river, and was reached via a narrow, unpaved road. By the time they came ashore, a small crowd of traders, settlers, slaves, voyageurs and Indians had gathered. Dufort assigned two men to guard the canoes, then he and another husky voyageur carried Maurice toward the village, using a stretcher hastily constructed from two stout tree branches and a blanket.

Arbut had been a zealous nurse, but Maurice's condition was obviously critical. Despite their attempts to keep his wounds clean and freshly bandaged, the lieutenant's arm was swollen and discolored, and had begun to emit a foul odor.

"Head toward the church," Jean Baptiste instructed Dufort, pointing toward the largest building in the tiny settlement. For ten years the lad had been educated by the Jesuits at Montreal, and he knew they prided themselves on the breadth as well as the depth of their learning. Missionaries assigned to the wilderness posts usually acquired significant medical knowledge through tending to the needs of their flocks, even if their formal medical training was rudimentary.

In this regard, Maurice and the other injured men were fortunate, although Father Jean-Paul Mercier was not a Jesuit. Born in Quebec and educated at the seminary in that city, in 1718 he had been assigned to the Saint-Famille Mission which the seminary maintained among the Cahokia tribesmen. In the succeeding thirteen years, the kindly priest had acquired a good deal of practical medical knowledge, having tended the wounded resulting from the frequent intertribal warfare as well as the even more common drunken brawls that plagued the various Illinois tribes. Now thirty-six years of age, with thinning blond hair and a very spare, almost emaciated physique, his dark robe billowing in the warm breeze, he spotted the new arrivals approaching and greeted them at the rear door of the church.

"Bring the man on the stretcher in here and put him on the table."

Dufort and the other voyageur did as they were told, placing Maurice on the indicated table after the priest removed a chess position he had been studying. The room seemed to be a combination bedroom and study for the priests and lay brothers of the mission. The furniture was plain and sparse, but sturdily built. The priest motioned to the other injured men from the convoy to sit on the beds scattered around the room.

"What happened to these men?" the priest asked. In as few words as possible, Jean Baptiste recounted the events of the past week.

"I wonder if this will ever end. I thought the slaughter last year ended the Fox threat, but I was mistaken. Please, those of you who are unhurt, would you be so kind as to wait outside while I see to these men? Thank you."

Jean Baptiste had noticed Maurice looking at the chessboard as the youngster talked to the missionary. As the uninjured men filed from the room, the lad heard his brother mutter "White to move and mate in three."

Dufort went back to the landing. He had to find a secure spot for their trade goods and equipment, to avoid the possibility of pillage by the numerous Illinois who lounged around the village. Jean Baptiste waited near the church so that he could learn of his brother's condition as soon as possible.

The sky was very clear, with only a few soft looking, fluffy clouds off to the west. This was the lad's first opportunity to study his surroundings. The combination church/residence was a substantial structure, about thirty paces in length and half as wide. The church property also included a barn and a stable, along with cabins for the slaves. The latter were responsible for the garden, the orchard and the acreage under cultivation. By all accounts, their efforts had been crowned with notable success. The village contained about two score buildings in all. The houses of the permanent residents (seven in number) were clustered together, each with broad eaves and prominent verandas and surrounded by a fence and garden. Several blockhouses were in evidence, the largest near the east edge of town.

The land here in the Illinois Country, bounded by an upland that roughly paralleled the river about a league inland, was reputed to have the richest soil of any of France's New World possessions. Looking east through a break in the trees, Jean Baptiste could see the wheat and rye fields about which he had heard. Turning back toward the river, he studied the buildings down the slope from the church. Numbers of Indians and Frenchmen were gathered around three of them. He assumed these to be trading houses, where everything from sewing needles and blankets to hatchets and muskets could be obtained, primarily in exchange for furs. He assumed that the trade items attracting significant attention at the moment were wine and brandy.

"Jean Baptiste!" The lad turned and saw Father Mercier motioning to him. He directed the youngster to accompany him as he walked a short distance from the church.

"The others will recover completely in a few weeks, the Lord willing, but Maurice's condition is grave. The wound in his side is healing well, but I'm afraid he must lose the arm. There is no alternative. I've seen this before – the swelling, the smell, the unnatural color. If the arm is not removed soon, the sickness will spread and he will die."

Jean Baptiste was numb. Thoughts of the past flooded into his head. Two years ago, when he celebrated his fifteenth birthday, his father told him that he should join the marines as his brothers had before him. The Jouberts were a power in the Montreal fur business, partially because having family members in the marine officer corps aided the family enterprise. Officers at the various interior posts were allowed to participate in the fur trade with the local tribes, and officers from the best-connected families tended to receive the most lucrative assignments.

Jean Baptiste had been unsure that he was ready for the challenge. He knew his father did not merely want him to join the marines, but expected him to rise to the rank of lieutenant or even captain. The Joubert name could probably guarantee appointment as a cadet, or officer trainee, but the rest was up to him. He had felt his stomach begin to churn until his father assured him that he could be placed in Maurice's company at Michilimackinac. As he grew up, Maurice had treated him well (this had not always been the case with Louis and Jacques, his other brothers). When home on leave, Maurice would take the lad fishing or hunting, and spent time teaching him chess and various card games. Although he could not show overt favoritism once the boy became a cadet, Maurice helped him as much as possible with his study of Indian dialects, and introduced him to various members of the nearby Ottawa village. Maurice made sure that Sergeant Fournier was Jean Baptiste's primary instructor. The sergeant was a hard man, but a fair one, and he worked diligently to make officer material of the boy.

The reality of the present situation began to sink in. The lad was sure that their father could use Maurice in the family fur business, but it was the end of his career in the woods he loved. Two arms were needed to function effectively.

"Let me speak to him," requested the boy.

" He already knows the situation and said he would follow my advice. Your brother has courage in large measure."

Jean Baptiste went inside to see his brother. The boy had tears in his eyes.

The lieutenant was lying on his back, drops of perspiration on his forehead. When he saw the youngster, his face brightened.

"Don't be so sad, brother. I was getting tired of paddling canoes anyway. I'll be spending more time at home, with opportunities to chase some of the buxom beauties in Montreal. Being a wounded hero of the Fox Wars should immeasurably boost my social life. By the way, don't forget to notify the commandant at Fort de Chartres about the Fox. The fort is a dozen leagues south of here. And don't worry – I'll be fine."

The cadet knew it was his responsibility to travel to Fort de Chartres and report in person to the commander, Lieutenant St. Ange. He decided on another course because he wanted to remain near Maurice until the crisis was past. He originally thought to send Etienne Dufort in his stead, but the affable voyageur did not want to go either. He had grown fond of the brothers during this trip, and he also wanted to make certain of Maurice's recovery.

"Send La Pointe," Dufort suggested. "He's an educated man. He'll be able to give a clear account of our trip. Besides, I have a few outstanding debts there from awhile back. It's probably best that I remain scarce in those parts."

Jean Baptiste summoned La Pointe, the heavily armed clerk. "Rene, I want you to travel to Fort de Chartres and tell the commander about the ambush. The Fox have raided in this area for many years. After their defeat last year, most people thought they were finished militarily. We have to let the local marine establishment know so they will be on their guard. Take a local man as a guide and one of our voyageurs. I should be the one to go, but I don't want to leave my brother."

"If the Fox catch and roast me over a slow fire, you'll never forgive yourself," joked La Pointe. "I'll do my best and get back as soon as I can." He then borrowed a musket, a hatchet and Dufort's monstrous hunting knife to augment his already formidable armament, and set off on his errand.

Just then Father Courier, one of the very young priests of the mission, approached Jean Baptiste and told him that Father Mercier was ready to attempt the surgery and needed his assistance. Dufort volunteered to help as well. When they entered the priests' quarters, one of the lay brothers had just finished administering copious quantities of brandy to the wounded officer, and the latter was quietly singing snatches of various voyageurs'songs.

Father Mercier offered a prayer for the injured man's recovery, and then asked Maurice if he was ready. The young lieutenant nodded.

"Jean Baptiste – hold his legs.  Etienne and Brother Paul, the arms.  Let us begin."

Maurice held a thick stick of wood between his teeth to bite when the pain became intense.  Beads of sweat multiplied on his forehead, and he looked frightened.

"Don't worry brother; I'm here," said Jean Baptiste. He and the others maneuvered to hold Maurice's body in place.  Then it began.

Jean Baptiste could hear the grinding sound as his brother bit into the stick when the priest began to saw. After a few minutes, a scream escaped the patient's throat despite the stick.  Mercifully, he lapsed into unconsciousness at this point, and the operation was completed while he was insensible. The arm was removed about a hand's breadth above the elbow.

"He should sleep for many hours now," said the priest as he finished bandaging the stump. "He is young and strong. If he gets through the next two days, I think he will survive, with the Lord's help. Brother Paul, please remove the arm. We'll bury it in the parish cemetery. Now, everyone out and let the man rest."

As the cadet and Dufort left the church, the older man said "Come lad, let's go to Legard's trading house and get something to drink. I know I could use it and I assume you could too."

Jean Baptiste offered no objection. He needed to forget the sight, sound and smell of what had just happened, if only temporarily. Night had fallen, and it felt wonderful to be out in the fresh air.

The air in Legard's was less fresh, due to the number of men smoking pipes in the confined space. Legard was a former *coureur de bois* who had been badly mauled by a bear some years before. No longer able to roam among the tribes and trade for furs, he decided to open a trading house near the Cahokia mission. By all accounts an honest man, his business had prospered. Despite some ugly scars on his left cheek, souvenirs of the bear, he still had the look of a man who enjoyed life. He was married to a Cahokia squaw, and through her tried to make sure that some of the more attractive women of the tribe were on the premises, thus assuring the presence of numerous male customers, both white and red.

As they entered, a bearded trader named Gaspard Roziere was complaining to anyone who would listen that something had to be done about the scarcity of trade goods normally shipped from New Orleans.

"How are we supposed to do business? The Illinois on this side of the river as well as the Iowas, Otoes and Missourias on the other side trapped plenty of beaver as well as other animals last winter. Their villages are loaded with prime pelts, and here we are, with little or nothing to offer in exchange." The two men with him, French-Cahokia *metis* named Claude and Michel, were in the process of agreeing with him when the three of them noticed Jean Baptiste and Dufort.

"Here are the only traders with merchandise, this young whelp and his ugly friend from Montreal. Can you believe it? The Illinois Country is no longer part of Canada, but is now part of Louisiana. Profits from the fur trade here should benefit our people, but it looks like the only ones who will do well this year are these curs from Canada. All because our suppliers in New Orleans are too timid to send us anything unless it is guarded by an army."

"Pardon me," interjected Dufort. "I couldn't help but hear you call me the 'ugly friend from Montreal.'" Without further ado he broke a stool he had picked up over Roziere's head. As the latter sank to the floor, Dufort continued "I'll have you know I'm originally from Trois Rivieres." He grabbed Claude and Michel by their throats and asked "Will there be any unpleasantness from you two gentlemen? No? – That's good. Revive your friend and let's all have a drink."

Maurice survived the next two days, and as the priest had predicted, he began to return to health. On the fourth day after the amputation, La Pointe returned to Cahokia, along with a sergeant and nine marines from the Fort de Chartres garrison. He had also added to his personal arsenal by somehow acquiring a sergeant's halberd. The troops took possession of the large blockhouse on the east edge of town.

"Why do you need that pike?" inquired Jean Baptiste.

"One needs to be prepared for any emergency. Besides, Sergeant Cavallier lost rather heavily when we were playing cards at the fort. He can't pay his debt at the moment, so as security I accepted his halberd. He has to pay up before Lieutenant St. Ange has another inspection, or he will have a lot of explaining to do. The situation has not improved the sergeant's somewhat sullen disposition."

"I'm glad you were able to bring some men to help protect the town. How were things at de Chartres?"

"I'm not an expert in military matters, but it seems to me that the lieutenant knows his business and runs a well disciplined post, though the structure itself looks in need of repair. He is very concerned about new trouble with the Fox. Over the years, the Illinois Country has suffered much at their hands. Farmers have been killed while working their fields, couriers have been attacked while trying to communicate with outlying settlements, entire families have been slaughtered with appalling cruelty in their homes, woodcutters and hunters from the fort have died within sight of the palisades. The various Illinois tribes in the nearby villages have been defeated so often that their survival has been in doubt at times."

"At any rate, as I said, I'm no soldier. One thing that puzzles me is the location of this fort. It is between the two largest centers of population, Cahokia and Kaskaskia, but is many hours travel from either town. I suppose it is well situated to offer sanctuary to the settlers if they know an attack is coming, but in the case of a surprise assault, I don't see how the garrison could offer timely assistance. I felt it my duty to slightly embellish the story of the ambush, estimating the enemy force at fifty to sixty. That persuaded the lieutenant to recall a patrol that had left for Kaskaskia several hours before. He decided to send them here, a more exposed location."

"Well done, Rene. You must be tired from hauling all that hardware around. Why don't you store all but the most essential two or three weapons and get some rest."

"Sounds good to me. Oh, I almost forgot. Lieutenant St. Ange sent a cask of his best wine and said he hopes Maurice recovers quickly."

Jean Baptiste knew it was time for a strategy session. The mission to the Sioux had come to naught, but their trade goods were intact and he had confirmed what the trader Roziere had said about the plentiful furs in the Illinois villages. Confident that the Fox threat had been eliminated by their crushing defeat last year, the various Illinois villages had dispersed into their much smaller winter camps the previous autumn, and they had harvested a huge number of furs. Their lodges were filled with pelts and they were eager to trade. Most of the Indians were low on powder and shot and new muskets were needed, as well as cooking pots, sewing needles, awls and steel knives. Brightly colored cloth, blankets, ribbons and beads would also find a ready market. Jean Baptiste's party had all of these things. He needed to talk to his brother.

"Maurice, the color is returning to your face. You look well. How do you feel?"

"Sometimes, it feels like my arm is still there and it hurts, but overall, I'm much better."

"Rene La Pointe has returned from the fort with ten men from the garrison to protect Cahokia. The whole area is on the alert. Now I think we need to plan our future actions."

"Buy Rene a bottle from me. What do you have in mind?"

"I've spoken to Dufort, and he seems to have some good ideas. We've got our trade goods stored at Legard's trading house. It's the biggest one in the area, and from what Dufort has discovered from talking to honest settlers as well as visiting every den of corruption within ten leagues, Legard is a fair man."

"Due to Indian trouble on the lower Mississippi, trade goods are scarce in the Illinois Country. We would have no trouble disposing of all our merchandise right here, exchanging it for the furs of the Illinois tribes. There is a problem, though. We are from Canada, and although the Illinois Country used to be part of Canada, some years ago it was placed under the administration of Louisiana. Although both colonies are French, competition for furs between traders from the two areas has been keen for a long time. I've even heard that some here think that our Governor General Beauharnois did less than his best to end the Fox threat, because the disruption they caused in Illinois territory benefitted the trade of Canada."

"Scandalous talk, though I've heard much the same thing at Michilimackinac. Supposedly, Beauharnois approached the Fox problem with little enthusiasm until his position was threatened by the Minister of Marine, unless he took effective action. I'm not sure what his attitude was earlier, but for the past several years, he has been a deadly enemy of the Fox. Maybe it was the minister who focused his attention."

Getting back to his original subject, Jean Baptiste continued. "The locals will not be happy if we trade our goods to the Illinois, their long-time customers. Roziere and the others won't like to see us depart with all the profits while they have to sit and watch due to a lack of goods from New Orleans. There might be trouble, and we have no desire for that, especially since these people have been kind to us in our time of need. Dufort suggests that we sell half of our goods to the local traders (at a modest profit of course), and trade the other half to the Illinois. In that way, we dispose of our goods, make a decent profit, the Indians are happy, and the local traders have benefitted as well."

"Sounds like a good plan," said Maurice. "I've been thinking about our military situation and have decided to send you back to Michilimackinac to report the ambush and the failure of our mission to the Sioux. Captain Montigny will need to report to Montreal as soon as possible to find out what action is required. Concerning the trading, we can ship our furs down river to New Orleans. Father has dealt with the trading firm of Hebert and Prevost on a number of occasions. They will ensure that the furs bring a fair price, and will credit father's account, less a commission.

"Without the furs you will be able to return to the straits unencumbered, and will be a less tempting target. In addition to our surviving voyageurs, hire some of the local men for extra protection. After wintering with their Illinois wives and their wives' relations, you should be able to find some Frenchmen willing to go. Promise them double the normal wages.  You can try to hire some of the Illinois as well, but news of the trouble has reached their camps, and I doubt you will find many volunteers.  I think the Fox will leave you alone this trip.  Your party will be strong and their scouts will notice that you will be carrying neither trade goods nor furs.  To attack would mean a hard fight with little profit.

"As for myself, I think I'll stay here awhile, rest and play chess with Father Mercier.  He must spend time studying things other than the Bible – he has a strong game.  I'll keep Arbut with me.  When I'm stronger, I'll head down river to New Orleans.  Who knows, a wounded hero of the Fox Wars may be attractive to the women there as well.  When he has completed the sale of our furs, Jean Hebert should be able to arrange passage for me back to the St. Lawrence valley.  I'll wager I'm home before you."

Jean Baptiste wanted to protest, but he saw the wisdom of his brother's plan. It was agreed.  The young cadet rose from the bench on which he had been sitting and prepared to set the plan in motion.  He hesitated. "Maurice, we have talked often about your experiences in the marines.  Concerning most subjects you are very open, but whenever last year's Fox campaign is mentioned, you change the subject with as little comment as possible.  I know we won a great victory.  Why does it trouble you?"

"I'm not sure I'd call it a great victory.  I've been thinking of the events of that summer often in the last few days, at times thinking that this wound is my just reward for the part I played in that nightmare."

Jean Baptiste started to protest, but Maurice motioned him to silence with his remaining hand.

"It's true. Our arms won little honor, despite the victory. Probably the Fox deserved a portion of what they got. They are fearless warriors, but their weapons were always pointed at us or our Indian trading partners, usually at the instigation of the English or their Iroquois allies. They attacked our friends, killed our voyageurs and kept the entire region in turmoil. When we negotiated with them, they would sometimes temporarily halt their depredations, if it suited them to do so. In fairness, their chiefs have little control over their younger warriors. At the slightest provocation, these young men would rekindle hostilities in the hope of winning renown through war. The English, always trying to disrupt our fur trade and divert it to Albany or Oswego, promoted the aggression of the Fox whenever possible.

"By the summer of 1730, the Fox found themselves completely isolated in their homeland along the Fox River. Their erratic and hostile behavior, usually demonstrated by the younger Fox warriors seeking glory, had alienated even former allies such as the Kickapoos, the Mascoutens and the Winnebagos. They had to face the enmity of the French and all their neighboring tribes, or relocate near potential allies. Most of the tribe, close to one thousand men, women and children, decided to leave Wisconsin and emigrate two hundred and fifty leagues to the east. They planned to settle among the Seneca, westernmost of the Iroquois nations, near our post at Niagara."

"At that time, I'd been sent by the captain with a supply of powder to Fort St. Joseph. I had spent several pleasant, though exceedingly hot summer days with Nicholas-Antoine Coulon de Villiers, the commander of St. Joseph. Late one steamy afternoon, an exhausted

Mascouten warrior approached the fort and was admitted. He said a hunting party of the Cahokias had encountered a Fox hunting party on the Illinois prairie. A skirmish resulted, after which the Cahokias discovered that the Fox hunters were part of a large migration heading east. The Mascouten warrior begged for assistance. Burdened with their aged as well as their young children, the Fox were forced to move slowly. This was an opportunity to destroy the major part of these hated foemen.

"Lieutenant Villiers assembled about three hundred Potawatomis, Sacs and Miamis, along with some Frenchmen, and determined to aid in the project. I foolishly volunteered to accompany that force, and was put in charge of the Sac contingent. I could communicate with the Sacs fairly well and had some slight acquaintance with several of their chiefs.

"After a march of seven days, we reached our destination, far out on the Illinois prairie. Beside a small stream and within a grove of trees, the Fox had made a stand. They had cut down some of the trees and had been fortifying the grove for the past two weeks. I inspected the site later and found it honeycombed with dugouts and connecting trenches to shield the Fox from our fire. Many of the dugouts were covered with reed mats and a layer of earth to make them musket proof. The position was strong, too strong to storm without great loss. It was defended by three hundred warriors, backed by the women of the tribe, who were known to fight like demons in defense of their families."

"We had the Fox fort completely surrounded with our colorful army. Lieutenant Robert Groston de St. Ange, the commander of Fort de Chartres then and now, had arrived with a large force of French and Illinois warriors the same day we reached the scene. We were soon joined by four hundred Weas and Piankashaws with a score of Frenchmen from Fort Ouiatanon. Counting the Illinois who had first encountered the Fox exodus, we had about twelve hundred men, more than one thousand of whom were Indians from the allied tribes. Sensing the complete destruction of their hated foes, these warriors, especially the Illinois and the Potawatomis, leaped and shouted and fired their weapons in the air, calling out for Fox blood. It was a whirl of red, yellow, green and black paint and feathers, most of the warriors stripped to the waist in the heat and humidity.

"A siege was decided upon to minimize allied casualties. Some warriors were detached to hunt food for the army. Towers were built allowing the French to fire directly into the Fox camp. The enemy had access to water because of the proximity of the stream, but they could not hunt for food. The plan was to starve them out.

"Negotiations started. The Fox wished to continue on their journey, or failing that, offered to surrender on the promise that the prisoners be split among the various tribes to learn pro-French ways. Mostly at the insistence of St. Ange, whose people had suffered for years at the hands of the Fox, these proposals were rejected. No quarter would be given. Later, Nicholas-Joseph des Noyelles of Fort Miamis further reinforced our army. He also carried a message from Governor General Beauharnois to the effect that no negotiated settlement should be accepted. It was to be to the death.

"Word reached me that my Sacs, kinsmen of the Fox, were planning to meet with the latter secretly. I spoke to Red Snake, one of the Sac chieftains, and he assured me that the meeting was to arrange for the safety of the Fox children. I agreed to let him go on that errand, but for no other purpose. He brought back nearly fifty youngsters, who would be kept safe in the Sacs' camp. Word of this activity spread throughout our army, and suspicion of the Sacs naturally resulted, but I felt it a small price to pay.

"Finally, one afternoon about two weeks after we arrived, a terrible thunderstorm struck. Few sentries manned their posts as the torrential rains poured down. Everyone sought shelter. The Fox, suffering mightily from hunger by this time, decided to escape by filtering through our lines during the storm. The crying of the children, frightened by the lightning and thunder, alerted us before they got completely away. By this time it was dark and the downpour continued. Since the Fox could not move quickly because of their families, we decided to wait until morning to pursue, so that we could differentiate friend from foe.

"We caught them about four leagues away the next day. The Fox warriors, greatly outnumbered and weak from hunger, died like men. The women and children were hunted down and hundreds were butchered. They did not die quietly, however. I witnessed numerous instances of the ferocity of the Fox women when cornered. One example will have to suffice. I was following about a hundred paces behind three of our Potawatomis, who were looking for one of the fifty or so Fox warriors who had escaped. The fugitive had plunged into some unusually tall grass. As the three warriors approached this tall grass, they passed the spot where a young Fox woman was concealed. She rose silently as the third warrior passed and buried a war club with an iron spike in his head. I ran forward as the other warriors wrestled her to the ground. She managed to tear out the left eye of one of them before the half-blinded brave and his companion finished her with their hatchets.

"I saw many such things that day. Rape and torture of non-combatants was common. About three hundred women and children were killed. Several hundred more were captured and divided among the victorious tribes. Much to our shame, we allowed many of these helpless captives to be tormented and then burned to death. There was probably nothing the small number of French could have done to prevent the carnage, given the enmity of the allied tribes toward the Fox. However, some of our people even participated in these excesses. This was not war. There was no honor or glory in it.

"Though the Governor General was overjoyed at our success, upon reflection, some of the tribes began to doubt the wisdom of their actions. If Onontio, the French Father in Montreal could destroy the Fox, why would he not do the same to them if they angered him in some way? Our ruthless slaughter of the Foxes still causes problems to this day because even our allied tribes do not fully trust us."

"Not a pretty tale," said Jean Baptiste, "but I can't see why you are so hard on yourself. You weren't in charge, and you did help save those children."

"I know. But the whole affair is a nightmare that never leaves me. I consider it a stain on my honor."

The Canadians' trading plans went well. The local traders stopped their grumbling when they found out they would be included in the commercial activity. The Cahokia living in the area, as well as many members of the other Illinois tribes crowded toward Legard's trading house when word was released that merchandise would be offered for trade at noon on the sixth day after their arrival. Dufort was in charge of haggling. He had a sharp eye for fur quality and that was important this far south, where fur quality as a whole was inferior to that found in more northern areas, such as the lands of the Crees and Ojibwas.

"How are we doing?" Jean Baptiste asked.

"Great" replied La Pointe, who was recording the transactions. "The fur trade is the essence of great commerce. Each side thinks they are putting something over on the other. The French trade hatchets, needles, whatever – perfectly ordinary utensils in their society, for furs which can be converted into great wealth. The most prized furs are the ones the Indians have sewn into robes and worn for a few months, because the eventual hat making process in Europe is aided by the furs being worn. From the Indians' standpoint, they are trading smelly fur robes for the wonderful metal implements they can't make themselves. Like I said, this trade is a beautiful thing."

Dufort was negotiating the sale of some scarlet cloth to a pretty Tamaroa squaw. At the same time he was trying to arrange a rendezvous later that night.

"I don't understand. How can she resist a handsome specimen like myself?"

"I don't know," said Jean Baptiste, "but she seems to be managing somehow."

"Perhaps a few sips of brandy, my dear, will lower your inhibitions, though I've never known an Illinois girl to have many of those.  Yes, I can see it.  I think she's falling in love."

"Good luck Etienne, but don't plan on a long relationship.  La Pointe thinks we will complete this business tomorrow.  The next day, we start north."

## CHAPTER 3

The next morning, the sky was clear and bright, but with a stiff west wind that agitated the waters of the Mississippi. The party assembled at the Cahokia boat landing to hear some remarks from Maurice before the return trip to Michilimackinac began. He had discussed possible return routes with Jean Baptiste and Dufort, and it was finally decided to retrace the steps that brought them to Cahokia. Given the ambush, this may have seemed foolhardy to some of the men, particularly when the Illinois River route to Lake Michigan was available. Although he would not be a part of this voyage, as commander Maurice felt it would be beneficial to explain the reasons why the Wisconsin River route was selected.

The men had finished packing their gear, and were awaiting the lieutenant's arrival from the mission. While they waited, Dufort and Gaspard Roziere instructed Rene La Pointe on the rudiments of using the war club he had acquired from a Shawnee visiting the area. He had traded Sergeant Cavallier's halberd for this new addition to his armament. He had also persuaded the Shawnee to contribute six beaver skins, to make up for the debt he would not collect when the sergeant found out about the trade (upon reflection La Pointe thought it prudent not to mention this transaction to the sergeant). The war club was made from a cut down musket stock, with a five inch steel spike added for effect. It was a fearsome weapon, and Rene's clumsy practice swings threatened destruction to anyone in the vicinity, be they friend or foe. Dufort and Roziere thought it in the best interest of the expedition to provide some training.

The two instructors had become good friends (a relationship that commenced as soon as Gaspard regained consciousness in Lagard's trading house). The two men were veteran voyageurs who had similar interests: strong drink, pretty women and games of chance. Roziere was tall; Dufort had more of a barrel shape. Both were flamboyant dressers – in addition to their beaded moccasins, brightly colored shirts and feathered caps, they vied with each other to locate the most striking sash in Cahokia to complete their ensembles. Most seemed to think Gaspard was victorious in that regard, his multi-colored sash of orange, yellow and black deemed more stylish than Etienne's red one.

It was an hour after dawn when Maurice arrived at the landing, moving slowly and supported by his younger brother.

"Men, though I'm not able to go with you, I wanted to wish you Godspeed. We have decided you will return by the same route we came. Of course, it's possible to head northeast on the Illinois, and after several portages, reach Lake Michigan. From there you could hug the eastern shore all the way back to the straits. Dufort, my brother and I decided against that option for several reasons. For one thing, we can't show fear to the Fox.

They are much depleted in numbers and at this point, have no firm allies among the tribes. If it looks like we fear them by avoiding their territory, it will only make them bolder and more aggressive. We also don't want to appear weak to the Mascouten and Kickapoo, former allies of the Fox who could return to the fold.

"We also want to find Leveau. He's a good man and it's possible he was spared after his capture, maybe even adopted into the tribe. I wish we could have prevented his capture, but the least we can do is try to determine his fate.

"I doubt the Fox will be very troublesome this time. When we were ambushed, our party was smaller and we were carrying a rich cargo that I'm sure the Fox needed desperately. This time there are twenty-six of you, including your two Ottawa scouts, and you will be carrying neither trade goods nor furs. It's possible the Fox will harass you a bit, and you need to stay on your guard, but I doubt they will mount a full scale attack on a party of this size, with so little to gain in the way of material goods."

With that, the men came forward to wish the lieutenant well. Dufort said "When I see you again I'll make you a club that can be attached to your stump, so you can still do good execution in battle, though it may prove less handy in an intimate encounter with a comely wench."

Somehow Maurice was able to control his joy. "Thanks Etienne. I'm certain the device will prove invaluable."

The two brothers said their farewells. "Good-bye Jean Baptiste. I'm sure I'll be seeing you at father's house before long. You're in command now, but it would be wise to confer with Dufort when in doubt. You have plenty of good, experienced men on this trip. I know you'll do fine. Now let me get back to the mission. I'll rest awhile and then try to even things up with Father Mercier. He's beaten me four chess games in a row."

La Pointe carefully stowed his new weapon, making sure it was accessible on short notice, and the twenty-six men set off in nine canoes, led by the Ottawa scouts. Dufort had met these Ottawas in the Cahokia village. They were from the Ottawa village near Michilimackinac, and readily consented to join the French expedition as they were headed home anyway. Raven Wing and Sky Singer were their names, the former, oddly enough, a cousin of The Turtle, their unfortunate former guide. The two were promised a liberal quantity of brandy when Michilimackinac was reached, but until then they had to content themselves with the large supply of good quality tobacco purchased from Legard. Jean Baptiste was pleased when told the identity of the new guides. He knew both of them from his frequent visits to their village, had been hunting several times with Sky Singer, and knew both to be brave and reliable.

High winds and the adverse current made northward progress on the Mississippi slow. La Pointe was encouraged to make vigorous use of a paddle rather than practice with his new toy. The men seemed in high spirits despite the labor involved. The ones who lived at the straits were anxious to see their families or girlfriends again. Those recruited in the Illinois Country were glad to be active again after the long period of enforced leisure due to the lack of trade goods. Jean Baptiste was sad at leaving Maurice behind, but was eager to perform well in his first solo command. He traveled in the same canoe with Dufort and Roziere.

It was early summer now, and the heat on the river was intense. Swarms of mosquitoes were a constant irritation, but the scenery along the shores was pleasant, with stands of oak, walnut, mulberry and cedar interspersed with prairie land. The wind had died for the most part, and all perspired profusely as they battled the current. Occasionally, Indians were encountered paddling down river, either singly or in small groups. These strangers proved friendly, though unable to provide any information on the mood or dispositions of the Fox. When camping for the night, Jean Baptiste chose an island location if possible, and had four men on guard at all times.

The young cadet came to know and like Roziere as the trip progressed, and he and Dufort had always been on excellent terms, but perhaps his closest friend was Rene La Pointe. La Pointe had studied history, literature, geography and mathematics in Marseilles prior to a brush with the law that made a hasty trip to New France seem expedient. His quick wit and education opened doors for him in the colony's biggest commercial enterprise, the fur trade. He worked for Jean Baptiste's father in Montreal for a year, learning the required bookkeeping as well as several Indian dialects. He learned quickly and was the obvious choice to handle the business activity at the proposed Sioux trading post.

When work was finished at the end of each day's travel, the two youths (Rene was twenty-two) would talk for hours. Rene had copied a number of maps he had seen in Montreal, and helped Jean Baptiste with his geography. The latter saw clearly for the first time that the French were well situated to dominate the North

American continent, at least from a geographic perspective.  France controlled the St. Lawrence River which led to the Great Lakes.  From the Great Lakes, the French had the choice of a number of river routes to the Mississippi River, the Missouri River and the interior of the whole land mass.  All of these routes were at least nominally under French control.

The English, on the other hand, were largely stymied by geography.  Their only viable route to the interior was the Hudson River/Mohawk River passage to Lake Ontario.  The English had recently built a fortified post  at Oswego on the lake, but English hopes for expansion in that direction were largely thwarted by the nearby French positions at Niagara and Frontenac.  Farther south, the Appalachian Mountains blocked English expansion to the west.  Easy access to the interior was denied them.

Many of the voyageurs began to take an interest in these discussions.  When La Pointe began discussing geography or the political situation in places such as Hudson Bay or the Mississippi Valley, many of the weary travelers would inch closer to the fire.  They learned useful things when the topic was North American geography, but the most popular talks concerned ancient history, a favorite subject of La Pointe's.

The merits of various military leaders, such as Alexander, Julius Caesar and Scipio Africanus were analyzed, but La Pointe insisted that the greatest leader of antiquity was Hannibal of Carthage.

"Why do you think him the greatest?  Asked Jean Baptiste.  "If I remember correctly, Alexander never lost a battle and conquered an empire much larger than that of Carthage."

"True, but Hannibal's accomplishments were incredible if you take into account the difficulties he faced. Read Polybius and Livy. Hannibal spent fifteen years in enemy territory, prosecuting his war with an army made up almost entirely of mercenaries. By definition, these men fought for money, not any patriotic motivation, and yet they fought on Italian soil for all those years with no record of discord or rebellion. His men were even known to fight to the death rather than choose an honorable withdrawal. Strange behavior indeed for men who fought for money. How could they collect their wages if they were dead? Hannibal must have been a truly inspiring leader."

Jean Baptiste would advocate other champions, and the voyageurs, warriors in their own right, were fascinated by these tales of the distant past. Some began to express their own opinions, using information provided by the two young men. In this way, the evenings passed quickly, as progress was made upriver and they began to approach the lands of the Fox.

## CHAPTER 4

Three days later, Jean Baptiste, Gaspard Roziere and Sky Singer crouched motionless in a dense thicket, watching a small Fox encampment a hundred paces away through the trees. It was a cloudless day, the heat was stifling and the mosquitoes hovered in clouds. The Ottawa had applied some evil smelling concoction to his skin before the convoy departed, and seemed little bothered by the flying blood suckers. The two Frenchmen, on the other hand, had to endure the bites of the little pests without response or complaint, though from the look on Roziere's face it was all he could do to stop himself from erupting into a string of curses.

Jean Baptiste could sympathize. In order to find a vantage point that offered an adequate view as well as concealment, they had slowly circled the enemy lodges for over an hour, until they had found this spot. Fortunately, the nearest oak provided shade; otherwise, they would have been unable to remain there very long. As it was Jean Baptiste felt like he was being basted in his own juices. Sweat ran freely inside his borrowed buckskin shirt, and he had to repeatedly wipe his brow to keep the salty perspiration from running into his eyes. He even wished he had used the Ottawa's rancid skin lotion, even though the smell was so bad he feared it would alert the Fox to their presence.

Yesterday the convoy had reached the spot where they had been ambushed six weeks before. Dufort and eight men had landed on the north bank of the Wisconsin about a league west of the site and proceeded through the woods slightly in advance of the convoy, intending to flush out anyone lurking in the woods. They encountered no one, and the portly voyageur greeted Jean Baptiste as he sprang ashore.

"Good afternoon, youngster. I trust your voyage was more pleasant than our walk. I'm getting a bit stout for all this exercise, especially considering all the bugs and snakes. We didn't see anyone, but I felt like we were being watched a couple of times. I'm sure one or more Fox scouts have had their eyes on us, at least since we entered the Wisconsin."

Raven Wing had been with Dufort's party and had continued along the riverbank when the rest of the patrol met the boats. He emerged from the trees after being gone only a few moments, and signaled to the others. Ten men stayed with the canoes; the rest fanned out and moved toward the Ottawa scout. Then they saw the reason for his signal.

It was Leveau, or at least, what remained of him. The scorched post and burned area around it provided information on the method of his passing. After they finished with him, the fox apparently dressed the body in his capote and fatigue cap, and retied it to the post. Had the French proceeded a bit farther upriver before landing, the post would have been visible from the river, as intended by the Fox. Their grisly sentinel had not remained as they left him, however. The beasts of the woods had been at work; only scattered bones and torn pieces of cloth remained. No trace of The Turtle was found.

"Gather up what's left," said Jean Baptiste. "We'll give him a decent burial on the island. It's the least I can do for him."

After a brief funeral, the young cadet conferred with Dufort, Roziere and the two Ottawas. "We're on our way back to Michilimackinac, but we don't have any current information on Fox activities. Sky Singer and Raven Wing have searched the area, and from the number of moccasin tracks moving about the area over the last month, they feel that a Fox camp can't be far. I propose that we find that camp and capture a prisoner who can be questioned."

Raven Wing immediately volunteered to aid in the project, but the cadet felt that this eagerness reflected the Ottawa's desire to avenge The Turtle, his dead kinsman. Any Fox prisoner within reach of Raven Wing's knife would have an extremely limited life expectancy. "No Raven Wing, I want this prisoner to live so that we can get information from him. Let me take Sky Singer and Gaspard this time."

Etienne Dufort started to protest, but Jean Baptiste reasoned with him. "Gaspard has long legs and a good deal less weight to propel if we need to make a run for it, which is a likely possibility. I need you and La Pointe to devise a method for the three of us to slip away from the convoy unnoticed by whomever might be watching from the woods. We'll camp on the island tonight and give you a chance to think."

After dark, Dufort called Jean Baptiste over to the small camp fire he, La Pointe and Roziere shared. "Young sir, I think we know what to do. If they do have someone watching, he probably knows how many are in our party, and he will make sure he can account for everyone. I've had several of our canoes beached behind some bushes where they can't be seen from the north bank. Tonight, we will fashion dummies for the three of you out of spare clothes and whatnot, and dress the dummies in the outfits you have been wearing. We'll put them in the canoes while it's still dark, and set off before first light, so the Fox scout cannot get a good look. You three will stay on the island until we are out of sight, then swim to shore and capture your prisoner. What do you think?"

"I think you want to get your hands on my beautiful sash, that's what I think," said Gaspard.

Etienne gave his best injured-innocent look. " How can you say such a thing! I'm at my wit's end trying to devise a foolproof plan, and all you can say is I'm trying to steal your sash. Besides, I like mine better."

"We can't wear our normal clothes anyway, Gaspard, especially you. I'm afraid your preferred mode of dress is too noticeable among the trees. OK, we'll donate our clothes and find something plain to wear that will blend in with the forest." Gaspard grumbled his agreement and lurched off to see Laurent, the only voyageur in the group large enough to have spare clothes that would fit him.

"Assuming we are successful and catch our man, how will we rejoin you?"

"We've been thinking about that, too. About two leagues upriver is that island with the small lagoon. Do you remember it from our trip down river?"

"I think so."

"I'll have some of the men pretend that they've hit

a rock and need to stop for repairs on the canoe. We'll take our time about it, and will even spend the night there if you haven't returned yet."

"Good. Make sure Gaspard brings some rawhide along that we can use to bind the prisoner. I've heard Roziere is a powerful swimmer; it will be his job to tow the Fox to the island without drowning him."

Things went according to plan, at least until now. The dummies were dressed in the clothes of the three, Gaspard vowing horrible revenge against Etienne unless his sash was returned in perfect condition.

Rene volunteered to loan Jean Baptiste whatever weapons he might require. The cadet made sure that he and his two companions were well armed. Each man carried a knife, hatchet and pistol in addition to his musket. Powder horns were filled and each carried at least fifty rounds of ammunition. A fallen tree would be used as a raft on which they would place their powder horns and a pack with provisions.

Before dawn, the convoy left and the three made their way to the north bank. It took about an hour for Sky Singer to find what looked like the most likely path to the suspected village. It led northeast from the river. They followed it very cautiously for another hour until they reached the small town. The village held only a dozen lodges and appeared to be temporary in nature. It was at this point that they had searched for a good observation point in the sweltering heat.

They remained in their haven for quite some time. They saw little movement in the village, and had no opportunity to take a prisoner. Jean Baptiste signaled for his two companions to shift to a spot about twenty paces to the left. He was concerned that their original hiding place was too close to the path, and that a Fox might blunder into them and raise the alarm. When they moved, Jean Baptiste was startled by something he saw attached to a pole outside the largest lodge; it had not been visible from their previous location – an English flag!

At that moment, inside the meeting lodge, Jacob Cutler, Tiny Mason and Robert Whittington, along with the six Iroquois warriors who had accompanied them on their western journey, met with Kiala and several of his principle warriors. The three Englishmen were dressed in buckskins, and except for Mason, wore tri-corn hats. Tiny, a giant of a man over six and a half feet tall and weighing more than three hundred pounds, wore no hat but instead had his dark hair adorned with eagle feathers. Whittington was a man of normal height and weight, his most memorable feature being his left ear, which had been cut in two during a bar fight in Albany eight years before. The two halves were held together by a highly decorative gold earring, given to him by his Mohawk mistress. Cutler was undoubtedly the leader of the three. A man in his early forties, his brown hair was graying at the temples. After twenty years in the wilderness, competing with the French for the furs trapped by the various Indian tribes, he was physically strong, mentally alert and possessed great skill in dealing with the warriors and chieftains he encountered.

Accompanying them were three Mohawks and three Senecas from the Iroquois Confederacy. Members of the easternmost and westernmost tribes of that league, whose territory extended along the Mohawk River from Albany to the French Fort Niagara, they sat impassively as the discussion continued.  Middlemen in the fur trade between the merchants in Albany and the western and northern tribes that trapped the beaver, they were here to help the English during this mission to the Fox.  For more than a century, the Iroquois had been deadly enemies of the French, ever since the Frenchman Champlain had sided with enemy tribes of the St. Lawrence valley.  Many wars had been fought against the French and their numerous Indian allies since then, and the Iroquois were diminished in strength as a result.  But the individual Iroquois warrior was still feared and supremely confident.

These six warriors were representative of their people.  Though the Mohawks lived close to the English and Dutch at Albany, as a group they had not fallen victim to alcohol addiction and sloth, such as had occurred with many other tribes living in close proximity to the Europeans.  The Senecas, living near the great falls on the Niagara River, had been less exposed to European influences.  Because of the summer weather, the six wore only breechcloths and moccasins, but still were able to express individual tastes with a variety of adornments.  Most were bald except for a tuft of hair at the top of their heads, had their earlobes slit and stretched by an assortment of heavy earrings and wore necklaces and metal armbands.  Two of the Mohawks were proud of nose rings they had recently acquired.

Jacob Cutler spoke.  "Thank you Kiala, for flying the English flag as a sign of the  love of the Fox people for our great king.  The Governor of New York will hear of this gesture and be pleased.  I am saddened to hear of the extent of your loss last summer at the hands of the French.  We had heard some rumors about the business, but did not believe that the result had been so disastrous."

Kiala responded, "Yes, most of our tribe decided to join those who had moved to Seneca territory years ago. We heard good things about their life there, and were surrounded by enemies here in our ancestral home. But Wisaka did not aid us in this venture. Many of our people died, even women, children and the old."

"If your people would like to try again, the Seneca still have lands available." As he spoke, Cutler looked at the Senecas present, who nodded in reply. At the same time Cutler thought, *I'd rather they stayed here and continued to harass the French, interrupting their trade as much as possible.* He continued, "If, on the other hand, you decide to stay in Wisconsin, I would urge you to end the recent quarrels you have had with old friends, such as the Mascoutens and the Kickapoos. In the past, the three tribes stood as one, but because of some minor differences caused by the ardor of your young men, old friendships were forgotten. *Some minor differences – the homicidal idiots murdered Mascouten and Kickapoo hunters without just cause.* If you could reestablish friendships with those tribes as well as your kinsmen the Sacs, you would be able to hold on here indefinitely.

Kiala replied "Those that remain alive want to stay here. Much of what you suggest has already been done. We have spoken to the Mascoutens and the Kickapoos, and also to the Sacs. They feel that the French want to wipe us out, and though they have recently been our enemies, with this they do not agree. These tribes have already begun to return Fox captives taken last year on the Illinois prairie. They have also sent emissaries to the Potawatomis and the Miamis to try and free the prisoners held by those tribes."

Cutler said "The friends of the Fox in New York will help all they can.  Once you are again allied with the other tribes, your combined strength will be feared.  At Oswego you will find the rum, guns and trade goods you want in plentiful supply and at good prices.  *Right, that bastard boss of mine, Mr. Thomas Blackthorne, will see to it that the men you send east to trade are filled with cheap liquor and cheated in every way possible.*

"I know you will want revenge for all those who have died.  We are not at war with France and so cannot march with you, but I want to assure you that we can help in other ways.  Our agents have traveled far and are causing trouble for the French with the tribes around Detroit and also near New Orleans.  The French will be unable to concentrate on you because they will have to deal with difficulties in many other places as well."

Kiala knew he really had no option.  *French attempts to trade guns to our hereditary enemies, the Sioux, are what started the trouble with these white men. Then, when hostilities with the Sioux eased and we would have allowed the French-Sioux trade, the French wanted to pay us nothing for using our territory to reach Sioux lands, and trouble with the French started again. In addition, the French are firm friends of tribes such as the Ojibwas and the Illinois, with whom we will always be at war. If we are to have any hope of maintaining ourselves, we must have guns. If we can't get them from the French, we must get them from the English.*  "My people thank you for your kindness.  With your help, we will have our revenge."

## CHAPTER 5

Jean Baptiste, Gaspard and Sky Singer were still watching for a good potential hostage. Several women had left the village and walked a short distance along the bank of a nearby stream. Still within sight of the hidden observers, they stripped off their cloth blouses and leather skirts, sat on a fallen tree trunk to remove their moccasins and began to wade in the water. The object of the mission was momentarily forgotten as the three watched the women from their vantage point fifty paces behind the fallen log.

"The one on the left has a rump like I've never seen," muttered Roziere quietly.

This remark roused Jean Baptiste from his silent reverie, and he did his best to give Gaspard a stern look. He pointed back toward the village, indicating that he wanted everyone's attention focused in that direction. Several children were playing among the lodges, and an old woman had started a fire in order to prepare a meal. Several other women were busy weaving cedar-bark mats. No likely candidates for abduction yet.

Then a lad emerged from one of the dwellings. It was difficult to say from this distance, but Jean Baptiste thought the boy might be about his own age, maybe a bit younger. Though probably not a seasoned warrior, he was old enough to have been included in tribal discussions, and so might possess the information they sought. The French cadet was especially eager to question the Indian about the English flag. The Fox youth moved off alone through the trees to the east, and three silent shadows followed, the largest of the three lingering for a moment to cast another glance at the naked women splashing in the stream.

It appeared that the Indian had set off to hunt. He did not wear paint, carried a bow and arrows rather than a gun and was not wearing the traditional warrior's roach headdress made of deer and porcupine hair. In addition to the bow, the lad carried a knife, but no other weapon. The eastward direction he followed pleased his pursuers, because they intended to go east by south to reunite with the convoy. They would let the lad continue for some distance before attempting the capture, making sure they were well away from the village.

After a half-hour, the boy stopped, took off his quiver and a bag in which to put small game, and began to practice with his bow. He fired at small marks set in front of a hillock, the bare earthen sides of which made arrow retrieval easy. On the far side of the hillock rose a large outcrop of rock, perhaps six times the height of a man, its width about three times larger.

The boy gave no sign that he intended to leave any time soon, so Jean Baptiste's party drew farther back into the trees, where they could devise a plan.

"First of all, remember I want him alive and able to talk. If possible, I'd like him to be conscious when we take him, so that we can question him and then get out immediately. The longer we stay in the area, the greater the likelihood that we will be spotted."

Sky Singer spoke. "I can work my way between the hillock and the rock outcrop, and then climb the back side of the hillock. When he walks toward the hillock to retrieve his arrows, I'll jump him, and the two of you close in."

"That sounds good. Gaspard?"

The big voyageur nodded his assent while still half-thinking about female body parts recently observed.

Things went pretty much according to plan. When Sky Singer leaped, the youth saw him a little quicker than anticipated, and dodged to his right while pulling his knife. The Ottawa struck him a glancing blow as he landed, knocking the Fox off balance. Before he could recover, Jean Baptiste had grabbed him from behind. Gaspard struck him a blow that stunned him; before he fully returned to his senses, he was bound hand and foot.

While Gaspard looped a piece of rawhide around the boy's neck and favored him with a baleful glare, Jean Baptiste asked the Ottawa to find a good spot to conduct the interrogation. Sky Singer quickly returned and said that a path existed to the top of the large rock. From the top they would have a good view of the whole area. Gaspard picked up the captive, slung him over his shoulder and the climb began.

When they got to the top, the young marine surveyed the area. The long axis of the rock outcrop ran from northwest to southeast. A stream ran from the northwest along the northern and eastern sides of the enormous boulder toward the Wisconsin River. The rocky ground on the other side of the stream and the boulder itself pinched the streambed and created a deep pool at the base of the outcrop.

While Sky Singer kept watch, Jean Baptiste was able to make himself understood in the Ottawa tongue. As the Ottawa had always acted in the role of the middlemen in the fur trade, their language was understood over a wide area. "Do you know who we are?"

"French and Ottawa," replied the boy.  He attempted to appear unconcerned about his predicament, but was not entirely successful.

"You realize your life is in our hands.  But, we have no desire to harm you as long as you answer our questions truthfully.  Do you understand?"

The boy nodded.

"Good.  Last winter, envoys of the Fox met with the French chief Villiers at our post on the St. Joseph River. They promised that the Fox would stop attacking the tribes allied to the French, and would cease harassing French fur traders. Yet less than two moons ago, we were attacked only an hour away from this spot. Why was this done?"

"I have heard of the attack, but was not present and don't know why it was made.  My brother and I were away at the time, gathering spruce roots for canoe building." *After the slaughter last summer, my people will have their vengeance, though they might have to make some empty promises to buy time until they have recovered their strength.*

"Let me have a few minutes alone with the lad," interjected Roziere as he fingered his knife. "I'll carve a few pieces off of his hide; I'm sure it will do wonders for his memory."

"Now Gaspard, I'm confident the boy wants to cooperate.  I'll give him one more chance before I turn him over to you.  What is your name boy?"

"Wolf."

" Now Wolf, I don't want to have my friend here slicing off parts of your body. Tell me, why is the English flag flying at the village and when were they here?"

Looking warily at the big Frenchman, Wolf responded. "Three Englishmen and six Iroquois are meeting with our war chief Kiala right now. They have been here several days, and I listened to what was said when they arrived. The Englishman Cutler is pleased that the Fox still fight the French and says that the merchants at Oswego will supply what we need to continue the war." *No big secrets here; everyone knows the English hate the French and want to divert trade to Oswego.*

"And what do you think?" asked the cadet.

"My father was a supporter of Ouchala, a leader who favored peace with the French. We need the weapons and tools of the white men to fight our enemies successfully. In order to get them, we must be on good terms with either the French or the English. Kiala favors the English, but my father had traveled far to the east and spoke to warriors from many tribes. They said the English often cheated them of their furs and did their best to force them off their lands. The English are numberless and their hunger for land insatiable. The French are far fewer in number and care more about the fur trade than acquiring territory. Though some Frenchmen are bad men too, they are more likely to trade fairly." *Oddly enough, I believe these sentiments to be true, and am not trying to curry favor with these Frenchmen.*

"Gaspard, is there anything you'd like to ask?"

"As a matter of fact, there is. Would you happen

to know the young lady with the round bottom, a reddish birthmark on her right cheek?"

Before Jean Baptiste could object to this line of questioning, an arrow flew past his head and shattered against nearby rock.

"What the hell! Sky Singer, I thought you were keeping watch!"

"I never saw anything until the arrow sailed by. Then I made out movement in the trees. I believe there are at least seven of them."

"Great. Keep your eyes open. Since we have the high ground I doubt they'll rush us."

"There is no reason for them to rush us. They can surround us up here and send one man back to the village for help. Then they can just sit down there and starve us out."

"Just when I was about to gather important intelligence, this has to happen," groused Roziere.

"Gaspard, if we don't figure a way down off this rock very soon, that will probably be the last derriere you ever see."

"I've been giving our departure some thought," replied the big man. " Sky Singer, if you see them trying to surround us, discourage them for a few moments. Jean Baptiste, I suspect that our friend Wolf here was expecting these guests."

"It's true," said the young Fox. "I had planned to hunt with some of the young warriors from a village to the north. We were to meet at this rock, a well-known landmark, when the sun was highest in the sky. Because we are so low on powder and shot, I was going to hunt with a bow. I got here early so I could practice. When you captured me, I knew all I had to do was delay you, and help would arrive. While I think Kiala is wrong to favor the English over the French, at present you are our enemies, and should be treated as such."

While this exchange was proceeding and Sky Singer took a shot at one of the shadows in the trees, Gaspard was exploring their fortress, apparently looking for something in particular. During those moments when he exposed himself to their fire, he attracted one or more arrows from the Fox down below, but none struck home. He now returned to the prisoner and securely tied one end of a rawhide thong to the rawhide binding Wolf's wrists.

" I trust those gentlemen down there are good friends of yours," remarked the big man.

"Yes, I've known most of them all my life."

"Excellent. Oh, and tell me son, are you a good swimmer? Well, no matter." With that he reached down and picked up a piece of rock that must have weighed as much as a man.

Wolf's eyes widened when he saw that he was attached to this boulder by the stout rawhide. One end of the rawhide bound his hands. The other end was wrapped a number of times and securely tied around the rock.

"Sky Singer, Jean Baptiste. It's time to go." With that Gaspard hoisted the boulder over his head and tossed it far out over the pool below. Wolf shrieked as he was jerked off the top of the outcrop into what looked to be deep water. "Let's get out of here. It should take his friends a little time to fish him out. Maybe that will give us enough head start."

## CHAPTER 6

As the three hurtled through the woods they remained silent, preferring to concentrate on the task at hand. After a time they heard the first sounds of pursuit, the distant howling of the Fox hunters who had so suddenly converted to warriors. Jean Baptiste signaled to his companions to stop. "We'll never be able to outrun them, because we're weighted down with our guns, and I think they are all carrying bows. I don't believe they shot anything but arrows at us back there."

Hearing no dissent from the others, he continued, "I'm not sure about the direction we need to take to hit the island where the convoy is waiting. I think we are going about right, but our noisy friends will catch us long before we reach Etienne and the others. Let's wait here and give the Fox something to think about. Fire only your muskets; keep the pistols in reserve. You fire first Gaspard, then drop back fifty paces and reload. Sky Singer, then you do the same; I'll cover your retreat. I'll be last and Gaspard can cover me while Sky Singer reloads. Then, we keep repeating the process, always moving south and a bit east toward Dufort and the others."

"Sounds like a good idea to me. As long as we only

have to contend with these whelps and their arrows, I think we'll be alright." Gaspard braced his musket against the adjacent tree and calmly waited as the howling grew louder.

Meanwhile, the meeting between Kiala, the Englishmen and the Iroquois had just concluded when a young Fox hunter burst into camp and announced that Wolf had been captured. "Eight of us from my village had arranged to meet Wolf at the big boulder to hunt. When we drew near, Eagle Beak thought he saw movement at the top of the rock. We approached with caution and saw Wolf, his hands bound, talking to two men. We fired at them and then I was sent here to get help."

"How many of them are there?" asked Kiala.

"It's hard to say. I doubt they could number more than eight or ten. My companions will surround the big rock and keep them there."

Jacob Cutler had noticed the commotion and walked over to see what was happening.

"One of our young men has been captured, undoubtedly by men from the convoy of canoes we have been watching. We are going to get him back. Will you join us?"

"Of course. I never miss an opportunity to bloody a French nose. Tiny! Robert! Get your guns and bring the Iroquois. It looks like this trip is going to liven up at last!"

The first pursuer burst into the open moving at a dead run, dead being the operative word. Gaspard fired as soon as the warrior appeared. The heavy slug struck the man square in the chest and hurled him backward into a large bush. His body jerked once or twice, then he was gone. The others had been strung out behind him; all immediately dove for cover.

"Nice shot Gaspard. Now, fall back about fifty paces and reload. Sky Singer – cover him."

The big man fell back. As he ran, a Fox stepped out from behind a tree and took aim with his bow, but Sky Singer saw him in time and fired a quick shot. The ball missed its mark, but blasted a chunk of bark from the tree above the archer's head, spoiling his aim.

"Sky Singer, as you fall back, keep alert. They are sure to try to outflank us. All right, go! I'll make sure they keep their heads down."

For the next hour, the three managed to maintain the status quo. The Fox grew to respect the accuracy of their musket fire and held back. As a result, the arrows they fired in return did no harm. Steady progress was made to the south and east. The French party thwarted several flanking attempts with precision musket fire. Finally, one warrior did succeed in getting behind them, but all three charged him at once, routing him from his position.

"I'm pretty sure I saw young Wolf awhile back," said Gaspard. "I'm glad the swim did him no permanent harm, though I'm not sure it improved his outlook on life. He almost got me a short time ago. By the way, rumor had it that you weren't much of a marksman, Jean Baptiste. You picked a good day to improve."

"I am doing better than usual, and I certainly can't complain about the timing of the improvement. How is your powder and shot holding out?"

"I'd guess about twenty to twenty-five more shots. Sound right to you Sky Singer?"

The Ottawa checked and nodded. "If we don't find Raven Wing and the others soon, we may need to think about a new plan."

Gaspard fired and pulled back. Jean Baptiste's musket had misfired on his last shot, and he was having some difficulty reloading, so Sky Singer signaled him to fall back while the Ottawa covered his retreat. This was accomplished, and Jean Baptiste signaled Sky Singer when he was ready.

Jean Baptiste aimed at the familiar shadows lurking back in the trees as the young Ottawa turned and sprinted toward them. As Jean Baptiste watched for potential targets, he heard a musket shot from the left front. Sky Singer was lifted off his feet from the impact of the round and hurled against a tree.

"Don't worry lad, I'm on my way!" bellowed Gaspard. He tossed his musket to Jean Baptiste, drew his pistol, and charged toward his fallen companion.

Jean Baptiste saw the smoke from the musket shot and fired at that spot, hearing a cry of pain in response. Apparently, help from the Fox village had arrived. Now they faced an unknown but larger number of assailants, and these newcomers were well armed. A volley of arrows and musket shots was directed at Roziere as he ran forward, but he remained unharmed as furrows were plowed in the ground around him and branches shot off nearby trees.

Gaspard reached the motionless Ottawa, and without stopping, grasped the boy's buckskin shirt in one hand, lifted him off the ground and headed back toward Jean Baptiste. The cadet saw a Fox draw a bow, and the young marine snapped off a shot with Roziere's musket. He missed and the Indian's arrow struck Gaspard in the hip as he neared Jean Baptiste's position. "I'm not sure lad," the big man gasped, "but we could be in some trouble."

Gaspard and the cadet experienced a short respite. The cry of pain Jean Baptiste heard came from Cutler. Instead of ducking behind a tree after he felled Sky Singer, he held his ground, admiring his shot. Jean Baptiste's ball caught him at the junction of neck and shoulder, breaking his collarbone. He sat down heavily, blood streaming down both chest and back. Kiala turned away from directing the action to see how badly his ally was hurt.

"I don't think the wound is dangerous," the Englishman grunted. "It hurts like hell though."

"I saw the shot. It was the boy who fired."

"Do me a favor, Kiala. I'd like to see whoever is left over there roasting over a slow fire within the hour."

"It will be as you ask."

Sky Singer was dead. The shot shattered his spine and he probably died before he hit the ground. His two friends had no time to mourn him now. The arrow in Gaspard's leg had missed the bone; the point stuck out a hand's breadth from the inner thigh. Jean Baptiste broke off the arrowhead and pulled the shaft from the wound. They tied a length of rawhide tightly around the leg above the injury.

"I don't know why they haven't finished us off by now lad. They're giving us a chance to get ready for them. It won't make any difference in the outcome, but we'll take some of them with us." As they looked around, both Gaspard and Jean Baptiste feverishly reloaded.

"By the way, son, no one would think badly of you if you tried to break out alone. With this leg, I'm a goner in any event, but I might be able to keep them busy long enough for you to make it."

"No, I abandoned a man once before, and have regretted it ever since. I'm not going to make a habit of it. Besides, one or two more shots, and I think they might surrender."

Roziere chuckled. "You're a good lad and would have been a fine officer. If this is it, I couldn't ask for a better comrade." As he spoke, he checked the priming on his pistol, and laid it, along with his hatchet and knife on a fallen trunk where they were in easy reach. Jean Baptiste checked his weapons again and peered out to the north. "Here they come!" he warned his injured companion.

Numbering twenty-four in all, the Fox, English and Iroquois fanned out and moved in for the kill. Jean Baptiste shot a Seneca through the head and Gaspard wounded a Fox. They received a shower of arrows and musket balls in response, one of the balls striking Roziere's left hand.

Then they closed in. Roziere picked up his pistol and shot a charging Mohawk in the stomach. Then, dropping the pistol and picking up his hatchet with his good hand, he waded into a cluster of his enemies, flailing left and right. A Fox shrieked as the blade nearly severed his hand at the wrist. A backhand rip across the throat finished another Mohawk.

The rush was upon him before Jean Baptiste could draw his pistol. He swung his musket like a club, striking a glancing blow to the side of a Fox warrior's head, drawing blood. The man recovered his balance and looked at the cadet, an expression of rage on his face. Jean Baptiste was bowled over by the shoulder of a huge, onrushing white man, who then tripped over the fallen cadet and landed some distance away. The furious Fox warrior had drawn his knife and was about to leap on Jean Baptiste when the prostrate boy saw a blur strike the man, knocking the blade from his grasp.

It was Rene La Pointe! War club in hand, the clerk now proceeded to pulverize his astonished opponent, turning the brave into a crimson mass of bruises and holes.

Jean Baptiste, groggy from the blow he had received, turned and saw a tide of his friends pour out of the woods and strike the enemy in the flank. Initial shots were fired, then the French closed in with clubbed muskets, hatchets and knives. A voyageur disemboweled a young Fox with a sweep of his blade. A Mohawk brained one of the Frenchmen with his musket butt. Men rolled on the ground, stabbing, punching and biting.

The enormous white man who had knocked Jean Baptiste down had at last disentangled himself from the bush into which he had fallen. The first person he saw was Etienne Dufort, who barred his path. Dufort dropped his empty musket and drew his knife, insulting the giant's parentage to the best of his ability with his broken English. The giant dropped his musket as well and drew his knife, a look of pleasure spreading across his dull features. Though Dufort was a large man, this Englishman was a monster, a good head taller and much heavier. The size difference apparently occurred to Dufort as well. He drew his pistol and fired, though the ball only creased the  side of the Englishman's head. Stunned, the giant staggered back out of the fight.

It seemed as though the world was moving in slow motion as Jean Baptiste dragged himself to a sitting position and surveyed the battlefield. Several injured men from both sides were pulling back from the fray, walking or crawling away. Many of the Fox and their allies were trying to regroup from the furious French assault. Jean Baptiste noticed that a middle-aged Fox, dressed in ceremonial finery, seemed to be in charge.

"Rene! The one over there with the roach headdress and the beaded deerskin shirt!"

La Pointe looked in the indicated direction and nodded. As the clerk loaded a discarded musket he had found, Jean Baptiste slowly drew his pistol and took aim. He fired but the ball struck the ground to Kiala's right. With a curse, Jean Baptiste began to reload. La Pointe was ready and now he took aim. His round struck the war chief in the shoulder, spinning him around as he fell.

That shot ended all aggressive moves by Kiala's men. They helped their chief to his feet and began to withdraw. The badly mauled Englishmen and Iroquois did not persist either, joining the retreat back to the village. Within a few minutes, all the firing had stopped, and except for the enemy dead and a few wounded who had been left behind, the field was in the hands of the French.

"Where's Gaspard?" asked Etienne, a worried look on his face.

"I haven't seen him since Hell broke loose. The last time I did see him he was near that birch tree, chopping Fox and Mohawk to kindling with his hatchet."

Etienne and Rene found him lying on his back

atop a mound of his late enemies. He was lying still and from all the blood they thought he was dead. They looked down sadly, when suddenly the corpse began to speak. "Help me up, would you? I just needed to rest following the afternoon's exercise. I'm glad you boys are here, but I'm sure the lad and I had the situation under control." In addition to the wounds he had received earlier, Gaspard had a long knife gash along his ribs, and had been knocked senseless by a stone war club, the impact from which had left the entire side of his head bruised. All in all, he was quite a sight.

With Rene and Etienne's help, Gaspard staggered over to the cadet. "Well lad, it looks like you've won your first battle. How are you?"

"I know I feel better than you look, but I'm happy we're both alive."

Mention of that reminded him of Sky Singer and he asked about Raven Wing.

"He's fine," said Dufort. "Just got a few bumps and bruises. He saw Sky Singer's body and immediately found and dispatched the enemy wounded."

"Ask him to see me, please." Jean Baptiste finally rose to his feet. His whole body ached and he felt nauseous, but he remained standing. Raven Wing approached, a number of dripping scalps attached to his belt.

"I wanted to tell you how sorry I am about the death of your friend. He was a brave warrior and died a warrior's death. His deeds will be remembered around the campfires of the Ottawa for many winters."

"I want to thank you for saving his body from the knives of the Fox. I studied the ground and read the signs of what happened."

"Gaspard Roziere recovered your friend's body. Charged right into a hail of shot to do it too. He is the one you should thank."

The Indian nodded and left to find Roziere. It was not a difficult task as the big voyageur was roaring at the top of his lungs while rough surgical repairs were in progress. "Henri, I swear, when I am feeling a bit better you will pay for this butchery!"

While the wounded were being tended, Jean Baptiste met with Etienne and Rene and explained the events leading up to the battle. "You certainly arrived at an opportune moment. Despite Gaspard's bluster, we knew we were done for."

"You did a good job finding your way back to the island. It's only a short distance from here," replied La Pointe.

"Rene spent all his time listening for your approach. When the war started, he ran to the canoes, grabbed his war club, dove in the river and swam to shore. He raced toward the sound of the firing despite my attempts to get him to wait for us. I left three men with the canoes and the rest of us grabbed all the weapons we could carry and came running."

"How many did we lose?" asked the cadet.

"Three dead and three seriously hurt, including Gaspard. All the wounded will live, although Gaspard lost the little finger on his left hand. My guess is we hurt them a lot worse."

This was an accurate guess. It was late that night before the Fox and their allies made it back to the little village. Tiny carried the semi-conscious Cutler the last several hours. The big man was not seriously hurt, but would bear a long scar along his cheek and the side of his head. The ball had also clipped off the top of his left ear. All three of the Mohawks were dead, as was one of the Senecas. Many of the Fox were dead or hurt.

Kiala had Cutler moved to his lodge, where both of them could have their wounds tended.

"I recognized the one who shot you," the war chief told the Englishman. "He was there when we ambushed the French two moons ago. Your agent in Montreal, the one who let us know the supply convoy to the Sioux was coming, maybe he can identify this boy."

" I hope so," replied Cutler with a groan. "I intend to meet that boy again."

## CHAPTER 7

Jean Baptiste had the men make litters for the wounded and also search the battlefield for anything useful. They found several serviceable muskets and some powder and shot. None of the enemies lying dead on the field were white men, a fact that disappointed the cadet. He was hoping to gather some information on the Englishmen, such as their point of origin.

He visited Gaspard and the other wounded men. Roziere was a sight, with more parts of his body bandaged than not. "How are you, Gaspard?" inquired the boy.

"I've felt better," admitted the voyageur. "They tell me those bastards shot off my little finger. It could affect my fiddle playing, will undoubtedly make it harder to cheat at cards, and who knows what effect it will have on my social life when the ladies discover I'm no longer physically perfect?"

"If those are your major concerns, I guess you're planning to live. Don't worry. As soon as the litters are finished, we'll move you and the others to the island. We'll be able to make you more comfortable there and also be able to observe uninvited guests before they arrive."

"Etienne, make litters for our dead as well. We'll bury them on the island."

"Yes lad.   I've had time to check everyone.   In addition to our dead and seriously wounded, we have five men with slight wounds, none of which are incapacitating."

"It could have been worse.   I think we should spend the night on the island where our canoes are beached, letting the injured rest a bit, then push on toward Green Bay in the morning.   We can leave the seriously wounded at Fort La Baye, then move as quickly as possible to Michilimackinac."

That night, they buried Sky Singer and the two slain voyageurs.  Gaspard insisted on being present, so his litter was moved to the grave site and he was propped against a tree so he could see. "He was a brave lad," was his only remark.

They left the island at daybreak.  Fog covered the water and shrouded the heavily forested island as well as they paddled out of the small cove. Jean Baptiste looked back at the final resting-place of his companions, until the island was lost in the mist.

By nightfall, they reached the portage to the Fox River.  Once on that stream, they would be traveling with the current, though rock-strewn shallows, and occasional rapids would make additional portages necessary.

That night, as they camped at the beginning of the portage, Jean Baptiste was unusually quiet as the others conversed on a variety of subjects, most of which involved women.  After a while, he excused himself from the fire, saying that he wanted to check on the sentries. He found all four in place, then walked down to where the canoes were beached and gazed out at the moonlight on the river.

"You seem lost in thought this evening."

"Hello Rene. You noticed."

"What's wrong? Are you thinking about Sky Singer and the others?"

"Yes. I realize that those men are dead because of decisions I made, and I don't know if those decisions were the right ones. Should I have tried to capture a prisoner or not? Going back farther, should I have shot Leveau when I had the chance? If I had, he'd still be dead, but it would have been much quicker and less painful."

"I think you can only do your best, and hope that is good enough," replied his friend. "You are a soldier, and the kinds of decisions you make often result in death for someone, friend, foe or both. While you can't spend the lives of your men foolishly, your decisions can't be based on whether someone might be hurt or killed. If you did, you would never accomplish anything, for almost any venture entails some risk. These men know that many of them will not live to enjoy their grandchildren. That is the lot of a voyageur. Sickness, an arrow, a hidden rock in a river, - these things end the lives of many canoe men. They know this and still they have chosen this work. If long life were important to them, they would have become farmers or innkeepers. Just as long as the man leading them does not throw their lives away for no reason. I imagine your marines feel the same way. Concerning Leveau, if you had shot at him, what makes you think you would have hit anything?"

Jean Baptiste smiled. "Thanks for the vote of confidence. For awhile yesterday, my marksmanship was pretty good, though I did miss the one we think was Kiala. Luckily, you managed to put one in him."

Kiala had reached a decision. *At present, the Fox are in no condition to defend themselves. We need to buy time, and with this time rebuild the strength of the tribe. In the future, the young boys in the villages will become stout warriors, but the Fox people do not have that much time before they face the wrath of Onontio and his marines. I have to effect the return of the Fox captives held by the various tribes, and also need to forge military alliances. The Fox have intermarried frequently with the Mascoutens, the Kickapoos and the Sacs. In the past, all had been strong allies. If I appeal to them in the right way, they will be again. Then I will have sufficient manpower to weather the storm.*

"Kicking Bear," Kiala called to a warrior at the far end of the lodge. "Find your brother. I wish to speak to the two of you."

Soon the two returned and stood before the war chief. "Kicking Bear, Eagle Claw, last winter, the two of you met with the Frenchman Villiers at Fort St. Joseph. You talked with him and were able to convince him that we were no longer interested in war. He wanted me to surrender and go to Montreal, where I would be held hostage as a guarantee for the tribe's good behavior. I do not trust the French and did not place myself in their hands, but I ask you to do so now. Go to Montreal. Negotiate with Onontio. Make whatever promises you need to make to delay their warriors. I need time to gain the release of our people who were captured in Illinois last year, and also to regain the friendship of the

Mascoutens and the Kickapoos. Do you accept this task?"

Eagle Claw nodded to his elder brother, and Kicking Bear spoke. "Though we know this journey may mean our lives, we will do our best, so that the people of Wisaka might live."

As the two left, Jacob Cutler turned painfully toward the chief. "Kiala, my men and I will be leaving as well. I know you are in a bad way, and maybe I can help. Even though England and France are not at war at the moment, the Iroquois are certain to want to avenge my dead Seneca and Mohawks. I'll also have Iroquois runners sent to the St. Francis Abenakis. I know the Fox have been on good terms with them for many years. Perhaps they will send aid. I'll also make sure my employer stocks Oswego with everything you will need to carry on the fight. Guns, powder, shot, hatchets, knives. Bring all the furs you have to Fort Oswego in the spring, and you'll leave with everything you need to achieve victory over your enemies."

"Thank you my friend. Are you well enough to travel?"

"I've traveled farther when hurt worse. I'll make it all right. How is your wound?"

"It troubles me more than it would have were I still young, but I will recover. I must recover; I have much work to do."

Far to the south, a small flotilla of bateaux neared New Orleans. Maurice Joubert was almost completely recovered from the effects of the amputation. Two weeks before, he had finished organizing this little fleet for the trip down river. Father Mercier had urged him to rest for a few more weeks, but he felt much better, and playing chess with the good priest was frustrating him immensely; the lieutenant had lost all twenty-nine games played.

Followed by the faithful Arbut, he visited the Cahokia village and recruited men to act as guards. The Frenchmen living there were easy to recruit; Maurice paid top wages and the work would be easy, as they would be going with the current. All they had to worry about was the possibility of horrible death at the hands of rampaging Natchez or Yazoos near the gulf. But, looking at the situation more positively, as these Frenchmen tended to do, they could just as well die a horrible death in the Illinois Country at the hands of rampaging Foxes. At least if they went on the trip south, they were getting paid to take their chances.

Maurice arranged for a bateau to carry the furs they had obtained. He thought there was safety in numbers, so he encouraged other merchants from all parts of the Illinois Country to ship their wheat, flour, tobacco, furs and lead down river as well. In all, six bateaux were loaded with the goods of "Upper Louisiana," each with its own *patron* or captain. Crews needed to steer the bulky craft down river were small, three men for each being thought sufficient (certainly many more would be needed to muscle the large vessels upriver on the return trip). Maurice and the merchants hired eighteen guards in all. The lieutenant was delighted to learn that Francois Legard wanted to make the trip too.

"I haven't been to New Orleans for some time, and I need to try and find an agent who robs me less than the one I'm using now. My wife is perfectly capable of running the trading house in my absence, and I think the relationship will benefit from a period of separation."

Maurice did not need elaboration on that final point, but was glad to have the former coureur de bois on the trip. "Happy to have you along. I'll be using Hebert and Prevost to dispose of the furs we acquired. I'd be glad to introduce you to them when we arrive in New Orleans. They have a reputation for honest dealing that rivals your own."

"You must be expecting trouble, based on the number of guards. Your caution is undoubtedly wise. Trouble with the Natchez has been really bad for several years, and many boats on the Mississippi have been attacked. Of course, the Yazoos and the Chickasaws are always roaming around looking for trouble, encouraged by the English traders in their villages. It could be an interesting trip."

Father Mercier saw them off at the Cahokia landing. There was only one bateau at this, the starting point. They would pick up the rest as they proceeded down river. "Maurice, Francois, may God watch over you on this journey. Alexandre Arbut! Be certain to change the lieutenant's bandage regularly, and do it the way I showed you."

"Yes, Father."

"I'll never be able to thank you enough for all you've done," said Maurice. "I'll send a generous donation to the seminary when I get back to Montreal."

Then they shoved off. Maurice watched the figure of the priest recede into the distance until it became indistinguishable against the tree line in the background. It was only an hour after dawn and the heat and humidity were already nearly unbearable.

This morning, the patrons estimated that they were four days from New Orleans. They had camped on islands whenever possible, and for the past three days, Maurice had kept the guards on full alert, or at least as near to it as was possible in the broiling sun. They occasionally had seen tribesmen along the shore or in canoes or dugouts, but thus far, had experienced no trouble.

Maurice's bateau was the last in line, and the patron signaled for his attention. Maurice walked to the stern, where the captain manned the tiller. "Lieutenant, in a short while we will pass the best spot on the river to set an ambush. A point of land juts out into the river. What lies behind the point is invisible to river traffic until they are almost even with it. What is worse, the river bottom has been shifting in recent years, and the only safe channel for bateaux this heavily laden is very near the point. If we were to steer more toward the center of the river, we would run aground."

"Thanks for the warning. Look to your weapons. I'll talk to the men."

After speaking to the guards and to those manning the sweeps, Maurice approached Legard and Arbut. "Francois, Alexandre, the patron says we are approaching a good spot for an ambush. We'd better get ready."

Arbut silently withdrew to check his weapons and that of the lieutenant. Legard drew a pistol he wore at his belt and reloaded it. "Blame for this war with the Natchez can be laid at the feet of Governor Perier and the idiot commander of Fort Rosalie, the Sieur de Chepart. Two years ago, de Chepart insisted that the Natchez abandon their chief village, the one containing their most holy places, and turn the land over to him. De Chepart and the governor were to be partners in a plantation to be built on the site. Predictably, the Natchez did not care for this plan, and instead tried to massacre every Frenchman within reach. The war has continued ever since. Of course, the English have been only too happy to help our opponents. In fact, the governor tries to blame the whole situation on a vast conspiracy masterminded by the English, in order to deflect blame from himself."

Arbut returned with his musket slung over his shoulder, a knife and hatchet at his belt. He carried two pistols for Maurice, and the officer's sword. "Thank you Alexandre. Take your position near the patron."

"Unusual to see a sword, except on the parade ground," commented Legard.

"I know. I usually bring mine when I am out in the field. Just a superstition, I guess. I thought it brought me luck." Looking at his empty sleeve, he continued, " I may have to change to a different good luck charm. I'm glad to have the sword now though. With one arm I need to keep a foe at a distance."

"This could prove handy as well." Legard pulled a war club from his baggage to augment his pistol, musket and hunting knife. It had a massive stone head attached to a long wooden handle. "It's been a long time since I had occasion to use this. I hope I've not grown too old and feeble."

The point of land the patron mentioned was visible now, protruding from the east shore of the river. Trees and heavy undergrowth hid the reverse side of the point from view. Following the channel, the bateau moved closer to the east shore. Maurice had positioned all three guards on the port side facing the point. They crouched down, muskets ready. All seemed to be well. The other five bateaux had already passed the point without incident, and they gave no indication that they saw anything troubling on the south side of the small peninsula.

Suddenly, the man at the port side sweep cried out, lost his grip on the oar, and fell overboard, a long arrow stuck in his neck. A volley of musket shots and arrows followed immediately, but none of the other Frenchmen were hit.

"Hold your fire until you have a definite target! Keep down until you're ready to shoot!"

At that moment five dugouts appeared simultaneously along the south edge of the point, each carried by eight to ten warriors who sprinted with their burdens toward the water. Maurice understood the enemy plan in an instant. Since the little fleet headed down river, the manpower aboard was fairly minimal. The Indians allowed the first five bateaux to pass, knowing they would have a very difficult time reversing direction and coming to the aid of the last bateau when it was attacked.

The dugouts had all been launched, and were bearing down on Maurice's bateau. The lieutenant drew one of his pistols, and calmly shot the lead warrior in the closest dugout. Legard killed the second man in the same vessel, and this Natchez overturned the dugout when he fell in the river. Now the range was point blank, and the three guards stood up and fired into the mass of boats closing on them, doing fearful execution. The Indians rammed the side of the bateau and tried to scramble aboard before the French could reload. The guards dropped their muskets and defended the rail with hatchet and knife.

Arbut shot a warrior in the side as he climbed aboard, then he, Maurice and Legard surged forward. One warrior gained the deck, war axe in hand, naked except for a breechcloth, his body covered with tattoos, his face a swirl of black and yellow paint. Maurice sidestepped the Natchez' off balance swing and then ran him through with his sword. Legard fired his pistol into the warriors alongside the bateau, then dropped the great war club to the deck. Instead he drew his hunting knife, and using the empty pistol like a club, dove right onto the mass of warriors below. Arbut picked up Legard's club and took a mighty swing at a brave trying to gain the deck. The force of the swing and the weight of the club swept the warrior off the deck, immediately followed by Arbut, who could not regain his balance.

As suddenly as it began, the action ended. The fifth bateau could not turn around, but was still close enough to Maurice's craft to provide fire support. The Natchez, expecting a quick victory and discouraged by their losses, backed off and either rowed or swam to shore. Suddenly, Maurice's vessel lurched to a stop. They had run aground!

## CHAPTER 8

Jean Baptiste was relieved to see the palisades of Fort Michilimackinac coming into view to the south. Since Sky Singer's death, the trip had been comparatively uneventful, but physically taxing. The portages on the Fox River are numerous, and despite the best efforts of their companions, the seriously wounded suffered greatly as they were carried around rough water. One of the injured men, a voyageur named Charles, died unexpectedly while being carried from a canoe. He had been a popular comrade, always ready to help when there was work to be done, always ready to sing when the canoe men plied their paddles. His wound had not been thought to be mortal, and his demise cast a pall over the entire party.

At Fort La Baye, they received permission to leave Gaspard and the other badly wounded voyageur to recuperate. Roziere had been loud in his protests of such treatment, insisting that he wanted to remain with the convoy. He raved on and on until he saw the nurse that Dufort had found for him, a buxom Menominee woman of about twenty. Etienne brought her to the lodge where Gaspard lay, which was located just outside the palisades of the recently rebuilt fort. The young woman, of average stature but heroic proportions, smiled shyly at her noisy patient. Gaspard ceased bellowing in mid-complaint, and looked at the new arrival in stunned silence.

"Gaspard my friend, I told you that if you behaved yourself I'd find someone to help you through your time of need. Well, even though you have turned out to be the biggest pain in the ass in the history of New France, I scoured the nearby Menominee village and brought you this dove anyway, hoping she would divert you from your ranting. Her name is Humming Bird."

Gaspard rose painfully to a sitting position. "No one ever had a truer friend than you Etienne. I'm forever in your debt. Now, can't you see I'm suffering. Take the young cadet and go. Let this angel of mercy tend to her work."

After resting at Green Bay for two days, Jean Baptiste's party set out on the last leg of their return trip to Michilimackinac. Roziere assured them that he'd be along as soon as his delicate health permitted, but mentioned that Humming Bird felt it might be some time until he attained his full strength.

Jean Baptiste could not wait to reach home. He felt that when they reached Michilimackinac safely, he would have a huge burden lifted from his shoulders. He wanted to sleep, fish, hunt, explore through the woods or do anything other than worry about the Fox Indians and what they might be doing. On the third morning after they arrived at Green Bay, the flotilla set off, proceeding northeast along the western shore of the bay until they reached the north shore of Lake Michigan itself.

Two days later, as they hugged the shore heading east, a powerful storm struck with little warning. It had been a beautiful summer afternoon, not too hot and with a following breeze. They had rigged sails on their canoes, and were traveling in comfort when Dufort gave a shout and pointed astern. Huge thunder heads had formed to the west, the wind picked up suddenly and they saw several flashes of lightning in the distance.

"Furl the sails and get to shore!" yelled Dufort. Everyone grabbed their paddles and headed for safety. Already, the sky darkened, the wind reached gale strength and with it, brought giant waves. All but two of the canoes reached shore safely. One of the canoes was swamped by a wave and sank; another was overturned just before it reached the sand. All the men were saved, and aside from a thorough soaking, no one was the worse for the experience.

Now, three days later, they were within sight of home. They reached the site of the Mission of St. Ignace, across the narrows separating Lake Michigan and Lake Huron. On the opposite side of the narrows, perhaps a league away, was the fort. As they paddled, Jean Baptiste strained to make out details of the place, a spot that he had come to take for granted and with which he was bored only a few months before. Now he could see the white banner of France floating in the gentle breeze. The sentry post above the water gate was now visible, as were those at each corner of the palisade along the beach. As they drew closer, the sentry over the water gate fired his musket in the air. Soon heads began to appear along the wall as the garrison took their defensive positions.

Dufort fired his musket in the air and began waving his paddle over his head. By now they were close enough to be recognized, and the water gate was thrown open, a stream of marines, settlers, traders and Indians issuing forth.  Dufort kissed two Ottawa and three Ojibwa women of his acquaintance and enthusiastically accepted a brandy offered by one of the traders.  Jean Baptiste watched a number of joyous reunions take place as his voyageurs greeted Ottawa or Ojibwa wives or sweethearts, often with squealing metis children hugging their legs. He also recognized several women who came to the beach in vain; their lovers were buried back in Fox country.

As this solemn thought crossed his mind, Jean Baptiste saw Sergeant Jacques Fournier pass through the water gate and approach the spot where he stood.  The sergeant had been working with a party of marines replacing rotted timbers in the south wall.  He walked stiffly, feeling all of his fifty-four years and also the effects of an old arrow wound to the knee.  He walked with a limp, and his only recognizable military clothing was his blue fatigue cap with tassel, but his shoulders were thrown back and his air of authority was unmistakable.

"My young cadet returns.  But where are the other marines?  Leveau?  Murat?  Arbut?  Where is your brother?  Why is that clerk La Pointe with you instead of tending to business in Sioux country?"

"Hello, Sergeant.  It's good to see you, but I'm afraid I bear bad news.  Our mission ends in failure. Leveau and Murat are dead, and we never made it to Sioux country.  As far as I know, Arbut is well.  Maurice was seriously wounded, but survived, though he lost an arm."

Jean Baptiste long remembered the look of shock mingled with sadness on the sergeant's face.  Everyone at Michilimackinac knew that the sergeant took responsibility for the men under his command.  He did his best to teach them what they needed to know to survive, and he took it hard when his efforts were in vain. The cadet knew that the sergeant, Leveau and Murat often fished and hunted together, and even pooled their slender resources to enable them to do a bit of trading with the local tribes.

"Tell me the details later, lad. You need to see the captain and explain the situation to him. He's meeting with a delegation of Nipissings at the moment, so you have time to make yourself look like a soldier before you report to your commanding officer."

"Yes, Sergeant."

Jean Baptiste retrieved his weapons and other belongings from his canoe, told Rene La Pointe that he had to clean up and report to the captain and hurried to his barracks. He stripped off the torn and filthy rags he was wearing and washed as thoroughly as he could with a basin of water, vowing to bathe in the lake as soon as he finished reporting to Captain Montigny. He donned new moccasins, deerskin leggings, a fresh shirt, blue veste and fatigue cap, and immediately reported to the commanding officer's house, where the captain often met with native emissaries.

The marine standing guard outside the residence sweated in the full uniform the captain required of those performing this duty. He wore the gray-white coat with blue cuffs and lining (turnbacks fastened in place per the captain's instructions), blue waistcoat, breeches and stockings, white cravat and tri-corn hat with gold trim. His musket gleamed, and he carried the regulation bayonet in its scabbard, rather than the hatchet normally seen at frontier posts.

As he was about to state his business, the door

opened and three Nipissings emerged with the captain.

"Big Crow, I am pleased that you and your sub-chiefs made the trip here to Michilimackinac. You know that Onontio is always anxious to trade with his red brothers, particularly the Nipissings, who travel far to obtain beaver pelts from many tribes. I'm not surprised that you are not pleased with the treatment your people have experienced at the Hudson Bay posts of the English, as well as the English trading post at Oswego. The English care nothing for the Nipissings, only for the wealth the beaver pelts bring them. If they can cheat you and pay little or nothing for the skins, so much the better. We, on the other hand, want to do business with you, your children, and your children's children. Relationships like that must be based on trust and honesty. Trade here at Michilimackinac, and you will be treated fairly and with respect."

"We will tell our people what you have said. If they agree with my wishes, we will return here to trade."

At that moment, the captain noticed Jean Baptiste for the first time. "Cadet La Croix, it's good to see you again. Please go into my quarters and have a seat. I must take these Nipissings to the King's storehouse and distribute some gifts for them to take back to their tribe. I'll be back directly. I'm anxious to hear your report."

Jean Baptiste entered the commandant's residence, which served as both home and headquarters for the captain. He entered the room where Montigny met with his officers, wrote reports and generally spent the bulk of his duty hours. A large desk sat at the far, or north end of the room, a window behind it provided light for reading and writing reports. On the wall to the right of the desk was a large, though somewhat crudely executed, map of New France. Next to the map, crossed swords were mounted about head-high, a decorative Ottawa hatchet suspended from the fastening as well. In fact, the room contained numerous mementos from the many Indian conferences held here, both during Captain Montigny's tenure in command and before. Perhaps the most striking item on display was a gigantic buffalo skull brought by the Sioux some years before. The cadet selected a chair near the desk and sat down. While he waited, he reflected on what he knew about the captain.

Jacques Testard de Montigny was sixty-eight years old, much older than most commanders of wilderness posts. He had been a marine for nearly forty years, and his had been a storied career. Before the turn of the century, he had fought with Iberville in Newfoundland, winning renown many times through audacity and his skillful handling of Indian allies. Early in the new century he had again been active in Newfoundland and Acadia, and again his efforts met with success. About twenty-five years ago, he traveled to France to present the Abenaki chief Nescambiouit at court, the two having been comrades during these campaigns in the east. Montigny made captain in 1706 (the highest rank to which a marine in the field could aspire), and was awarded the Cross of the Order of Saint-Louis in 1712, for his long and meritorious service to the crown. Despite his advanced age, he had been assigned to Michilimackinac because of the respect the tribes had for him.

Jean Baptiste's thoughts were interrupted by the captain's arrival. The cadet leaped to attention, but Montigny signaled him to resume his seat. The old officer was dressed in his finest, in honor of the guests just departed. His justaucorps was made of fine quality, off-white material trimmed in blue. His blue waistcoat was edged in gold, and his gorget was highly polished and gleamed in the sun. Of greatest interest to the cadet was the white Cross of Saint-Louis pinned to the captain's left breast, suspended by a red ribbon. The elderly officer looked tired, and sat down heavily behind his desk.

"I assume you have bad news for me, else I would be talking to your brother right now. Give me the essentials in a few sentences, then start at the beginning and tell me the whole story, omitting nothing of significance."

When Jean Baptiste finished, the captain said nothing. He leaned back in his chair looking at the ceiling, lost in thought. Finally, he spoke. "Well, lad, I am truly sorry about your brother and the men who were killed. Maurice is a fine officer and the service will miss him. Leveau was my orderly for several months, probably would have been even now if he could have shined boots better. Based on what you have told me, my only criticism of your actions is that you did not kill him when you had the opportunity, saving him from the torment that came later."

Jean Baptiste's face became flushed. "I have thought about that moment often. I hoped I was giving him a chance for life, perhaps adoption by the Fox. When I saw how things turned out, I wished I had finished him."

"That's over; put it behind you. My God, you saw more action in the last few months than most marines experience in ten years. Your brother's wounds even gave you a valuable opportunity to command, and you seem to have done it well. Heavier losses than I like to see, but probably couldn't be helped. One thing puzzles me. Why do you think the Fox attacked you? I'd have thought they would have licked their wounds from last summer for quite awhile."

"I think they needed the supplies we were carrying. On the return trip, I'm sure they were watching us, but made no attempt to hinder us until we kidnapped the boy, because we were carrying little of value."

"Some might question the wisdom of seeking a captive, but I'm glad you did. This business of the English and the Iroquois causing trouble again, this time inciting the Fox, is information of value. It will have to be reported to Montreal. I know you are tired. Rest tonight. By noon tomorrow, have a full written report of the expedition on my desk. I will then write a report that will accompany yours. Relax for a few days and regain your strength. I may have need of you soon."

Jean Baptiste walked to the storehouse where his father's business was transacted. He wanted to inform the clerk, Claude Guyotte, about the trip, most notably why they had departed with several boatloads of trade goods but had returned with nothing. When he arrived, he found Rene La Pointe already relating the tale.

"Friend Claude says the difficulties we encountered don't surprise him. He says it seems like a dark cloud hovers over your father's business affairs. Formerly, everything your father touched turned to gold. His business, originally founded by his father before him, was the most successful trading venture in New France. Your family seigneury on the St. Lawrence above Montreal is ideally situated to exploit the fur trade, and for years, success followed success. But for the last few seasons, evil luck has been the rule. Supply convoys from Montreal have been attacked or simply disappear; the same with shipments of furs to Montreal. Of course, all traders are affected to some extent, but your father certainly more than most."

"It is true," said Claude. "I hope that your brother Maurice is able to get a good price for the furs sent to New Orleans, and that his trip is smooth and uneventful."

"As do I.   Is your brother Gilles still at Michilimackinac?"

"No, he really doesn't like the upper country. He came out in the spring to help with the ledgers, but as soon as that was completed he joined the first fur brigade returning to Montreal."

## CHAPTER 9

Maurice was experiencing anything but a "smooth" and "uneventful" trip. When the bateau ground to a halt, everyone still on board was thrown to the deck. The lieutenant yelled to the patron, asking what had happened, but received no response. Maurice stood up, feeling bruised but not broken, and turned aft to look at the tiller. The captain still manned his post, standing next to the steering oar and seeming to peer forward, but he would never respond to anything again. Two arrows had passed completely through his body and pinned his corpse to the tiller. Maurice pulled the arrows free and lowered him to the deck.

"Help those men out of the water! Careful! Don't expose yourself to fire from the shore more than necessary."

Legard and Arbut were fished out of the river. Several arrows were fired at the bateau during this rescue mission, but all landed harmlessly.

"I'm glad to see you're both alright," said Maurice. "Unfortunately, we're not out of trouble. The captain is dead and we're stuck on a sandbar. Does anyone know the best way to get us afloat?"

Unfortunately, none of the survivors were

experienced river men.  Finally, Maurice concluded, "Well, we'd better get over the side and try to shove her back into deep water.  If we stay here, we are tempting the Natchez to make another try at us."

Legard said, "We need one man to stay on board and keep an eye on the Indians.  We'll prime all the pistols and muskets and leave them with him. Lieutenant, you should stand guard.  You don't have your strength yet, and with only one arm, could provide only limited help to us.  Keep a sharp watch and we'll get us off."

Maurice reluctantly agreed.  He stayed on board with one of the guards who had received a mortal wound in the recent melee.  The other six men went over the starboard side of the bateau, arranged themselves along its length, and began to shove.  After a time, Legard called, "It's no use.  The bateau is so heavily laden that the six of us can't budge it.  We need more men."

Maurice looked to the south to assess the situation on the other bateaux.  The boat nearest them, the one that had supported them during the fight, had set its anchors, and was moored about a musket shot away. With its small crew, it would have difficulty making headway upstream to come to their aid.  Farther south, the other four bateaux had cleared the dangerous channel near the east shore and also had dropped anchor.  It looked to Maurice that help might be on the way, however.  One of the dugouts lost by their attackers had drifted downstream and had been recovered by the crew of one of the bateaux.  Several men from each of those vessels had boarded the dugout, and the rescue vessel had begun to make slow progress upstream.

"Help is on the way, men.  They caught one of the

Indian dugouts downstream, and you should have many more hands to help with the work soon."

"Thank God," said Arbut. "The six of us couldn't move this thing if we worked at it until the river froze over."

"Keep in mind, Alexandre, that the Mississippi doesn't freeze over, especially this far south," said Legard. "By the way, that was certainly a beautiful swing you employed to clear the deck of that Natchez. While I'm thinkng about it, have you seen my club anywhere?"

Arbut's face reddened. "I'm sorry. I didn't realize how heavy the thing was. I swung it as hard as I could, and once everything started moving in the direction of the swing, I couldn't stop. Your club is on the bottom of the river."

"It's alright little man. Though I was pretty busy, I was able to catch you from the corner of my eye. Seeing the look on your face as you sailed out over the water was worth the loss of the weapon. Although I have had it..."

One of the guards, the man positioned at the stern of the bateau, screamed and fell backward, clutching his neck. A Natchez had swum underwater until he reached the tiller, then slashed the unlucky guard across the throat with a blade he carried in his teeth. Maurice put a pistol ball through the top of the Indian's head. He then turned and stared hard at the river between the bateau and the point of land on the east shore. He saw several other shapes gliding under the water. He fired twice more; the first missed, but the second resulted in a cloud of red matter floating to the surface. The swimmers retreated.

"Andre's dead," said Leveau as he crouched over the guard's body floating in shallow water.

"Here comes the dugout with our friends," called Maurice. The dugout had picked up two more men from the nearest bateau, and now contained ten Frenchmen in all. In a short time it bumped against the side of the stranded bateau.

"We saw you were in trouble. It looked like you weren't moving and we guessed you had run aground. If so, you would need more muscle than you had aboard to get you off. It's lucky this dugout was handy."

"We appreciate the assistance. The fellows on shore were becoming troublesome again."

As Legard took his place with the others, preparing to muscle the bateau back into the channel, Maurice mused, "Based on the tactics employed by our Indian enemies this trip, I believe I will recommend that spear fishing be a required part of the training for marine cadets."

Even with ten more strong backs, it took the better part of an hour to free the bateau. All six bateaux then drifted about three leagues further downstream until they found a defensible island, where they landed and made camp for the night.

Three days later, the little flotilla of bateaux reached New Orleans. Founded only thirteen years before, it was an impressive spot. From the beginning, the growth of the community had been planned, with streets symmetrically designed in preference to the haphazard growth found elsewhere. Facing southeast on the Mississippi, the central waterfront was dominated by the Place d'Armes, an open square bordered by government and religious buildings. The river front on both sides of the Place d'Armes contained the commercial areas of the new settlement. Back away from the river were the residential sections, neatly arranged on geometric streets, many of the home sites still vacant at this early date. Some brick construction was beginning to replace the older wooden structures. Trees, flowers of many vibrant colors and gardens were much in evidence, and the private residences featured large verandas, some of which entirely encircled the homes. Maurice noticed that freshly dug entrenchments covered the approaches to the town.

Maurice still traveled in the sixth bateau. His companions in the other vessels had selected dock facilities upriver from the government buildings, and had secured their bateaux. Maurice pulled in near them and jumped ashore.

"Arbut, stay here and keep an eye on things. Francois, come along with me if you like, and we will find the firm of Hebert and Prevost."

They walked along the wharf and studied the activity going on around them. Legard had mentioned that a high percentage of the town's exports originated nearby, such as naval stores, indigo, tobacco and hemp. More for consumption by the local population were the locally produced rice, fish, figs, oranges, vegetables and meat. The grain of the Illinois Country also found a ready market here in New Orleans. Furs obtained nearby or from the north were shipped to France to be manufactured into apparel. The port was alive with activity.

"If all this loading and unloading is any indication, business appears to be good," commented Maurice. "If much of this is for export, as you say it is, there should be a lot of manufactured imports stored here somewhere, ready to be shipped to the Illinois. Our reception on the trip down river makes me more sympathetic to the merchants who don't want to ship trade goods north unless they are well protected. What do you think?"

"I suppose there is no alternative but to hire a number of guards, unless the governor can be prevailed upon to provide a military escort. We merchants can hire guards ourselves, but will have to raise our prices if we want to make a profit. We don't compete much for business against the English in the Illinois Country, but those French areas that do, including here in Louisiana, already have trouble, due to the low price and high quality of English goods. English trouble making here and elsewhere improves their already advantageous trade position."

"I have to meet with the governor later, a matter of courtesy since I am an officer from Canada. I'll see what I can do about a marine escort for your return trip. Ah, here's the place we are seeking. Hebert and Prevost. Shall we go in?"

Jean Hebert and Cesaire Prevost ran a modest establishment on the river front a short distance above the Place d'Armes. Maurice and Francois introduced themselves to a gentleman of about fifty with sparse brown hair and watery eyes. The man's face brightened when the "Joubert" name was mentioned.

"Would you be related to Daniel Joubert by any chance?'

"Yes, he is my father."

"Welcome then, welcome. Your father and I have never met, but have had business dealings on a number of occasions. A man of absolute integrity. Excuse my bad manners! I am Jean Hebert, one of the proprietors here. What can I do for you gentlemen today?"

"We've come with a convoy of bateaux from the Illinois Country. Most of the boats contain grain. I don't know if you are the agent for any of the other merchants or not. I'm only concerned with thirty-two packs of prime pelts obtained from the Cahokias. I'd like you to get the best price you can for those. If memory serves, several merchants in Montreal honor your bills of exchange. I need to return to Canada soon, and I'd like to take a credit with me so that father can use it to obtain more trade goods. I'd also like your help finding passage to the St. Lawrence. Will you do it?"

"That's why we're here, son. Show me where the furs are located when we finish talking, and I'll get right to work. And you, sir," Hebert said, looking at Legard. "Is there something I can do for you today?"

Later, after Hebert's men began off-loading the furs, Maurice decided it was time to report to Governor Perier. He had Arbut go through their belongings, trying to piece together some type of presentable outfit. The result was a laughable amalgam of items, but did include Maurice's gorget indicating his rank, and Arbut was able to give it a reasonable shine.

It was late afternoon when Maurice arrived at the seat of government at the Place d'Armes. He approached a guard wearing the familiar white uniform trimmed in blue of the Companies franches de la Marine. The lieutenant stated his name and his business and the man came to attention, then asked him to wait a moment. The guard entered a room, and returned a few minutes later with a young man in a well-tailored officer's uniform.

"Lieutenant Henri Gaultier at your service. News

of your arrival has preceded you and the governor has looked forward to this meeting. I am his aide and would be happy to introduce you. Please come this way."

The white clad lieutenant led Maurice into a room that appeared to be the antechamber to a much larger room. The antechamber contained Gaultier's desk, several chairs for visitors, and on the wall, the flag of the East India Company, the organization presently governing Louisiana. Lieutenant Gaultier motioned to Maurice, and they proceeded through double doors into the governor's office. The room was large and richly appointed.

Governor Etienne Perier rose from his desk to meet them.

"Governor, I'd like you to meet Lieutenant Maurice Joubert, Sieur de Tremblant."

"I apologize for my appearance, Governor. It's been a difficult trip."

"Nonsense, my boy. We realize that traveling in this wilderness is not like a Sunday row on the Seine. Think nothing of your clothes. We will find something appropriate. Henri, would you take care of that please?"

"Certainly, Sir." And with that, the dapper lieutenant left.

"Please sit down, Lieutenant, and tell me of your journey." So, Maurice recounted the salient facts of the trip, omitting the numerous remarks he had heard which indicated the residents of Louisiana held their governor in low regard.

When he concluded, Perier said, "I am truly sorry about the arm. What are your plans now?"

"When my business with Jean Hebert is concluded, I want him to help me locate a vessel sailing to the St. Lawrence. I can't spend much time here or it will be too late in the season to make Montreal before winter."

The governor did not respond immediately. He seemed to be concentrating on something as he paced back and forth. Finally, he seemed to make a decision and turned to Maurice. "I think I have the answer to your problem. In three days, Lieutenant Gaultier is supposed to sail to Canada aboard the *Pelican*, a fast schooner I have at my disposal. Given your rank and family background, it will do no harm to tell you his mission.

"Louisiana is being destroyed by the Indian trouble instigated by the English. You have seen the difficulties we face trying to transport merchandise to and from Upper Louisiana. This war has been going on for years, and it is strangling our commerce. We are a small colony from the standpoint of population, but have a large land area to defend. I have only a few companies of soldiers, the militia and some loyal tribes with which to do the fighting. Rumor has it that the Company of the Indies, which manages Louisiana for France, has despaired of ever making a profit here. They wish to return the colony to the crown. That may or may not happen, but I'm sending the lieutenant to appeal to the governor-general in Montreal for military assistance. My feeling is that control of this province will revert to the crown, but if the transfer takes much time and we are left without help, there may not be much left to transfer.

"Since Lieutenant Gaultier is headed to the St. Lawrence anyway, we should have no difficulty making room for you on board the *Pelican*. You might even be able to corroborate his tale once he reaches Canada."

"It is a most generous offer, and I'd be a fool to refuse it. I have a marine with me and would like him to go as well."

"Certainly. That will not be a problem. Do you have a place to stay?"

"Yes, my fusilier has arranged for rooms at an inn."

"Fine. Why not get a good night's rest? Let Henri know where you are staying, and by this time tomorrow, you should have suitable clothing. Then you can join us in the evening for dinner, and perhaps a little diversion later."

"I'll look forward to it."


Lieutenant Gaultier returned to the governor's office a short time later.

"Ah, Henri. Have you found something suitable for our guest?"

"He's about my size, perhaps a bit thinner. I've sent one of my uniforms to be altered. It will be ready in the morning."

"Excellent. I've been thinking, this Canadian is well placed to further the real aim of your mission. If Governor General Beauharnois does consent to send military help, that would be wonderful, but the chances of that are slight. I'm more concerned that our financial goals are met. I think Dominique might be helpful in that regard. Why don't you send her to me?"

"I'll locate her immediately, Uncle."

## CHAPTER 10

M aurice slept like the dead that night, as did his roommate, the fusilier Arbut. The lieutenant awoke about three hours after dawn; Arbut still snored noisily. Maurice went downstairs to the common room in the small inn. One of the serving girls was cleaning the tables and smiled brightly as she recognized him.

"And how are you this morning, sir?"

"Fine, but my stomach feels like I haven't eaten in a month. Could you find some bread and cheese, along with some wine, for myself and my companion?"

"Yes, sir." Before she left, she curtsied daintily, making sure Maurice got an eyeful of her cleavage. She winked at him mischievously and then was off.

*Well, I must not be totally repulsive to all women, even with one arm. That's good to know.*

As he waited for the food, the door swung open and a small man in his sixties entered, carrying a marine officer's uniform.

"I'm looking for a lieutenant named Joubert."

"You are in luck. I am Joubert."

"I'm Adrien Dupleiss, the tailor selected by Lieutenant Gaultier to alter this uniform. I don't like doing alterations without measuring the subject myself.

Leads to an unsatisfactory result, if you know what I mean.   You may be smaller in the waist than the lieutenant said. Well, there's only one thing to do. Please try the uniform on."

"I'm sure it will be fine."

"I insist, sir.  My professional reputation in the community is at stake.   Besides, the lieutenant didn't mention anything about your special situation.  I'll have to pin up that sleeve in a becoming manner."

"As you wish.  Come upstairs with me." As they started upstairs, the serving girl appeared with the food. "Could you bring the food up to my room, ah, I'm sorry, I forgot your name."

"Annette.  And I'll be right up."

Alexandre Arbut awoke at last and gave a low whistle when he saw Maurice. "Where did you find such a handsome uniform on such short notice?"

"Lieutenant Gaultier, the man who will be traveling to Canada with us, located it somewhere." And it didn't even cost anything.   The little tailor had already been paid for his services. It really was by far the best uniform he had ever worn. Though officers' uniforms were usually made of better quality material than those of enlisted men, he had never worn one such as this.  The material was extremely comfortable and of lighter weight than those issued in Canada.  The blue veste with the gold edging denoting an officer and the near white justaucorps were a perfect fit. The left sleeve of the latter was neatly folded and pinned near the shoulder to keep it out of his way.

"Alexandre, see what you can do about obtaining clothes for the trip.   By the time we reach the St.

Lawrence, it will be getting cold."

That evening, he went to the governor's office as planned, and found that a sumptuous meal had been prepared, and awaited him in the meeting room next door. The governor and Lieutenant Gaultier were already present, as were several prominent New Orleans merchants. When he arrived, all were seated, and servants began bringing heaping dishes of delicacies. Thin-sliced beef marinated in wine, capon and venison were the main courses, but several rice dishes, fish and a number of desserts featuring figs and sliced oranges were also served. And the wines were excellent, undoubtedly the best Maurice had ever tasted.

"I never realized how sick I was of eating pemmican until this moment," said Maurice as he sampled a morsel of capon.

"Eat hearty sir," spoke up a rotund merchant named Raimbault. While you're on board ship, I doubt the food will be this good."

"I'm sure you are right; this food is so good, I don't think I want to leave at all."

After dinner, while all enjoyed a glass of brandy, the merchants added their voices to that of the governor and Lieutenant Gaultier. "Please, sir, do all that you can to convince Governor General Beauharnois to send troops. We are in desperate condition. The savages have attacked our convoys on the Mississippi again and again. Either we spend ruinously to provide adequate protection, or we lose the convoys. Either way the commerce of the colony will soon wither to nothing."

"Gentlemen, after the courtesy I've been shown here, I will certainly champion your cause. But please keep in mind that I am only a lieutenant of marines, and I've never met the governor-general. I'll be happy to share my rather harrowing experiences on the Mississippi with him, but whether that will do any good, I have no way of knowing."

"You can only do your best," said the governor. "Well gentlemen, if you have all had enough to eat, perhaps we should repair to Madame Linctot's, where we can play cards or billiards, and associate with members of the opposite sex. Anyone opposed? I didn't think so. Let's be off."

Madame Linctot's was a wooden structure located a short distance downstream from the Place d' Armes. Undistinguished looking on the outside, it was elegant inside. Costly fixtures lined the walls, the main room boasted thick green carpeting with ornate geometric designs and a large chandelier hung from the center of the ceiling. Four billiard tables lined the far wall, while nearer the entrance, six tables were set up to accommodate New Orleans' wealthy card players. To the left was a well appointed bar, near which several women in eveningwear conversed.

"Well Maurice, what appeals to you here?"

"I've never played billiards, and it's unlikely I will ever become proficient now. I will probably also have significant difficulty playing cards. What do you suggest?"

"Dominique!" The governor gestured to a tall, raven-haired woman, who broke off the conversation she was having with two other women and approached.

"Maurice Joubert, I'd like you to meet Dominique Lamarque. Maurice is a lieutenant in the marines, stationed at Michilimackinac far to the north. As you can see, he suffered some misfortune of late. Dominique is the most beautiful woman in New Orleans, as I'm sure you'll agree."

"I'll certainly not argue with that." In fact, Maurice could readily believe it. The woman standing before him was stunning. Many of the women in Canada were pretty too, but none he had seen had this combination of natural beauty augmented by a beautiful scent, exotic use of cosmetics and a dazzling coiffure. She wore a shimmering blue dress gathered tight around her small waist, the length of the garment extending almost to the floor. The bodice was extremely low-cut, and the woman smiled as Maurice could not help looking at her breasts. He looked up and noticed her eyes for the first time, a very light green color, with long, dark lashes. The eyes themselves and the eyebrows had been carefully outlined in black.

"I'd like a drink if you can manage it."

"Certainly, I'll be back in a moment." Maurice noticed for the first time that the governor had left them and had begun a conversation with several men seated at one of the card tables. *Not such a bad fellow after all.*

Maurice brought two glasses of brandy to where Dominique was standing. "I hope you like this. I didn't even ask what you wanted."

"Brandy is fine. So tell me, how did a marine from Michilimackinac end up in New Orleans? If my memory serves me, Canada is a royal colony, while Louisiana is run by the East India Company, which means there is not too much official business between the two. In fact, there has been quite a bit of bad blood from time to time."

"You are well informed. If you like, I'll tell you the tale of how I started for Sioux country and ended here, if you will promise to tell me how you came to this city."

"Fine. Several of the gaming tables are not being used. Why don't we sit and make ourselves comfortable?"

Maurice spent the next hour recounting his recent adventures. He was amazed at how easily he could communicate with her, even about difficult subjects like the loss of his arm. She listened attentively, asked many insightful questions and appeared genuinely interested. At times, he wasn't even sure what he had been saying due to his preoccupation with her eyes, nose, hair and various other physical features. If he stuttered, or stopped suddenly in mid-sentence, she gave no indication.

When he finished, he found she was holding his hand in her right hand, gently rubbing the back with her left. He was enormously thirsty, but wouldn't have moved his hand at that moment, even to save his life. She must have read his mind because she raised her glass to his lips and he drank.

"Now it is your turn," said Maurice.

"I was one of the *casquette* girls who arrived from France in 1727. I was born and raised in Brest. In school, the nuns told us many stories about the New World. It seemed like a terrible place in many ways, with priests being martyred, Indian wars and trouble with the English. But it also seemed like a place where opportunities existed that were absent in France. Even a poor man could own his own farm. If he decided he didn't like the spot he lived, he could move elsewhere. New towns were being built, and people tried new business ventures, like the lead mines in the Illinois Country. I decided to try my luck.

"With three Ursuline nuns as escorts, a group of girls from my school and others took ship for Louisiana. As a parting gift from the king, we each received a box or casquette containing our trousseau, for we were to be married upon arrival. When we arrived, we were placed in a guarded house. Men from the surrounding area came to the house during daylight hours to select their brides. Though I wasn't sure I liked his looks, I was wed to Antoine Lemarque, a cotton farmer near here. He turned out to be a good husband, but a year after we married, he died from a fever. I decided that cotton farming was not for me, sold the place, and moved into the city. Elaine Linctot is the sister of one of my cotton farm neighbors, and I had met her a number of times when she came out to visit. I liked her nice clothes and expensive perfume and when I moved to New Orleans, I decided to see if she would hire me. After a few short lessons in making myself presentable, here I am. I don't plan to stay here forever, but this is the place to meet the influential in this city."

Two tables from where they sat, a small crowd had gathered. Only two seats were occupied, both by female employees of the club. Around the table, a half dozen men had gathered to watch the proceedings.

"What is happening?" asked Maurice.

"It looks like Gabrielle and Marie had another of their little disagreements, and have decided to settle it by playing "twenty-one.""

"Don't they get along?"

"Not especially well. It often happens that they both try to catch the eye of the same man. Rather than resort to violence, I must admit that they have devised various interesting methods to get the beau's attention."

As she spoke, Maurice studied the contestants. Gabrielle, a tall redhead wearing a green dress similar in style to Dominique's, was shuffling the cards and would act as dealer. Marie was a petite blond wearing a dress of pale yellow. Both women were very attractive, as were all Madame Linctot's employees.

Maurice was too far from the table to make out any of the cards being played. Gabrielle dealt, and Marie looked at her hand. She requested another card, and then another. She then threw her cards on the table (presumably the total for her cards exceeded twenty-one), indicating she had lost. She turned to a young naval officer to her left, smiled up at him, then slowly pulled one arm, then the other, from the sleeves of her dress. She then grasped the bodice of the gown and pulled it out and down, exposing an exquisite pair of breasts that bounced slightly as they were freed from the material.

"That definitely seems to have gotten the man's attention."

"Gabrielle won't be easily outdone. Watch."

The redhead dealt another hand. This time Marie decided to play those cards. Gabrielle looked at her cards, drew one more, then the two showed their hands. Gabrielle smiled, rose from her chair, and slowly exposed her bosom much as Marie had done. Her breasts were smaller, with pale pink aureoles around the nipples. Then she turned her back to the ship's captain, who was near apoplexy by this time, and slipped the entire dress down to her ankles, revealing that she wore nothing underneath. Winking at him as she wiggled her butt and stepped out of the gown, she walked to the officer, placed his arm in hers, and the two walked to the bar to get drinks. Marie seemed momentarily unhappy, but recovered quickly when all the other men standing at the table tried to strike up a conversation at once.

Maurice was dumbfounded. He had never seen anything like that, at least by white girls. Of course, many of the Indian women were wonderfully uninhibited, and exhibiting their feminine charms seemed to come naturally. But this was new to him. Suddenly he remembered he was with Dominique and tore his eyes away from the scene before him, blushing deeply.

He was amazed to find her laughing at his discomfort. "Perhaps you'd like to go for a walk," she said. "It's a beautiful evening and the moon is full."

He mumbled his assent, afraid that his tight-fitting breeches would reveal the extent of his enthusiasm for the card game. They walked to the door, then out into the night. They strolled arm in arm along the river front, upstream past the Place d' Armes and into the commercial district.

"I thought I should get you out of there before you had some sort of fatal attack. After all, you are in a weakened condition, having recently been wounded. How would it look for the governor to have to report that you survived multiple Indian attacks only to succumb to the sight of a pair of quivering cheeks?"

"Go ahead and laugh. I just wasn't expecting something like that is all. Does that sort of thing happen often?"

"As I mentioned, Gabrielle and Marie can be inventive when they choose to be, as can some of the other girls."

As they walked, they came to an unoccupied wharf with several benches. It was late and no one was in sight. The moonlight was beautiful, shining on the water.

"Why don't we sit here and enjoy the evening, Dominique?"

They sat and then Dominique lifted her skirts above her knees and placed her right foot in Maurice's lap. "Help me with my shoes please, if you want me to be comfortable."

After he removed her shoes, she stood up suddenly and said, "Let's go for a swim!"

Without another word she peeled off her gown, stockings and undergarments, the moonlight shining on her voluptuous body. Maurice gaped at her and stood mute, unable to move. "Come on, take off your clothes. What's the matter, don't you like me anymore?" While asking that last question, she stepped forward and grasped his crotch gently. "No, that doesn't seem to be the problem, though I'm not sure that's because of me, or still because of Gabrielle and Marie."

Maurice laughed aloud, then immediately stopped himself. He didn't want to arouse the neighborhood, and spoil the moment. He started to remove his uniform, but progress was slow due to his single arm.

"Here, let me help you. You do the top and I'll get the bottom." He sat down and she pulled off his boots; then he stood up and she unbuttoned the fly on his breeches. She pulled his breeches off and revealed his erection. "Look at that. That's quite impressive, but I fear I must take action immediately, or else you won't enjoy your swim." Then she reached for him.

## CHAPTER 11

Jean Baptiste awoke with a tremendous headache. The pain was centered behind his eyes, and even slight movement provoked waves of it, as well as nausea. His mouth was so dry it felt as if he'd had nothing to drink in weeks, though he knew that was not the case. He vaguely wondered why he could not have continued in blissful unconsciousness when a snort beside him caused him to start suddenly, an action he instantly regretted. When the throbbing in his head subsided a bit, he turned over very slowly and carefully, and saw that he had a companion.

Memory slowly returned. Yesterday he had completed and submitted the report to the captain. Afterward, he could not decide what he wanted to do. What he really wanted to do was walk to the Ottawa village a short distance to the southwest, and spend weeks hunting and fishing with his friends. He couldn't do that though, because the captain said he might have a job for him. He had to stay close to the fort.

In the end, he walked along Rue Dauphine through the water gate and sat on the beach to the left of the pier, near a line of bateaux pulled up on the sand. He sat peacefully gazing across the strait to the spot where he imagined that Father Marquette had ministered to his flock. He idly wondered what, if anything, interesting was happening there. While he daydreamed, Rene La Pointe walked up and sat down next to him.

"Jean Baptiste, I've been looking all over for you. How did your report turn out?"

"Well, I tried to be as factual as possible. I think Captain Montigny will be able to follow the sequence of events, but I doubt the report has much literary merit."

"I assume my indispensable role in the proceedings was duly noted," laughed the young clerk.

"Your contributions as chief advocate of Hannibal the Carthaginian were prominently mentioned." The two sat silently for a time, then Jean Baptiste continued. "I wonder if events actually happened the way they were described by your Livy and Polybius. Our recent experiences in battle certainly were nothing like Hannibal's. He was in control in almost any situation. He would shrewdly analyze a situation, including his opponent's mental abilities, and create an appropriate plan of action. More times than not, events occurred as he foresaw.

"Our experiences, on the other hand, would indicate that battle is a place of confusion where much happens by chance. Not much grand design. Certainly not a lot of control."

"Based on what I've read, chaos is the result for most soldiers," replied the clerk. "With experience, it is possible to achieve a degree of control by doing a better job anticipating what your opponent will do. Also, a veteran commander builds options into his plans, so that he may react successfully to an array of his enemy's counter-moves. Hannibal's ability to do these things well made him the best. He was successful even though the Romans enjoyed overwhelming manpower advantages. If I were you though, I wouldn't worry that you don't compare to Hannibal. No one does. You just need to learn from your experiences and improve, as is the case with all mere mortals. While you're thinking that over, why don't we get something to eat? I heard from Dufort that the rations of bread, salt pork and dried peas are being issued today. Then we can try to catch some whitefish to augment this rather limited diet."

Jean Baptiste smiled. "Let's go."

The two youths spent the afternoon fishing from the pier next to the fort, and they enjoyed a good deal of luck, catching seven plump whitefish between them.

"I wonder where Dufort is hiding this afternoon?" asked Jean Baptist.

"He said he and your Sergeant Fournier were going to hunt for some fresh meat. He thinks that too much salt pork is bad for the digestion. If they bag a deer, we'll have a feast tonight. How are the vegetables in your garden plot?"

"I should be able to find some beans to contribute to the meal. Why don't you start cleaning the fish and get a fire going. I'll see what I can find in the garden, and also try to locate Etienne and the sergeant."

Dufort had brought down a fine buck with a shot from seventy paces, so the four comrades feasted well that evening on the beach outside the fort. The sergeant provided several very acceptable bottles of brandy, and when those were empty, went away for awhile, reappearing out of the darkness with three or four more. Soon everyone was in a very mellow mood, especially Jean Baptiste, who had drunk very little in his short life.

Dufort and La Pointe decided to visit the nearby Ojibwa village in search of entertainment. The cadet elected to stay with the sergeant and finish the brandy.

"You have been in a somber mood since your return, my young cadet."

"Yes, I can't stop thinking about Leveau, Murat, Sky Singer and the others."

"You might have a hard time believing this now, but it is good that you think about them. Some officers care nothing for the welfare of their men. The men are mere tools to be used on the path to promotion. If they are killed or disabled, they are discarded and forgotten. Of course, troops will do no more than is absolutely necessary for a commander who throws their lives away. A man who gains the respect and trust of his men by spending their lives prudently to achieve significant goals can accomplish great things. The man in charge needs to weigh the cost against the value to be gained. The men you mentioned died for a reason; they were not mindlessly sacrificed."

The sergeant continued. "My feeling is that being a good officer, one that can attain the proper balance in his actions, is more difficult here in New France than in many other places."

"Why is that?"

"Usually, officers are given military objectives and resources to achieve them. Their role lies in planning how to attain the desired goals, and leading their men into action. Here in New France, the policy allowing officers to participate in the fur trade, theoretically to offset some of the expenses at the frontier posts, complicates the situation for many commanders. Instead of being concerned with purely military duties, the temptation is great to emphasize involvement in trade. It is possible to become very wealthy by trading with the tribes. The more effort that is expended on commercial activity means that less is available for official duties.

"Of course maintaining the flow of trade goods to the Indians is how they are kept friendly, but I think the role the post commanders play in this commerce is a mistake. It takes a strong man to involve himself in the trade only as much as good Indian relations require. Many are not strong enough. An aspiring officer must decide if his main focus is to perform his duties with honor, or to become rich. I'm confident that in your case, like your brother before you, you'll make the right choice."

Jean Baptiste and the sergeant sat without speaking for a length of time, both staring into the fire. The young cadet reflected long on the sergeant's words. He knew the sergeant was aware of his family background. His father was an honest man, but he encouraged his sons to join the marines in large measure to benefit from the trade opportunities open to officers on the frontier. If the sons obtained desirable postings, the family business would prosper. With a start, Jean Baptiste realized that much of the difficulty he had experienced in recent years from his twin brothers Louis and Jacques was related to what the sergeant had just said. They were four years older than the cadet, and both had achieved the rank of ensign. Louis was currently assigned to a company in Montreal; Jacques had recently been sent to Fort St. Joseph. Jean Baptiste realized now that one of the big reasons he identified much more with Maurice than with the twins was that Maurice de-emphasized direct participation in trade and stressed achievement of military objectives. The twins took a different view. By reputation an excellent marine officer himself in his day, their father wanted his sons to be successful in both arenas.

He couldn't think about this or anything else right now. He decided he'd had too much to drink. He felt a bit dizzy and his head had begun to hurt.

"Well, Sergeant, thank you for sharing your thoughts." Jean Baptiste stood up, lost his balance, and almost fell into the fire. He regained his footing and said, "I think it's time for me to get some sleep."

He started back toward the gate when he encountered Dufort, La Pointe and three Ojibwa women walking unsteadily toward him.

"There he is! Jean Baptiste! Join us! These ladies have found some delightful Ojibwa-made spirits. A nice change of pace from brandy."

Though he tried to decline the invitation, his friends were insistent. Very little of what happened after that was clear to the cadet on this, the following morning, as Jean Baptiste looked around and realized he was lying in one of the Ojibwa lodges near the fort. He knew the location because he could just make out one of the fort's sentry posts through the opening that served as a door. His companion, one of the women from the night before, snored fitfully beside him. He noted that she was nude and had very vague recollections of feverish groping at some point in the darkness.

He had always heard that no matter how old you were, or how many women you had been with, you always had special memories of the first time you made love. Moving very slowly to minimize the concussion of the artillery exploding in his head, he got dressed while

wishing he had some memories of the event, special or
otherwise.

## CHAPTER 12

Maurice was in a quandary. The *Pelican* was scheduled to sail tomorrow morning. There was really nothing to prevent him (and Arbut) from sailing on the vessel, unless some problem arose connected to the sale of the furs. Even if some snag did arise with the sale, he trusted Jean Hebert and knew his father would receive a fair price and a complete accounting when the difficulty was resolved. He really did not have to remain in New Orleans until this (possible, or maybe hoped for) difficulty was no longer an issue. Though the governor had been exceptionally accommodating, Maurice could not possibly ask him to delay the voyage. Lieutenant Gaultier was entrusted with a mission important to the survival of the colony, and the season was already so far advanced that the vessel would barely make it to the St. Lawrence before ice closed it to navigation.

The lieutenant hated the thought of leaving Dominique so soon. They had just met, but he knew he wanted to see much more of her (both literally and figuratively). He recalled the night they had spent at her house, which was located two streets from the river front, not far from Madame Linctot's.

117

It was a memory that would live with him forever, and he did not like thinking about boarding ship in the morning, probably never to see her again. He knew his duty was clear; he was not on leave in New Orleans. He needed to return to the St. Lawrence valley at his earliest opportunity, both to report the results of his mission to his military superiors, and also to bring needed funds to his father. He told Arbut to finish packing, and said he would return after visiting Hebert and Prevost. He then wandered gloomily to the trading house, secretly hoping some commercial disaster had occurred.

The pleased look on Jean's face as he entered the establishment provided an early warning that no financial crisis was at hand. "Maurice, good news! I got a fine price for your furs and the transaction can be completed this afternoon. When you sail on the *Pelican,* you will have our bill of exchange with you. Let me see, the gross sale price was 31,680 livres, less our commission. By the way, due to my long association with your father and the high price you paid to obtain these furs, I've only charged seven per cent instead of the normal ten. That leaves you with 29,462 livres to take home. A tidy sum."

"Thank you Monsieur Hebert. I'm sure my father will have good use for the funds. You have been most efficient as well as kind, and I will encourage him to utilize your services whenever possible."

"You are most welcome. Please return late this afternoon, and I will have your funds."

With that, this most unwelcome conversation was concluded, and Maurice returned to the inn to help Arbut finish packing.

At that moment, the governor had a visitor.

Lieutenant Gaultier led the guest into the governor's office and announced, "Madame Dominique Lemarque to see you sir."

"What an unexpected pleasure. Let me help you to a comfortable seat."

As the lieutenant turned to leave, Dominique motioned and said, "Please stay, Lieutenant. What I have to say concerns you too."

The governor nodded in assent and the lieutenant remained by the door.

"Before we begin on the business of interest to you, I wanted to thank you for entertaining our Canadian marine. I assume the evening went well. The two of you made an early exit and never returned."

"The evening was satisfactory from my point of view. I normally don't speculate on these things, but in this case I'm confident the lieutenant considers the evening well spent. Oddly enough, he is a big part of the reason I'm here now."

"Please go on."

"Maurice mentioned that you have been extremely helpful to him since he arrived, and have even arranged passage back to the St. Lawrence for him aboard the *Pelican.*

"Merely helping an officer from a sister colony. Nothing remarkable about that."

"Without trying to cause offence, governor, I've noticed that you rarely exert yourself strenuously unless you stand to profit."

"What an unkind thing to say, my dear."

"It was not meant to be an insult. I tend to be motivated in much the same way. For example, the five hundred livres you gave me to entertain the lieutenant gave me significant incentive to excel.  In fact, I may have played my part too well.  I wouldn't be at all surprised if his desire to leave New Orleans has cooled considerably."

"That would be unfortunate," said Gaultier.

"I have been thinking about the situation for hours," replied the woman.  "Let me tell you what I've concluded.  Maurice spoke at some length about his family, and I gather that the family business is a fur trading enterprise of substance, headquartered near Montreal.  My place of employment brings me into contact with most of the influential men in the community, and I make it my business to listen to their conversations, whether or not that was their intention.  I hear many interesting bits of information.  I hope I don't offend you when I say that much of what I have heard concerns business enterprises of yours, Governor, many of which would not be covered by even a liberal definition of your official duties."

The governor's cheeks reddened and he started to protest.

"Please sir, allow me to speak frankly.  Whether what I have heard is true or not, I cannot say, and I in no way condemn you if these accusations are true.  I mention them only because they concern my analysis of the situation.  If these accusations are true, you presumably have accumulated a good deal of capital.  One other bit of gossip I have heard on numerous occasions is that Louisiana is about to revert to royal authority, rather than being governed by the Company of the Indies.  If that happens, it will probably mean you will be recalled to France."

"I suppose that could happen."

"If it does, you may be looking for ways to, how

shall I say it, diversify your investments. It wouldn't do to return home obviously enriched by your term as governor. Embarrassing questions might be asked, possibly by people in authority. It might be a good idea to involve some of your funds with reliable partners in far off colonies. It would be one way to hide your sudden prosperity."

Governor Perier's anger had by now changed to wonder. He had known this beautiful woman was intelligent, but that she could divine his thinking this well amazed him. "Please continue. I want to hear the conclusion of your theory."

"I'm almost finished. Maurice is a member of the Joubert family, owners of the largest fur trading business in New France. The fur trade is by far the biggest commercial enterprise in Canada. He can provide you with access to his father, who may or may not need an investor. If he is not interested, he will probably know of someone who is. If you treat his son well, he will treat you well, at least that is what you are hoping."

"I'm impressed Dominique. Your theory is substantially correct. But I am a bit puzzled. Why have you come here today to tell me what I already know?"

"As I said, I believe I've made a very favorable impression on Maurice. Perhaps it is an overstatement to conclude he will be reluctant to leave New Orleans, but even if it is, I can aid your scheme considerably."

"How so, and why would you want to?"

"What if I were to sail aboard the *Pelican* as well? Knowing your plans, I can whisper the right words in his ear at the right time. Nephew Henri will prove to be a valuable agent I'm sure, but I have certain assets that he lacks."

Now it was Gaultier's turn to blush. His kinship to the governor was not supposed to be public knowledge. The advantages he enjoyed were supposedly the result of hard work, not family connections. Henri vaguely remembered alluding to his uncle when drinking with Dominique at Madame Linctot's some months before.

"Concerning why I would do it, the answer is simple. Money. Before I step on board the *Pelican*, I want a bill of exchange in the amount of five thousand livres. That would seem to be a modest figure. I'd like to be able to draw on the trading company of Hebert and Prevost. I understand they are reliable and have business associates in Montreal. Also, I'm beginning to think I want to live elsewhere. The Company of the Indies wants to give up on Louisiana. Maybe they are right. Maybe it will never develop into anything. Canada, on the other hand, is better established. It may provide more scope for my activities, though if Maurice is a typical Canadian, I may have to be a bit more shy and demure in my approach. Well, what do you think?"

The governor looked at Henri, who nodded almost imperceptibly.

"Very well, Dominique, you will receive the documents you desire within the hour."

"Thank you very much, Governor. Henri, I knew you would see the wisdom in my suggestion. I had better leave now. I don't have much time to prepare for the trip."

Henri Gaultier saw her out and then returned to talk to his uncle. "What do you make of all that?"

"I think I believe most of what she said," replied the governor. "What bothers me are the things she didn't say. The most important of those being how she feels about our friend Maurice. As long as financial gain is her primary motive, she can be a big help to us in this enterprise. I wonder though, if this sudden attraction to colder climes might not have been influenced by feelings she has developed for him, or at least for him as a member of a wealthy Canadian family. Her usefulness will be considerably compromised if she forgets her place in this scheme and becomes really attached to Joubert. It's a good thing that you will be on the voyage as well. Keep a very close eye on Madame Lamarque. Do what is necessary to bring this plan to fruition. My God, after today's conversation, I am relieved she is leaving New Orleans, though Madame Linctot's will be less amusing without her. I feel sorry for the poor fools in Canada; they have no idea who I am about to drop into their midst."

Maurice felt miserable. Yesterday, he had been somewhat buoyed by the thought that he would see Dominique on his last evening in New Orleans. When he finished with the packing and concluded his business with Jean Hebert, he dressed in the uniform provided by Lieutenant Gaultier and hurried to Madame Linctot's. He scanned the entire room when he arrived, but did not see her. He saw the proprietress speaking with two of the bartenders, waited for the conversation to end, and then approached. "Ah, Madame, you are looking lovely this evening. Could you please tell me where I might find Dominique?"

"She stopped by this afternoon and said she would not be coming to work this evening. Apparently, she had some business to conclude related to her late husband's affairs, and said she would return to town late tomorrow afternoon."

"You wouldn't happen to know where she was going?"

"No, she did not say. I'm sorry. I know you two seemed to enjoy each other's company, but perhaps someone like Marie could help you enjoy the evening just as well." As she spoke, she started to motion to the petite blond, but Maurice stayed her hand.

"You are very kind, but I just remembered several tasks I must attend to before I sail in the morning." Then a thought struck him and he asked, "May I borrow some writing materials, that I may leave Dominique a note?"

"Certainly. I have a small office in the back. Follow me. You won't be disturbed. Put your note in one of the envelopes and leave it on the desk. I'll see that she gets it tomorrow evening when she arrives at the club."

So he wrote her a letter filled with sentimental nonsense, and sadly returned to the inn.

The next morning, he and Arbut arose early. The serving girl, Annette, brought them bread, cheese and wine for breakfast, and then they got their gear together in preparation for departure. Before they left the inn, Maurice knocked softly at Francois Legard's door. After a few moments, the trader sleepily opened it. "Good morning, Lieutenant. I'm glad you stopped before you left. It looks like a convoy of trade goods will be headed upriver in a few days with an escort at least partially provided by the governor. I've also concluded a business arrangement with Monsieur Hebert that should result in greater profits for me than those I experienced when I had a thief for an agent."

"I'm glad to hear it. Give my regards to your wife."

Maurice Joubert and Alexandre Arbut then settled their bill at the inn, shouldered their packs, and set off for the docks. They soon found the *Pelican*, a sleek schooner, riding easily at anchor. They were greeted by the vessel's captain, one Lieutenant Pierre La Force, who proved to be none other than the lucky man Gabrielle and Marie competed for two nights before. "Good morning, Lieutenant. I am Lieutenant Tremblant and this is Private Arbut. The governor arranged passage for us."

"Yes, I was informed. There is not much luxury below decks on this vessel, but we have constructed several small cabins for passengers. I've reserved one for you, Lieutenant. Your man can bunk with the crew." Addressing Arbut, he said, "Take that ladder down. You can leave your officer's gear in the first cabin on the right. Then report to the mate and he'll show you where to stow your pack."

After Arbut left, Maurice said, "I was at Madame Linctot's two nights ago. I'm glad to see you survived your evening with Gabrielle."

"It turned out to be two evenings actually. I'm glad to be leaving New Orleans. A few more nights with her and I'd have to be hospitalized. What a hellcat. But enough of that. Let me show you around the ship. We're really proud of her. The governor thought I did well on several assignments he gave me, and he spoke to the right people at the Ministry of Marine. That's how I was able to be permanently assigned as the *Pelican's* captain, even though the governor owns her."

"He owns her?"

"Yes, the *Pelican* as well as two other vessels, a sloop and a brigantine. He has a variety of business ventures in many locales, and I suppose he thought it made sense to own the ships he needed rather than pay someone else for the use of theirs.

"At any rate, the *Pelican* is a one hundred ton schooner. I designed the rigging myself, seeking maneuverability as well as speed. She also has a very shallow draft, allowing us to operate in virtually all coastal waters. It is large enough to carry a crew of seventy-five, but we wanted to save space for cargo, so I normally sail with a crew of about forty.

"With the small crew and desire for maximum cargo space, defensive capability was a concern. Normally, a sloop this size would carry eight six-pound cannon as well as four swivel guns. Instead of that, we decided to arm her with fewer, but larger guns with greater range. We had to strengthen supports in various places, but as you can see, we now carry four twelve-pounders and two swivel guns. Some of our voyages are to dangerous places, but the size of our shot and the accuracy of our fire have saved us more than once. We are plentifully stocked with ammunition, and the crew's gunnery is excellent."

"I'm pleased to be in experienced hands. I'd prefer this voyage to be a quiet one. I've had enough excitement in the last few months to last the rest of my life."

"We'll try to keep things peaceful, though it is not always possible. Organized piracy was for the most part eradicated from the Carolinas and the Bahamas years ago, but from time to time, men with little to lose give it a try."

The captain excused himself to handle some last minute paper work. Maurice was happy to be left alone, though happy was probably an inappropriate word to use at the moment in conjunction with the young lieutenant. As the vessel gently rocked in the river current, he absent mindedly studied the activity on the dock. Barrels and casks of food and drink for the voyage had already been loaded. At the moment, late arriving bales of cotton were about to be hauled aboard. Pulling in upstream from the *Pelican*, two Choctaw dugouts carried a load of deerskins to trade. Negotiations were being conducted all along the riverfront, with various goods being bartered for each other.

Maurice watched this activity with limited enthusiasm. Though it was a gloriously bright, sunny day, with gulls wheeling about the ship and a favorable breeze giving promise of a good start, he felt frustrated. He had no idea if any type of relationship would have resulted if he had more time with Dominique, but he certainly wished he had the opportunity to find out. She knew he was leaving this morning, so he was surprised and disappointed that she had not postponed her business for one day, so that they could have seen each other last night, and she could have seen him off today. Perhaps their one night together had meant little to her.

"Maurice, there you are!"

The brooding marine officer turned to see Henri Gaultier, resplendent as usual and apparently eager to be off.

"Hello, Henri. I did not see you come aboard."

"I arrived over an hour ago. Did Pierre give you his tour of the vessel? He loves the *Pelican*, especially since his suggested modifications were adopted. She's a fine ship, and I'm sure we'll have a quick passage to Canada."

Maurice nodded but did not respond, watching the final preparations before they shoved off. He looked back at the dock once more, knowing the one he sought wouldn't be there.   He felt a light tap on his shoulder, turned and was shocked to see Dominique, radiant in the morning sun, the breeze blowing through her thick, shiny hair.  "Good morning Maurice.  I hope you are happy to see me."

## CHAPTER 13

J ean Baptiste walked gingerly back to the barracks, trying to avoid all movements that started his head throbbing. He walked with his head down, concentrating on the patch of ground in front of his feet, hoping not to be stopped by anyone or delayed in any way. That was not to be. Corporal Charbonneau saw the lad carefully stepping through the gate, apparently headed for his bunk.

"Joubert!"

Jean Baptiste recognized the corporal's voice, snapped to attention, and instantly regretted doing so.

"Joubert, you look disgusting. Where in the hell have you been? Playing hide-the-carrot over in the Ojibwa village I suspect. Well, it's time the marines got some work from you, my lad. We haven't finished replacing the rotted palisades in the south wall yet. You've been gone and haven't done your fair share. Today will be your chance to catch up. Put on some work clothes and report back to me at the south wall immediately."

"Yes, Corporal."

The cadet hurried to the barracks, suffering all the way. He poured some water from a pitcher into a bowl, then splashed some of it on his face and washed his hands. He put on a pair of deerskin breeches and moccasins, along with a well worn, though clean shirt. He completed the outfit with one of his blue fatigue caps.

As he headed to the south wall, he realized he could expect no mercy from the corporal. Corporal Louis Charbonneau had once been Sergeant Louis Charbonneau until Lieutenant Maurice Joubert, Sieur de Tremblant had caught him drunk while he was sergeant of the guard. Maurice had recommended he be reduced in rank to corporal, and given sixty days extra duty.

The punishment could have been, and probably should have been, much more severe, but in view of Charbonneau's overall good record, the post commander agreed with Maurice and decided to be lenient. The ex-sergeant, however, didn't see things that way. He'd loved being a sergeant, with its extra pay, better quality uniform and absolute authority over the fusiliers. Being reduced in rank severely hurt his pride, and embarrassed him in front of those he'd commanded. Whenever he wore his justaucorps, he'd look down at the cuff, where the gold edging on the buttonholes used to be, and curse the lieutenant under his breath. He knew there was little he could do to the officer, but Cadet Jean Baptiste Joubert was a completely different matter, particularly now that the lieutenant was not around to protect his little brother.

Jean Baptiste reported to the corporal and was put to work trimming any remaining branches from the trees that had been felled and piled near the south wall. He and another man removed the remaining limbs, sharpened both ends of the trunks, and then carried the trunks to the wall where a crew was fixing them in place.

Fortunately, the sky was cloudy and threatened rain, and the temperature was cool for mid-summer. Even so, Jean Baptiste had never felt so ill in his life. The pain in his head every time he swung his axe made his nausea even worse. He did his best to hide his infirmity; if Charbonneau knew how he felt, he was certain the corporal would get really inventive on this work detail.

Finally, the workday came to an end. Jean Baptiste had eaten nothing during their rest breaks. In fact, he moved far away from the other men while they lunched on pemmican. Had he been in the vicinity while they were eating this dried meat mixed with animal fat and berries, he would have lost what was left of yesterday's dinner for sure. He staggered back toward the barracks and finally made it there unmolested. He fell onto his bed and slept without bothering to remove his clothes.

The next day was Sunday, and Jean Baptiste felt much better after a full night's sleep. He changed into a fresh shirt, veste and a pair of wool breeches, and attended mass at the church inside the west wall of the fort. He thanked the Lord for his deliverance during the trip to the Illinois Country, and prayed that Maurice had recovered from his injuries. He felt at peace in the church, far removed from the anxiety and terror of his first command, and when he emerged, he had a more positive outlook than he'd had in weeks.

When he stepped out in the daylight, the first people he saw were Etienne Dufort and Rene La Pointe. Both were lounging outside the trader's store next to the church.

"You two should have gone to mass. After the other night, I'm sure an extended period in the confessional would be warranted."

"Jean Baptiste, we looked for you yesterday to see how you liked the lovely Blue Otter, but saw you were in the clutches of that nitwit Charbonneau, and decided it was best to leave you alone. You looked positively green. Are you better now?"

"Yes, but I think it will be awhile before I'm up to eating salt pork. I'll have to make do with just biscuits and some vegetables for a few days."

"Blue Otter was asking about you this morning," said La Pointe. "I'd have to say that you made a positive impression on that woman. How did you do it?"

"I wish I remembered. I believe I'll stay away from her for awhile too. The captain said I should relax for a few days because he might have an assignment for me. He must have forgotten to mention it to Corporal Charbonneau. And from what little I recall, being with Blue Otter is anything but relaxing."

"Sounds like you should stay close to the fort," said La Pointe. "How about a little hunting this afternoon? We won't stray too far."

"I'd like that. It will be the first time in awhile that I shot at something that wasn't shooting back. What about you Etienne?"

"Sure. You youngsters need someone to show you how it's done. By the way, and I know I speak for Rene as well, if your "new assignment" is something more interesting than replacing old timbers, try to include us."

The few hours spent in the woods looking for game did wonders for Jean Baptiste. He laughed and joked with his friends, making enough noise to ensure that their conversation would not be interrupted by the presence of any animals. "I swear that Charbonneau is never going to forget being busted to corporal. I almost wish they'd consider promoting him again, except I'm sure that move would weaken the nation."

"I've given some thought to that man," said Dufort. "But I can't seem to devise a totally fitting course of action to correct his attitude. I think I'll wait until Gaspard rejoins us. I just know he would have an inspired thought."

After awhile, the three abandoned any pretense of hunting and sat under some birch trees near a small pond south of the fort. They sat quietly and watched a hawk circling high above them. Finally, Jean Baptiste spoke. "It's hard to believe all the fighting and dying that occurs here in America so that European gentlemen can wear beaver hats."

"I suppose it used to be possible to justify the bother due to the tremendous profits that could be made," responded La Pointe. "Late in the sixteenth century, traders would make profits ten, twenty or even thirty times the cost of the goods they traded to the Indians for the furs. The amazing thing is that the bloodshed continues even though the big profits disappeared long ago. Of course, the fur trade involves more than commerce now. Britain and France have come to realize that the country that controls the fur trade will control the interior of the continent as well."

"It sounds to me like the learned Rene La Pointe is about to deliver a lecture," sighed Dufort.

"If he is, it's one I'd like to hear. If my hair is destined end up gracing a Fox lodge pole, I'd at least like a greater understanding of the reasons we are fighting."

"If it will not bore you too much Etienne, I'll explain what I've learned. As you know, I have a great interest in history. What has occurred here in the Americas is not of the same vintage or interest as the Punic Wars, but some sense of events is possible through a careful reading of documents available here in Canada and also in France. In fact, I'd been an avid reader of *The Jesuit Relations* since I was a little boy. When I arrived in Canada and started working for your father, Jean Baptiste, I searched for whatever information I could find to augment the writings of the martyrs of the Society of Jesus, whether it was in the form of diaries, personal letters, official correspondence or conversations with retired coureurs de bois.

"Apparently, the fishermen who came to eastern Canada nearly two hundred years ago also traded for furs with the native tribes. In Europe, these furs were without unusual value until French hat makers discovered that beaver skins could be made into very stylish hats. These hats found wide acceptance among the affluent, and suddenly, beaver skins were very valuable indeed. The Dutch, the English and the French all traded cloth, tools, guns and liquor to the Indians in exchange for the furs.

"Interestingly, it is not the coarse outer hair on the pelt that is utilized by the hatters, but rather the soft undercoat next to the animal's skin. In most cases, the beavers are trapped in winter, when the fur on the pelts is thickest. Indian women process the hides and sew a number of them together to make leggings or jackets. These items of apparel are worn with the fur side next to the body for warmth. After a year or two of wear, the coarse outer fur is worn off, leaving the much softer fur prized by the hat makers. These are the skins for which we pay the most when we trade. Beaver pelts that have not been worn are worth less because of the additional labor necessary to convert them into felt for hats.

"In the beginning, profits from the fur trade were enormous. Gradually, as the various European nations entered the trade and competition increased, the Indians learned to negotiate prices. When a customer can choose between several sellers, and the sellers are eager to buy the customer's goods, the customer gets more in exchange. So the Europeans had to pay more for the pelts, driving down profits.

"From the Indians' perspective, they stopped hunting for subsistence and now hunted on a commercial basis, to obtain the furs they needed to trade for the wonderful implements the white men offered. They no longer killed only the animals they would consume, but now killed as many as they could, so they could buy more iron cooking pots, steel knives, guns and brandy. Old methods of making tools and weapons were neglected or forgotten because the products of the white men were superior. As the old ways were forgotten, goods obtained from the Europeans were no longer luxuries, but had become necessities. To harvest the pelts as efficiently as neighboring tribes, your tribe had to have the same steel tools as the neighboring tribes.

"Of course, the unrestrained harvesting of the beaver quickly depleted their numbers. Prime trapping areas retreated farther and farther from the centers of European population, ever farther to the west and northwest. Nearly a century ago, the Iroquois initiated a series of wars of annihilation against the Hurons, the Neutrals, the Eries and others. By that time, beavers were scarce in the Iroquois homeland, but the Five Nations still needed the white man's products. In order to regain access to a supply of beaver, they needed to conquer territory that still contained beaver, or they needed to force distant tribes to obtain their goods in neighboring Albany, and assume the lucrative role of middlemen in these transactions. The numerous wars fought by the Iroquois in the last century were to attain these ends.

"Our difficulties with the Fox originally stemmed from their unwillingness to let us supply the Sioux, their hereditary enemies, with muskets and steel hatchets. Later, when relations between the Sioux and the Fox improved, we continued to have problems with the Fox because they wanted to assume the middleman role, and we didn't want to share the profits.

"Even though the profits of the trade have shrunk tremendously, it still continues. And do you know why?"

"No, but I'm certain I'm about to find out," interjected Dufort.

"Thirty years ago, beaver pelts rotted in store houses because we had far more than we needed, even though beaver hats remained in style. Still, we traded for more. The reason was and still is that we are prisoners of the trade as much as are the Indians. The Indians are dependent on European trade goods and will trade with whomever gives them the best deal. Tribes that trade with the French will side with the French if war looms between France and England, because they need to keep the supply of merchandise flowing. If a tribe that traded with us should suddenly stop doing so, and trade with the English instead, then we have lost an ally and gained an enemy the next time we fight the English. We must continue to trade for beaver skins even if we have no economic reason to do so. Control of and alliance with the tribes, and by extension the land where those tribes reside, is completely dependent on maintaining good trade relations with them. The fur trade is now driven by perceived political advantage rather than profits."

Jean Baptiste quietly reflected on his friend's words, as the two of them gazed at the small pond before them. Etienne Dufort dozed peacefully, all this historical analysis apparently too much for him.

After Etienne finished his nap, the three of them returned to Fort Michilimackinac. They arranged to reunite an hour after sunset for supper, which would apparently consist of monotonous marine fare, since their hunting had produced no game. When Jean Baptiste returned to the barracks, a fusilier named Le Duc told him he was to report to the captain, so he made himself presentable, and repaired to that officer's quarters.

Captain Montigny seemed pleased to see him. "Sit down, Cadet. I imagine you'll be pleased to learn that I've decided to send you to Montreal with dispatches. I've delayed this long because rumor had it that some of the traders were sending one last convoy east before the onset of winter. If they are, they're being damned slow about getting it organized. I can't wait any longer. The information in your report and the one I wrote to accompany it must get to the governor general without further delay. Have you recovered sufficiently to make the trip?"

"Yes, Sir. I can be ready to leave in the morning. I'd like to ask two favors, Sir."

"What are they, Joubert?"

"I'll go in a single canoe, and with your permission, would like Etienne Dufort and Rene La Pointe to accompany me."

"That's fine with me. With Dufort out of the way,

there's less likelihood of murder being done by a jealous husband. I'm not familiar with the other man."

"La Pointe was to be the chief clerk at my father's Sioux trading house. Since that didn't work out and Claude Guyotte can handle things here by himself, he needs to go where he can find work."

"Now I believe I recall who you are talking about. Isn't he the lad who's always walking about armed to the teeth?"

"Yes, I'm afraid that's him."

"Odd behavior for a clerk. Oh, well, you are welcome to him. I'm glad you don't need any men from the garrison. I'm eleven men under strength at the moment. And your second favor?"

"I'd like to take some leave. As you well know, my family lives west of Montreal, and I haven't been home in more than a year. Hopefully, Maurice will be home soon from New Orleans, but I wanted to forewarn them about his arm."

"Of course. It would be folly to try to return here before the snow anyway. Spend the winter with your family. Be sure to say hello to your father for me. I'm sure I mentioned that he and I served together in Newfoundland more than twenty-five years ago."

"Yes, I believe you have mentioned that on several occasions."

"Your father and I campaigned with Auger de Subercase in 1705. We were victorious from beginning to end, but I'm afraid with few lasting results. The next year, he accompanied me to France when I was sent to present Nescambiouit, the great Abnaki chief, to the king. King Louis was so pleased by this stout ally of France that your father and I both benefitted. I was made captain and your father was promoted to lieutenant. Those were great days." The aged captain sat behind his desk, mentally reliving this highlight of his career. Finally he said, "Enough of this blather. You have preparations to make. I wish you success, and enjoy the time with your family."

Jean Baptiste returned to the barracks and began packing what he would need for the trip. At the appointed hour, he met Dufort and La Pointe. Etienne informed his companions that he had spent the time since they parted wisely. He had been shooting dice with three marines and won a string of whitefish. "Now we don't have to eat salt pork and dried peas again. Just to show you gentleman what kind of friend I am, I've already started the fire down on the beach and cleaned the fish. I've got two for each of us, so you can make your selections, and we can get started roasting them."

As they walked down to the beach, Jean Baptiste explained his assignment. In conclusion he said, "I asked permission for the two of you to accompany me, and the captain was only too happy to comply."

Both were enthusiastic. Dufort said, "I wasn't looking forward to being snowed in here, even though they seem to have a nice assortment of female companions this year. Montreal probably has more to offer, at least in a cultural sense."

La Pointe gave the trader a disgusted look, but was also eager to go. "I like it here at Michilimackinac, but would like to return to Montreal and line up some gainful employment. Hopefully your father can still utilize my services."

"Excellent. Then we're agreed. Let's hurry and eat these fish, then we'll find Guyotte and obtain the supplies we need.  I told the captain we'd leave in the morning."

## CHAPTER 14

Kiala had been working to strengthen the Fox tribe as quickly as his slowly healing wound would allow. He had met again with representatives of the Sacs and the Kickapoos, and so far, results had been as promising as could be expected. Both of those tribes had been disturbed by the apparent desire of the French to completely destroy the Fox people, and had agreed to complete the repatriation of any Fox captives they still held. In time, the tribe would regain its strength as its young boys and adolescents grew to manhood. But he needed warriors now. He could only muster about one hundred men between the ages of fifteen and fifty. The Sacs, close kinsmen of the Fox with whom they had frequently intermarried, seemed receptive to an alliance, but also seemed to want some sign that French anger toward the Fox had cooled. The wound in his shoulder did not reassure them.

The Kickapoos were former staunch allies who had been alienated by the stupid actions of all but uncontrollable Fox hotheads. Three years before, the Kickapoos held several French prisoners. A group of young Fox warriors traveled to the Kickapoo village and demanded that the prisoners be turned over to them.

When this demand was rebuffed, the frustrated Fox youths inexplicably killed Kickapoo and Mascouten hunters they later encountered, despite the fact that these tribes were allies of the Fox. These murders cost the Fox virtually their only remaining friends, and were a direct cause of the disastrous decision to emigrate east, which ended in the massacre on the Illinois prairie. The Kickapoos had agreed to return any captives they still held, but had been non-committal concerning an alliance. Kiala felt that the Kickapoos sympathized with the plight of the Fox, but they didn't know if the younger Fox warriors could yet be trusted.

Tomorrow he would meet with Kuit, the Mascouten. This man had fought at the side of the legendary Fox chieftain Pemoussa, nearly twenty years ago at the great battle near Detroit. Kiala was confident that he could rekindle Kuit's anger at the French for the role that they had played in that bloody defeat. Yes, Kiala was beginning to feel that he might piece a workable alliance together. His biggest concern was that the French would act before he was ready.

Far to the south, Maurice tried unsuccessfully to recover his composure. Try as he might, he could do nothing but stammer at the unexpected but thrilling sight of Dominique on board the *Pelican*. He thought he had almost reached the point that he could string two or three intelligible words together when he realized that the ship was moving away from the dock, and Dominique was making no move to disembark. The realization that she intended to stay on board caused him to have a relapse.

Henri Gaultier, merely an amused spectator to this point, could contain himself no longer and burst out laughing. "If you could only see yourself Maurice. I would have thought a veteran officer of marines would keep a cooler head during a time of stress."

"Really Maurice, are you all right?" said Dominique. "I realize now that this was a bad joke, but when I first thought of it, it seemed like it might be fun."

The distressed lieutenant was apparently recovering, because he no longer looked like he'd swallowed his tongue. "I... I don't understand," he croaked.

"You see, when my husband died of fever, I caught it too, but recovered. I've had it twice since and the doctors told me I had to move to a cooler climate or the sickness would finish me. I arranged passage on the *Pelican* two weeks ago. The governor knew we would be sailing on the same ship and so arranged for us to meet at Madame Linctot's. Instead of telling you I'd be on board, I decided on a whim to surprise you instead. I even enlisted Elaine Linctot in the conspiracy. I thought you might go to the club last night, so I had her tell you I was out of town. Had you stopped by my house, you'd have found me feverishly packing. I have a tendency to let things go to the last minute."

"Why, this is wonderful! So you plan to live in Canada?"

"Possibly. I'll spend some time there and see if it agrees with me. Otherwise, I could return to France. My late husband's property turned out to be worth a considerable sum, so if I do return, it will be as a woman of substance."

"Have you decided where in Canada you will stay?"

"I don't know. Once I knew I was going, I talked to everyone I knew who had been there. Quebec sounded like it might have a bit too much of a religious flavor for my taste. Perhaps Montreal."

"I hope you continue thinking that way. If you'd allow me, I'd like to offer you lodging at my family's seigneury just outside Montreal."

"Oh, I don't want to be any troub..."

"You won't be," he interrupted. "My family home is large, and unless my parents have produced a significant number of brothers and sisters in my absence, I'm sure we can find a room for you. At least until you have a chance to get settled and find a place of your own."

"Your offer is extremely generous. We can discuss it during the voyage. Now, can you show me around a bit?"

As she put her arm in Maurice's and the two of them turned toward the stern, she glanced over her shoulder at Henri Gaultier and winked.

Thomas Blackthorne viewed the "fortress" at Oswego with disgust. A stone blockhouse eighteen paces long by eight wide, it was garrisoned by twenty-four nearly worthless provincials. As a man with a keen eye for valuable real estate, Blackthorne was impressed. The site, on the south shore of Lake Ontario, at the outlet of the Oswego River, was priceless. It posed the first serious challenge to French domination of the waterways to the interior. Until this post was erected in 1727, the French controlled the entire route from the St. Lawrence River through the Great Lakes to the immense, fur rich areas to the west and northwest. They had erected forts and trading stations at many key points along the way, such as Frontenac, Niagara, Detroit and Michilimackinac.

Trade goods flowed from Montreal to the interior posts, where they were exchanged for the furs that subsequently traveled the same route, but in the opposite direction.

Oswego changed the picture completely, at least in theory. Located between Frontenac and Niagara, the English post was on the flank of the French trade route. Tribes that had traditionally traded with the French now had an option. Without going far out of their way, they could now compare English merchandise and prices with those offered by the French. Concerning many commodities, particularly blankets and various types of cloth, Blackthorne knew English goods were superior. They were also more easily obtainable because the English colonies had many ports that were open the year around. Canada did not.

Oswego was a military, as well as a commercial threat to New France. It was an excellent staging area for an assault on either Frontenac or Niagara. If either of those posts fell to the English, France's lifeline to her interior posts would be cut, and her ability to compete for furs would be greatly diminished.

Considering the importance of the site, the minimal effort expended on its fortification was criminal. Blackthorne had opened a trading establishment here, as had a number of other Albany merchants. In fact, he was tempted to move the bulk of his operation here, despite the difficulty of the Mohawk River route. This is where the real money could be made, but to risk a major portion of his assets at Oswego was madness. Protection of his trade goods and storehouses was entirely inadequate. A company of French marines would take that blockhouse away from the provincials in a quarter of an hour, and then where would his merchandise be?

Burned to ashes or carted back to Canada, that's where. He had to speak to the governor about stronger defenses and more troops.

Thomas Blackthorne was thirty-eight years of age and a respected member of Albany's merchant class. In his early twenties, he used funds borrowed from his father to outfit a 280-ton merchant ship. Selection of cargo was entirely based on profit potential, so over the next seven years he made numerous voyages to the Slave Coast in West Africa, usually realizing tremendous profits. Only one of these voyages lost money, and that was because he was becalmed west of the Cape Verde Islands for five weeks. He ran short of food and water and was forced to toss most of the cargo overboard. Other than that one time, profits had been exceptional.

Eventually, despite the money it produced, Thomas Blackthorne decided to get out of the slave trade. The long months at sea, listening to the constant wailing and crying below decks, had begun to affect him. He also noticed that despite his wealth, a significant segment of New York City society shunned him because of the way he earned his living. He decided he needed to involve himself in something more respectable. Now, instead of listening to a West African mother wail for weeks about the children she had lost forever, he could watch as a drunken Algonquin warrior, primed with free rum and singing off-key, traded a year's catch of furs for a few bottles of cheap liquor and some worthless beads. Now this was more to his liking!

Still, the Indian was a fickle customer. Many of those he traded with this year might well go elsewhere to trade next year. Perhaps the French would develop a new color for their blankets that appealed to the savage eye.

In that event, his customers would leave him, even those he treated fairly.

A new thought had been slowly rising to the level of consciousness. Instead of trying to maximize profits on each trade for furs, maybe he should start thinking more long range. It was common practice to extend credit to Indian hunters in the fall, supplying them with ammunition, clothing, traps and whatever else they might need during the winter hunting season. The credit was to be repaid with furs the next spring. Perhaps, instead of being very conservative with the amount of credit he extended, he should be more generous. Of course, his clerks could still get the hunters drunk and tempt them into spending most of their furs foolishly. The end result would be that the credit extended in the fall would not be repaid in the spring. When the debt became so large that it could not possibly be repaid, a concerned Thomas Blackthorne would make a suggestion.

In order to offset the debt, would the hunter be interested in selling a piece of land?

Blackthorne knew this idea posed problems. Indians did not buy and sell land because they did not believe that a man could any more own the land he stood on than he could own the air he breathed. Despite that, if Blackthorne could get a responsible tribal member to sign a bill of sale, and later a dispute arose, it would be decided in a white man's court of law, a place that did recognize private ownership of land. New York was a growing colony, and her English and Dutch inhabitants needed room to expand. The land needed would be obtained, one way or another, and he was determined to be involved.

However, all that was a concern for another day.

Right now he needed to focus on Oswego and making it the preferred trading destination for as many tribes as possible. That reminded him, where were Cutler and those two companions of his, the dull-witted giant and the one with the jewelry holding his ear together? He hoped that they were succeeding at their twin goals: causing trouble for the French and directing trade to Oswego.

## CHAPTER 15

J ean Baptiste was impatient to be off.  The sun had been up for two hours.  Rene La Pointe and he had completed packing the weapons, supplies and food in the canoe.  Now all that was missing was Etienne Dufort.  Finally they spied him running from the Ojibwa camp while trying to pull his buckskin shirt over his head.  He arrived at last, panting and with a sheepish look on his face.

"I'm sorry I'm late, lads, but I had a number of good-byes to make over in the village.  These poor women.  Hearing their anguish and lamentation at the news of my impending departure would melt a heart of stone.  I was forced to do my best to comfort them, and that much comforting takes time.  I'm not as young as you fellows.  Oh no, look at this! I'm too late to help with the packing.  I will undoubtedly hate myself for days as a result.

"Well, why don't we get started?  I'm a bit fatigued, so I think I'll arrange a few bundles like so and take a short nap, if you don't mind.  Be sure to wake me if you have questions.  By the way, I'd advise taking the old French River – Lake Nipissing – Ottawa River route to Montreal.  It's more direct than going by way of Detroit and Niagara, so unless you don't mind taking a chance of ending the trip on snowshoes, you should heed my suggestion. Naturally, since this is a military mission, you're in charge, Jean Baptiste. I'm just having my say."

Having completed this oration, the portly Dufort snuggled down among the bundles in the center of the canoe and promptly went to sleep.

"I can see he will be an amazing asset on this journey," remarked La Pointe.

"I had been giving the route some thought and I believe I would like to use the Ottawa River. We could shorten the alternative path by following the Toronto Carry, but let's avail ourselves of the route favored by our forebears. I don't want to delay bringing my dispatches to the governor general, but as he will be unable to act until the spring thaw, time is not really of the essence."

"You're in charge. Which way?"

"We'll cross the strait here and paddle along the north shore of Lake Huron."

With that they pushed off from the beach and headed north with Rene in front, Jean Baptiste in the rear, and the already snoring Dufort in the middle. After a few paddle strokes, the cadet looked over his shoulder at the water gate. The sentry noticed and raised his musket; Jean Baptiste waved his paddle.

He anticipated with pleasure seeing the route they planned to cover. A century and more ago, the Ottawa River route to the Great Lakes had been the one used by virtually all the old explorers. He especially recalled the travels of his favorite adventurer, Etienne Brule. Brule, a lad not much older than the cadet when he came to Canada, had been the subject of several writings in *The Jesuit Relations*, books about the early years of New

France that Jean Baptiste had eagerly read as a boy. Traveling the Ottawa River a number of times early in the seventeenth century, Brule lived among the Hurons near the southeastern tip of Georgian Bay. From there he embarked on numerous voyages, and it was said that he discovered all the Great Lakes save Lake Michigan. He also explored to the south, in lands claimed by the English. Once captured by the Iroquois, he was tortured but managed to talk his way out of the predicament by convincing his superstitious captors that a sudden summer storm was a sign of his God's displeasure at their actions.

Jean Baptiste smiled when he recalled that one of the Jesuit writers condemned Brule because of his frequent sexual liaisons with Indian women. Less amusing was his hero's demise. For some reason the Hurons, with whom he'd lived and been friends for twenty years, killed and ate him. When the Huron tribe was later decimated by smallpox, many of the survivors blamed the spirit of Brule's sister, who they said flew over the country, breathing pestilence.

Once Dufort awoke, he picked up a paddle and worked with a will. They sped past the north end of Mackinac Island heading east. A brisk breeze rose out of the southwest, and Dufort suggested they rig a sail. Clouds began to form ominously, but when Jean Baptiste asked if they shouldn't furl the sail and get closer to shore, Dufort shook his head.

"No, I don't think they'll be a problem. Those clouds are limiting our sunshine, but they won't bring rain. Leave the sail up. If the wind holds, we'll cover a distance that would have taken three days paddling."

He was essentially correct. At one point early in

the afternoon, they felt a few drops of rain, but it soon stopped, and the wind and waves were always easily manageable.  That night, they made camp on the east bank of a small stream that emptied into Lake Huron. While Rene found suitable firewood and set up the camp, Jean Baptiste and Etienne hunted.  Their efforts were rewarded, and they returned with two rabbits and four plump pigeons.  During their absence, Rene was able to catch two whitefish.  It took some time to skin, clean and remove the feathers from their various entrees, and by the time they were ready to start roasting, darkness had fallen.

It was a beautiful evening.  Light from the moon reflected off the water, and the breeze brought a welcome chill to the air.  The three friends watched the game roast on several spits.  While they waited, Dufort brought a bottle of brandy from the canoe, and they passed it around several times.

"Rene, I remember you telling me that you came to New France because the authorities began to take too much interest in your activities.  What was that all about, if you don't mind me asking?  If you would prefer not to talk about it, just say so."

"Not at all, Jean Baptiste.  Let me see, where to begin?  Are you gentlemen familiar with the pirate kingdoms on the North African coast?"

"Yes, some of the sailors bringing supplies from France have talked about them," said the cadet. "In fact, I think one of them said he'd been captured by pirates from Tripoli some years back, and spent six months as a galley slave before he was able to escape."

"My brother is in the navy, stationed in Marseilles," said Dufort. "He has fought several actions against them.

Nasty fellows, from what he has told me."

"Yes, they are a plague on commerce in the Mediterranean. They attack all kinds of vessels, from many nations. When they capture someone wealthy, they hold them for ransom. Prisoners without substantial financial resources are sent to the galleys."

"What does that have to do with you?"

"I was coming to that. My uncle was appointed to negotiate the release of a number of French citizens being held by the Bey of Tunis. The Bey is really a charming fellow; if he feels a prisoner's family is slow to respond to his ransom demands, he begins removing parts of the captive's body and sending the pieces to his relations. Just to motivate them to greater efforts.

"My uncle knew of my interest in Carthaginian history, and since Tunis is located on virtually the same site as ancient Carthage, he asked if I wanted to be part of his entourage. I leaped at the chance and was able to spend a good deal of time exploring the ruins, though the Romans did a very thorough job when they destroyed it. Not much was left. One exception was the circular lagoon where naval vessels were anchored. The island in the center of the lagoon also still exists. On the island, the Carthaginian admiral had his quarters, along with sheds for maintenance and storage of naval vessels.

"While I was exploring, my uncle effected the release of eleven captives, two of them from well placed aristocratic families. He received high praise and a substantial pension from the king. He also inherited the job of negotiating with the North Africans on a permanent basis. When he went to Tripoli or Algiers, I was not interested in going, but he made a number of trips to Tunis, and I always accompanied him there. Aside from exploring, I searched the bazaars for Carthaginian artifacts and questioned as many people as possible, gathering information on the old city and its people."

"They must have thought you'd been out in the desert sun too long," grumped Dufort. "Why else would you spend so much time and effort finding out about a city that vanished nearly two thousand years ago?"

"One day I was approached by a man named Yusuf, the son of Hasan. His father owned an antiquities shop very near the naval lagoon. He wondered why I asked so many questions about Carthage. I told him that I had read the Roman accounts of Hannibal's exploits, and my interest in the family of Hannibal Barca and the people of Carthage grew from there. He said he too, had always loved the old tales about the wars with Rome, possibly because a family tradition asserted that they were descended from Hannibal's Numidian ally Syphax. I spent much time in Hasan's shop, looking at his wares, but also listening to tales that originated before the time of Christ. Many of the stories dealt with the Punic Wars and the role played by the Numidian cavalry in Hannibal's army. The old man loved to repeat the tales, also stressing those dealing with the mighty war elephants of Carthage.

"Hasan grew to know and trust me, and after a time asked if there was a market for Roman antiquities in my country. Several of my uncle's friends had started collections of Greek and Roman statuary that had been found in the south of France. A number of his other acquaintances had said they would like to acquire pieces as well, if more were available. Legally collecting antiquities from outside France was difficult and expensive because of duties imposed by the government.

I told Hasan that good quality antiques would find a ready market in my homeland, except for the high duties involved. He took me into the back room of his shop where he kept a number of pieces of excellent quality, including a life size statue of Mars found in the nearby Roman ruins.

"'Talk to these people,' he said, ' and if they really have an interest, Yusuf, you and I will figure a way to get them what they want.'

"So that is how I became a smuggler. My uncle was a respected envoy, and the vessels on which he traveled were not closely inspected either in France or in North Africa. I told my uncle what I was planning to do, and he had no objection; in fact he gave me the names of five of his friends to contact about possible purchases. I made several highly profitable trips to Tunis, Hasan paying me twenty per cent of the purchase price for the pieces he sold.

"The next time I sailed to Tunis, I went straight to Hasan's shop, but the old man wasn't there, which was odd. He lived nearby, so I walked to his home and was admitted by Yusuf, who looked as if he had been crying. He took me into his father's bedroom, and there was the old man, ill and apparently at the point of death.

"'Yusuf, Rene, come close,' the old man whispered. 'I doubt I'll live through the night, and so will be unable to complete a task I set for myself. Ten years ago a desert man brought a metal box into my shop. He said it had been uncovered by the wind near where he had taken shelter to wait out a sandstorm. The box had an intricate latch, but he had managed to open it, finding only old papers within. He thought it probably was worth little, but would I be interested in buying it?

"'The box was solidly built and appeared to be made of copper.  What immediately caught my eye was the disc and crescent emblem of Carthage on the lid.  I gave the nomad a few coins and he went on his way.  I could scarcely wait for him to be lost in the crowd, so that I could look at these papers.  It took some minutes, but at last I also solved the riddle of the clasp, and I was able to open the copper top.  Inside was the record of a journey made in the second century before your Christ by a Greek named Dionysus of Cyrenacia.  He had lived in Carthage for fifteen years, acting as tutor to the children of Hannibal's descendants, members of the Barca family.  This was nearly forty years after the death of Hannibal, and the great city of Carthage had been made to suffer since the defeat at Zama.  Stripped of most of her territory, forced to disband most of her armed forces and pay a huge indemnity to Rome, the Carthaginians were nearly helpless.

"'Many in Rome remembered the depredations of Hannibal on Italian soil, and were determined to destroy their ancient enemy completely.  When, about the middle of your second century before Christ, the Romans invaded North Africa, the Carthaginians knew the end was near.  The Barca family selected Bomilcar, grandson of Hannibal's brother Hasdrubal, to travel two days ride south into the desert, accompanied by the faithful Dionysus, to recover the Barca treasure.'"

"Treasure!  What kind of treasure?"  Dufort had been dozing through most of the story, but came instantly awake at the allusion to great wealth.

"Hannibal's father, Hamilcar, had conquered Spain between the first two Punic Wars," explained La Pointe.  "He planned on fighting an all out war against the

Romans, and since the Carthaginian army was made up predominantly of mercenaries, he knew he needed a vast war chest. The gold and silver mines of Spain provided the funds he needed. In fact, the mines provided much more than was needed. Legend has it that even after Hannibal's war, much of the Barca fortune remained, a good portion of it converted into precious gems. The family found a secluded spot in the hills south of Carthage, and had an impenetrable vault built by trusted retainers.

"Hasan told us that Bomilcar and Dionysus were to recover the treasure and carry it by caravan far to the west. The Romans now controlled the Mediterranean, so the journey would be made by land. The treasure was to be carried to the shores of the Western Sea, meaning the Atlantic Ocean, and concealed at a place named Cerne, a distant place with ties to the Barca clan. On the highest point of land at Cerne was a small temple dedicated to Melkart. One hundred paces due east of the temple was a tiny opening in the hillside, which led into a large cave where Bomilcar and Dionysus hid the treasure, a treasure intended to be used to aid any survivors from the doomed mother city.

"Carthage was destroyed when the Romans attacked, and virtually all her citizens were killed or sold into slavery. Hasan guessed that Bomilcar and Dionysus were attacked by desert tribesmen on their return journey, and knowledge of the whereabouts of the Barca clan's fortune died with them, until the Greek's journal was accidentally uncovered by the wind. Hasan had meant to search for the treasure, but had no idea where Cerne was located. He knew I had read much that was written by the Greek and Roman historians. Yusuf was his only child, and while resourceful in familiar surroundings, was illiterate and unfamiliar with the wider world. Hasan decided he would tell both his son and myself about the contents of the Carthaginian box, because he thought we would have to work together to have a chance to locate the treasure.

"Yusuf and I promised the old man that we would cooperate with each other and share the profits equally. Hasan died during the night, and two days later, I returned to France with my uncle. I told Yusuf that I did not know where Cerne was either, but would study the matter back home when I had access to my books. I told him I'd see him when we returned to see the Bey.

"Unfortunately, there was no next time. A short while after we left, the Bey was too enthusiastic in the mutilation of one of the captives to be ransomed. The man died, and he turned out to be the brother of King Louis' favorite concubine. Negotiations for prisoner releases and travel to North Africa were suspended while the Minister of Marine considered bombarding Tunis. At this inopportune moment, a crate I had sent from Tunis was dropped on the dock in Marseilles. It broke open, revealing a fine bust of Aphrodite without the proper import documents. It was at this time that I decided I needed a change of scenery, and wound up here in New France. I had to leave so quickly I left behind a jeweled scimitar that would have been handy in all these melees in which we find ourselves."

"An interesting story, though a bit long," commented Dufort. "Diamonds and emeralds and such. But since you don't know where Cerne is, it seems like the trail has reached a dead end."

"That may be the most intriguing part of the tale.

I just realized I do know where it is, or at least I'm confident I could find it."

## CHAPTER 16

"**N**o, I'm not kidding," said La Pointe. "In fact, now I can't wait to get back to Montreal. I stored most of my books when I got the assignment to go to the Sioux country. The book I need to verify what I just remembered is one I left behind. In fact, Jean Baptiste, your father was kind enough to store my books and surplus gear at your family's seigneury."

"What is it that you just remembered?" asked Dufort.

"Ever since Hasan mentioned 'Cerne,' the name of the place has bothered me. It seemed like I had seen it before, but no matter how hard I tried, I could not remember where. I had very little time to study the matter before my hasty departure from France, but the study time I had on the voyage to the New World and later in Montreal produced no results. It's really frustrating to think you've encountered the key piece in the puzzle at some point in the past, but be unable to duplicate the feat.

"I hadn't thought much about the problem for the past few months, probably because I didn't have access to most of my books, and so couldn't really research the situation anyway. When you asked about my narrow escape from the law, Jean Baptiste, and I narrated the whole story, it suddenly occurred to me where I'd seen the word 'Cerne' before."

"That's great you remembered. How long do you think it will take to get there?" inquired Dufort.

"It probably is not quite that easy. Let me explain. As I discussed Dionysus' journal, I remembered reading an account of a voyage to West African waters by a Carthaginian named Hanno. I believe it took place about 500 B.C. Hanno's mission was to found colonies on the Atlantic coast of Africa. One of the colonies he founded was situated on an island on an indented stretch of coast. If my memory is accurate, the name of that colony was Cerne."

"Is the account of the voyage sufficiently detailed to enable you to locate the place?" Asked Jean Baptiste. "I would think that most of the place names are different now, since more than two thousand years have passed since Hanno's day."

"Keep in mind that I haven't read Hanno's report for a number of years, but I remember when I did that I was struck by the details he included, such as the number of days required to sail between specific points, and detailed descriptions of geographic features. Polybius, one of the historians who wrote about the Punic Wars, was responsible for having the text translated into Greek from the original, which was posted in the temple of Moloch in Carthage, and recovered when the city was sacked. I believe I have a complete copy of the translation included with my Polybius material. Now that I've remembered where I heard the word 'Cerne,' I can't imagine why it took me so long."

Rene La Pointe had a sudden inspiration. He

stood up and announced, "Gentlemen, I propose that after I verify what I have told you, and we gather sufficient resources to fund an expedition, that we three find my friend Yusuf the son of Hasan, and together the four of us recover the Barca treasure."

"And since there are no Carthaginian survivors to help, I guess we'll just keep all the gold and jewels," said Dufort.

"Right. Keep in mind though, that Yusuf gets half the treasure. The three of us will split the other half. Even then, we'll all be as rich as Croesus."

It was agreed. Jean Baptiste now enjoyed the trip even more keenly. Not only was he returning home and seeing new territory in the process, but also the possibility of becoming rich presented itself to his mind's eye. Thinking about that was much more pleasant than worrying about English intrigue, Fox ambushes and slow death by torture.

The trio sped on their way, propelled by visions of prosperity. They paddled along the shore of Georgian Bay, after a time entering the mouth of French River. They were forced to fight the current, and progress was slow. The surroundings were beautiful, however. The soil did not appear fertile, being both hilly and full of rocks, but the forests were thick, the blue waters of the river flowed around numerous rocky but well wooded islets and the sun smiled on their expedition. They also took a little time to vary their diet by gathering some of the plentiful blueberries and wild raspberries of the region.

At last they entered Lake Nipissing, and all felt that the worst was over. Certainly many portages lay ahead, but the rest of the paddling would be on the lake, or with the current on the Mattawa and the Ottawa. Lake Nipissing boasted numerous verdant islands and a shoreline that began to reflect the various yellows, oranges and reds of early autumn, but the three travelers paid less attention than was due; their minds were on gold ingots, emeralds, rubies and diamonds.

If the three took the bounty of nature for granted, they nevertheless enjoyed themselves immensely. Though each of them knew recovering the Carthaginian treasure was at best a remote possibility, evenings were spent discussing what they would do with their newfound riches. Each time the subject was discussed, desired goals became more outrageous. Dufort finally decided that he would become a Moslem, depose the Bey of Tunis and end piracy on the North African coast. He vehemently asserted that the recent discussion they had concerning the Bey's harem privileges had nothing to do with his humanitarian impulses.

Finally, they reached the Ottawa, and though they had a long way to go along this lengthy river, Jean Baptiste felt like he was almost home. They made excellent progress, then one afternoon decided to pull into shore and camp early, because the sky gave indications of stormy weather ahead.

They still had half the meat from a deer Jean Baptiste had dropped the previous day. The buck had come down to the river to drink and the cadet had shot him from a range of more than one hundred paces while seated at the rear of the canoe. Dufort had almost upset the vessel when suddenly awakened by the report of the gun, and the daydreaming La Pointe had grabbed his war club in order to repel boarders, but all were happy to have the venison.

No one was interested in pemmican to complement the meal, but Dufort did have a taste for more raspberries and blueberries. Jean Baptiste and Rene said they would start supper while Dufort looked for dessert. The stocky trader checked the priming on his musket, and disappeared over a hill south of their campsite.

"In some ways, I'll be sorry to see this trip end," said Jean Baptiste. "I want to see my family, but I feel good right now. Besides, when you study your Polybius, you'll probably find out that the island mentioned was not 'Cerne," but rather 'Cernix,' or 'Cervix,' or something like that. Then all our dreams will be dashed. At least now they are only unlikely. On top of that, Etienne will undoubtedly kill you. He really wants the be the Bey."

The two youths laughed, but their merriment was cut short by the sudden reappearance of the potentate to be, who ran down the hill, signaled for silence and brought no berries.

"Quiet!" Etienne whispered. "The other side of that hill is swarming with Mohawks."

## CHAPTER 17

Rene quickly kicked dirt on the fire they had just started. Jean Baptiste pulled the canoe behind some nearby shrubbery, hiding it completely. Etienne gathered up all the items that had been unloaded, and hurriedly deposited them back where they originated. The three of them then scrambled into a dense thicket, checked their weapons and tried to analyze the situation.

"How many are there?" asked Jean Baptiste.

"At least twenty, probably more like thirty. I would have walked right into their midst except I heard a sound to my right, looked over, and saw one of them pissing against a tree. Lucky for me he was facing away from me. I ducked behind some bushes, waited for him to finish his business, and then followed in the direction he went. In moments he joined his fellows, and I was able to get a good look before I remembered you would be starting a fire for cooking dinner. So I hurried back to warn you."

"What could they be doing here?" asked Rene. "We are not at war with either the English or the Iroquois, at least not at the moment. And these Mohawks are definitely not where they belong."

"They're not a hunting party. I noticed a number

of them touching up their face paint, like they expected action soon. Probably not too soon though, now that I think about it, because many of them were lounging about, and they all seemed pretty relaxed. I'm not sure, but I think there were a few Oneidas and Onondagas with them."

At that point, the storm that had threatened burst upon them in full fury. The three crawled to their canoe, emptied it and turned it over to use as a shelter against the rain that was building in volume. They were careful to keep under cover, though there was little chance that the enemy would do much roaming during the downpour. Using bearskins that normally served as their bedding, they were able to rig a shelter that kept them tolerably dry. They carefully wrapped the locks on their muskets, to keep them dry and serviceable.

"One other thing," mentioned Dufort, "though it is evidence that advancing age is taking its toll on my memory. I recognized the spot where they camped as being about one hundred paces from the beginning of a long portage. There's a lengthy stretch of rough water downstream from there. It requires a carry of a third of a league or more. God apparently did not mean for us to die today my friends. He sent threatening skies, which prompted us to quit early, and he befuddled my mind, so that I forgot the location of the portage. If I'd remembered it, I'd have encouraged us to push on and camp there. If we had, we'd have paddled right under their guns. War or no war, I'm sure that would have been the end of us."

"This storm is a good opportunity for me to see for myself," said Jean Baptiste. "I'm sure it's not an accident that they camped along the Ottawa near a portage trail.

They must be waiting for someone, though they won't be alert now because they will assume that travelers would seek shelter from the wind and rain. I'm going to take a look. No sense bringing a gun out in this weather; it probably wouldn't fire anyway. I've got a hatchet and knife; they will have to do."

"I'll join you, lad," said Dufort. "I know just where the bastards are skulking."

"No, Etienne. One of us blundering about out there is plenty. You and Rene sit tight. I not only want a look at the Iroquois, but also at the terrain. If you need something to do, keep watch upstream, in case an unsuspecting friend is about to venture in harm's way. My suspicion however, is that the war party is looking for someone coming upstream. If they were interested in traffic coming downstream, any scout looking that way would have seen us before we pulled into shore."

It was still light, probably an hour before sunset, though the landscape was gloomy and uninviting in the extreme. The rain was pouring down. Jean Baptiste was careful when he left their makeshift shelter, trying to keep it as water tight as possible. Fortunately, the air was warm, though the rain was colder than he would have preferred. Moving slowly and taking advantage of all available cover, he was able to reach a vantage point overlooking the Iroquois camp in about a half-hour. No one was to be seen. Apparently the warriors had planned to stay at this spot for some time. Jean Baptiste didn't know when they arrived, but they'd had enough time to erect temporary lodges, in which they now apparently resided.

The cadet made a circuit of the enemy camp. He was sure it was invisible from the portage trail, as it was intended to be. Several heavily wooded hills to the southwest commanded the hidden camp. Before darkness became complete, Jean Baptiste found a sentry post with an excellent view downstream and along the portage trail. The grass at that spot was well trampled, and bones from rabbit and deer had been discarded, the refuse from many meals eaten by the sentinels. He had seen enough. He made his way back to his friends.

Not wanting to be blown to shreds by Rene's over sized pistols, Jean Baptiste was careful to make his presence known as he approached the overturned canoe. Once under shelter, he stripped off his dripping clothes, dried himself with a blanket and put on buckskin breeches and a shirt.

"I'm sure they're waiting for someone coming from Montreal. I'd have to guess that whoever the someone is will be unpleasantly surprised when they arrive here. I'm certain we could slip away undetected, but I think I want to stay here and see if we can't upset the Iroquois' plans. Of course, we could avoid the Iroquois and warn whoever is approaching, but they would still have to pass this way to reach the lakes. I think we may be able to help them more by maintaining ourselves on the Iroquois' flank and rear. Etienne, how do you think the Iroquois plan to ambush the new arrivals?"

"Since they selected the end of the portage trail for their camp, I assume they'll hit their target nearby. If it's a convoy bearing trade goods and supplies, as I suspect, the voyageurs will have to make a number of trips from the lower end of the trail to this, the upper end, carrying boxes, kegs and bundles. The Iroquois will want to catch them by surprise, and when the whole party is together. I believe they'll wait until all the goods are piled up at this end of the trail, ready to be reloaded, and then attack. They probably won't wait for the canoes to be reloaded because of the possibility that the canoes would overturn during the attack, resulting in lost or spoiled trade goods."

"I'm confident you're correct. In the morning, I'll circle around the Iroquois and return to the river at the beginning of the portage trail. Then I'll continue down river about a half-league, just to ensure I can't be seen. I'll hail whoever is coming from shore, and warn them of their peril. I want you two to move our canoe and goods to a spot so secluded that even you will have difficulty finding them again. Then move to those hills I mentioned southwest of the Iroquois camp. You will be within musket range of their ambush positions, so you'll have to be very quiet, but be prepared to hold on. I'll rejoin you before the shooting starts, and try to bring some men with me.

"Let's see," continued the cadet, "We'll need some way of knowing when all the supplies have reached this end of the trail, and when all the voyageurs are together, so that we can start the fireworks. That's it. Etienne, I know for a fact you never returned Gaspard's sash. Let me have that orange, yellow and black monstrosity. We'll have the voyageur carrying the last of the supplies put on the sash. When he puts his load down at this end of the trail, that will be the signal to open up."

"I decided to hang onto the sash so that Gaspard did not remain overlong with Humming Bird," replied Dufort defensively. "When he recalls it is missing, it will spur his recovery."

They awoke before dawn the next morning. The storm had passed and the sky was clear. Bare patches of ground were very muddy, slowing movement and increasing the possibility of discovery through footprints.

"Hide the canoe and our extra gear well. When things dry out, some of the Mohawks may decide to stretch their legs. You'll need to find excellent concealment for yourselves up on the hills as well. I'll start now and try to reach my observation point by dawn. If nothing develops today, I'll meet you on the hills an hour after dark."

Jean Baptiste worked his way around the Iroquois camp, hearing nothing and seeing no one. When he was well clear, he increased his pace, being careful to remain hidden by the foliage. At first light he estimated that he was near the start of the portage trail. He stopped for a moment to get his bearings. As he was about to resume his journey along the riverbank, he heard voices and immediately dropped from sight.

He was about twenty paces from the landing where those using the trail unloaded their canoes. In the uncertain light, a single canoe holding two men was pulling in. Jean Baptiste could not see them clearly, but could hear them conversing in low tones. Their voices carried across the water to his hiding place, though he could not make out what was being said. He elected to watch the new arrivals before deciding whether to reveal himself or not.

The two landed their canoe. One of the men took both muskets and both packs, the other hoisted the canoe over his head, and they headed up the trail. They passed within ten paces of the cadet, and now he recognized them. Mohawks! They wore breechcloths and moccasins, along with leggings to protect them from branches along the trail. Both wore a variety of ornaments dangling from their stretched earlobes. The man carrying the canoe wore no shirt, but had a sheathed hunting knife suspended from his neck. Somewhat uncharacteristically, he wore his hair long, hanging loose about his shoulders. The other warrior wore a shirt that had not been washed in some time. He had only a small tuft of hair at the top of his skull, to which several feathers of different types were affixed.

What really interested Jean Baptiste were the crucifixes both men wore around their necks. These Mohawks were mission Indians, probably from Caughnawaga near Montreal. The young cadet had a decision to make, and very little time to make it. Adherents of the Catholic Church as were virtually all the Frenchmen in Canada, these tribesmen were in theory allies of the French, and had left their homeland along the Mohawk River to relocate in the St. Lawrence valley. If they were friends, they were headed for trouble.

Though tempted, something stopped him from calling out. Maybe he recalled the words of his father, who insisted that all Mohawks were the enemies of New France, whether they took to wearing crucifixes or not. Daniel Joubert had noted a marked reluctance on the part of the Caughnawagas to oppose their brethren still living along the Mohawk River, and felt welcoming these converts to the Montreal area was no less than inviting the enemy inside your defenses.

Whatever the reason, Jean Baptiste allowed them to continue on their way, while he moved down river to look for the expected convoy. He found a good spot and tried to make himself as comfortable as possible, since he assumed he would have a considerable wait. Fortunately, the day turned warm and bright and the ground dried quickly, making his vantage point more livable.  He decided he must be well hidden, because a variety of animals practically trod upon him as they came down to the water to drink.  The wildlife included a doe, a fine buck and even an elk of tremendous size.  The cadet knew that hunting was out of the question, and sourly contented himself with eating the pemmican he had brought.

No one else appeared at the landing after the passage of the two Mohawks.  Late in the day, the wind swung around until a brisk breeze blew from the northwest, dropping the temperature considerably.  Jean Baptiste was most uncomfortable by the time darkness fell and it was time to return to his companions.  He had sat nearly motionless all day, and his legs were stiff when at last he stood up.  After he started walking back, the stiffness departed and he felt warmer.  He hurried as much as safety allowed, being anxious to learn the fate of the two Mohawks.

It was full dark when he climbed one of the hills where he'd asked his companions to wait.  He moved cautiously in the gloom, seeing nothing of his friends.  At last he heard his name whispered and felt a hand on his shoulder, which turned out to be Dufort's.

"We're grateful to see you again.  When those two devils showed up at the Iroquois camp this morning, we were afraid you had blundered into them and come to grief."

"I saw them, and for a moment almost warned them about the Iroquois camp."

"Why would you do that?  They're Iroquois too, aren't they?"

"Yes, but they're Caughnawagas.   They're

supposed to be on our side."

"Well, it looks like someone forgot to tell them," said La Pointe. "We saw them arrive. The whole camp instantly became a hive of activity. The new arrivals spoke for a few minutes to the men of the encampment, then preparation for something began in earnest. The lethargy of yesterday was no longer evident. It looks like whatever they are planning will happen at this end of the trail. A dozen warriors began moving fallen logs in place to provide breastworks as protection against fire from the landing."

"Interesting," said Jean Baptiste. "I'd guess that whatever is going to happen will occur tomorrow. You seem well hidden here. Did you have any trouble?"

"About noon, two warriors climbed this hill, thinking to improve their observation point. Though it's somewhat higher than the one they are using, the foliage is too thick, so they gave up and went back down. I doubt any of them will find our canoe. It is five hundred paces from the river and well hidden."

"Good," replied the cadet. "Tomorrow, we'll repeat what we did today, except I think the expected guests will arrive."

"Jean Baptiste," said La Pointe, "I've been thinking. We need something to turn the odds in our favor. If it is a convoy bringing supplies, why don't you see if they have these items, and bring them back here when you return with the reinforcements. I may be able to create a few surprises for the Mohawks below, whether they be Christian or heathen."

## CHAPTER 18

Before dawn the next morning, Jean Baptiste retraced his steps to his observation point on the riverbank. He tried to get as comfortable as possible, in case he had another long day ahead, and reflected without enthusiasm on the lump of pemmican he had brought to provide sustenance. Thinking positively, the day gave early indications of being warm and dry. He remained vigilant, scanning the river constantly, but for the first two hours saw nothing.

Then, he thought he heard rather than saw something. He wasn't sure what it was at first, but then recognized snatches of "Alouette," one of the voyageurs' songs. Gradually, the singing grew louder, and finally he could see four of the large *canot du maitre* approaching against the current. The channel apparently flowed near his place of concealment, for the canoes were angling across the river toward him. When they were about fifty paces off, he stood and held his musket over his head to get the convoy's attention. The singing stopped immediately, and muskets replaced paddles in the hands of a dozen voyageurs.

"I'm a friend!" Jean Baptiste called to the canoes, cupping his hands around his mouth in order to direct the sound in the desired direction.

"Who are you, friend?" inquired a tall paddler with a gray moustache, seated at the rear of the first canoe.

"Joseph, Joseph Varin, is that you? I thought you'd grown too old for these trips into the wilderness. I'm Jean Baptiste Joubert, on my way to Montreal from Michilimackinac. Have all your canoes come ashore here. There's a decent landing place. Come quickly and quietly, if you value your lives."

Varin was an employee of long standing in Daniel Joubert's fur business. Thirty years ago, he started as a voyageur noted for his strength and stamina. When returning from the interior with furs, he would carry three packs at once during portages, never stopping to catch his breath until the assigned resting places, or *poses*, were reached. Years of exposure to the elements had hastened the onset of crippling pain in his hands and knees, and in recent years he had remained in Montreal, though still an efficient and dedicated worker. He prepared trade goods for shipment to the *pays d'en haut*, and when furs were received from the far country, he broke up the bundles, sorted, graded and marked the pelts.

The old man exited the canoe and shook hands with Jean Baptiste. The cadet noted that the old voyageur's grip retained much of its strength. "It's good to see you, lad, though you gave us a start. What is the problem?"

"There are about thirty Iroquois lurking at the far end of the next portage. We've been watching them for several days, and they haven't moved. Evidently, they are waiting for you. How many men do you have?"

"Thirty-two, including myself, and I probably am

getting too old for this much exercise. But, your father has experienced one financial reverse after another. Convoys have disappeared; his losses have been ruinous. He decided he had to get these supplies through to Michilimackinac, to make up for earlier shipments that never arrived, even though the season is well advanced. I volunteered to lead these men. You'll recognize many of them. Quite a few are past their prime, as is their leader. But few voyageurs were available in Montreal, and these men, though aged, have years of experience. We may move a little more slowly on the portages, and we may carry less weight than in the old days, but we still don't rest until the task is done. As Daniel's son, these men and I are at your disposal. What would you have us do?"

Jean Baptiste asked if they carried any of the ornamented powder horns occasionally used in the trade. He was pleased to receive an affirmative response, and requested that six be located. He asked that four of the best marksmen accompany him, bringing with them the extra powder horns, as well as a keg of powder and one of shot. As the four men located the desired supplies, Jean Baptiste explained the situation to Varin and the others.

"How many trips will be needed to transport everything to the far end of the portage trail?" asked Jean Baptiste.

"Each man will have to make three trips."

Jean Baptiste handed Gaspard's sash to the old voyageur. "Have the man carrying the last load on the last trip wear this sash. We will be on the hills behind the Iroquois. When the man with the yellow, orange and black sash puts down his load, that will be our signal to fire. As you drop off the goods at the upper landing, stack them to provide cover for yourselves. Keep your weapons at hand. We think we know what they will do, but Indians can be unpredictable."

"Good luck to you, lad. We'd better be on our way. The Mohawks will be expecting us and we don't want to be late. I know I don't. I've been carrying a Mohawk arrowhead in my back for twenty-one years. I never thought I'd evened things up for that."

As Jean Baptiste and his four recruits made their way to Dufort and La Pointe, the cadet reflected on the words of Varin, and the look in the eyes of the other voyageurs. They regarded the Iroquois, and especially the Mohawks, as enemies of their blood. New France had fought the Five Nations for more than a century, and it was felt that no truce with these tribes would ever be lasting. These aging canoe men had fought the Iroquois many times, often during periods when no official war had been declared, and the scalps of old comrades hung in Mohawk, Oneida and Onondaga lodges. They all seemed eager to even the score.

The five just started the climb up the reverse slope of the hill where they would fight, when they encountered Dufort. "Bad news, Jean Baptiste. About twenty more Iroquois just arrived. We decided I should find you and let you know before you put our plan in motion, but I can see I'm too late." Dufort silently shook hands with the four new men, all of whom he knew.

"Well, we'll have to continue on with it. By now Joseph Varin and the rest of the convoy will have reached the portage trail and begun unloading the trade goods. The Iroquois are sure to have seen them. An attempt to pull them back now would bring the whole pack down on them and cost us whatever element of surprise we have."

The cadet then led his five companions up the hill where they joined Rene La Pointe.

"I guess the ball has started," commented La Pointe. "We could be in a little trouble. The Iroquois have settled into their positions, and I was able to count fifty-five in all. How many do we have?"

"Thirty-five, including us. We'll have to hope that your bomb making is a success. Luckily, the convoy was carrying everything you asked for."

"While you were gone, I cut the sleeve of a shirt into pieces, and made fuses from them. Here, let me see what you've brought me."

"I contributed also by emptying one of our brandy bottles, going down the reverse side of the hill for a few moments, and quietly breaking the bottle into a few hundred shards of glass," mentioned Dufort, seemingly very pleased with himself as he belched contentedly. "I thought the broken bits would be good to pack in the bombs as well."

"I'm beginning to wish we had a few pieces of artillery up here," said Jean Baptiste. "But we'll have to do the best we can with what we've got."

"How much time do you think we have until we see the man wearing Gaspard's sash?" asked La Pointe.

"I'd guess the last load would arrive at the landing below around noon."

La Pointe began making his bombs, packing the powder horns with a mixture of powder, musket balls and broken glass. Each was fitted with a fuse, and one of the voyageurs gathered dry kindling so they could start a small fire with which to light the fuses. Because of the keen sense of smell possessed by their enemies, and the fact that they were upwind of the Iroquois position, they wouldn't be able to light the fire until the shooting started.

Jean Baptiste sat with La Pointe and helped his friend prepare their secret weapons.

"You know," said the clerk, "I'm not sure how long these fuses will burn. After Etienne finished gathering his broken glass, he stood watch while I left the hill to burn a couple of the fuses. Based on my experiments, it should take about a slow five count from the time it's lit until it explodes. I also practiced throwing my powder horn a number of times to determine the best way to do it. I think I know. Grasp it like so, the barrel of the horn in the palm of your hand, the spout with the fuse projecting between index finger and thumb. The problem is, there's no way to throw a bomb anywhere near the Iroquois position from where we are now. They're just too far away."

"Maybe your bombs won't be used at all. Indians are usually quite sensible in the way they fight. Keeping their own casualties to an absolute minimum is the first priority. The men of the convoy should be able to provide a volume of fire sufficient to discourage a direct assault. There are only seven of us, so even though our rate of fire won't be much, the fact that we've caught them between the convoy and ourselves may dishearten them. Maybe they'll decide to quit the field and fight another day."

"I'd say that was a big maybe."

"I guess you're right. In case they don't agree with my analysis of their priorities, and decide to come up here after us, hopefully your bombs will discourage them. Well, I'd better check how the other men have positioned themselves."

After satisfying himself that each man had taken the best cover possible without resorting to noisy digging or cutting, and ensuring that both flanks as well as the front were covered to the extent possible by seven men, he found a good spot in the center of their position, and watched with interest the scene unfolding below. Apparently, a number of voyageurs had already reached this end of the portage trail, because Jean Baptiste could see several kegs, as well as about a dozen bales of merchandise stacked at the landing. The cadet had been busy with their preparations, and had not seen the men arrive and drop off their loads. He gave a silent prayer of thanks; at least to this point, the enemy was doing as they anticipated.

As he watched, two voyageurs appeared, approaching the landing from the southeast. They moved with the steady shuffling trot characteristic of voyageurs on portage, each carrying two packs on his back, leather tumplines looped around their foreheads and the lower of the two packs. These tumplines allowed the voyageurs to lean well forward as they moved, properly balancing their loads. Jean Baptiste couldn't help but marvel at the courage of these men. They stuck to the plan and carried their loads to the landing, right into the sights of fifty muskets. They dropped their loads and headed back for more; several carried their acting to an extreme and casually lit pipes at the landing, apparently enjoying a short smoke before returning to the lower landing. After seeing these displays of quiet valor, the cadet was more certain than ever that these men would acquit themselves well in the coming fight.

Time passed slowly. Jean Baptiste studied the Iroquois positions. If they were able to fire the first volley at an unsuspecting foe, he had no doubt it all would be over very quickly. They would probably fire once, then close in on the dazed survivors and finish them with their hatchets. He wished things would start. Waiting like this was hard. His mouth was getting dry; his palms were getting sweaty.

He tried to focus on the situation. He was sure he had seen the voyageur setting his load down now on two previous trips. In fact, about a dozen voyageurs were now gathered about the landing, smoking and relaxing a bit. Jean Baptiste noted that they had done a good job piling the sacks of trade goods to provide some protection. All stayed close to their muskets. It wouldn't be long now. More and more of the canoe men arrived, dropped their final loads, and scattered about the landing. Finally, Jean Baptiste saw Joseph Varin emerge from the trail, wearing no cap, his gray hair and moustache clearly visible. The old man carried what looked to be two packs of pemmican, the voyageurs' food supply while traveling. Around his waist he wore a yellow, orange and black sash.

## CHAPTER 19

J ean Baptiste signaled to his six companions atop the hill to get ready. As soon as Joseph found some cover they would let loose. The cadet saw the men at the landing inching toward the bales of merchandise or convenient trees that would provide some measure of protection from the Iroquois' fire. Joseph set his load down, and with agility that belied his years, dove into a thicket to the right of the landing.

"Fire!" shouted Jean Baptiste. He had been watching the Iroquois positions below and had picked a stocky warrior who seemed to issue instructions to his companions from time to time. The cadet fired; the ball missed its mark, whistled by the ear of the warrior and struck the ground to his left. Jean Baptiste cursed and began to reload, keeping one eye on the tribesmen below to see if the ragged volley fired by his companions had any effect. He heard cries from several who were hit, saw two fall, and then his vision was obscured by smoke from the musket fire.

"Rene!" he shouted. "Start the fire so we can use your bombs if need be."

Using a steel striker, La Pointe had already started on the fire.

Jean Baptiste looked to the base of the hill and saw that the Iroquois were in confusion. Some fired at the voyageurs at the landing, but to little effect. Others looked up the hill to see who was shooting at them. Jean Baptiste could see the stout warrior, the one he had missed, had recovered his composure and was rallying the others.

"Dufort! Do you see that fat bastard down there with his face painted red and yellow? Try to eliminate him."

Etienne nodded and took careful aim. He fired and from the look of satisfaction that spread across his face, Jean Baptiste knew he'd gotten his man. The men at the landing were firing into the Iroquois as well, but per his instructions only one-third of them at a time, so that the Indians would not have an opportunity to rush them when all their muskets were empty. With at least one of their leaders out of the fight, the cadet hoped a few more well placed volleys would cause the Iroquois to retire.

After a few minutes, he began to lose hope that this fight would be easily won. The warriors seemed to recover from their initial panic, and other leaders began organizing them to face both the hill and the landing. One Mohawk who was very active was the shorthaired mission Indian he'd seen at the lower landing yesterday morning. He had gotten a dozen Iroquois to turn and face the French at the top of the hill. Their fire was intended to keep the heads of Jean Baptiste's men down while the other Iroquois concentrated on Joseph's voyageurs. Smoke obscured much of what was happening below, but the cadet felt that his little band had better get all their defensive firepower ready.

He turned to La Pointe and saw that the blaze was well started. Rene had a burning brand handy, and had passed another to a voyageur on the far left of their position, along with two of his bombs.

"Rene, they've figured by now there aren't many of us up here. With all the smoke to hide in I've got a feeling they'll try working their way up, using all the cover they can find. When they get close, they'll rush us. Be ready."

The cadet could see very little of what was happening below, but it sounded to him like the French at the landing were holding their own and keeping their more numerous attackers at bay. Through breaks in the smoke he was sure he saw warriors making their way up the hill. Twenty paces below the French position was an outcrop that would provide some protection for the climbers. Suddenly the voyageur to Jean Baptiste's right cried out, clutched his head and fell backward. The lad looked to see if there was something he could do to aid the man, but he'd been struck in the forehead and had paddled his last canoe.

"Rene, that outcrop below us. They're gathering there for the final rush to the top. When I give you the signal, light the fuse and let's see how it works."

Jean Baptiste peered down the slope and could see four or five warriors working their way around the left side of their position. He saw another of his men stretched on the ground, probably dead but certainly out of the fight. The man had been hit in the upper chest; a pool of blood had already formed beneath him. The voyageur on the left with the bombs saw the danger below from the flanking maneuver, and lit one of his fuses. He was about to hurl the bomb when he was struck in the head, the explosive dropping from his lifeless fingers.

"Everybody down!" screamed Jean Baptiste. He dove behind a tree moments before the device detonated. Musket balls and pieces of broken glass ricocheted off rocks, trees and the ground. The cadet felt a pain in his wrist and saw that a musket ball had struck the back of his right wrist and exited cleanly on the other side.

"Is everyone all right?" he called while ripping off a piece of his shirt to bandage his wound.

"It's a miracle," gasped Dufort. "There's not much left of Augustin, but Paul, Rene and I are still among the living."

La Pointe had recovered from the concussion the fastest of the four survivors on the hill. He saw that the knot of warriors at the outcrop had already risen from concealment and had begun the final ascent. He had only seconds to act. He lit the fuse halfway down its length and threw the missile at the feet of the nearest climbing warriors, who by this time were only a few steps away. Jean Baptiste lunged for cover again as the explosion rent the air, accompanied by the screams of the injured and the dying. The cadet looked up, his ears ringing, the smell of burnt flesh in his nostrils. Only paces away, smoke rose from a pile of Iroquois. Some were still alive, though terribly wounded. They were attempting to crawl back down the hill to their friends. Three or four lay still and would never move again.

As this carnage was registering on his mind, he saw the warriors that had flanked them on the left surge over the brow of the hill. Etienne and the surviving voyageur had seen them coming and dropped two with pistol shots at point blank range. The other two were on them before they could draw either hatchet or knife. The Frenchmen grappled with their assailants, trying to tie up their arms to prevent fatal thrusts. Rene ran to the aid of the voyageur, clubbing his Oneida attacker to death with his spiked war club.

Jean Baptiste tried to finish Dufort's attacker, but the Mohawk saw him coming and was able to keep Dufort between himself and the cadet. This Iroquois was a brave man. Though now alone, he gave no thought to escape, caring only about killing his enemies. His whole body had been painted red, except for the areas around the eyes and nose, which were white. In spite of the red paint, Jean Baptiste could see the man had been wounded in the side. The cadet finally dove on top of the interlocked combatants, and was able to drive his knife between the Indian's ribs.

La Pointe had snatched up a firebrand and one of the bombs, and was pointing down the hill. "Come on, Jean Baptiste. Let's finish this!" With that the young clerk gave a wild cry and sprinted down the hill at the remaining Iroquois, who were still firing at the men at the landing. Jean Baptiste grabbed a pistol and La Pointe's bloody war club, and started after him.

Up ahead, Rene was now two-thirds of the way down the hill. He paused to light his bomb. One of the Iroquois, a veteran warrior of many campaigns, chanced to look over his shoulder to see how the fight for the hill was progressing. He didn't see any of his comrades, but did see a young Frenchman trying to light something with a torch. The warrior, an Onondaga, turned and raised his musket.

Jean Baptiste saw Rene's danger at that moment. In one motion he raised and cocked the pistol, praying that his aim was true and the pistol was loaded. The report of the weapon satisfied him on the second point. The ball struck and shattered the stock of the Onondaga's musket, and the weapon discharged harmlessly in the air. Rene had the bomb lit now and tossed it up in the air over the Iroquois, dropping to the ground as he did so.

The ensuing explosion gave the main body of the Iroquois their first taste of the French "heavy artillery." It was also the last taste they intended to experience that day. They had enough, and began streaming off the field to Jean Baptiste's right, heading down river. Joseph's voyageurs gave them a few parting shots to speed them on their way. In a few moments, all the firing ended and it was quiet, except for the cheers of the Frenchmen, several of whom hoisted La Pointe on their shoulders while they thanked him for making his charge down the slope to their rescue.

When he was back on firm ground, Jean Baptiste clapped his friend on the back. "Well done Rene. You were the one who got them on the run." The cadet didn't want to say anything now to dampen Rene's spirits, but La Pointe's recklessness was becoming a concern. How many of these fights could he survive? They would have to talk later.

"Where is Etienne?" inquired the clerk.

Jean Baptiste looked around. He didn't see their portly companion. In fact, he didn't recall seeing him since the last of the Iroquois was killed at the top of the hill. They looked at each other, apparently had the same thought, and sprinted back up the hill. Dufort was sitting with his back against a tree, near the dead Mohawk in the red and white paint. He was humming the tune to a voyageur song, sipping brandy from a bottle he had stashed nearby.

"Well men, it sounds like the war's over, and since you're up here looking for me instead of being chased through the woods, I take it we won. Sorry I wasn't around at the finish. Thought I'd stay here and replace some of the liquid I lost. That asshole came close to costing me a share of Hannibal's gold." With that, Dufort dropped the bottle and fainted. Rene sat him up, and as he did, felt wetness on his own right hand. Blood. Etienne had been stabbed in the left armpit and had bled much.

"How is he?" asked Jean Baptiste.

"I think he'll be all right. As near as I can tell, the blade didn't hit anything vital. I'll tie this up, and he should be good as new in a few weeks, though it's an excellent excuse for him to avoid any work on the rest of the trip. Go ahead and see how the others are doing. I can manage here."

Jean Baptiste found old Joseph picking a variety of burrs and thorns out of his legs and backside. He'd apparently made an unfortunate selection when he dove for cover into the bushes. "Young Joubert! I'm so glad to see you well. How are those who were with you?"

"Paul is the only one of the four I borrowed who is still alive. I'm sorry. Dufort is hurt but I think he'll pull through. And you?"

"Ignace Menard is dead and four others are hurt. Counting you and Dufort, we've got four dead and six wounded. I had hoped you hadn't lost so many up there. Those bombs turned out to be the difference, I think."

Men were assigned to bury the dead. The wounded were gathered at the landing, and Joseph proved to be an adept nurse, having had much practice tending to wounds in his long career.

"I think all will live," he told Jean Baptiste late that afternoon. "The problem is that I'm not sure we have enough uninjured men to successfully fight the current."

"Dufort, La Pointe and I need to continue to Montreal. We'll leave in the morning. I'd advise that you stay here and tend to your wounded. I'll get replacements for you as soon as I arrive on the island. We'll hurry. What you're carrying is important and it's getting late in the season."

"Fine, lad. It's probably our only option anyway. Move as quick as you can though, and watch out for those Mohawks. They retreated in the direction you're going."

"I know. You keep a good watch too. I think they've had enough for the moment, but it's hard to be sure."

After he helped the voyageurs convert their part of the battlefield into a semi-permanent camp, Jean Baptiste decided to climb the hill where they'd made their stand once again. The sun was low on the horizon. It would be dark soon. The voyageurs were digging a large pit that would serve as a communal grave for the enemy dead, though they still lay where they had fallen. The Frenchmen had not moved them; they'd only made sure that the wounded would cause no more trouble.

The cadet wandered over to the cluster of bodies caused by Rene's bomb. One of the figures looked familiar. The dead man was lying on his stomach, his long hair covering his face. Jean Baptiste turned the body over. At least four musket balls and probably a half dozen shards of glass had hit the man. Death had been quick. He wasn't really interested in the man's gruesome appearance, but rather in what he surmised was hanging around his neck. There it was. A metallic crucifix, dented now after being struck by a musket ball. Jean Baptiste removed the object and returned down the hill.

A short distance away, Strong Hand, a sub-chief of the Caughnawaga Mohawks, bathed his face in cool river water, the pink-stained liquid splashing on his gold cross. He was in great pain, for when the Frenchman threw the powder horn that exploded, grains of burning powder had been blown into his face and right eye. He had abandoned the fight, along with two or three others who survived unscathed. As he rubbed salve on his injuries, one of the Mohawks who had ascended the hill with him returned from a short scout of the area, and told Strong Hand he had found the trail of the main band of retreating warriors.

The Caughnawaga signaled the others and they left the scene of this humiliating defeat. *But perhaps all was not as it seemed,* mused Strong Hand. *We had thought to ambush this convoy, but instead had been ambushed ourselves. Mr. Thomas Blackthorne uses spies to get information. Maybe someone is spying on him. Many Iroquois died this day. Someone will pay for that.*

**CHAPTER 20**
September, 1731

K icking Bear and Eagle Claw, envoys of the Fox nation, were escorted into the presence of Governor General Beauharnois by Nicholas-Antoine Coulon de Villiers, the commander of Fort St. Joseph. They had passed overland from his post to Detroit. From there, they proceeded by canoe the lengths of Lakes Erie and Ontario and down the St. Lawrence to Montreal. They arrived toward evening, the western sky showing lightning and billowing thunder heads. The two warriors requested that they have the night to refresh themselves so that they might make the best impression possible on the mighty Onontio on the morrow. Lieutenant Villiers granted their request, and accompanied by four marines, they left the dock area to spend the night at a marine camp outside the town walls.

At the appointed hour, the two Foxes were summoned to the governor general's residence. Their instructions from Kiala had been clear. They were to buy time by promising whatever the French required. This was the first time either of them had seen a European town other than small collections of settlers outside places like Fort St. Joseph and Fort La Baye. They were sufficiently impressed by its size and relative grandeur that they came to believe more fully in the importance of their assignment. If Wisaka's people were to have any chance to survive the wrath of the French, much time would be needed to prepare.

Both brothers had taken pains with their appearance, appropriate in view of the occasion. Kicking Bear had seen thirty-four summers and was the larger of the two. His body bore the scars of a dozen wounds, most received in combats against the despised Illinois confederacy. Like his younger brother, he wore a red horsehair roach headdress attached to his scalplock, augmented with hawk feathers. Both men had a number of silver ornaments attached to their ears, and wore deerskin shirts and leggings of the finest quality. Beautifully made deerskin moccasins, beaded in bright colors with intricate designs, completed their attire.

Eagle Claw, two years younger, was not as renowned a warrior. In his youth he had shown promise of legendary proportions, raiding alone deep inside Sioux country on four occasions, each time returning with two or more scalps. Ten years ago, an Ojibwa musket shot had struck him in the shoulder and left him with a withered right arm. He still fought when needed, but since his injury had turned his considerable energies toward studying the history of his people, as remembered by the old men of the tribe. He tried to understand what had happened before, to better know what should be done now. When decisions were needed, his voice carried weight at the council fire.

Charles de Beauharnois de La Boische was nearing his sixtieth birthday, and whatever patience he had possessed concerning the Fox problem had long since disappeared.  These troublesome savages had disrupted the fur trade, particularly the potentially lucrative traffic with the Sioux, in which the governor general himself had an interest.  Their incessant warfare against practically everyone they encountered caused an inordinate amount of toil and expense to be expended to alternately cajole, threaten and attack them.  No permanent solution had been found, and the Minister of Marine had sent a number of scathing letters on the subject.  Beauharnois meant to conclude the matter.

The governor general and most of the important officials of the colony had gathered to hear the words of Eagle Claw, who would present the Fox petition.

"Onontio, we come here today to ask mercy for the people of Wisaka.  We realize we do not merit your forbearance, but ask it nonetheless.  We have suffered grievous losses in the past few years, not only of warriors, but also women, children and the aged.  We are no longer a threat to you, and ask that you not remove us completely from the earth.  Please grant us peace in order to use it to atone through our submission for the enormous crimes that our unfortunate stubbornness made us commit.  Please send someone to govern us who, in representing your illustrious person, will inspire in the rest of our young men the respect and submission that they owe you."

Beauharnois was pleased when these words were translated to him, but his response reflected little charity.

"The crimes committed by the Fox over the years are too numerous to count.  All the reasons that you could bring to lessen the magnitude of your perfidy could never include anything which could be used as justification.  You two are unworthy even to appear before me, but because of my exceeding kindness, I will grant you your lives. I do however, require additional guarantees and security for your faithfulness. One of you will remain here as a hostage while the other returns to the lands of the Fox. I demand that Kiala and four other chieftains travel to Montreal and throw themselves at my feet. If the five do not appear here next summer, I will see to it that the Fox are destroyed to the last man, woman and child."

Kicking Bear and Eagle Claw were led from the room. Villiers allowed them to decide which of them would remain as a hostage. He walked away so they could confer in private.

"Brother, I believe your speech accomplished what we came here to do, though it was difficult to bear his insults in silence."

"Yes, it would seem that Kiala has nearly a year to prepare. Since at that time every warrior will be needed, it is fitting that I remain here. You are a whole man; I am only half. I doubt we will see each other again. Remember, when next you are in battle, you must strike for two."

Despite the lateness of the season, Kicking Bear left immediately to bear the words of Onontio to Kiala. After he left, Eagle Claw was shackled and thrown into a damp, windowless basement cell.

At that moment, the *Pelican* was entering the St. Lawrence River, sailing past the south shore of Anticosti Island. Maurice was a happy man. His stump caused virtually no discomfort anymore. Dominique had insisted on being his nurse, shooing Arbut away when it was time for his bandages to be changed. The lieutenant had not wanted her to be involved with that unpleasant business, but she insisted, and he had difficulty denying her anything.

The voyage itself had been uneventful, for which Maurice was grateful. Lieutenant La Force's mention of possible pirate activity had made him uneasy. In case of trouble there was no absolutely safe place for Dominique on board.

He was exhilarated by the fresh sea air and generally cool breezes, particularly once they headed north along the Atlantic coast of the English colonies. The weather had been generally fair and their progress had been swift. La Force kept the crew sharp by drilling the men frequently. Never one to favor idle hands, the captain also kept the men busy washing and scraping the deck, and kept a goodly number constantly on watch. Maurice observed that though La Force worked his men, they respected and even seemed to like him. He demanded discipline and performance, but without the brutality common on the sea.

Maurice had not known how to act toward Dominique. They had been intimate in New Orleans, but that had seemed a very private affair, removed from the eyes of others. Here, on board ship, in close contact with forty sailors, the situation was different. The first night on the vessel, he had bid his lovely companion good night and then lay awake for hours, knowing she was in the next cabin, only a thin wall separating them. The next morning when they ate breakfast in the tiny captain's cabin, she had given him a quizzical look that had him thinking all day. They spoke at various times, usually on topics of little consequence, and then it was night again. They went to their respective cabins and Maurice lay down on his cot, wide-awake again. After a time, he heard a soft knock on his door. He opened and there she was.

"I'm lonely. Would you mind some company tonight?"

What a question, recalled Maurice. But since then, the voyage had been the most pleasant experience of his life (with the possible exception of the night he met her). Henri had allowed the two of them much time without interference, spending the bulk of his time learning the fine points of seamanship from La Force, and even taking enthusiastic part in the gunnery drills.

Now that they were on the St. Lawrence, Maurice mused that this idyllic interlude would soon end. But there was no reason for Dominique to be absent from his life. After all, she was planning to live in Montreal, at least on a trial basis. He had to make sure she was happy there.

Two days after Beauharnois' meeting with the Fox envoys, the governor general had other callers. Led by a Huron war chief named La Forest, a delegation of Hurons from Detroit and Christian Iroquois from the Lake of Two Mountains Sulpician mission requested an audience. After initial pleasantries were exchanged, the Huron made a proposal.

"Our father, we seek your permission to attack the Fox homeland. Since the days of our fathers this tribe has caused trouble for all in the lakes region. Recently they have met defeat and their losses have been severe, but they still exist, and will grow stronger with the passage of time. The Hurons have old scores to settle with them. Our friends from the Lake of Two Mountains wish to demonstrate their loyalty to you, Onontio. Many have whispered that the Iroquois who have accepted Christ and live in Canada still have English hearts. To prove this is not so they wish to strike the Fox, mortal enemies of the French."

"Though my heart smiles at this show of devotion from my Huron and Iroquois friends, I cannot give the permission you seek. Only two days ago I met with representatives of the Fox and granted that tribe their lives. Let me explain my position more fully by saying this. I cannot approve your planned expedition, but at the same time would not oppose any effort you choose to undertake. In the event any disputes arise as a result of your attack, I can promise that I will remain neutral between you and our enemy."

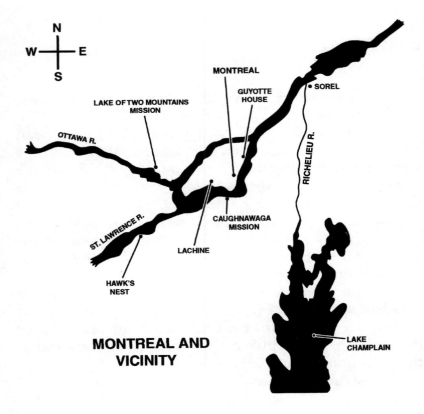

N
W   E
S

MONTREAL

GUYOTTE
HOUSE

• SOREL

LAKE OF TWO MOUNTAINS
MISSION

OTTAWA R.

RICHELIEU R.

ST. LAWRENCE R.

CAUGHNAWAGA
MISSION

LACHINE

HAWK'S
NEST

LAKE
CHAMPLAIN

**MONTREAL AND
VICINITY**

## CHAPTER 21

Jean Baptiste was getting excited. He was almost home. To their left was the Lake of Two Mountains mission. The Island of Montreal was dead ahead. As their canoe sped downstream, they could see four canoes carrying about a dozen braves arriving at the mission from the direction of Montreal. Situated on a point of land projecting into the Ottawa, the fortified missionaries' house and church were clearly visible.

"Those boys in the canoes were all dressed in their ceremonial finery," commented Dufort. "I wonder what they were up to?"

"That reminds me," said Jean Baptiste. Lake of Two Mountains has Iroquois as well as Algonquins and Nipissings. Perhaps the two Christian Iroquois who aided the ambush of Joseph's convoy were from there rather than Caughnawaga."

"I'd bet they were from Caughnawaga," replied Dufort from his comfortable seat in the middle of the canoe. I've heard plenty of talk in the last few years that the Caughnawagas have retained strong ties with their kinsmen along the Mohawk River. Of course it's common knowledge that our Mohawks and the English Mohawks cooperate to smuggle English trade goods into New

France."

"The authorities not only know about the illegal trade, but allow it to continue," interjected La Pointe. "The English goods are needed, because except for our gunpowder and our brandy, most Indians prefer the English alternatives. English cloth, clothing and utensils are of better quality and more readily obtainable than ours. They certainly prefer the lower prices the English goods cost. I've heard that at least a few warriors prefer English rum to our brandy, irrespective of price."

"No wonder they're called savages," commented Dufort. "Though I must admit, if your main goal when drinking is to become insensible as quickly as possible, rum will certainly do the job, and at a very reasonable cost."

"I want to tell my father that the attacks on his voyageurs don't appear to be random, but first I must report to the governor general about the failure of our mission to the Sioux. Naturally, I'm really looking forward to that. Etienne, I was thinking that Rene and I would leave you at Lachine while I report to Montreal. We'll pick you up on the way back, and then start for my family's seigneury. By the way, how do you feel today?"

"Vastly improved. I wouldn't doubt that in another day or two, I'll be recovered enough to take my turn with a paddle."

The city of Montreal sat on a large island in the St. Lawrence River, near its confluence with the Ottawa. The city was on the south side of the island, but the south channel of the St. Lawrence between the western tip of the island and the city, a distance of three leagues, was impassible due to the Lachine rapids. A town had grown on this western tip of the island, also named Lachine. It was connected to the city by a road that became a sea of mud in the spring, and not much better at other times of the year. Montreal traffic to and from the far west passed through this town, in order to avoid the rapids. Warehouses for storage of furs and trade goods were much in evidence. Voyageurs, clerks and various artisans passed each other on the narrow streets, along with Indians from a dozen tribes.

Jean Baptiste could identify many of the passing native men and women. A tall Winnebago from the Green Bay area unloaded prime pelts from his canoe while his wife steadied the bark vessel. A Cree from the far north calmly smoked his pipe, watching people come and go. He looked like he had finished his business for the day, and the young cadet wondered how the French offerings compared to those the Cree could have gotten from the English at the Hudson's Bay posts. Ottawa and Nipissing canoe men, the most astute and numerous of the native traders, jockeyed for position and analyzed possible items for purchase. Jean Baptiste was amused by the sight of a Nipissing, probably in his forties, offering an expensive looking-glass to a comely Algonquin maiden from one of the missions. She preened in front of the mirror while he made his pitch for financial or other considerations.

"Let's find a place to stay. It's well before noon, so I'll have time to get cleaned up and report to the governor general this afternoon."

"Rene, go with him and make sure he doesn't waste any time. I'm anxious for you to read your history books and pinpoint the location of the treasure. While you two are gone, I'll hire some men and send them to Joseph."

They found an inexpensive inn and deposited Dufort in a room with a somewhat more costly bottle of brandy. "I'll be right here when you boys get back. Maybe we'll even be able to make it to your seigneury tonight. What do you think?"

"I think we had better wait until the morning, Etienne. Don't worry. I'm sure my father is taking excellent care of Rene's books. If the treasure has remained undisturbed for two thousand years, one day more or less won't make any difference."

Jean Baptiste washed quickly but thoroughly and unpacked his uniform. It had not survived the journey especially well, but it would have to suffice. He donned a wrinkled shirt and his blue breeches, put on his blue veste and asked Rene's opinion.

"Put on your justaucorps and hope it conceals the deficiencies in the rest of your clothes. I've been trying to put your tricorn into some sort of reasonable shape, but it's hopeless. Take it off as soon as you arrive at the governor general's, and keep it under your arm until you leave."

Jean Baptiste donned the justaucorps, always his favorite part of the dress uniform. It was in fair condition, and he wore it with the skirt tails hooked backed, revealing the anchor symbols on the inner lining. The coat itself was off-white with blue cuffs; he was grateful that none of the gold buttons on the coat front, pockets or cuffs were missing. He wore the cartridge box with the anchor symbol at his waist, along with a hatchet and powder horn. He regretted that his only pair of regulation shoes had deteriorated to uselessness months ago. Instead he wore moccasins with deerskin leggings.

"Well, this is the best I can do. Let's go see

Monsieur Beauharnois."

Rene had changed into a less worn set of buckskins, new moccasins and was just putting a new red woolen tuque on his head. "Let's walk into Montreal," he said. "I need to stretch my legs a bit after all the canoe riding we've been doing."

The walk into town was pleasant, but the two young men were unable to enjoy the sights to the degree they might have wished because they had promised Etienne they would return to Lachine that night so that the three could get an early start in the morning. Wagons, horses and people afoot crowded the narrow path between Lachine and Montreal. Furs from the interior headed toward Montreal while trade goods moved in the opposite direction. The day was warm and sunny, and it appeared that there had been no appreciable rain for at least a few days, because the dirt of the roadway was dry and firm.

They encountered five young marines led by a corporal who were cooking an early supper by the side of the road. Jean Baptiste and Rene stopped to talk and found that these young recruits were destined for Michilimackinac.

"Captain Montigny will be happy to have more strong backs," said Jean Baptiste. "I'm sure much work still needs to be done on the stockade."

The new recruits had arrived from La Rochelle in July, and had been receiving the rudiments of their training from Corporal Daux. Two of the new lads were from Poitou, one from Aunis and the others from Saintonge. When they found that Jean Baptiste was stationed at their new post, they asked many questions.

After answering to the best of his ability, he concluded by saying, "My friend and I must be on our way. Remember three things. Make sure you have plenty of warm clothes if you are wintering at the straits. Develop a taste for whitefish, because that will be the main course on many, many occasions. And do everything in your power to avoid drawing the attention of Corporal Louis Charbonneau, unless of course you enjoy digging latrines in howling snowstorms."

"I know Charbonneau," said Corporal Daux. "So he's a corporal now. I'm sure that didn't do anything to improve his cantankerous disposition. The cadet is right, boys. Stay out of Charbonneau's way. He's an asshole."

As they continued down the road, La Pointe commented, "Maybe we should have accepted the corporal's offer to join them for supper. I know it was only a stew of salt pork and peas, with a few odds and ends thrown in, but I'm hungry enough that it actually smelled good."

"I could certainly stand something to eat myself, but we'll be able to find something better in town."

As they neared Montreal, they passed the fortifications that had been started some fourteen years before and which had advanced to the point that they might offer significant protection to the population. Once inside the walls, they walked down Rue Saint-Paul, the main thoroughfare closest to the river. Rene remarked that more and more of the houses and commercial buildings were being built of stone, a materials selection reflecting both the relative affluence of the population and the ordinances urging stone construction as a protection against fire.

By the time the friends reached the market place,

they were famished. They each bought loaves of bread so fresh they were still warm to the touch along with slices of beef cooked very rare. Several glasses of brandy concluded the meal.

"That is enough drinking for me," said Jean Baptiste. "I have to be coherent when I give my report to the governor general."

"Why don't you make your report and meet me back here. This seems like a good spot to loiter."

Jean Baptiste had noticed his friend eyeing one of the serving girls, a pretty wench who didn't seem to mind the attention at all. "Alright, but don't wander off or we'll be blundering around in the dark trying to find our way back to Lachine."

"I know. I know. Etienne will be mounting a rescue mission if we're late. He needs to relax a bit, don't you think? I'd like to find the treasure too, but do you think he's concentrating on it too much?"

"He'll be fine. I think it's just that he never thought about doing anything other than what he's always done. This new and completely different option has him excited. He told me that he knows the treasure may be gone even if we find where it was hidden. I guess he's just motivated by the thrill of the hunt. That, and the possibility of having his own harem."

A short distance from the market was his father's business office in Montreal. Though he knew he should go directly to the governor general's palace, he decided to make a quick stop. His father was not there, not surprising since he spent much of his time at the seigneury. Three clerks were hard at work. One he did not know. The others were Denis Labonte and Gilles Guyotte, the latter the brother of Claude, the clerk at

Michilimackinac.

The two he knew had been in his father's employ for many years. The new man was introduced to him as Jullien Rivole, a clerk hired when Rene La Pointe was sent to the pays d'en haut. "I'm sorry I can't stay and talk awhile, but I'll be in Montreal until spring, so we'll have many chances to catch up."

Jean Baptiste hurried past the main hospital in Montreal, continuing to the governor general's palace, located at the intersection of Rue Saint-Paul and Rue Saint-Charles, and only a short distance from the Montreal headquarters of the Jesuits. Though the building was imposing in size, Jean Baptiste felt that "palace" was something of an exaggeration. A stone structure three stories in height, it was larger but similar in appearance to several homes of wealthy merchants that he had passed. Dormer windows protruded through the steeply pitched roof on the top floor. Numerous rectangular windows lined both of the other floors, plush yellow curtains concealing any view of the interior. A broad stairway led to the main entrance, which was flanked by marine fusiliers in the most immaculate uniforms he had ever seen on private soldiers. He stated his business and the fusilier to the right of the door asked him to wait and disappeared inside.

As Jean Baptiste waited, the other guard spoke. "So you're posted to Michilimackinac, are you?"

"Yes, I'm Jean Baptist Joubert."

"Bernard Cretien. Glad to make your acquaintance. Been a marine for eleven years and now I'm thinking of taking my discharge, getting my piece of land, and settling in the colony. The question is, where do I want my land to be? I spent three years at Detroit, so I know that area well.  What's it like at Michilimackinac?"

"Really cold in the winter, and there's not much to do. It's beautiful there though."

"Everywhere in Canada is cold. I guess I'll have to give it more thought. Of course, my woman is from Caughnawaga and she doesn't want to be far from her family."

At that moment the door opened and the guard who had gone inside motioned Jean Baptiste in. A small man, probably about fifty years of age, dressed in an expensive-looking pale green waistcoat and breeches, waited just inside the doorway.

"I'm Michel Vaudoir, secretary to the governor general. You have dispatches from Michilimackinac?"

"Yes, here they are." Jean Baptiste opened the water tight pouch that he'd carried inside his veste and handed the packet of papers inside to Monsieur Vaudoir.

"Please make yourself comfortable in one of those chairs. The governor general is finishing a meeting at the moment. He will want to read what you have brought him at his earliest opportunity. Remain here in case he has questions."

Jean Baptiste began experiencing very uncomfortable moments as he sat in the foyer of the governor general's residence. All the insecurities he had felt about his actions flooded back into his mind. Everything that had happened was noted in his report on the expedition, or Captain Montigny's remarks, or both. The highest official in New France would read how he had abandoned Leveau to a ghastly fate, quit the projected mission to the Sioux and risked the lives of his men by seeking to capture an enemy to be questioned. Beads of sweat began forming on his forehead. Perhaps he should offer to resign, to save his family the embarrassment of a formal inquiry.

As these dark thoughts passed through the cadet's mind, the door to the governor general's office opened and Governor General Beauharnois himself stepped out, accompanied by a marine officer who looked to be in his middle forties. "Lieutenant Villiers, I'm giving you the post at La Baye because you know how I want the Fox treated, if any are still lurking in their old haunts. Execute my instructions properly, and you will soon be made captain. Have a good journey."

Jean Baptiste had snapped to attention when he saw the governor general and the marine officer. Villiers walked out the front door without further comment. The governor general noticed him, and appeared to remember something. "Oh yes, young Joubert isn't it? Well, return to your seat if you please. It will take some time to digest what you have brought me."

Jean Baptiste resumed his seat, not at all comforted by the knowledge that the moment of crisis was nearly at hand. Perhaps a change of career was a good idea. Maybe a coureur de bois, roaming the woods, trading with the Indians. His mother had wanted him to enter the priesthood, but he doubted that was still an option after his encounter with Blue Otter. He could always work as a clerk for his father, if the old man wasn't too shamed by his youngest son's failures.

From time to time the cadet's state of mind was made even more precarious by the frequent bellows of dismay and strings of curses issuing from the governor general's office. At last the door opened and Monsieur Vaudoir waved him in.

"You mean those bastards attacked you without any provocation when you were on your way to Sioux country?" fumed Beauharnois.

"Yes, Sir. We had made no contact with the Fox prior to their attack."

"They're telling Villiers in January that all they wanted was to live in peace. Shortly after, they attack you without warning and destroy the Sioux project about which we had such high hopes."

"They didn't get our goods, Sir, and we were able to do a good deal of business in the Illinois Country."

"That will certainly burn Perier's ass when he hears of it down in New Orleans," chuckled Beauharnois. "That's about the only good part of this entire business."

His brow darkening, Beauharnois returned to the subject of the Fox. "Only a few days ago, Fox emissaries pleaded for mercy right here in Montreal. And the worst part is that I gave it to them. Well, a hand other than mine still might strike them, and if that happens, their punishment is richly deserved."

"I should report, Sir, that the Fox seemed to be in great want. The boy we captured intended to go hunting with his friends, but they were all using bows because their supply of powder was so low. What they did was certainly wrong, but maybe they're getting desperate. The huge losses they suffered last year in Illinois had to have a profound effect on last winter's hunt. If that was unsuccessful and they had few pelts with which to barter, maybe they felt they had to take what they needed to survive."

"With any kind of luck, their survival will be of short duration. I assume you will be seeing your parents after leaving here. Give my best to them for me. Enjoy your stay in Montreal before you return to duty."

Jean Baptiste felt like an enormous weight was lifted from his shoulders as he left the official residence. No reprimand. No official inquiry. No firing squad. He was still a marine! Still, he wondered what Beauharnois had meant when he talked about the limited life expectancy of the Fox Nation.

## CHAPTER 22

"**H**awk's Nest" was the name of the Joubert family seigneury located on the south side of the St. Lawrence River, about six leagues west of the western tip of Montreal Island. The property had been granted to Jean Baptiste's grandfather, Adrien Joubert, a captain in the Carignan-Salieres regiment. That legendary unit had been posted to New France in 1665 to combat the threat posed by the Iroquois nations. At the conclusion of several years' service, the officers and men of the regiment were offered incentives to remain in the New World to bolster the population of the fledgling French colony. Adrien Joubert decided to take advantage of the opportunity for officers to own a large tract of land, an opportunity he would not enjoy in France.

He was not sure where he wanted his holding. Once he decided that the fur trade would be the focus of his energies, he applied for and received a tract of land west of Montreal, on the path to the rich fur country to the west and northwest. At that early date, the site he selected was an extremely dangerous one. The Iroquois threat was far from over and this seigneury sat alone and far from help. The nearest holding was that of Charles Le

Moyne and his considerable brood of future heroes, but Chateauguay, the Le Moyne seigneury, was separated from Hawk's Nest by five or six leagues of undeveloped wilderness.

Eight men from his old company elected to throw in their lot with their former commander. The first priority was making the exposed position defensible. These nine men certainly had the requisite training and experience, and on a high point of land about one hundred paces from the river, they built a stout blockhouse. Some effort was expended clearing land and planting wheat, several vegetable gardens and a small orchard. The main business activity, however, was to be the fur trade. Adrien Joubert had saved enough money over the years to finance the purchase of three canoe loads of trade goods. He, four of his ex-soldiers and a dozen men hired for the trip set off on the first of what proved to be many expeditions into the interior. Financial success was swift. The Joubert fur business was soon well established.

The site of Hawk's Nest proved fortunate. Trading facilities were erected right on the seigneury, and many voyageurs, Indians and coureurs de bois returning from the west with canoes filled with pelts, stopped there to trade rather than continue to Lachine and Montreal. Soon Adrien stopped traveling to the west himself, finding his time better spent managing the trade at Hawk's Nest and establishing business contacts in Montreal. These contacts facilitated acquisition of trade goods at favorable prices as well as the sale of pelts.

From his first day in business, the cornerstone of his operation was that fair dealing was the order of the day. He recognized, as did many others, that Indians were often unusually susceptible to the attractions of alcohol in its many forms. Many cheated the Indians when they came to trade, befuddling them with drink and then buying a year's harvest of furs for a pittance. Adrien refused to do this for what he considered sound business reasons. Yes, it was possible to cheat a warrior once, but when his head cleared and he realized what had happened, he would never return. Joubert was trying to establish a business that would flourish not only during his lifetime, but also during the lifetimes of his sons and grandsons. It was entirely possible for both sides in the fur trade to conclude their business and leave the table happy. Why not arrange it so?

Concern for the future became an issue when, in 1671, at the age of forty, he married Henriette Lavaux, daughter of a prominent Montreal merchant. A substantial squared log house, with framing around the doors and windows, was erected immediately. Three years later Daniel, their first child was born, followed in quick succession by two more boys and three girls. Young Daniel was soon recognized as the obvious choice to succeed his father at the helm of the family business enterprise. The boy was intelligent and proved to be a shrewd judge of fur quality, whether it was beaver, otter, deer or a host of other skins. He also had great facility with Indian dialects, and readily continued to stress honesty in the Joubert operation. Recognizing the business advantages of having family members placed in command at the lucrative western fur trading posts, Adrien arranged for Daniel to join the marines in 1688, just after his fourteenth birthday.

Disaster struck the next year. It was late summer and Adrien had been in Montreal conducting business.

He intended to return to Hawk's Nest that night, but concluded his affairs late. By the time he reached Lachine, night was falling and a heavy storm was brewing. He decided to stay there and return home to Henriette in the morning. That night, a massive Iroquois assault, numbering 1,500 warriors, was launched against the unsuspecting town. Many Frenchmen were killed, including the aged Adrien Joubert, who died sword in hand, his face toward the enemy. Most of the town was burned to the ground. The elder Joubert had by this time become a person of note, even to the Iroquois. As related by a French prisoner who subsequently escaped, the Mohawk who killed the old man recognized the body, cut off its head, and paraded through the smoking ruins of the town holding his trophy aloft, impaled on his lance.

News of the disaster spread panic through New France. Hawk's Nest was prepared for a desperate defense, but the blow never came. Adrien's body was located and brought back to his beloved seigneury to be laid to rest. Daniel comforted his grieving mother and hoped the two of them had learned enough from his father to prevent the business from faltering. Fortunately, Henriette proved astute as well as tough. She became the new leader of the clan, ably assisted by her eldest son.

Though he probably could have gotten a discharge, Daniel felt it his duty to continue in the marines. For most of his first five years of service, friends of his father saw to it that he was posted in the Montreal area, close to his mother and siblings. When not on duty, he devoted himself totally to the family business, investing as much of each year's profits as possible in ever-larger consignments of trade goods. By the turn of the new century, the Joubert name was known throughout the Great Lakes region. Though officials in France noted the glut of furs and issued edicts curtailing the trade in the wilderness, officials in Canada recognized the value of the trade in cementing good relations with the Indians. They turned a blind eye when restrictions on the trade were ignored, especially if the trader allocated a portion of his profits to them. When the necessary trade goods were scarce, Daniel secretly acquired them from English and Dutch merchants in Albany. Canoe brigades bearing the distinctive hawk emblem of the Joubert family on their vessels plied waterways throughout the interior, exchanging cloth, brandy, tools and weapons for the furs harvested by the tribes.

In 1699, Daniel wed Toinette Redon, the daughter of a former sergeant in his father's regiment. Clement Redon was one of the men who helped Adrien Joubert found Hawk's Nest. He was a freeholder on the seigneury, and the Redon home was less than a hundred paces from the Joubert residence. Daniel had known Toinette since they were children growing up together. She was tall and skinny as a child, and preferred hunting and fishing with the boys of the seigneury to playing with the girls. Oddly, the boys accepted her without serious complaint, probably because of her fishing skill. She always seemed to find the spot where the fish were biting, and generously shared the information with her confederates.

After his father died, Daniel had little time for enjoyment. His duties with the marines and his fur trade work occupied all of his time. He saw some of his boyhood friends as they grew older and signed on as canoe men, but of course, Toinette was not one of them.

He thought of her occasionally, meaning to visit the Redon family when he was at the seigneury, but somehow never did. One day, in the summer of 1698, Daniel was heading toward the riverbank where the canoes were beached when he encountered a beautiful woman with dark, shiny hair and large brown eyes. She was carrying a basket of cucumbers and melons from the Redon family garden, a gift for his mother. Though he scarcely recognized her, the woman was his former childhood companion. He decided at that moment to delay visiting the Redons no longer. Daniel and Toinette were married the next year.

The couple were to have six children. Francois was the oldest, but he died of a fever at the age of three. Maurice was next, followed by Jeanne, the only girl child. The twins, Louis and Jacques, preceded Jean Baptiste, the baby of the family.

The morning after the meeting with the governor general, Jean Baptiste and his two friends paddled upriver from Lachine toward Hawk's Nest. They crossed to the south shore of the St. Lawrence, passing Caughnawaga. The longhouses of the Iroquois residents were surrounded by a palisade. Directly to the west of the Iroquois lodges was a European fortification that housed the missionaries and a small garrison maintained on the site.

"We need to find out if the two mission Iroquois at the ambush came from there," Jean Baptiste commented to his companions as they glided by Caughnawaga.

"I might be able to find out something," said La Pointe. "Before I was sent to Michilimackinac, I spent quite a bit of time in the company of Marguerite

Desauniers. She and her two older sisters have been running a store at Caughnawaga for the past five years. Not much happens there that they don't know about. I'll talk to her."

Soon the mission fell away to the rear as they made their way upriver. Though the day was bright, with very few clouds, the wind was from the northwest. Many of the leaves on the trees had turned yellow, orange or even brilliant red, and were falling into the river whenever the gusts strengthened. Jean Baptiste and Rene had to work hard to make headway against the current, but they were grateful for the exercise, because it helped ward off the chill. Dufort, still too injured to participate, nestled down under a bearskin robe.

"There's the Le Moyne seigneury," said Jean Baptiste. "They are our closest neighbors. The land between here and Hawk's Nest is virgin forest that has been granted to no one."

"I'm not sure that is still the case," said La Pointe. "While I was waiting for you at the market yesterday, I heard a lot of idle gossip on a variety of topics. Whether it was true or not I don't know but I heard two Sulpicians mention that the land directly west of the Le Moyne's had been granted to none other than our esteemed governor general."

"If that's true I hope he develops the seigneury," responded Jean Baptiste. "That will provide some protection for the eastern end of Hawk's Nest."

They traveled about five more leagues. Jean Baptiste was the first to spot a break in the heavy foliage along the shore. Trees had been cleared, and a number of canoes and bateaux were pulled up on the narrow beach. As they got closer, they saw more signs of human habitation. Several storage sheds stood near the riverbank. Farther back were the houses of the tenant families, mostly of the squared log style. Up the slope was the large log house where the cadet had been raised. Next to it was the stone structure that was to be the new Joubert family home. A two story building with a steeply pitched tile roof and three chimneys, it boasted a large parlor, three bedrooms and the kitchen downstairs, and five bedrooms upstairs.

It looked like work on the new house had been completed, at least on the outside. Jean Baptiste knew his father planned to retain the old family home as well, to provide rooms for the many guests that stopped to visit the Jouberts. These included merchants from Montreal, missionaries and parish priests, old marine comrades of Daniel's, Ottawa, Nipissing and Huron chiefs, voyageurs, public officials and even the odd coureur de bois. Hospitality was always in evidence, and included some of the best eating in New France, courtesy of the kitchen of Toinette Joubert.

Jean Baptiste had tried not to think too much about his mother's cooking all the times he was choking down pemmican or salt pork while on duty. It was bad for his morale. Now that he was home he eagerly anticipated the sight, smell and taste of all the dishes his mother prepared so well.

As the boy savored these pleasant thoughts, he heard his name shouted from the far end of the strand. The cadet could see several men standing among packs of beaver pelts and beached canoes. Another man was waving his arms and coming toward Jean Baptiste and his friends. He seemed a bit unsteady with age, and his hair was now completely white, but the boy recognized his father's distinctive gait, and ran down the riverbank to meet his sire.

"Jean Baptiste!"

"Father." The two embraced, and said nothing else for a long moment. Finally, the older man spoke.

"I'm surprised to see you. Since it is so late in the year, I didn't think there was any chance you would get leave until the spring. How long will you be able to stay?"

"Captain Montigny sends you his greetings and said I need not return to Michilimackinac until the spring."

"Excellent. I'm sure we can find plenty for you to do to occupy your time. Who have you brought with you?" The older man squinted and said, "Why, that looks like Rene La Pointe! What is he doing here? He should be four hundred leagues away in Sioux country."

"I'm afraid I have bad news concerning that mission, but let us speak of it after you welcome my friends."

A cloud of concern passed over his father's face. He desperately needed a good return on the trade goods he had supplied for the Sioux commerce. But the look was replaced with one of genuine pleasure at renewing acquaintances with two respected employees.

"Rene, it's so good to see you well. A more active life seems to agree with you. Your shoulders and chest have filled out, and you now look the picture of health."

"A more bloodthirsty monster was never loosed upon the inland waterways before," chimed in a voice from behind La Pointe.

"Etienne Dufort! Is that you, you old drunk? What are you doing there, all wrapped in that old bearskin? Come out of there, and let me have a look at you."

The commotion had drawn the attention of those in the stone house. When Jean Baptiste looked up, his sister was running down the slope toward them, followed as quickly as she was able by his mother. After the cadet had squeezed them for a long moment, he remembered his manners and made the proper introductions. Madame Joubert had met Rene before, while he worked in the company offices in Montreal. Neither woman had met Dufort previously. The portly trader bowed low to the two ladies, gallantly sweeping off his cap at the same time.

"That I should be introduced to two such beautiful women at the same moment is almost more than I can bear, but in deference to your relations I shall act the detached gentleman rather than follow the dictates of my heart."

The Joubert women were amused by the jolly rascal, and in turn offered their hands, which he kissed with great ceremony.

"Come up to the house, all of you," said Madame Joubert "Dinner is just about ready, and I'm certain we have plenty for everyone. Daniel, are those the Aurique brothers you were bargaining with? Invite them to dinner as well. They're good boys, for the most part."

As they trooped into the house, the delicious smells from the kitchen greeted them, and Jean Baptiste was drawn back to his reverie about his mother's cooking. He recognized the aromas of the main courses. They were going to be treated to meat pie filled with deer and moose meat as well as pie filled with several varieties of fowl, probably partridge, snipe and teal. The cadet could also smell as well as see six large loaves of wheat bread that had just come from the oven. A large bowl was filled with apples as well as raspberries and cranberries. For those who preferred their fruit in another form, strawberry, currant and cherry jellies and jams were present. A smaller bowl contained imported lemons and oranges. Brandy, rum and cider were the choice of drinks.

Discussion of family business would be delayed until all had eaten their fill and the Aurique brothers had taken their leave. Jean Baptiste hoped they would not stay too long, because he knew his mother was anxious for news of Maurice. She was gracious to her guests as always, but her youngest son recognized lines of tension at the corners of her mouth. He dreaded telling her the news, though of course that news could have been much worse.

After the meal, which was eaten at the long table on the left side of the great parlor near the kitchen, the men enjoyed a smoke. The Auriques knew that Jean Baptiste had been gone a long time and took their leave as soon as etiquette allowed, so that the family could discuss their affairs. Dufort and La Pointe were going to take a stroll outside as well, but Jean Baptiste motioned them to stay.

"I think Rene and Etienne should stay, father. They know everything I'm going to tell you, and they might be able to remind me if I forget something of importance."

The family members nodded in agreement.

"First, let me say that Maurice is alive, though he was badly wounded in a Fox ambush. He was being cared for by Father Mercier at the Indian mission at Cahokia in the Illinois Country. He did lose his left arm."

At those last words, sobs escaped both from his mother and his sister. Daniel Joubert's expression did not change, but his hands involuntarily clenched until the knuckles turned white.

"How did this happen?" asked the head of the family. So Jean Baptiste related the relevant events that had occurred since the previous spring.

## CHAPTER 23

"It is as I suspected," said Daniel Joubert as Jean Baptiste finished his tale. "The bad luck we have experienced has not been bad luck at all. Someone has been planning all of these business reverses. Every trader loses goods in transit and voyageurs die while performing their duties, but not to the extent that these things have happened to us."

As soon as he mentioned voyageurs dying, he caught himself and looked at Jeanne, his only daughter. Three years ago, when she was twenty-one years of age, she married Guy Chaloche, a young voyageur who grew up in Three Rivers. They built a home at Hawk's Nest and looked forward to raising a big family. Guy was a high spirited youth but a hard worker of whom all in the family heartily approved. The summer after the marriage, with Jeanne already heavy with baby, Guy set off for Michilimackinac with a convoy of trade goods. Somewhere along the French River, he elected to run a stretch of rapids rather than portage his canoe. The fragile vessel struck a submerged log and Guy and the other man aboard were thrown into the water. The other voyageur was saved, but Guy hit his head on a rock and drowned before he could be rescued. His son, named

Guy in honor of his father, was born two months later.

Continuing his train of thought, Daniel said, "From what you have described about the ambush on the Ottawa, it would seem the Iroquois were waiting for old Joseph's convoy. It is only through the greatest good fortune that you happened by when you did and foiled the attack. We must find out who is directing this campaign against us. If these disasters continue much longer, the Jouberts will be bankrupt. As it is, I pray that Maurice is well and was able to sell the furs he brought to New Orleans for a good price. If I can't pay my creditors in Montreal a substantial amount this winter, I won't be able to buy the trade goods we need to stay in business next spring."

"I know I speak for Etienne as well as myself," interjected Rene. "We'll help in any way that we can, whether it be looking for your enemies, sorting furs, paddling a canoe or whatever else would be helpful." Jean Baptiste couldn't help but notice that as his friend made this announcement, he looked purposefully at Jeanne, who held his glance for a moment and then looked down.

"Good," responded Daniel. "Your assistance this winter will be both needed and appreciated. One thing I can promise. You won't go hungry. Our fields have produced excellent yields of wheat, corn, peas and beans, and the celery, onions, carrots and cucumbers from the garden are also plentiful. We've also laid in a good quantity of game, as well as salt bacon and eel.

"By the way," continued Daniel, "Let me see that crucifix you took from the dead Mohawk."

Jean Baptiste removed the cross from around his own neck and handed it to his father.

"Yes, I believe you are right to concentrate your search at Caughawaga.  If my memory is accurate, this is the type of cross purchased by the Jesuits for their missions.  The Sulpicians at Lake of Two Mountains prefer a slightly different style, a bit larger and more ornate.  Talking to Marguerite Desauniers might be an excellent idea, Rene.  Jean Baptiste, you said one of the mission Iroquois was among the dead, but not the other?"

"I think both of them were in the bunch that rushed the hill and were decimated by Rene's bomb.  I only found the body of one, though if the other one lives, I'd wager he was badly hurt."

"If he lives, he got close enough to the top of the hill to have seen, and possibly recognize you.  Though with all the smoke you described, luck may be on our side.  In any case, you did get a good view of him, Jean Baptiste, when he and his companion landed at the portage trail.  Maybe all three of you should visit the Desauniers sisters and see how the store at Caughnawaga is doing.

"Of course, even if you find this warrior, he is not the spy we seek.  The man providing the information on when our convoys are leaving, their composition and the routes they are taking is the man that we really want to find.  It has to be someone associated with our operation in some way.  We really have not taken pains to keep this information confidential, so it is not necessarily an employee of the firm.  Possibly someone we hire frequently to haul goods.  I certainly hope none of our people are involved.  I can't believe that they are.  Most have worked for us for many years."

"Except for Jullien Rivole," said Jean Baptiste.

"Oh, you've met Jullien, have you?  It's true that

he has only been employed by the company for a short time, but I can't believe he would be the one. He comes from a good family in Quebec. I've known his father for twenty-five years. Besides, our problems started before he was hired. I guess we have to start somewhere though. Very well, we'll start keeping an eye on him.

"Gentlemen," continued Daniel. "I assume you could use some rest from your long journey. Let me show you to your rooms. We have plenty of space at the moment right here in the main house. You'll excuse us if the furnishings in your rooms are a bit sparse. We intend to leave the old house standing and have left most of the furniture we had in it. I've built more for the new house, but not nearly as much as it needs. Rene, you can have the room where I've stored your books."

This last remark caused the three new arrivals to look at each other and smile. Jean Baptiste had not alluded to the Carthaginian treasure when relating their adventures. The gold and jewels certainly would be a godsend if they were available now.

It was late September, and Kiala was pleased with the progress that had been made. Fox diplomacy was beginning to bear fruit. The seemingly never-ending round of talks he had with nearly all the neighboring tribes had been a success. While they had not committed to an actual alliance with the Fox, tribes such as the Mascouten, the Kickapoo and the Sacs had released most of their Fox prisoners, and these were slowly making their way to the Fox camp which Kiala had consolidated on the Wisconsin River.

The war chief of the Fox was planning to take a gamble. Ordinarily at this time of year, the tribe was preparing to disperse into numerous small groups, which would scatter to the various winter hunting grounds. Because the freed hostages were straggling back home, often weak from hunger, Kiala wanted them to be able to locate their kinsmen easily.  For that reason he decided to keep the tribe together this winter, gambling that the few hunters available could provide adequately for all. He left word with the Mascouten and the other tribes releasing hostages as to the location where they should be sent.  He hoped that Kicking Bear and Eagle Claw had been successful in their mission, but to be on the safe side, he had men watching the French forts at La Baye and St. Joseph.  No unusual activity at these posts had been reported, indicating that the French had no assault planned for the near future.  Soon Kiala would recall these lookouts and they could participate in the hunting. The snow would  blanket the forest in the near future, and he would feel safe from French guns until the spring.

The air was very chill this evening, and his wound, though healed, ached a great deal.  A sign that he was getting older he supposed.  His wife was sewing a patch on a worn moccasin.  Kiala smiled as he looked at her face, thinking of all the years they had been together. Just then she looked up, as though sensing his gaze.  He opened his buffalo robe and she crossed the lodge to join him.

"Here it is!" shouted Rene as he burst into Dufort's room, where Jean Baptiste was helping the latter sort through the gear they had brought up from the canoe.

"You've found the Carthaginian gold?" asked Dufort excitedly.

"At least I've got a good idea where Cerne is

located. Though it took far too long to resurrect, my recollection concerning where I had seen that name was accurate. I found the account of Hanno's voyage to West Africa in an addendum to my Polybius papers."

"What does it say?" inquired Jean Baptiste.

"I've brought the pages with me. Let me read you the relevant portions.

*"The Carthaginians commissioned Hanno to sail past the Pillars of Heracles, and to found cities of the Libyphoenicians. He set sail with sixty vessels of fifty oars and a multitude of men and women to the number of 30,000, and provisions and other equipment.*

*"After putting out to sea and passing the Pillars we sailed beyond them for two days. Here we founded our first city, which we named Thymiaterium. Under it a wide plain opened to view.*

*"Thence we stood out westward and made Cape Soloeis, a densely wooded Libyan promontory.*

*"Having founded a temple of Poseidon at this point we sailed on for half a day to east, until we arrived at a lagoon full of high and thick-grown cane. This was haunted by elephants and multitudes of other grazing beasts.*

*"We skirted the lagoon for about one day's journey. Then we founded sea-side towns which we named Carian Fort, Gutta, Acra, Melitta, and Arambys.*

*"Putting out from that point we reached a big river flowing from Libya, the Lixus. Lixite nomads pastured their flocks on its banks. We made friends with them and stayed with them for a time.*

*"Beyond these dwelt inhospitable Ethiopians. Their land is infested with wild beasts and is broken up with high mountain chains, from which the Lixus is said to flow. These highlands are inhabited by a freakish race of men,*

*the Troglodytes, who are said by the Lixites to run faster than horses.*

*"From the Lixites we took interpreters and coasted along the desert southward for two days. Thence we turned back east for one day. There we found at the top of a gulf a small island, with a circuit of five stades. Here we founded a colony named Cerne. We estimated from the distance traversed that it lay in a line with Carthage; for it was the same distance from Carthage to the Pillars and thence to Cerne."*

"Our fortune is made," remarked Dufort. "Those instructions are as good as a map to the hidden treasure."

"I wouldn't be quite that confident," corrected La Pointe. "I'm not an expert on African geography, so I need to do some research on the place names mentioned to see if they still exist or if they their modern equivalents can be identified. I'm not sure what is meant by 'it lay in a line with Carthage,' though the clause immediately after that seems clear enough. The distance from Carthage to the Straits of Gibraltar is the same as the distance from the Straits to Cerne."

"What happened on the rest of Hanno's voyage?" asked Jean Baptiste.

"The Carthaginians experienced a variety of adventures. Sailing further south, they sighted a high mountain range, but were prevented from landing by wild men dressed in animals' skins who threw rocks when the vessels approached. Later, they landed on an island. At night they heard the sound of pipes and cymbals, and the shouts of an unseen mass of people, and saw the light from many fires being lit. In fear they fled the island. They reported a river of fire and saw a mountain they called the Chariot of the Gods. Perhaps the strangest entry occurred near the end of the journey. I'll read it to you.

*"Following the rivers of fire for three further days, we reached a gulf named the Southern Horn. In the gulf lay an island like the previous one, with a lake, and in it another island. The second island was full of wild people. By far the greater number were women with hairy bodies. Our interpreters called them Gorillas. We gave chase to the men, but could not catch any, for they all scampered up steep rocks and pelted us with stones. We secured three women, who bit and scratched and resisted their captors. But we killed and flayed them, and brought the hides to Carthage.*

*"This was the end of our journey, owing to lack of provisions."*

"I've never tried that approach when a woman bit and scratched me," mentioned Dufort. "I'll have to keep it in mind."

"Do you think you can find Cerne with the information in Hanno's report?" asked Jean Baptiste.

"Maybe. But I've still got a lot of work to do before I can give you a more definite answer."

"I'm sure you'll have time this winter when the snow piles up. Until then we need to remember that we have other priorities."

## CHAPTER 24

T he next day was Sunday and the Joubert family, along with members of many of the tenant families, traveled to the Le Moyne seigneury to hear mass. Early on Monday Jean Baptiste, Etienne and Rene left to see what they could discover at the Jesuit mission of Caughnawaga.

"I should admit to you at the start that while I know Marguerite Desauniers quite well, and if the warrior we seek is at Caughnawaga, she probably knows him, she may not be interested in identifying him for us," said Rene.

"And why might that be?" asked Dufort.

"When she and I stopped seeing each other, things became a bit unpleasant."

"How unpleasant?"

"She chased me around the store, threatening to do me bodily harm with a large skinning knife she was waving around. I distinctly heard the word 'castration' mentioned. I'm sure she didn't mean it though. She was just a little distraught."

"And what was the reason for this ill-humor?"

"She found out that I was also seeing the daughter of Lachine's tanner. Apparently she was more possessive than I realized."

"You might have mentioned this sooner," said Jean Baptiste.

"Well, that was a long time ago. She's probably forgotten the whole thing by now. Even if she hasn't, I can usually tell when she's lying. That should be worth something."

"I've been thinking about finding our spy, and I believe locating this Indian is the key to the problem," said Jean Baptiste. "He probably could not be made to tell us what we want to know, but perhaps he could be tricked into revealing the information we seek."

"I just hope we find our man and put an end to all these attacks," said Dufort. "I've never been involved in so much fighting, and we're supposed to be at peace right now. I'd like to be able to relax a little bit and not worry about running into a volley of arrows and musket balls at every bend in a river."

They were paddling with the current, and so reached the Jesuit mission quickly. They beached their canoe on the south bank of the St. Lawrence, just west of the French fortifications. The three walked around the back of the fortification and entered the nearest gate in the palisade surrounding the Indian lodges. They then walked briskly to the Desauniers sisters' store, located just to the east of the French works. Now that the moment of truth was at hand, Rene La Pointe's courage seemed to be deserting him. He hung back as they reached the entrance to the store.

"Come on Rene. Like you said, Marguerite has probably forgotten that unfortunate incident from the distant past."

"I've thought about it some more, and have

reached a new conclusion. If I step through that doorway, it may be my last act on this earth."

"Don't worry. We'll protect you."

"Just make sure there are no edged weapons within her reach."

The three entered the store and there she was, or more accurately, there they were. All three sisters were working at stocking the shelves along the west wall. The three unmarried sisters had been running this store for about five years. There were always rumors of illicit trade with Albany, but if the sisters were trading with the English, they were acting much like many other Montreal merchants. Marie-Madeline was the oldest; Marie-Anne was in the middle, and Marguerite was the youngest and most attractive. Marguerite had hair the color of corn silk and a rather pleasing though unsmiling face coupled with an attractive figure. By reputation a determined woman with a fiery temper, she had the look of someone not to be trifled with.

Marguerite turned from the shelves to face the newcomers. Then she recognized Rene. "You!" she screeched. She immediately began searching for something that could be used as a missile.

"Peace! Peace!" entreated Jean Baptiste. "We are here on a mission of mercy, and want no trouble." As he spoke he maneuvered the angry woman away from a display of steel hatchets near her right hand.

"You're one of the Joubert boys, aren't you?" asked Marie-Madeleine.

"Yes, the youngest. Jean-Baptiste."

"Well, we're running a business here. Missions of mercy sound more like something the Jesuits next door could aid you with. I'll help you if I can, though."

"A few days ago we had a powder explosion near our warehouse in Lachine. A mission Indian was hurt, but he ran off before we could see to his injuries. I don't know his name, but I think he was from Caughnawaga. We wanted to make sure he is all right. Have you seen anyone like that, someone with fresh burns?"

"I don't know of anyone. What about you, girls?"

Both of the other sisters said they knew of no one. All the while this conversation developed, Marguerite cast venomous glances at Rene. Jean Baptiste had fortunately taken the precaution to hold both her hands gently, but firmly, in his own.

"Thank you ladies," said the young cadet. "We won't disturb your work any longer." The three friends left the store, Jean Baptiste and Etienne shielding Rene with their bodies.

"Rene, you really have a way with the ladies," said Dufort as they walked away. "I do believe Marguerite wouldn't bother to piss on you if you were on fire."

"She still seems a little tense, I admit. She was lying about not seeing a burnt Indian though. I can always tell when she lies. Something about the right side of her mouth."

"I think they all know the Indian in question," said Jean Baptiste. "They won't volunteer the injured man's name, but Marie-Madeline did offer a good suggestion. We should visit the Jesuits. A warrior from this mission needing medical attention would probably have paid them a visit. Let's see if we can find Father La Bretonniere. If I recall correctly, he enjoys quite a reputation as a healer. He also was on de Lignery's expedition against the Fox three years ago, so we might be able to get on his good side by relating some of our adventures along the Wisconsin."

They found the good priest sitting on a bench inside the fortification, enjoying the autumn sunshine while he worked to perfect his command of the Iroquois language. He had labored at Caughnawaga for ten years, and could converse with the Indian converts when everyday topics were discussed, but picking up foreign tongues was not one of his strong points. He worked hard to improve his fluency so that he could understand the nuances of Indian thought.

Jean Baptiste introduced himself and the others, mentioning that they had just returned from the land of the Fox. As the cadet had hoped, this prompted the priest to recount his experiences when he accompanied members of his flock on the campaign of 1728. After everyone contributed anecdotes about their travels in Fox country, the cadet recounted his story of the powder explosion in Lachine, and asked the priest if he knew of a burned warrior.

"That sounds like Strong Hand. I treated him myself two days ago. He wouldn't say how he had been hurt, but one side of his face was badly burned, and he has lost one of his eyes. I'm sure he was in a great deal of pain. The savages seem to think that I am a gifted medicine man, and I have been able to help some of them from time to time. I did what I could for him, but I'm afraid the most I could do was to make him more comfortable. I don't believe his injuries threatened his life, but I'm sure he will be heavily scarred. Since this accident occurred at your family's facility, perhaps you can make it up to him in some way. I appreciate you taking the time to follow up on the matter."

"Would you happen to know where we can find

him?"

"No, shortly after I treated him and gave him an additional supply of medication, I saw him leave Caughnawaga in the company of two warriors. I happened to be walking along the wall over there, enjoying the breeze off the river. The three of them got in a canoe and headed down river, toward Montreal."

"Thank you so much for your help, Father. We want to ensure that Strong Hand gets what he deserves."

The three friends left Caughnawaga, convinced that they knew the identity of the Indian they sought. Of course, they had not located him yet. They decided to return to Hawk's Nest.

"I believe I met Strong Hand on several occasions when I used to come to Caughnawaga to see Marguerite," said Rene. He's a minor chief here. Rather a sullen fellow if I remember correctly."

"I've got one question," said Dufort as they launched their canoe and headed up river. "How major a sin is it to lie like that to a Jesuit? And he even seemed like a decent fellow."

"That probably depends on the identity of your confessor," opined Rene. "The next time you go to confession, Jean Baptiste, I'd advise that you seek the services of a Sulpician. He'll probably go easier on you."

As they headed upriver, they began to overtake a large bateau headed in the same direction. Two men were rowing the vessel and they carried three passengers and their effects, two marines and a woman. As they got closer, they all noticed that she was quite a woman. She was seated in the stern of the bateau, next to one of the men. Wisps of dark hair were visible under her bonnet as she watched the canoe approach, peering back over her left shoulder. They could all see her large, pale green eyes now, regarding them with amused detachment.

"Will you look at her," said Dufort. All three men in the canoe found themselves paddling with a great deal more gusto.

"If you drooling fools will avoid ramming us, I'll introduce you to the lady in due course," stated a familiar voice. Jean Baptiste tore his eyes away from the woman in order to look at the man seated next to her. "Hello, brother," said Maurice. "I see you are still keeping bad company, in spite of all my advice. Rene! Etienne! I'm glad you all made it back. Since both boats seem to be headed to Hawk's Nest, I'll make the necessary introductions when we arrive."

## CHAPTER 25

Another heartfelt reunion ensued, this time bringing the entire Joubert clan together save only Jacques, who was on duty at Fort St. Joseph. Louis, Jacques' twin brother, had taken several days leave from his marine unit at Montreal, and was visiting Hawk's Nest when Maurice arrived.

The canoe and the bateau traveled the remaining distance to the family seigneury together. When they landed, Jean Baptiste sprinted up the slope to the new house to break the news. In a few minutes, not only the family, but also many of the neighbors, had gathered by the riverbank. Toinette Joubert held her crippled son close for long moments, tears filling her eyes despite her attempts not to weep.

"Mother, don't cry. I've had time to deal with my situation and I'm all right. Really. Now I'll be able to help father here in Montreal. After all, he is in his declining years and no doubt needs the assistance."

Daniel chuckled and embraced his eldest surviving child. "You're probably right. My eyesight is not what it once was. Those tiny entries in the ledgers seem to get smaller each year."

"Before I forget, I know you must be concerned

about the sale of the furs in New Orleans. I have a bill of exchange in my pocket from Jean Hebert for something over twenty-nine thousand livres. He sends his greetings, and I wanted to let you know that he took less than his standard commission on the sale due to his long association and friendship with you."

"Thank the Lord. We probably shouldn't be discussing commerce during this moment of reunion, but this news relieves a good deal of anxiety for me. We'll talk more later."

"Mother, father, I'd like you to meet Madame Dominique Lamarque, late of New Orleans. For health reasons she had to leave that tropical climate, and I hope I was not too presumptuous when I offered her lodging here for the time being."

Toinette greeted the new arrival warmly. "Of course you can stay. We have plenty of space and my daughter and I would love to hear some news of the outside world, particularly from a woman's perspective. I'm sure New Orleans has a much more active social life than we have here in the frozen north. You must bring us up to date."

"Yes, the entertainment there can be quite diverting. I know Maurice found it so even during his short stay."

Maurice felt his cheeks redden, but was saved from further embarrassment by a polite cough to his left. "Oh, I'm sorry, Henri. I'd also like everyone to meet Lieutenant Henri Gaultier, also of New Orleans. He's here on official business on behalf of the Governor of Louisiana. Do we have room for him as well?"

"You are most welcome, Lieutenant," said Daniel Joubert. "You can bring this backwoods hamlet news of the world from a masculine point of view."

That evening, after dinner, the women retreated to the kitchen to discuss New Orleans society (a topic which caused Maurice a bit of concern). The men stayed at the table, smoked their pipes and each recounted his experiences in turn to the group. After the conversation died down and the men enjoyed a final brandy, Henri Gaultier excused himself, and retired to his room to unpack.

"He seems to be an efficient officer," observed Daniel Joubert.

"Yes," agreed Maurice. "He's trying to arrange an appointment with the governor general, but Monsieur Beauharnois is at the moment inspecting fortifications along the Richelieu River. He's expected back in Montreal in a few days."

"We need to discuss business," said the elder Joubert. "No, that's alright, Rene. You and Etienne can stay." He continued, "The funds you brought today are of critical importance, Maurice. The bulk of the money will be paid to merchants here in Montreal to cover purchases made last spring. They won't cover all my debts, but enough that I'll be able to get credit next spring to supply our convoys to the interior.

"In addition, I need people to travel to Albany as soon as possible. I realize it's late in the year, but the supply ships from France did not bring many of the trade items favored by the Indians. If we are to have the trade goods we need at the start of the season in the spring, we need to get them at Albany now, before the heavy snows."

Everyone at the table immediately volunteered, even Maurice. "Maurice, I believe you should stay behind, and probably you as well, Rene. We still need to locate our spy. The two of you can spend time in the Montreal office. Rene, you can refresh Maurice's mind on our bookkeeping practices, while both of you keep an eye on Jullien Rivole. After spending time there, move on to the wharves and warehouses. I think our security problem is more likely in one of those places. You can also continue your search for the injured Caughnawaga.

"If there are no objections then, Louis, Jean Baptiste and Etienne will gather nine additional men and take two canoes to meet our Albany business contact. I'll go to Montreal in the morning and buy ten thousand livres worth of furs for you to trade to the English. Because of all the recent trouble, what little fur I've received from the west this year I've already sold to meet my obligations. The trade items we need that are in short supply include blankets, firesteels, thread, yarn, fish hooks, needles and various items for personal adornment, especially necklaces and finger rings. I'll send a runner to the commanders of the various strong points along the Richelieu, requesting that they not scour the woods for smugglers during the period when you are heading to Albany. Take Bernard La Motte as one of your voyageurs. On the way back send him ahead to the strong points. He'll visit the commanders and clear the way for you. He's done this job a number of times before; the officers at the forts know they can expect compensation in return for this dereliction of duty.

"Louis, you're a marine ensign; you will be in charge. I'll also send a runner to the merchant I deal with in Albany. He keeps a warehouse north of town stocked for customers such as ourselves, people whose business dealings would be frowned upon by both the

French and the English governments, at least officially. Today is Monday. Let the journey to Albany commence at dawn on Wednesday. Does anyone have any questions?"

Jean Baptiste asked, "Who is the merchant we will be dealing with?"

"His name is Blackthorne. Thomas Blackthorne."

Jean Baptiste anticipated no problems with his older brother Louis on this trip, even though they had had more than their fair share of difficulties in the past. When he was a boy, the twins seemed to go out of their way to torment him, possibly because of the affection showered on him by their parents, since Jean Baptiste was the baby of the family. Oddly enough, he had always gotten along well enough with both Jacques and Louis as individuals. It was only when the two of them were scheming together that the result was trouble for their little brother. Once when he was six and the twins were ten, they frightened Jean Baptiste by imitating the sounds of bears and other large animals while he camped alone for the first time in a tent behind the family home.

Their father found out and subsequently evened the score. The next time Jacques and Louis visited their favorite fishing spot, Daniel Joubert hired a Seneca from the Lake of Two Mountains mission. The man donned all his wartime regalia, including paint from head to toe. He surprised the boys while they fished and chased them all the way home, a distance of more than a league. By the time they arrived home and raised the alarm, both were exhausted and Jacques had wet his pants. The Seneca walked right up to the homestead as the boys hid behind their father. Their father laughed, paid the man, and asked the twins how they liked being frightened. Relations between Jean Baptiste and his brothers remained strained. As they grew older, things did improve somewhat, and since Jacques would not be present on this journey, Louis and he would probably have an amiable relationship.

Louis Joubert encountered Henri Gaultier the next morning when both were on the way to breakfast. The officer from New Orleans asked if Louis had time to show him around Montreal. Louis felt there was little risk in trusting Henri, and so told him about the expedition to Albany.

"If I had known of it, I'd have volunteered to go as well. After all that time confined aboard ship, I could use an extended period of exercise."

"What about the meeting you're supposed to have with the governor general?"

"I'll be here all winter, and he could take no action on my request for assistance until the spring, so if I don't talk to him for another week or two, no harm done."

"I'm sure it will be alright for you to accompany us. Just one thing, though. I know you are a lieutenant, and I am only an ensign, but this is family rather than marine business. I've lived in these woods my whole life and I've traded with these Englishmen a number of times before, so I'll be in charge."

"I've got no problem with that arrangement at all. I'm just along for the ride."

"And to provide some muscle with a paddle, and also when we have to portage."

"That too. By the way, I assume this traffic with the English is not entirely legal."

"You're right.  Officially, both governments regard this commerce as smuggling.  The problem is that we control the lion's share of the fur trade through good relationships with most of the interior tribes. Unfortunately, both the quality and the quantity of our trade goods leave something to be desired.  The English want a bigger piece of the trade than they are able to garner through friendship with the remaining tribes, and they have access to large volumes of good quality trade goods.  So the French trade some of the furs that the English want in exchange for trade goods that the French need.  Everyone benefits.

"Unfortunately, both European countries want only their own colonists to benefit from the trade, and so try to discourage the traffic between Albany and Montreal. Versailles ordered the erection of Fort Chambly and other posts along the Richelieu River partially to intercept smugglers.  Fortunately, the local authorities look at the matter from a more practical standpoint, and enforcement of royal edicts is lax.  I don't know if it is coincidental or not, but it appears that the colony of New York benefits from the trade in another, though non-monetary manner."

"How is that?"

"In time of war, it seems that our war parties strike at New England much more frequently than they do at New York.  Perhaps there is some other reason than the trade, but I for one don't think so.  By the way, if this traffic with the English troubles you, you may withdraw your offer of assistance."

"It doesn't trouble me at all.  We seek creative solutions to business problems in New Orleans as well."

Rene La Pointe found himself quite infatuated by both Jeanne Chaloche and her little son Guy. The tiny grandson of Daniel Joubert followed the clerk all around the house to the amusement of all. They wondered why the little man found this stranger so interesting. They didn't know that Rene had seen Guy try to raid the jar of imported figs. When no one was looking, Rene helped himself to some of the figs, putting them in his pocket. He sneaked pieces of fig to Guy on the sly, and soon the lad was following him around looking for more. Of course if Guy were in the vicinity, his mother Jeanne was also nearby.

Rene engaged Jeanne in conversation whenever the opportunity presented itself. She was an intelligent woman who shared his love of books. They began to go for walks together, usually with Guy. Sometimes one of them would carry the small boy; at other times he would walk between them, holding their hands.

"Isn't that lovely?" commented Dufort when he saw the three walking along the riverbank the evening before the trip to Albany was to commence. "Here we are with millions of livres worth of Carthaginian gold at stake, and what is our researcher doing? Walking in the moonlight!"

"I'm glad he is. He has all winter to study his geography. My sister has needed someone since the elder Guy drowned, and I can't think of anyone I'd rather that someone be than Rene. The two of them are a lot alike. She is probably the smartest of the Jouberts, and has always been thoughtful and kind, much like our friend. I hope they get along famously. Certainly he and little Guy are great friends already."

The next morning the two large canoes set off for

Albany. The twelve voyageurs were dressed as civilians, but were dressed for warmth, because the air was becoming much cooler, especially at night. All wore buckskin or cloth shirts along with leggings of wool or hide. Moccasins were the footwear of choice, and all wore capotes, or heavy blanket coats. Most of the men wore the blue tuque, or stocking cap of Montreal. Dufort was one of the exceptions; he insisted on wearing the white tuque emblematic of Three Rivers, the place of his birth. The men were heavily armed. This was supposed to be a peaceful trip, but they would be traveling very close to the ancestral homes of the Mohawks, easternmost of the Iroquois tribes. Given recent events, the men carried extra ammunition.

They landed at Lachine and portaged around the rapids to Montreal. There the Jouberts picked up the packs of furs to be traded and the necessary provisions; then they glided down river as far as the mouth of the Richelieu, where the small village of Sorel stood. The voyageurs landed on the south bank of the St. Lawrence a half-league before reaching the town and its garrison. They portaged around Sorel in order to avoid questions about why they carried furs south, and then continued toward Albany.

All knew that they were traveling on the great invasion route between New France and the English colonies. Even before these colonies existed, warring Indian tribes traveled between the St. Lawrence River and the Hudson River to the south using the Richelieu River, Lake Champlain, Lake Saint Sacrement route. It was by far the most direct path to the vitals of enemy territory. Not the least of the attractions of this route was that it allowed passage of heavy loads; in the case of the

Jouberts, the cargoes were for peaceful trade purposes, at least on this trip.

Henri Gaultier had been his uncle's aide for some time, and had grown a bit soft as a result.  Paddling a canoe blistered his hands, but that discomfort was trivial compared to the way he felt toting a pack of furs on portage.  Most of the men carried two packs at a time, but even with half the load, he found himself puffing like a bellows by the time he reached the rest stops.  He did, however, maintain good humor about the situation.  "Louis," he called to the man in charge as the two of them rested briefly, "When I said I wanted to go on this trip to get some exercise, I didn't intend for you to kill me."

"You're doing fine," interjected Dufort.  "By the time this trip is over, you will probably want to resign from the marines and become a coureur de bois.  That way you could spend all your time paddling canoes and lugging heavy loads around."

"I'm sure the idea will grow on me in time."

"The best part is yet to come.  Later on when we stop to eat, you've got a real treat in store.  When we loaded supplies in Montreal, I noticed the food consisted mostly of pemmican."

Jean Baptiste, who had just dropped off his packs at the rest stop, groaned when he heard this news.

## CHAPTER 26

W hile their comrades paddled along rivers and muscled their canoes over portages, Maurice and Rene set about the business of training the former on the company bookkeeping practices.  It was a painful experience both for the teacher and the student. Certainly Maurice had the ability to master the work easily, and Rene La Pointe proved to be both a skilled and patient teacher.    Maurice just had difficulty concentrating behind a desk after having spent so many years in the woods as a marine.  At first he had difficulty sitting still for more than a few minutes at a time, and his mind constantly wandered.  Where were Charles and Jean Baptiste at the moment?  In the event of trouble, had they armed themselves sufficiently?  How did Rene think they should try to locate Strong Hand?  Anything to keep from spending too much time on the blasted ledger books.

"How is your study of the African coastline progressing?" asked Maurice.  This was the fourth topic completely unrelated to bookkeeping he had broached in the last quarter hour.

"Not too well," admitted the clerk.  "I wish I had access to my brother Denis' library.  I have a limited selection of volumes here. His resources in Marseilles are much larger, and historical geography is a particular interest of his. I guess I shouldn't fret about a situation I can't control."

Then Maurice mentioned Jeanne, and Rene was only too glad to be distracted from the lesson. "So how are things between you and my sister?"

"Wonderful as far as I'm concerned. I don't know what she thinks. Who can tell for sure what is on a woman's mind? I hope she likes me half as much as I like her. I would be satisfied with that. But I'm sure I'm not the only one with romance on my mind. It would seem that you have made a very favorable impression on Dominique."

"No woman has ever driven me as crazy in such a short period of time. I think I was obsessed an hour after meeting her. I'm sure I would do anything she asked, up to and including swimming over the great falls at Niagara. Since I am that far gone, I certainly hope she likes me too. Otherwise, the future looks pretty grim. I have an idea! Tomorrow let's free our minds of all these entries and sums and take the women somewhere. There are a number of small islands in the St. Lawrence down river off Beauharnois' seigneury. Bring little Guy. We'll pack a lunch and make a day of it. I was just outside and I'm sure tomorrow will be a fine day."

"You'll do anything to avoid this bookkeeping, won't you? Sounds good to me though. I'll talk to Jeanne tonight."

The trip to the island the next day was a success. Everyone ate too much and were still able to enjoy themselves. Rene spent hours with Guy, teaching the lad how to skip stones across the waters of the St. Lawrence. The little boy's technique needed work, but he giggled with delight at even the smallest success. Then Rene ran back and forth along the little island's beach, carrying Guy on his shoulders. The boy loved it, and urged him on and on until La Pointe collapsed from exhaustion, carefully spilling his laughing passenger on the soft sand. Jeanne laughed almost as hard as Guy, then brought some brandy to the "horse " to revive him. As Maurice had predicted, it was a perfect day, not only unseasonably warm with light wind and bright sunshine, but filled with smiles and happy memories.

While the others frolicked on the beach, Maurice and Dominique watched from a nearby hillside. He had his arm around her, and she alternately laughed at the antics on the beach, and softly kissed him on the cheek. "Thank you for bringing me here today," she said. "This is the most pleasant afternoon I've had in a long, long time."

"Then I'm glad I thought of it. I was afraid you might be bored."

"Not at all. Your family and friends experience their share of trouble and more, but they really care about each other. I feel a sense of contentment like I've never known."

"Rest assured I will do my utmost to prolong the feeling."

The next day, Rene and Maurice returned to the bookkeeping, but the lieutenant was able to sidetrack his tutor by reminding him that they had to try to locate Strong Hand.

"I know. I'm not sure how to approach the search.

We must be careful not to scare him off."

"One of my boyhood friends lives in Caughnawaga, and I've asked him to make some discreet inquiries as to Strong Hand's whereabouts. He seems to have gone to ground. No one at the mission has seen him since the day he sought medical attention. He's probably found a spot where he can relax while he recovers from his injuries. We may just have to wait until such time as he decides to emerge. On the bright side, neither he nor the spy we seek can be causing much trouble at the moment since the fur convoys are finished until the return of warm weather in the spring."

In the meanwhile, the pair renewed friendships with workers in the Montreal office and took pains to become acquainted with Jullien Rivole, the clerk who had been hired when Rene went to Michilimackinac. They took lunch with Jullien as well as Denis Labonte and Gilles Guyotte, the other clerks. After work the five of them would have several rounds of drinks at one of the local inns. Sometimes they would play cards. Rivole mentioned that he enjoyed chess, and Maurice promptly challenged the young man, unfortunately enjoying the same success against this opponent that he had against Father Mercier of Cahokia. Jullien seemed a bright, friendly, uncomplicated young man who was interested in finding a pretty wife and raising a large family.

They also spent time at the warehouses and wharves handling Joubert business. There were plenty of questionable characters in evidence, but few who were around for any length of time, certainly not the whole of the last eighteen months during which the trouble had occurred. A few company employees had been on the job for many years, but they continued their work each day, still living in the same humble dwellings of their youth, with no sign of any sudden accumulation of wealth.

Maurice and Rene did not know how to proceed. On the chance that they did not locate the spy before the spring, the two drew up plans to change work assignments both at the office and at the warehouses. The purpose of the changes was to ensure that no one man had complete information on the composition, route and destination of Joubert convoys leaving Montreal. If they couldn't catch him, at least they could make things more difficult for whoever was leaking information.

Gradually, Maurice became more acclimated to working indoors, and soon grasped the various bookkeeping assignments fully. The other clerks were used to his presence now, and Maurice kept a sharp eye in order to detect anything out of the ordinary. So far, nothing. Jullien was the most talkative of the clerks, but his conversation centered mostly on a plump vegetable seller at the market who would pay him no heed. Denis and Gilles concentrated on their work and talked little.

After work one day, Rene mentioned to Maurice that Jean Baptiste had been working on a way to trick Strong Hand into revealing the man they sought. "If only we could catch the Caughnawaga. We have to work harder to find that Indian."

Dominique was becoming very popular with the Joubert women. Though she was a guest and did not have to work, she rose early in the morning to help prepare breakfast. She was not an especially good cook, but was a willing worker, and tried diligently to prepare the meals that Canadians loved. She found preparation of the meat and vegetable, as well as fowl pies particularly challenging, but after a few missteps, which the Jouberts choked down without complaint, her skill improved and finally she became reasonably proficient.

Dominique was an accomplished seamstress (she had made many of the dresses worn by herself and the other women at Madame Linctot's). Both Jeanne and her mother were anxious to learn how to make some of the new fashions (Maurice again became a little worried when he heard this). Dominique readily assented to teach them, as well as a number of other women from the seigneury.

"Before we begin, I need to go to Montreal and get the appropriate material. Nothing I've seen here will do for what I've got in mind."

"Let's go tomorrow," said Jeanne. "Would you like to go too, mother?"

"You two go ahead. I'll watch Guy. Enjoy yourselves. I don't believe Dominique has seen much of Montreal as yet. If the weather is decent, you can show her the sights."

La Forest would have his revenge. This Huron chief had borne a deadly hatred of the Fox ever since his brother had died in battle against that tribe some nineteen years before. That fight had occurred here in Detroit, the spot from which La Forest planned to launch a winter campaign against the Fox homeland. After his meeting with Onontio in Montreal, at which he had received tacit approval for his planned assault, forty-seven Iroquois from the Lake of Two Mountains Mission had accompanied the Huron home to his village near Fort Pontchartrain.

The French commander at Detroit, Captain Henri-Louis Deschamps de Boishebert, had aided the cause immeasurably. Knowing the enmity the governor general had for the Fox, Captain Boishebert supplied anything La Forest wanted in the way of weapons, ammunition and provisions. To that the Frenchman added large doses of encouragement, also free of charge.

La Forest had hoped to recruit many warriors from the Ottawa and Pottawatomi villages near Detroit, but in this he was disappointed. Chiefs from these villages informed him that many of their warriors had already scattered to their winter hunting camps. If the Huron would wait until the spring, more men would be available.

But La Forest was in no mood to wait. Late in the summer he had fasted for a number of days, hoping for a vision. For a long time he saw nothing. Then he dreamed that a mighty eagle swooped from the sky and killed a woodpecker as it sat on a branch. Seeking the meaning of this dream, he consulted the elders of the tribe. They concluded that the woodpecker represented the Fox, who revered this bird and whose roach headdresses were designed to emulate that creature's appearance. The eagle was La Forest himself, who would be the instrument of destruction.

Elated, he traveled to Montreal, hoping for the blessing and assistance of Onontio. The residents at the Lake of Two Mountains had been stung by accusations that the mission Iroquois favored on the English, as their kinsmen still in New York undoubtedly did. They had been looking for a way to prove their loyalty to the French, especially if that way did not include striking their relations to the south. When news of La Forest's intentions reached Lake of Two Mountains, he found many eager volunteers.

The Huron was impatient to duplicate the events of his vision, even though if they left now, the campaign would take place in the snow and cold. La Forest intended to proceed at once, and the Iroquois had no objection. Yes, the winter would cause hardship on the march, but the Fox would not be expecting trouble at that time. With luck, surprise would be complete and the Fox, already much reduced in numbers, would be completely erased from the sight of man. The expedition would proceed on foot rather than by canoe for several reasons. The season was well advanced and if they used canoes, they were certain to encounter ice long before they reached their destination. In addition, La Forest planned to recruit more men as they journeyed to various tribal villages along their line of march. It was about the middle of October when seventy-four Hurons, forty-seven Iroquois and four Ottawas left Detroit, intending to exterminate their hated foe.

## CHAPTER 27

The Joubert canoes were making good progress southward, especially once the last French strong point on the Richelieu was by-passed. Jean Baptiste was enjoying himself. He was relieved rather than unhappy that Charles was in charge. He could do his work and joke with his companions, leaving the worrying to his elder brother. He was certainly glad he'd gotten a warm capote from his mother. At night it was really getting cold. On the last two mornings there had been ice along the edges of the Richelieu when they had awakened.

Finally, they were out on the waters of Lake Champlain, a huge body of water much longer than it was wide. They would travel the full length of the lake from north to south. The water itself was clear and sparkling on this crisp autumn day. Jean Baptiste could see a number of wooded islands, the trees looking somewhat barren as most of the leaves had already fallen.

"Ordinarily, from this point on, we would expect to find no more Frenchmen, other than other smugglers," said Charles over his shoulder to his younger brother. "However, the governor general has decided to erect another fortification, all the way down near the head of Lake Champlain. Construction began this summer and I'm sure it will take years to complete. From what I was able to determine before we left Montreal, the men working on the project were to be released this week to return to their homes for the winter. If we see them, we should probably try to avoid being recognized."

"What is the English response to this construction?" inquired Jean Baptiste. "This new fort must be uncomfortably close to their territory, if I remember the geography of the area."

"I haven't heard if they've made any official protest, but I'm sure they're not happy."

When they got close to the site of the new fort at the narrows at the south end of the lake, the Joubert party was able to portage around the spot unobserved. The next day they passed Ticonderoga, a commanding position between Lake Champlain and Lake Saint Sacrement to the south. "That is the spot where they should be building their fort," commented Dufort.

"I agree," said Charles Joubert, "and I'm sure that's the next step to be taken."

They traveled along the east shore of Lake Saint Sacrement, taking extra care to be inconspicuous. They were very close to Mohawk country now, and even though no official war was in progress, relations between the French and the Mohawks had been bad since Samuel de Champlain sided with the latter's enemies more than a century ago.

"It certainly is a wondrous spot," commented Jean Baptiste as the sun dropped behind the mountains to the west.

"Pretty, yes, but keep a good watch every minute.

Those Mohawks would rather kill a Frenchman than just about anything," said Dufort. "I heard they even killed the Jesuit who discovered this lake."

That night they made camp on the east shore, and made sure to keep their fires low. Dufort distributed the ration of pemmican to the men in his canoe. He then made amends by being extremely generous with the cask of brandy, in order to "keep out the chill."

"I hope everyone is well rested," said Charles. "Well before mid-day tomorrow we will reach the head of the lake. We then have a considerable portage to reach the Hudson River. From there it should be a smooth trip to Albany."

"I'd like to suggest that we trade some of the furs for edible food," commented Henri Gaultier. Actually, the lieutenant had been doing reasonably well on the trip, all things considered. After becoming accustomed to the delicacies available in New Orleans, he thought Dufort was joking when the voyageur offered him this foul smelling stuff called pemmican for the first time. When he got hungry enough, he ate some of this concoction of dried meat, fat and crushed berries, but he didn't exactly thrive on it. Still, the spare diet and hard work had hardened his muscles and reduced his waistline.

"I wouldn't mind a couple of loaves of bread, still warm from the oven, along with a nice roast of venison," mused Dufort. "However, it would be unhealthy to do any hunting in these parts and we don't have an oven, so I guess I'll be satisfied with what is available. Pass me another fist full of pemmican please."

The portage from the head of Lake Saint Sacrement to the Hudson was of considerable length, and it required a day and a half to carry the canoes, the furs and all their supplies and equipment. Henri held up well this time; his conditioning had improved. Dufort helped him pass the time as they trudged under their loads by teaching the lieutenant several voyageurs' songs. At the conclusion of these lessons, Dufort remarked, "We have to bring Monsieur Gaultier on all of these little excursions. He has a voice like an angel." Henri's expression indicated he was not convinced this was a good idea.

After a few days on the Hudson, they saw an occasional stone house with accompanying broad wooden barn. Charles indicated that they were near their destination. "I'll go ahead alone from here. Keep the canoes concealed in this little cove. I'll walk to our English friends. I recognize where we are; it isn't far to the warehouse. Blackthorne's establishment is considerably north of the settled part of town, so we should be able to complete the trade and start back toward Montreal without arousing undue suspicion."

"Great," said Dufort. "We'll have time for a little snack. Pemmican anyone?"

Tiny Mason was not happy. He understood why Jacob Cutler wasn't helping with the work; the man's wound was not completely healed. But there was no reason that Whittington was sitting on his ass doing nothing. There he was, sitting on a keg, drinking rum while Tiny did all the labor. He'd have a little talk with his split-eared friend later. They didn't know when the French would arrive, but before he left for New York yesterday, Mr. Blackthorne told them to gather the requested trade goods, so that the exchange could be made as quickly as possible. At least Jacob helped him locate the items the Frenchman had sent on his list. Jacob read what was desired, and Tiny climbed over boxes, bales and barrels until he found it. Fortunately, most of the items requested were small in size and lightweight, with the exception of the load of blankets he was hauling out now. His stomach was beginning to grumble; he hoped Strong Hand would return momentarily with a fat buck for dinner.

Tiny dully wondered what had happened to the Indian. He arrived in Albany last night, looking for Blackthorne. When told that the boss would be out of town for several days, he elected to wait, but would tell no one else what he wanted. He also refused to comment on the cause of his injuries. Tiny knew that he was no prize in the looks department, especially with the new glowing pink scar along the side of his head, but Strong Hand was really a beauty. He wore a patch over one eye, and one side of his face and head bore numerous fresh burns. Tiny supposed it was understandable that the Indian was even more sullen than usual. No matter. The important thing was that the Indian agreed to hunt for fresh meat. Tiny told him they had some work to do at the old north warehouse, so the Iroquois agreed to meet them there with the results of the hunt.

Just as Mason set down his load of blankets outside the warehouse and started back for more, Robert Whittington called out that someone was coming. Tiny stopped and looked in the indicated direction, hoping to see the one-eyed Iroquois loaded down with game. Instead he saw Charles Joubert, the one who had come a number of times before to trade.

Etienne Dufort had just settled in for a comfortable

snooze when Charles returned to the small cove where the canoes were hidden, and said he'd made contact with the English.

"I've looked over the trade goods, and they've got most of what father asked for. They are a little short on the number of blankets, so I took some bolts of heavy cloth instead. Etienne, you'll be happy to know that they even threw in a free keg of rum, to help keep us warm on the return journey."

"These Englishmen seem to be getting more civilized over time. Well, I suppose we should start moving these furs so that we can pick up our goods."

The three Englishmen stood waiting outside the large barn-like warehouse as the first of the Frenchmen arrived with their bales of furs. Etienne was fourth in line, just ahead of Jean Baptiste. Dufort was bent forward at the waist, straining under two packs of furs. He could see the feet and legs of the man in front of him as the voyageur lowered his packs of furs to the ground. He moved slightly to the right to find some open space and saw two very large moccasins below legs that looked like tree trunks. He lowered his load and stood up, holding his aching back. Etienne found himself looking into the face of the man with the large legs, who proved to be none other than the giant he had shot at the battle near the Wisconsin River.

Tiny thought this man looked familiar, and somehow, he knew he did not like this stranger. Then he remembered the face, the flash of a pistol, the pain. With a roar he picked up Dufort like a sack of flour and tossed him over the packs of furs.

"What the hell is wrong with you?" screamed Jacob Cutler at his gigantic but dim-witted companion.

"He's the one that shot me in the face! I'll wager the one that got you is here as well."

At the sound of Tiny Mason's bellow and the sight of Dufort's flying body, Jean Baptiste dropped his load and pulled the pistol at his belt. He understood English and had heard the exchange between the big man and the man with his arm in the sling. The cadet assumed the latter was the man who had killed Sky Singer and whom he had shot in turn. He regretted that the man's injury was not more serious.

Charles was some distance away, back near the cove, so Jean Baptiste stepped forward. "Hold! We don't want any trouble here. This is supposed to be a peaceful exchange of merchandise. Let's leave it at that."

Jacob Cutler surveyed the situation. More Frenchmen were moving into the clearing in front of the warehouse. There were eight in sight and probably more on the way. He had only two companions. Cutler was content with a peaceful resolution of the situation. For now.

"Your English is excellent, monsieur," said Cutler in French. "May I ask your name?"

"Jean Baptiste Joubert, Sieur de St. Croix, cadet in the Companies franches de la Marine. And you sir?"

"Jacob Cutler, fur trader. Kiala said that a boy shot me. Would that have been you?"

"With due respect, I hope so. The Ottawa you killed was a friend of mine."

"We can settle our differences another time. As you say, our purpose here is trade. Let there be no violence on either side. Tiny," he addressed the giant, who stood glaring at Dufort, "that especially means you."

Etienne rose unsteadily to his feet, checking to see

if anything was broken. "I don't know what he's so mad about," he whispered to Jean Baptiste. "If anything, the scar and the loss of part of his ear has improved his looks."

Charles had by this time reached the clearing. When he learned of the situation, he agreed to complete the exchange and depart immediately.

Dufort wanted to ask if they still got the free rum. Rather than take the chance of a negative response, he signaled to Henri Gaultier, who was standing near the small keg. Henri understood and picked up the container, planning to get the liquor back to the canoes as quickly as possible. As he reached down to pick up an additional bundle, he saw an Indian enter the clearing, carrying a freshly killed buck on his shoulders. The warrior, wearing a patch over one eye, did not appear hostile until he looked at Jean Baptiste, who was talking to his brother and had not noted the Indian's arrival.

The warrior dropped the buck and began to raise his musket. With nothing else handy, Henri raised the keg of rum in both hands and hurled it. The keg struck the Indian in the shoulder, knocking the musket from his grasp. Strong Hand looked at Gaultier with venomous hatred, gave a wild cry, and bounded away into the woods.

"No pursuit, men," said Jean Baptiste. "No harm was done, and we've pledged no violence."

Strong Hand wondered what was happening as he escaped through the trees. He had wanted to talk to Blackthorne, the man in charge, about the ambush that had gone so very wrong. How was it possible that the ambushers had been ambushed in turn? How did the

French know where to set their trap? Now he goes to Blackthorne's storehouse and sees one of the men who cost him an eye and his face. What was he doing there? He had to know. He respected Cutler. He would wait in the woods until the French left and then talk to him.

The Jouberts hurried back to the cove where their canoes were beached.

"I assume that is the Iroquois you have been looking for," said Charles.

"Yes, and isn't it interesting that he turns up here, on the property of Thomas Blackthorne. We also know that Blackthorne's men were stirring up Kiala and the Fox, the same Indians that attacked us on the Wisconsin. It looks to me like father is obtaining trade goods from this Englishman, and Blackthorne is arranging to have the goods stolen back. I wonder how many times father has bought the goods we are carrying right now?"

"Why didn't you try to catch the Iroquois?" asked Charles. "We need him to find the traitor who has been giving Blackthorne information."

"True, but we need to be moving as quickly as possible. Cutler might change his mind and decide to pursue us. So we wouldn't have time to interrogate him now, and guarding him while we moved these trade goods would be difficult. Of course, we also pledged not to use violence. Anyway, if we took him by force I'm sure Cutler would have had his Mohawk kinsmen on our trail before morning. Burdened as we are, we'd never have made it to Montreal. The Indian will return to Caughnawaga sooner or later. We'll just have to keep a good watch. Henri!" Jean Baptist called. "Thanks for saving me. I didn't even see him."

"And the best part," said Dufort, "is that none of the rum was lost.  I recovered the keg in all the confusion and brought it to safety."

## CHAPTER 28

Thomas Blackthorne was enjoying himself immensely. New York City had so much more to offer in the way of entertainment than Albany. The gaming establishments, taverns and bawdyhouses were numerous and appealed to a variety of tastes. Even polite society opened its doors to him now that he earned his wealth from the fur trade rather than the slave trade. He was sufficiently prosperous that wealthy families with marriage-age daughters considered him a good catch. Of course, they didn't know about the Mohawk woman to whom he was already married, and he saw no reason to enlighten them on that point.

He received invitations to dine at the homes of the prominent. Attractive women glanced at him suggestively from the corners of their eyes, looks that sometimes promised much, and he found out if these promises ultimately had value. Businessmen eagerly sought his ear, telling him that with his Indian contacts, he was ideally positioned to profit from the ever-growing demand for land. Again he gave thought to how he could use the fur trade to induce sufficient indebtedness among his Indian customers that they could be persuaded to pay what they owed with land.

Blackthorne felt that his prominence in the community required the upgrading of his wardrobe. His new friends recommended a tailor and he had the man call on him at his rooms. He ordered five suits of clothes, and also bought several new pairs of riding boots and three beaver hats.

Of course, all of this took much more than the three or four days he had originally intended to spend in the city. This was not the busy season for the fur trade. He was confident that Cutler could handle whatever routine matters had to be dealt with, even if he wouldn't trust either Mason or Whittington to efficiently pour water from a boot. No reason to hurry back to Albany, a prospect made doubly grim by the impending onset of winter. Instead of a few days, he spent more than three weeks in New York. When he finally returned to Albany, it was mid-November.

When he found out what had happened when the Jouberts picked up their trade goods, he was beside himself with rage. "You mean you just let them leave? After what they saw here in Albany? I gave you credit for having some intelligence, Cutler. Obviously, I was mistaken."

"What were we supposed to do? There were three of us and a dozen of them. Anyway, I think you are being too pessimistic. They know Tiny, Robert and I were dealing with the Fox, but that was quite some time after they were attacked. There is no reason for them to think we were behind the ambush on the river, even though it was your inside man who tipped Kiala off. As for Strong Hand, they gave no indication that they recognized him and Jean Baptiste Joubert halted any pursuit. They probably think he is just some crazy Iroquois who hates all Frenchmen.  God knows there are plenty of those."

"Where is Strong Hand now?"

"After the French left, he came out from his hiding place in the woods.  He was very suspicious about how the French could have known to ambush him on the Ottawa River, and why one of the same Frenchmen who had injured him was here trading with us.  I talked to him for hours and gave him his own keg of rum, and finally he seemed satisfied.  He had begun to think you had betrayed him, but I pointed out that you had nothing to gain from such an act.  I could not explain the French ambush; I just told him that in war, sometimes luck favors the other side.  As to the trading here, I explained and he then remembered that the Jouberts have traded with you for years when certain trade goods were scarce in Canada.  He stayed in the vicinity of our north warehouse for a few days, roaring drunk most of the time.  When the rum was gone and he sobered up, he decided to return to Caughnawaga for the winter.  I told him to keep out of sight except for checking each week for messages from our contact in Montreal.  Then he left. That was three weeks ago."

"I don't agree that we have nothing to worry about. If Strong Hand recognized the boy from the fight on the Ottawa, there is an excellent chance the boy recognized him as well, even though he is now disfigured.  Strong Hand's presence here links us to the attacks on the Joubert convoys.   Connecting you to the Fox who conducted the Wisconsin River ambush does nothing to diminish that impression.  That's all for now.  I need time to think."

*What a disastrous turn of events.  While I was wallowing in the fleshpots of New York, my entire operation was turning to shit, and I knew nothing about it. At the least, I have to stop the attacks on the Jouberts for the foreseeable future. Daniel Joubert is an influential man in Montreal, and since England and France are at peace, could make me look bad if all this comes out in the open. He doesn't have any real proof at this point. I could have Strong Hand killed, but he is an important man among his people. Cutler said he was suspicious of me already. If he's told other Caughnawagas about those suspicions, and then was to die suddenly, I'd never get another good night's sleep. Each time I went to bed I'd expect to be awakened by the feel of a Mohawk scalping knife against my skull. Why did I decide to go to New York when I did? If I'd stayed in Albany, I could have prevented all this.*

Later in the day, Blackthorne summoned Cutler. "I've decided on the course of action we must take. Before they have an opportunity to gather any damning evidence against us, we have to eliminate the Jouberts. I propose a winter campaign against their seigneury. The Mohawks wish to avenge their dead from the fight in Wisconsin, but I don't want to start a war with the French. Some Fox have been living among the Seneca for a number of years. Quietly obtain some examples of their weapons and have our Mohawks prepare their arrows and lances with Fox markings. Any evidence left behind will point to the Fox and away from our friends. The Jouberts fought against the Fox several times this year already. The French will think the Fox along the Wisconsin sought revenge, and this assault on a prominent family will strengthen the French resolve to wipe out that troublesome tribe. I assume it will take several weeks to prepare. Get started at once."

At that moment in Montreal, Dominique and Jeanne were returning to the market to obtain more material. The sewing classes had become so popular that not only had all the women and teenage girls of Hawk's Nest started to attend, but even women from several of the seigneuries closer to Montreal had begun to travel to the Joubert's home to learn how to make the newest fashions. This was the third trip to town that had been necessary. Dominique was a wonderful instructor, and when she modeled some of her own clothes for the ladies, they redoubled their efforts. In most cases, the results would not look quite so breathtaking because the women did not possess Dominique's looks or figure, but she patiently helped each student look the best she possibly could. Of course, keeping the social climate in mind, she confined her classes to the more conservative items in her wardrobe.

The St. Lawrence was still navigable, but the weather was getting much colder and the wind was making the water very rough. Two of Daniel Joubert's voyageurs had volunteered to take the ladies to Montreal in a bateau. They sped along traveling with the current; the return trip would not be as easy.

At Lachine the women looked for a way to travel to Montreal that offered protection from the elements. They had no success until Jeanne saw Noel Sabattier, the son of a wealthy merchant. She had attended the Jesuit school in Montreal with Noel when they both were children, and had always regarded him as a pleasant, if not overly bright fellow. He was entering a covered carriage when she recognized him and called his name. Fine snow, driven by the wind, had begun to fall, and the women were extremely grateful when Noel eagerly offered them a ride to town.

Jeanne introduced Dominique and then made polite conversation, inquiring about the health and activities of his family. Noel's responses were correct, though brief, his eyes drawn frequently to Dominique's face. When they drew near the market area, the women were relieved to exit the carriage, though the ride had been very comfortable, at least in a physical sense.

"Has he spent the last ten years alone on a desert island?" inquired Dominique. "He was acting like he'd never seen a woman before."

"You did seem to impress him. And I'm afraid the social graces have never been one of his strong points. He's harmless enough though."

The snow had abated, at least temporarily, and the wind had died as well. The two decided to spend time browsing in the various shops before buying the material they needed. They spent a good deal of time at the shoemaker's, and Dominique bought a pair for herself and one for Jeanne before they departed. Next they decided to see if the candlemaker had anything interesting in stock. Dominique satisfied her curiosity in a short while, but Jeanne had some questions to ask the proprietor.

As that conversation continued, Dominique walked to the window and began to watch passers-bye on the street. The goldsmith's shop was on the other side of the street and a bit farther down. Dominique had seen a bracelet there several weeks ago and had just about decided to buy it, despite the cost. Directly across from the candlemaker's shop was that of the locksmith, and Dominique idly watched the man do his work. As she watched, someone in a hooded capote entered the locksmith's shop, at the same time throwing back the hood and shaking off loose snow. It was an Indian. She could clearly see the scalplock, but what was even more noticeable was the ravaged condition of his face. He wore a patch over one eye and she could see what looked like burns on one side of his face and head.

She could not hear the conversation across the street, but saw the locksmith nod and produce a piece of paper from under the counter, which he handed to the Indian. Apparently the paper bore a message which the warrior read. He seemed to be thinking for a few moments, then turned and exited the shop without further comment, again covering his head with the hood. He crumpled the note and dropped it in the street as he headed toward Lachine.

Dominique forgot about the goldsmith and headed out into the wind to see if she could retrieve the piece of paper. She didn't think they were the right ones, but she picked up several other pieces of paper she saw on the street, just to be safe. One was blank and the other looked like a child's drawing of two fish. When she found her elusive quarry, it led her a merry chase before she was finally able to grab it between gusts.

Dominique heard a voice laughing behind her and turned to see Jeanne, who had been watching with amusement as her friend chased bits of paper out in the cold.

"What are you doing?"

Dominique ducked around the corner of the locksmith's shop, motioning Jeanne to join her. They were now out of the wind, and in a spot not visible to the shop's owner.

"The Indian Rene and Maurice are searching for is

supposed to have a badly burned face. A man fitting that description just paid a visit to this shop, and was given this piece of paper by the proprietor." She carefully unwrapped the wad of paper, flattening it so it was again legible. It said:

*The Jouberts know who you are and are looking for you. Keep out of sight except for weekly trips for instructions.*

"Should we try to follow him?" asked Jeanne.

"I don't think so. He looked to be headed back toward Lachine. Once he got outside the city, he'd probably spot us, particularly since he's just been alerted to be careful. We've got one of his messages, and we know where he picks them up. In my opinion, we should tell Maurice and Rene what we know, and let them handle it from there. One more thing. Since we don't know who the spy is, but it's a good bet that it is someone close to your family, we need to act like nothing unusual has happened until we get back home."

"Does that mean we should finish our shopping?"

"That it does. We came to Montreal to get material for our sewing classes, and we will have that material when we return to Hawk's Nest."

## CHAPTER 29

J eanne and Dominique returned to Hawk's Nest well after the normal dinner hour. The bateau ride from Lachine to the seigneury had been rough; the wind blew strongly from the west, and the snow began again, heavier than before. The two voyageurs had fortified themselves liberally with brandy while waiting for their passengers, and the liquor helped keep out the cold as the men plied their oars on the return trip. Dominique was not used to traveling in such conditions, or even experiencing such conditions at all. She began to fear for their safety, but Jeanne reassured her.

"Don't worry, we are in good hands. Michel and Raimond will get us home safely. I've been transported by these men in much worse weather than this, and never had a problem."

"The beautiful mademoiselles could not be more secure if they were sitting before the fire in the great house," chimed in Raimond, the older of the voyageurs. "We will give our lives before we will allow a hair on your heads to be harmed."

Somewhat placated, Dominique sat back and tried to enjoy the ride, checking frequently to be sure the recovered message was still dry.

When they reached the seigneury, the women were surprised and happy to find that the trading party to Albany had returned. Dinner had been delayed pending the return of the two women from Montreal, though Dominique noted that Henri Gaultier and Etienne Dufort were sneaking pieces of venison from the table whenever possible. Usually business matters were deferred until the meal was over, but today that rule was waived, and the events of the Albany and Montreal trips were related to all. Daniel Joubert was angered by Thomas Blackthorne's apparent complicity in the attacks on Joubert men and property, but needed time to plan a response.

"So you saw Strong Hand in Montreal," commented Jean Baptiste to Dominique and Jeanne. "If not for Henri, that Indian would have killed me. Let me see the note you recovered if you please."

He examined the note at length. "So much for trying to take him unaware. No matter. With this sample handwriting and the knowledge that the pick-ups are made at the locksmith shop, we should be able to catch our man. Rene, Etienne, perhaps you'd like to accompany me tomorrow when I pay a visit to our friend the locksmith."

"I'm not sure I'll be finished eating by then," said Dufort. "I'll hurry so that I can accommodate you."

"Madame," said Henri, addressing Toinette Joubert. "I have experienced your cooking before, and found it uniformly excellent, but you have outdone yourself. This must be the best meal ever prepared by a mortal being. My compliments."

"Sounds like the lad had his fill of pemmican on the trip," laughed Daniel Joubert. "Don't worry, the stuff grows on you in time."

Jean Baptiste and his friends were able to canoe to Montreal the next day, though ice formation would prevent that mode of transportation soon. They landed at Lachine and headed straight for the locksmith's.

"Monsieur Bayaux," said the cadet as they entered that gentleman's establishment. "It has come to my attention that a Caughnawaga visits your shop from time to time and picks up messages."

"Yes, Strong Hand. Do any of you know what happened to him. I saw him yesterday for the first time in awhile, and his face was badly injured."

"I gave him that face," stated Rene in a matter of fact manner.

"Oh. Well, gentlemen, I'm quite busy today, so if you will please excuse me."

"Actually, we do have some additional questions for you," said Jean Baptiste. "I'm sure you won't mind answering."

"No, I'll cooperate," said the locksmith, regarding La Pointe warily.

"Who leaves the messages for the Indian?"

"A young boy drops them off. Not the same boy every time either."

"How was the drop off arrangement devised originally?"

"By letter. One of the lads brought me a letter stating that I would be paid twenty livres per month if I would accept messages periodically for an Indian named Strong Hand. I was to keep them here until the Indian came to get them. What the hell. Twenty livres a month for doing almost nothing. I agreed."

"When did all this start?"

"I guess nearly two years ago. I've probably gotten about a dozen messages in that time, and pay has always been prompt."

"Did you ever read any of these messages?"

"No, they were always sealed."

"Show me how." So the locksmith showed Jean Baptiste how the notes were sealed. "I am now going to confide in you Monsieur Bayaux. The notes that you have been giving to Strong Hand have been used to hurt my father, Daniel Joubert."

"I had no idea..."

"I'm sure that you did not. I'm going to give you an opportunity to make amends. I have a letter that you will give Strong Hand on his next visit. As soon as he departs, go to my father's place of business, and let one of the three of us know. Study our faces. Tell no one except one of us. My father's office is only a short distance from here. For doing this favor, you will be paid two hundred livres. Do you agree?"

"Certainly monsieur. The Jouberts are a powerful and respected family, and I would not knowingly have damaged their interests."

"My father is generous when dealt with honestly. But, when he is not..." The cadet did not finish the sentence, but instead looked at his companions, who were busy testing the edge on their weapons.

"You need have no concern. Your wishes will be carried out to the letter. The Indian was bad for business anyway. Customers usually left when he came in. The way he looks now, they would probably run out the door."

The trio left. Rene volunteered to stand the first watch in the office. He would stay for two days, sleeping on the bed in the back room, and be relieved by Dufort. Jean Baptiste and Etienne made their way back to Lachine. They stopped at an inn to have some brandy prior to their bone-chilling return trip.

"I don't think the locksmith will cause problems," said Dufort.

"I don't think so either, and once we have our hands on that Indian, I think we will find our spy very quickly."

Several days later, Henri Gaultier approached Daniel Joubert as the latter caulked the seams of his favorite canoe. Daniel was about to put the vessel in storage for the winter, but he wanted to return it to top condition first. It was nearly sundown, and a chill wind blew off the nearby St. Lawrence. Henri was acclimating slowly to the Canadian weather; he was shivering even though he wore a thick capote and mittens.

"Henri, taking a little walk before supper to stimulate the appetite?"

"No, I was looking for you. As you know, I saw the governor general yesterday to request military aid for Louisiana. He was polite, but non-committal about sending help. I am not surprised by his response, and I'm sure Governor Perier will feel the same way."

"I've heard about your Indian situation in the south, but as you are aware, we've got plenty of our own in the north. I doubt the governor general feels he has any excess marines. The damned English seem to be causing problems for us everywhere."

"Very true. I doubt that the military aid will be forthcoming. However, there is another aspect to my mission, unrelated to the request for military assistance, that I wanted to discuss with you.

"Certain parties in Louisiana, who wish to remain anonymous, have accumulated capital for investment purposes. Naturally there are many avenues open to them closer to home, and many of these avenues have been explored, but it was felt that it would be wise to invest in other locales in addition to Louisiana. When the gentlemen in question heard that I would be traveling to Canada, they asked me to investigate potential investment opportunities for them. Since I knew I would be here for the winter, I readily agreed.

"You have made no secret of the financial reverses you have suffered during the past two trading seasons. In spite of this, I'm impressed by your operation. The trip to Albany acquainted me with the high caliber of men in your employ. I hope you will not be offended, but while I was in Montreal, I made certain discreet inquiries, and despite your recent setbacks, you and your operation are held in the highest regard. I know I am taking a long time getting to the point, but I wanted to let you know that I would be willing to authorize investment in the Joubert fur company if you felt the additional funds would be advantageous."

"You have the decision making power?"

"Yes. Because of the great distances involved, if my recommendation had to be transmitted to New Orleans for approval, a year might elapse before word of the decision got back to the St. Lawrence. I am familiar with financial bookkeeping, and the investors have given me wide latitude to act."

"Certainly an infusion of funds would be welcome. However, before I would consider such a thing, we must be absolutely clear on one point. This is a family business, and control will remain in the hands of the Jouberts."

"Without question. You are the expert on how this business should be conducted. In exchange for the funds, the investors expect a percentage of the profits. Nothing more."

"How big a percentage?"

"That would depend on what I find when I investigate your books, and on how much help you desire."

"In general terms, what amount of assistance are you prepared to give?"

"It could be one hundred thousand livres, two hundred thousand, maybe more. The exact amount can be discussed later."

"I'm most pleased you have made me this offer. Naturally, I'd like to discuss the matter with my family, but I'll give you an answer by the end of the week."

"I've a favor to ask as well," said Henri. "If you could think of two or three other businessmen in the community who you feel are good investment candidates, let me know their names. If I might impose upon you further, letters of introduction to these gentlemen would be most appreciated."

"I'd be happy to help in that regard."

That night, Maurice knocked softly on Dominique's door. She had been preparing for bed, but admitted him without hesitation.

"Please forgive the late hour, but I needed to talk to you. Henri represents some Louisiana investors and has offered funds to my father in exchange for a share of his profits. We just had a family meeting to discuss the matter. No final decision was reached, but I wanted to talk to you. You may know nothing of these financial matters, but I trust you and have found in the past that you have a surprising amount of knowledge on many subjects."

Dominique did not respond immediately, but sat on her bed, regarding him thoughtfully. "I may regret what I am about to say, and at least part of it may hurt you deeply. If so, I apologize with all my heart, but I do so in an attempt to make things right. Let me start by saying that the welcome and kindness I have received from your family since I arrived have touched me. I love them all; in a short time, they have made me feel like in some small way I am part of the family too. Of course, I'd never have maneuvered you into inviting me here if I didn't have strong feelings about you as well.

"However, I lied to you about why I was on the *Pelican*. I'm not suffering from a tropical disease. Governor Perier paid me to accompany you, assuming I had a good deal of influence on your thinking. There are no 'investors.' Perier is the only investor, and he didn't always get his money honestly. The Joubert fur enterprise is known even in Louisiana, and the governor thought he could realize a good return on his money if he bought into your family business. I was supposed to get you to support the idea.

"I wouldn't refuse his assistance just because he's a scoundrel. At least some of the money might as well be put to good use."

Maurice was thunderstruck by these frank admissions. Actually, he'd hardly heard what she said after 'Governor Perier paid me to accompany you.' This woman, whom he thought about virtually every waking moment, had to be paid to spend time with him. He began to feel sick to his stomach.

"From the look on your face, I see that my remarks were a bit too blunt. I ask only that you not hate me. I was wrong to do what I did, and I'm only telling you the truth now so that you and your family have all the information you need when deciding whether to accept the governor's help."

"Where does Henri fit into all this?"

"He's the governor's nephew. I feel that basically, he can be trusted. Gaultier's heart is really not that of a crook. His uncle is another story.

"One other thing. As soon as it is convenient, I'll find lodging in Montreal."

"But why? You're welcome to stay as long as you like. You said you feel like a part of the family." Despite his disappointment, Maurice didn't want her to leave, even though Montreal was not far away.

"Well, I've decided to open a dressmaker's shop. I could do some business from right here at Hawk's Nest, but you have to agree that it is hardly centrally located. If I had a shop near the Montreal market, I'd have access to many more customers. Anyway, thanks to my underhanded dealings with Governor Perier, I can afford a place in town, maybe a shop downstairs and living quarters upstairs.

"Besides, I understand that while we both stayed at your parents' home, appearances required that we behave in a chaste manner. I'd like you to begin courting me in earnest, and I think I can promise you that I will make your trips to Montreal worthwhile."

With that she reached for the bewildered ex-marine, gave him a lingering kiss, pinched his manhood lightly, and pushed him out the door.

## CHAPTER 30

The trap was about to be sprung on Strong Hand. Three days before, Bayaux the locksmith entered the Joubert fur trade office late in the afternoon. The day had been extremely cold and Rene La Pointe did not recognize the man at first as his features were obscured by the tuque, scarf and capote he was wearing. The little man unwrapped his outer garments and spied Rene sitting in the corner, separate from the three clerks working on their ledgers. The locksmith looked at each man in the room until he recognized La Pointe. The two huddled in the corner, talking in low tones.

"The Indian just left my shop, monsieur. He picked up the message you wanted him to get."

"Were there any other messages for him?"

"No, monsieur."

"Good. Return to your shop and act as though nothing unusual occurred."

After the little man left, Gilles Guyotte asked, "Wasn't that Bayaux, the locksmith from the market?"

"Yes I'm thinking of buying a jewelry box for Jeanne, and wanted him to design a locking clasp. It looks as though he will be able to do it."

Rene then left the Joubert office and headed south

on the Rue Saint-Paul toward Lachine. He found Jean Baptiste and Etienne at the inn where the three had taken rooms. They found seats near the roaring fire in the common room, and drank brandy while Rene dried the chill from his bones. He told his companions of the locksmith's visit.

"Excellent. Etienne and I have completed work on the storehouse we will use as our jail. The room is stoutly built, but we have discreetly loosened several planks along the rear wall. Unless the Indian is blind in both eyes, he should escape in a few hours."

"All this manual labor has given me quite an appetite," commented Dufort. "I checked the kitchen a while ago and spotted some savory looking pigeon pies being prepared. I'm sure I can finish two or three myself."

Three days had passed. It was two hours past sundown, an hour before Strong Hand was scheduled to meet the spy, or so the Indian had been led to believe. Rene, Jean Baptiste and Dufort took up their positions. It was another cold night. Fine grains of snow blew from the west, seeking every opening in the heavy clothing of those who waited. Jean Baptiste and Rene crouched together alongside a building thirty paces in front of the storehouse. Etienne was protected from the snow if not the cold; his post was just inside the front door of the rendezvous point.

"Now we'll see if your writing was enough like that of our spy to fool Strong Hand," said Jean Baptiste.

"That should not be a problem. The informant took pains to hide his normal style. The result was very deliberate and easy to copy. All we have to do now is wait. We instructed him to come to this storehouse, three hours after sundown, on the first Thursday after he got the message. He should arrive very soon."

"Check the priming on your pistols again. If we have to shoot him, try not to kill him. We need him to be able to speak."

Time passed very slowly in the cold. Etienne tried moving his hands and feet at frequent intervals to keep them from freezing. He kept the front door of the storehouse open a crack so he could see if anything was happening. There was no light in the storehouse, but with the snow on the ground outside, he could see quite well. After what seemed a very long wait, Etienne heard soft footfalls crunching the snow to his right, along the side of the storehouse. The steps got louder as the person got closer to the front door. Etienne silently closed the door, tightly gripped the cudgel in his hand, and moved to the side of the door opening.

Nothing happened. Whoever was outside made no attempt to enter. Etienne slowly opened the door a crack and peered out. Directly in front of the building, not more than an arm's length away, stood the man he had heard. At least from the size of the individual Etienne assumed it was a man. Whoever it was wore a capote with the hood up. Adding to the identification problem was the fact that the stranger's back faced the storehouse door. According to the plan, Jean Baptiste would hail the spy. Rene would then step from the shadows and both would cover the man with their pistols. This was the tricky part because anything could happen. Etienne saw that the stranger carried his musket at the ready. He might make a fight of it or run, possibly escaping the trap. Etienne was supposed to strike the man when the others had his attention and they were sure of his identity.

*Oh hell,* thought Etienne. *Who else but Strong Hand would be waiting around in the cold, in pitch darkness, in front of a closed storehouse.*

The voyageur silently opened the door, strode forward, and struck the stranger a mighty blow on the head. He dropped without a sound, face first in the snow.

"So much for carefully laid plans," commented Jean Baptiste. "But assuming this is Strong Hand, you probably had too good an opportunity to pass up. You hit him awfully hard though; I hope he's not dead. Let's see who we've got."

They turned the unconscious man over on his back, and beheld the eye patch and scarred face of the Iroquois they sought. They also noticed that the Indian's continued breathing produced little puffs of steam in the air.

"Thank God," said Etienne. "Come, let's get him inside. I don't know how long it will be until he awakens from my little love tap."

They tied Strong Hand to a chair, and waited for him to regain consciousness. That event didn't occur for several hours. While they waited, the three friends ate dried venison and sampled wine.

At last, Strong Hand stirred. Jean Baptiste pulled his head up by the scalplock.

"So, you are awake at last. We began to worry that you had ignored the invitation of our new friend, and would not put in an appearance tonight. But, in the end, you did not disappoint us. Yes, I remember you from the fight on the Ottawa, though something looks different about you. Do you recognize him, Rene?"

"Yes, I believe so. I thought we had you the first time you were betrayed into our hands, but this time we will be able to give you more personal attention."

"Sleep well and think about your predicament," said Jean Baptiste. "We will cover you with blankets so that you do not freeze during the night. My friends and I are tired and go now to get our rest, so that we will be strong when we work on you tomorrow. I know the Iroquois respect a man who remains silent under torture. I doubt that you will, but it does not matter because at this time of year few people frequent this area. You may scream as loudly as you wish, but you will suffer for your attacks on my family. We go now to pay the man who summoned you to your doom, the friend of Monsieur Blackthorne."

With that the three Frenchmen left the Iroquois, locking the door to the storehouse as they departed. They started back to the inn.

"I figure it will take him about two hours to work his way out of those bonds, then another hour or two to break out of the storehouse," said Dufort. "Whoever the spy is could be in for an interesting day tomorrow. Do you think the man we're looking for is Jullien Rivole?"

"If it is, the man is the best actor I've ever seen," said La Pointe. "His mind seems totally fixed on the vegetable seller in the market. The wench deigned to speak to him last week, and it's all he's been able to talk about since. I have to think we're interested in someone else."

"By the way, what did you mean when you said 'I thought we had you the first time you were betrayed into our hands?'" asked the cadet.

"Just a shot in the dark," responded La Pointe. "He doesn't know our ambush on the Ottawa was a chance event. Since we are trying to shake his confidence in our spy, I thought I'd make him think the spy had double-crossed him before as well."

The next morning, the three returned to the storehouse and found it empty. Strong Hand had broken his bonds and the weakened section of wall, as they had planned.

"Etienne and I will repair the damage here, Rene. Keep your pistols handy and return to the office, in case Strong Hand decides to pay a visit to any of the employees. I have to finalize the sale of some late arriving furs to Jacques Delisle here in Lachine. Etienne and I will join you in the office late this afternoon, and we will await events."

As Rene trudged back to Montreal in the cold, he reviewed the facts over and over in his mind. Strong Hand was not particularly adept at hiding his emotions. The lies they had told him obviously had the desired effect; rage at his alleged betrayal was written all over his features. Rene had to believe Strong Hand would waste little time looking for his betrayer. But who was the man both they and the Indian were after? Now that he was well acquainted with the young lad, Rene was confident that Jullien was innocent. But if not him, then who?

Except for the Fox attack on the Wisconsin River, all the attacks on the Joubert convoys had followed a pattern. All had occurred in the vicinity of the Thousand Islands of the St. Lawrence, or along the Ottawa River.

For that reason, Jean Baptiste and he had doubted that the Fox attack was part of the conspiracy. Now, for lack of anything better to do to keep his mind off the cold, Rene theorized that the Fox attack was coordinated by the same man who initiated the others. If so, who would have been in a position to provide information to the Fox as well as the Iroquois? As soon as he posed the question in this way, the answer occurred to him. He would test his theory as soon as he got back to the office.

Gilles Guyotte was a very worried man. Ever since Monday, when he saw Bayaux the locksmith in the office, he'd been living a nightmare. If only he hadn't gotten so drunk that night two years before. When it was obvious that the cards were running against him, he would have been smart enough to quit rather than increase his bets to try to recoup his losses. That damned Englishman Cutler did a wonderful job putting him in a hopeless financial situation. In the morning, when his head cleared, Guyotte was confronted with the news that he owed Cutler almost thirty-four thousand livres. He'd never be able to pay that amount, and Cutler wasn't interested in waiting for his money.

He'd pleaded with the Englishman, and finally the man said there were a few favors Guyotte could do that would not only make Cutler more patient, but would actually reduce the amount of the debt. That's when it all started. After a time, Guyotte realized that he had probably been cheated in the card game, but by then it was too late. Several attacks on Joubert convoys had been made. Men had been killed. There was no going back.

He knew the Jouberts were looking for Strong

Hand. If they found him and made him talk, Gilles was doomed. He dared do nothing to the Indian. The scarred savage terrified him. If he tried to kill the Indian and failed, he did not want to think about the horrors he would experience in turn. When he saw Bayaux on Monday, he thought he would faint. Certainly it was no coincidence that the man who gave Strong Hand his instructions was here in the office, regardless what La Pointe said. He thought to escape, but it was too late in the year to sail out of the St. Lawrence. He realized he was no coureur de bois. If we wandered out into the woods at this time of year, all that would remain of him in the spring would be a few scattered bones. Guyotte was trapped, knowing disaster was approaching and unable to extricate himself.

Then this morning, the traitor received a glimmer of hope. He lived on the far northern edge of Montreal, with few close neighbors. A Mohawk entered his home before dawn and told him that a party of English and Iroquois was gathering at a meeting place Guyotte knew near Sorel. They would stay out of sight during the day, but wanted Guyotte to meet them that night, four hours after dark, or as soon thereafter as he could make it. Ordinarily, he would have been frightened to cross the river at this time of year, but now he embraced the opportunity. Though risky, it was still possible to navigate the St. Lawrence by bateau. He'd leave work early. The Mohawk he talked to this morning said two of his kinsmen had accompanied him to the Island of Montreal. They had a bateau hidden and would ferry him to the south shore. Snowshoes had been made and could be used if necessary to reach the rendezvous point.

Guyotte didn't know what the English wanted, and

he didn't really care. All he knew was that this was his only chance to escape. Cutler was undoubtedly at Sorel. He'd explain the situation, tell Cutler that the game was up. The Jouberts were closing in on him and would undoubtedly catch their traitor before the spring convoys left Montreal. His usefulness as a spy was at an end. He had to return with Cutler and the others to the colony of New York.

Guyotte decided to make a token appearance at the office. He'd brought one of the ledgers home to work on last night, and didn't want anyone from the office showing up on his doorstep looking for it. He'd bring the ledger back, work for a short while, then complain of illness and go home. He doubted anyone would question that he was sick; due to worry and lack of sleep, he looked like hell.

Gilles Guyotte was mentally reviewing which of his worldly goods he should bring to English territory when the office door opened, and Rene La Pointe appeared.

"Greetings everyone. Gilles, did you finish the Delisle ledger?"

"Yes, I've got it right here."

"Excellent. Would you bring it to my desk please? I had one or two questions I wanted to ask."

Gilles brought the ledger and his chair to Rene's desk, and made himself comfortable. Rene began reviewing the figures, looked at the same column for quite some time, then pushed the ledger away and turned to Guyotte.

"I can't concentrate. I didn't get any sleep at all last night. But the loss of sleep was rewarded. You know about the attacks on our convoys. We had determined that the locksmith shop was being used to pass messages from a spy in our midst to a Caughnawaga named Strong Hand. So we planted a message of our own which resulted in our catching the bastard last night."

Guyotte tried to appear calm while he fought feelings of imminent doom. *Was there anything nearby that he could use as a weapon?* "Really? That is certainly good news."

"But he escaped before we could get him to talk."

Waves of relief washed over Gilles Guyotte.

"Actually, that's not quite true. We allowed him to escape, figuring that his courage would be equal to the occasion and he could not be compelled to talk. However, while he was in our power, we convinced him that our spy had betrayed him. I've never seen anyone in such a rage."

Guyotte became so nauseous he thought he would vomit on La Pointe's desk.

"What is wrong Gilles? You don't look well at all."

"I haven't slept in several nights and my stomach is very upset. I only came to work today because I know how urgently we need to reconcile the Delisle account. In fact, I feel much worse now than I did when I arrived this morning. I'd better go home immediately and try to get some rest." *I'd better go home immediately and get my ass to Sorel as quick as possible before I run into that homicidal Caughnawaga. He'll kill me before I have a chance to explain that I had nothing to do with his getting caught.*

Gilles quickly donned his capote, tuque and mittens, and for a sick man, left the premises with admirable dispatch.

## CHAPTER 31

L a Pointe realized he had made a tactical error as soon as Guyotte left. Though he was certain that Gilles was the man they had been seeking, he had no real proof. What made him suspect Gilles was that he remembered that Guyotte had been at Michilimackinac visiting his brother Claude when the convoy left for Sioux country last spring. Gilles had arrived in the company of a friendly Abenaki along with a shipment of supplies from Detroit. La Pointe theorized that the Abenaki had been used to warn the Fox of their approach and thus precipitate the ambush.

Rene guessed that the spy would try to run, an action that would seal his guilt, but with Etienne and Jean Baptiste still at Lachine, pursuit could be a tricky business. With no other option, he told Denis Labonte and Jullien Rivole, the other clerks in the office, about his suspicions.

"Denis, I need you to go to Lachine immediately and find Jean Baptiste and Etienne. They should be at Jacques Delisle's storehouse. I assume Gilles is heading home to pack for a long trip. Do you know the way there?"

"Yes."

"Good.  Bring them to Guyotte's home as quickly as possible.  Jullien, I'll need you to come with me.  We'll keep an eye on his house.  If he starts to run, we'll take him."

"Take him how?  I'm not a soldier.  I'm afraid I handle a pen much better than a sword."

"Don't worry.  I've got a couple of spare pistols stashed here in the office.  You can use them.  I'll show you all you need to know as we're walking.  Let's hurry gentlemen.  We don't want to lose Gilles."

"There are quite a few pairs of snowshoes in the back," Denis mentioned.  "Maybe we should each take a pair in case the weather gets bad."

"Good idea," said La Pointe.  "Let's see.  I'm glad that Monsieur Joubert keeps weapons stored in the office.  Probably the result of all the Iroquois trouble in the past.  I'll take this musket and a pistol.  Here's powder and shot.  What a happy coincidence that I brought my Shawnee war club to the office to show my coworkers, and have not yet brought it back to Hawk's Nest.  Jullien, the pistols I mentioned are in my right hand desk drawer.  Can you get the snowshoes too?  Thanks."

Rene and Jullien hurried north along the Rue Saint-Paul, while Denis started in the opposite direction.  As they progressed, La Pointe made sure his companion's weapons were properly loaded, and that he had at least a vague idea how to fire them.  In a short while, they neared the north end of Montreal.  What buildings existed were widely spaced.  Relatively few people were visible at the moment.  Rene shielded his eyes from the glare of the sun on the snow.  Far in front he could see a solitary figure moving quickly in the direction of Guyotte's house. The figure was too far away to recognize, but he assumed it was Gilles.

"Let's pick up the pace a bit. I want to get closer."

In another quarter of an hour, their quarry reached its destination. It was Guyotte's house. As Gilles disappeared inside, Rene looked for good observation points. He found two that enabled them to see both entrances. He stationed Jullien in a little stand of trees that afforded a view of the rear entrance. Rene was about to move to a spot a short distance to the left, when Jullien said, "When I took this job, no mention was made that we were required to shoot fellow employees from time to time."

"Try to view this more positively. Once this disagreeable business with Gilles is over, you will be a more senior member of the firm."

Rene found a spot behind some shrubs that not only provided a good view of the front entrance, but also shielded him from the wind. He squatted down and prepared to wait. He hoped the wait was considerable, because that would give Etienne and Jean Baptiste a chance to rejoin him.

In that he was disappointed. After only a very short time, he heard a pebble land nearby and looked toward Jullien. The clerk was waving frantically. Rene kept low and moved to the other man's position.

"Gilles is leaving! And he's not alone."

Rene peered around the large maple tree in front of him and saw Gilles Guyotte leaving his house, accompanied by three Indians who appeared to be Mohawks. The four set off at once toward the river, which Rene knew was very near.

"Don't worry Jullien. I don't plan to start a war. In fact, I'm as surprised as you are about the Mohawks. Gilles and the others look to be carrying his spare clothes and some of his possessions. The first Indian has a kettle, and another has a keg of brandy. Looks like he's not planning to return anytime soon."

"What do we do?"

"I'm going to leave you here to watch for Jean Baptiste and Etienne. Then I'm going to follow Gilles. It looks like they are headed for the river, and probably will cross to the south bank of the St. Lawrence. Where they are going from there I don't know. Fortunately their trail, and also my trail, should be easy to follow because of the new snow. When Jean Baptiste and Etienne arrive, tell them what happened and send them after me."

Rene then left the relieved Jullien Rivole, and set off after the spy. Jullien wished him well and gave thanks that his part in this drama was nearly at an end. He wanted to wed the lovely Henriette, have ten children and die in bed of old age. Being riddled by Iroquois arrows held little appeal for him.

La Pointe reached the river after a short march and saw his quarry out on the water, angling toward the far bank. They appeared to be in a bateau. How could he follow?

This part of the island was lightly populated, but there were a few people. They must have boats of some kind. He searched up and downstream for a thousand paces, finding only an old bateau that he couldn't possibly handle himself. He began to feel panic; he didn't want Gilles to get too big a start.

Then, from the corner of his eye, he saw something that seemed out of place. Whatever the object was, it had been covered with brush. The brush had been disturbed by the wind, and the concealed object partially exposed. It was a canoe! He didn't know if the seams needed caulking; if they did, he did not possess the repair kit anyway. He would just launch the vessel and take his chances. He walked out on the ice near the riverbank, keeping the canoe on his shoulder. When he reached the edge of the ice, he waded ten paces in the freezing water, still keeping the vessel aloft, until he was sure the water was free of floating ice that would threaten the fragile skin of the canoe.

Rene started across, the current causing him to move diagonally. When he was halfway, his progress was observed from the island. Observed by one eye only, for the man's other eye was covered by a patch.

Jean Baptiste had concluded his business with Jacques Delisle and he and Etienne were halfway to Montreal when they encountered a panting Denis Labonte approaching from town. He told them about Gilles.

"We'd better hurry before Rene does something crazy," said Jean Baptiste. He instructed Labonte to return to the office at his own pace, and to apprise his father or brothers of the situation if they came by. He and Etienne moved at top speed to the office, where they picked up extra powder and shot, as well as snowshoes. "I know where friend Guyotte lives. Follow me."

They moved at a trot toward Guyotte's house, the stout Dufort doing the best he could. When they drew near, Jean Baptiste slowed the pace. Then they stopped and the cadet peered through some bushes at the house. Everything was quiet. Then there was movement off to the right. A man approached. Jullien. They uncocked their weapons.

"Gilles and three Mohawks left and headed for the river shortly after we arrived. Rene followed them. Less than an hour later I saw some movement near the house and thought it must be you. I almost left my concealment and called out when a man came into view. I nearly wet my pants when I saw who it was. It was the Indian with the eye patch you've been looking for. If he'd emerged a few seconds later, I'd have already called out, and he'd probably be roasting me right now."

"Where did he go?" asked Dufort.

"He went the same way everyone else had gone."

"How long ago was that?"

"About two hours."

"All right, Jullien. Thank you for your help. Please go back to the office. Denis is there. If my father and my brothers are still ignorant of events, send a message to Hawk's Nest. Come on Etienne. We've got time to make up."


On the south side of the river, Rene was having no difficulty following Gilles Guyotte. The trail of the four men was plain in the fresh snow. They were headed northeast, toward Sorel. He had pushed very hard to close the gap, and he guessed he was no more than a quarter hour behind them. He was helped by the fact that his quarry gave any French habitations a wide berth, while he continued along the riverbank. He was even able to make a quick stop at one of the farmhouses, picking up bread, cheese and a little wine.

He was actually enjoying himself; the snow had stopped and while the air was cold, the wind was bearable. His only regret was that he had not waited until Jean Baptiste and Etienne had returned to the office before he had his talk with Gilles. If he had, the three of them would be tracking the man now, or perhaps they would have taken him at his home, Mohawks or not. No sense worrying about that now. Besides, he was sure his friends would be along soon.

Jean Baptiste and Etienne were closing the gap as quickly as they could. They'd muscled the old bateau Rene had seen earlier across the St. Lawrence. As soon as they hit the far bank, they headed northeast in pursuit of their friend. They were sure Rene knew nothing of Strong Hand being on the trail also. At first, they were afraid the Caughnawaga would catch their friend and kill him before they could intercede, but it appeared that the Indian was content to follow Rene, at least for the moment.

Robert Whittington was not pleased. Normally Jacob Cutler would be in charge of an expedition like this. Cutler had in fact been in charge when they left Albany. It had been Cutler, Tiny Mason, himself and twenty-six Mohawks. He and Cutler had met with Thomas Blackthorne before they left Albany, and gotten their final instructions for the destruction of the Jouberts. The Iroquois were armed with weapons bearing Fox markings. Though unhappy about being forced out into the cold, Whittington didn't think the planned attack would be difficult. True, he had never seen Hawk's Nest, but it was Cutler's responsibility to work out the details. As usual, he and Tiny would tag along, able to concentrate their energies on emptying the keg of rum they'd brought.

Or so he had thought. Two days after leaving Albany Cutler slipped on some ice, fell, and broke his leg. Never a jolly companion, Cutler had been especially morose on this trip. In fact, his spirits seemed to improve after he was hurt and he realized he would be going back to Albany. They made a sled for him and he departed in the company of two Mohawks, who took the part of the sled dogs they didn't have.

That meant Whittington was in charge. He'd never been in charge of anything before, and suddenly the projected attack on Hawk's Nest seemed more challenging than it had previously. They trudged north, past Lake Saint Sacrement and Lake Champlain, finally reaching the south end of the Richelieu River. Twice they were caught in howling snowstorms. If he'd had any choice in the matter, Whittington would have turned back. But, he did not relish the thought of facing Mr. Blackthorne, trying to explain the expedition's failure by pointing out that it was cold outside. They had to be more careful now, because the French had built a number of forts on the Richelieu. Luckily, the Mohawks knew the location of these obstacles, and they were able to bypass them.

Finally, they reached their initial destination, a concealed vale in the woods southwest of the French town of Sorel. By this time, Whittington knew he needed assistance with the planning phase of the attack. Talking to Tiny had been as helpful as holding a discussion with a bag of musket balls. He'd send for Guyotte. He had undoubtedly visited Hawk's Nest many times, and could provide answers to his many questions. So, he sent three of the Mohawks to fetch him. He should be arriving any time now.

Gilles Guyotte was exhausted. He had been a clerk for too may years. Walking all these hours on snowshoes was too much for him. He knew they were near the meeting place because they had left the river and struck inland. He wanted to reach the English camp, get something to eat, and sleep for about two days. He refused to think about the number of days that it would take to walk to Albany. If he thought about that, he'd probably just sit down where he was and never move.

He'd been warned about loud noises. The French kept troops at Sorel, and they were close enough to hear a musket shot. Ahead, he thought he saw a few flickers of light in a small valley they were entering. Night had fallen, and the moon was bright. He could see figures moving against the background of snow. His Mohawk companions, who had barely spoken to him on the entire trip, did not seem alarmed, so he assumed they were among friends.

Rene was only five hundred paces behind Guyotte's party. He saw the small campfires and the movement in the vale as well. He decided to get close enough to hear what was happening.

Strong Hand wasn't sure what he should do, but was sure he would act very soon. He knew he would kill Guyotte at his first opportunity. He had only spared the man who had betrayed him this long because of his Mohawk escort. He did not want trouble with his kinsmen, and thought he might have a chance to catch the Frenchman alone. Now that Guyotte had reached this camp, that possibility was lost. Patience was not a virtue Strong Hand possessed in large measure. His rage was building again and sought release.

He should have killed the Frenchman following Guyotte when he first saw him. Strong Hand had not understood what was happening, and decided to watch awhile as he followed both Guyotte and the second Frenchman. He still didn't understand the situation, but the second Frenchman got so close to Guyotte's party that Strong Hand had to spare him as well for fear that Guyotte's escort would hear something if he tried to kill the man. It was especially galling because he had just realized that this was the Frenchman who threw the bomb that disfigured him.

Now he didn't care what was happening. He would have his revenge without further delay. Guyotte was with the English, who had undoubtedly instigated his betrayal. He couldn't count on the Mohawks in the little valley either. Maybe they had been completely won over by English rum. He had to get closer to get a clear shot at Guyotte. Then he'd finish the other Frenchman and escape.


Robert Whittington was not averse to having a little food and drink. When Gilles Guyotte arrived, he looked too tired to talk. Maybe some venison and rum would perk him up. Tiny was always enthusiastic about eating, and immediately began slicing the dried venison.

Guyotte was surprised when he learned of the proposed attack on Hawk's Nest. Upon reflection, if the attack was a complete success, it would benefit him greatly. If all the Jouberts were killed (along with Etienne Dufort and Rene La Pointe), he might not have to flee New France after all. When Gilles finished his rum, he felt much better. Tiny stoked the fire a bit so that the Frenchman could prepare a map of the Joubert residence.

"I'll do my best on this drawing. I'm trying to remember the other buildings in the vicin...."

The sound of the shot and the impact of the ball were simultaneous. The shot struck the back of Guyotte's head, killed him instantly, and pitched him into the campfire. Instantly, all was pandemonium.

Rene jumped at the shot, wondering what had happened. He looked at the spot where he thought the shot had originated, and saw movement. The movement was in his direction. In fact, whoever was approaching had broken into a run, and continued to head right at him. Rene cocked his musket and took aim, bracing the weapon against a tree. *Who was that? Friend or foe?* He still couldn't identify the man, but whoever it was, he dropped his musket and pulled a hatchet from his belt, throwing it at Rene in one smooth motion. The Frenchman fired, the ball striking the attacker in the center of the chest.

"Who the hell is doing all the shooting?" yelled Whittington. "This place will be crawling with Frenchmen in no time."

"Over there!" yelled Tiny. "I saw a musket flash over there."

The two Englishmen and their Indian allies had snatched up their weapons, not knowing from what quarter the danger lay. No more shots were fired.

"I know there's one behind that tree," said Tiny Mason. "I'm pretty sure I saw him drop someone else. Maybe they are the only two."

"And maybe there's fifty more waiting for us to stick our heads up," said Whittington. "But we can't waste time. Those shots will bring the French from Sorel. Go get the bastard behind the tree, and let's get out of here."

Rene La Pointe knew the game was up. Strong Hand's hatchet was buried in his thigh. The Mohawks would catch him in the first fifty paces if he tried to run. He could see them coming for him, indistinct shadows against the snow. He unstrapped the great war club from his back, drew his pistol, and stepped out from behind the tree.

## CHAPTER 32

"Oh God!" exclaimed Jean Baptiste as he heard the first two shots. He increased his pace, leaving Dufort behind.

"Go ahead!" he heard Dufort yell. "I'll be along as soon as I can."

Then there were more shots, maybe a half dozen this time. Jean Baptiste fired his musket in the air to let Rene know that help was on the way. Dufort did the same.

Jean Baptiste frantically increased his pace again, practically running on the snowshoes. The firing sounded close. He was sure he would be there in a few minutes. *Hold on for another few minutes.*

Jean Baptiste banished all negative thoughts and concentrated on attaining maximum speed. He knew what he was doing was foolhardy. Based on the number of shots fired, Rene was probably contending with Strong Hand, Guyotte and the three Mohawks. The cadet had no idea what the tactical situation was; unfortunately, there was no time to worry about that. He would go in making as much noise as possible, hoping to throw the Iroquois on the defensive until he could save his friend. He intended to have a stern talk with Rene when this was over, concerning the virtues of acting with more caution in the future. La Pointe should have waited at Guyotte's house until the three...

Jean Baptiste was too late. He burst into a small clearing in the trees, and saw a number of dark shapes lying on the ground.

"Jean Baptiste, is that you?" Rene La Pointe's voice, but very weak.

"Hang on Rene. I'll be right there." Whoever had been here had left very quickly. They had not even extinguished one of their fires. Jean Baptiste snatched up a burning brand and hurried to the spot where his friend lay.

A feeling of sick horror struck his stomach like a blow. Rene lay on his back, naked. The Mohawks had not had much time to work on him, but they had made the most of it. They had blinded and castrated him. La Pointe was feebly trying to keep his intestines from spilling on the ground from the long slash across his belly. He had been wounded at least a score of times. It was a miracle that he still breathed.

"Etienne will be here in a moment," said Jean Baptiste. He could think of nothing else to say.

"They planned to attack Hawk's Nest. I heard them talk."

"Don't speak any more. Save your strength."

"It hurts."

"I know old friend. Just rest now and think about your days in North Africa. It was warm and dry, and you were on the trail of the Carthaginian gold." As he spoke, Jean Baptiste reached a decision, drew his knife from its sheath, said a silent prayer for forgiveness, and plunged the blade to the hilt into the heart of his suffering friend.

He did not know how long he held the body in his arms. After a time, he noticed that a second torch burned near the one he'd gotten from the fire. Etienne was sitting a few feet away, tears running down his cheeks.

"They treated the lad very hard," the voyageur sobbed, "but he didn't go easily."

For the first time Jean Baptiste took a good look around the clearing. Five other bodies lay still on the snow.

"Strong Hand is one of them," said Dufort. "Rene shot that bastard. From the look of the wounds on the others, I'd say he made good use of the war club training Gaspard and I gave him. Guyotte is lying over there with his brains blown out."

"Help me get Rene dressed," said Jean Baptiste. "All the commotion should bring troops from Sorel. I don't want others to see him like this." So they dressed their friend, covering most of his many wounds. Etienne found a bearskin that had been abandoned in the hasty flight of the Iroquois, and they wrapped La Pointe's body in it.

"I'm going after them," Jean Baptiste announced after a period of thought. "Rene saved me once from an impossible situation, but I was too late to save him. I can't change that, but I will kill the men that did this."

"From all the tracks, I'd say there are at least twenty of them. How will you know which ones to go after?"

"I'm going to kill all of them." The young cadet said the words quietly, but without a trace of uncertainty.

"I intend to be with you." Dufort had never seen a look like the one on Jean Baptiste's face. Rage, sorrow and merciless determination were all evident.

"No Etienne. I'll be moving too fast for you to keep up. The patrol from Sorel should be here soon. You can follow when it arrives. I want you to make sure the wolves don't get Rene's body. I'd like to borrow that meat cleaver you call a knife, and I see that Rene's war club is still here. I'll put that to further use."

"I'll be a short distance behind you. Be alive when I get there."


Robert Whittington was in a panic. To hell with the attack on the Jouberts! He was getting back to Albany while it was still possible. French troops were sure to have heard all the shooting, and they would put their Indians on the scent directly. Sure, Blackthorne would be enraged, but whatever he would do was much better than what the French Indians would dream up if Whittington and his party were caught. He'd enjoyed watching the Indians carve up the Frenchman, and he had even participated a bit, but he had no interest in being on the receiving end of that kind of abuse. He was near the front of the mob scrambling south. Where was Tiny? It was probably best that he didn't know. Tiny didn't move well on snowshoes, and Whittington would not be slowed down for any reason. Then he heard a shot coming from the rear. Then another. The French! Whittington hoped the men in the rear put up a good fight, so that he had a chance to get away.


The cadet had been having no difficulty following the tracks in the snow. No attempt at concealment was made. The pursued were moving as quickly as they could, frequently abandoning equipment not thought absolutely essential along the trail.

Jean Baptiste gave no thought to strategy or tactics. Nor did he consider his own safety. These weren't men in front of him. They were animals. Who but animals would inflict such pain and mutilation on a helpless foe? Now they would see what would happen when the foe was not so helpless. When he caught up....

He rounded a fallen tree, and saw two Mohawks, not twenty paces away. He shot the one on the left, an older warrior with much gray hair in his scalplock, through the head. The other warrior fired too quickly and missed. Jean Baptiste dropped his musket, drew Dufort's knife, and closed with the surviving man. The warrior drew his hatchet, but Jean Baptiste grabbed the Mohawk's wrist before the blow could fall. He drove Dufort's blade into the Indian's stomach and ripped upward. A howl of agony escaped from his throat, and he fell mortally wounded.

The cadet only slowed long enough to retrieve his musket, then set off again at top speed. Tiny Mason was only yards ahead, struggling forward on his snowshoes. Two more Iroquois were a slight distance in front of the big man. Mason had heard the death cry of the Mohawk, and fearfully turned to see how close the pursuers were.

When he saw Jean Baptiste step into view, alone, a smile crossed his lips. Even if they were running, he would at least have the pleasure of killing this boy. He knew he didn't have much time, but perhaps enough to inflict wounds that would not kill immediately, like on the other Frenchman. Tiny drew his hatchet and knife, and was pleased when the Frenchman dropped his musket.

Tiny Mason had killed many men, sometimes even in fair fights. Because of his size, opponents usually were on the defensive at first, trying to figure a way to attack the behemoth. Tiny would often goad his adversaries into being more aggressive, to get them within reach of his massive arms.

"Well, little man, if I had known...." Even Tiny's limited intellect suddenly realized that no prodding was necessary. The young Frenchman unslung the great war club from his back, and strode purposefully forward. In his last moments, Tiny Mason realized that he was seeing the face of death.

When still several strides away, Jean Baptiste gripped the war club in both hands and aimed a mighty overhand blow at the giant. Mason raised his hatchet to block the stroke, but the war club sheared through the hatchet handle and the steel spike buried itself to the hilt in the big man's forehead. He fell backward without a sound, the weapon still attached to his head.

The two Mohawks had watched this brief encounter, and terror gripped even their stout hearts. Everyone thought the giant was invincible. That this boy could kill him with a single blow was incredible. They turned to flee, but Jean Baptiste pulled his pistols and shot both of them. One died instantly, but the other was only shot through the elbow. He bounded forward, telling and retelling the tale of Tiny's death to his confederates, spreading the fear to all who heard.

Jean Baptiste paused long enough to reload his firearms, then forged ahead. Fifty paces further down the trail, a Mohawk's thirst for glory overcame his anxiety. If he could kill the man who vanquished the Englishman Mason, he would gain the respect of all around the council fire. Of course, maybe this Frenchman was not a man at all, but some type of spirit in human form.

Possibly he could not be killed. Suddenly torn by indecision, the warrior's reverie was interrupted by the Frenchman's sudden appearance. The Mohawk fired, and the ball tore a chunk from Jean Baptiste's thigh. He was on top of the frightened warrior an instant later, and brained him with his musket butt.

The chase continued for several more hours. The cadet's disdain for his personal well being saved him a number of times. Knowing how a normal person would react, the experienced Mohawk warriors realized too late that they were not dealing with a normal person. By the time that realization became evident, the avenger was among them, dealing death with either hand.

Still, the Mohawks were renowned warriors for a reason, and they fought with skill despite their fear. Jean Baptiste was wounded six times, the most serious being a pistol shot in his side. Though he felt no pain, the loss of blood began to affect his vitality. He staggered forward, his desire to kill undiminished.

Finally, he saw only one man still before him. An Englishman. He increased his speed again.

Robert Whittington was near exhaustion. He could hardly believe what he had heard from several of the Mohawks, most recently from one with a bad wound near his elbow, who nonetheless had outdistanced the Englishman in the race south. The Indians had said that a single Frenchman was causing all the damage. He'd brained Tiny and had been slaughtering the Mohawks all the way from Sorel. The Indians had shot him many times but he was unaffected. He kept moving forward and killing. *The Mohawks must be crazy, or maybe their aim is off because we were too generous with their rum ration. Whatever the reason, I'm not going to let whatever is chasing us get close enough to kill me too.* For reassurance, Robert Whittington decided to slow a bit and steal a peek over his shoulder. He screamed when he saw the Frenchman. His pursuer was covered with blood, but moved relentlessly forward. Whittington threw his musket away to increase his speed.

Jean Baptiste was getting delirious. Maybe he would kill just this one more, and then he would rest awhile. He would find whoever was hiding in the woods after he'd gotten his strength back. He was tired. Very, very tired. He was close to his quarry now. The cadet dropped his musket, drew Dufort's knife, stopped and carefully measured the throw. He drew his arm back and let fly. Then he collapsed, and saw only darkness.

## CHAPTER 33

Kiala felt better than he had in many months. The snow and wind had arrived in full fury. Winter was usually to be feared, because food was often scarce. In that regard, this winter promised to be worse than most. During the spring and summer, traditional activities, such as the planting and harvesting of corn, pumpkins, beans and squash, had been greatly disrupted by the tremendous casualties suffered by the Fox the previous year, and by the real possibility that additional attacks were forthcoming. The few warriors available did less hunting than usual, because tribal defense was the top priority. The many diplomatic missions to neighboring tribes further diminished the time spent on food gathering.

These missions had been a success, at least from the standpoint that many Fox prisoners, men, women and children, had been returned to their homeland along the Wisconsin River. Their return, however, further aggravated the scarce food situation. Kiala had kept the tribe concentrated as much as possible until recently, in order to keep the warriors together. He had men watching the nearest French posts, but had withdrawn them when autumn was well advanced and there was no sign of hostile activity. These scouts and other available men and boys had been set to work hunting, but the game caught had not kept pace with the additional mouths to feed. Just two days ago, five more ex-prisoners had arrived in camp. The Sacs living near Green Bay had freed these five, a man, two women and two children.

On the heels of these new arrivals, the snow had come. Kiala felt that at long last he could relax a bit. This first big storm of the season had been very severe, and that fact elated the Fox leader. He viewed the snow as protection for his wounded tribe. Winter campaigns were somewhat rare. If the French had not come when the weather was good, why would they come now, when the weather alone put their lives at risk? Yesterday, he began dispersing the tribe so that the hunters could operate in areas where the game had not been depleted. Kicking Bear had recently returned from Montreal with Onontio's promise that there would be peace, at least until next summer. Kiala didn't know if he entirely believed this message, but it was reassuring nonetheless. Let the people relax and gather their strength. In the spring he would renew his attempts to form an alliance with the Kickapoo, Mascouten and Sacs.

With the wind whistling past his lodge, Kiala was able to spend time doing what he loved, teaching the young about the history of their people. Six children, including the two just returned by the Sacs, were seated in front of him. The war chief related to this young audience how the manitou Wisaka had created the earth and peopled it with the Fox tribe. These were molded from red clay; hence the name by which they knew themselves, Mesquakie, or the people of the red earth.

Wisaka and his brother Kiyapatha had been the most powerful of the manitous, but the lesser beings had conspired against them and killed Kiyapatha. Wisaka fought against the killers and was eventually victorious, banishing the defeated into the heavens or underground. Some of the defeated manitous were changed into Thunderers, guardians of the tribe who rode the south wind.

The children paid rapt attention as Kiala changed the subject to the more recent history of the tribe. On this occasion he discussed the great battle fought almost twenty years before at Detroit. Invited by the French to settle in the region, the Fox had antagonized other tribes living in the vicinity, notably the Ottawa and the Hurons. Trouble soon erupted and the Fox were besieged inside their fortified village by a host of Frenchmen and allied tribes. The Fox defense was led by the legendary chieftain Pemoussa, who at one point lectured his enemies, assuring them that the Fox people were immortal and could never be defeated, no matter how great the odds. In the end the Fox lost many men, women and children, but the tribe had survived as Pemoussa said it would. The tribe had survived then and it would survive now, Kiala emphasized, even though the odds once more were great.

The chief patiently answered the children's questions. After they left, he sat in silence, then absent-mindedly ate some venison stew and walnuts. It was the first food he had tasted in three days. Wolf, the lad whose capture by the French the previous summer had precipitated the running fight in the woods, stopped by the chief's lodge to let Kiala know that he and two of his companions were heading a day's march to the southeast in search of beaver.

"I know the location of a series of ponds where beaver have been plentiful for several years."

"Good," replied Kiala. "We need food, but we also need furs to trade. The Englishman said he would provide guns, powder, blankets or whatever we needed at the Oswego trading post. I doubt that he plans to give them to us, however, so we need as many beaver skins as we can get. Good hunting."

After Wolf departed, Kiala decided to take a short nap. All the sleep he had lost in recent months had taken its toll. He was exhausted. But now, with Wisaka covering his people with a blanket of snow, he felt safe enough to relax his guard.

La Forest was disgusted. The Huron war chief from Detroit had expected to recruit many allies during his march from Detroit to Fox country. Thanks to Kiala's diplomatic efforts, these expectations had not been realized. The Potawatomi living near Fort St. Joseph refused support, saying most of their warriors had already dispersed to their winter hunting camps. By the time the Chicago portage was reached, the weather had grown cold and blustery. A permanent winter camp was built, and several sick warriors, along with a man who had been injured by the accidental discharge of a musket, were left there. A nearby Kickapoo village refused help, also because the tribe had already scattered for the winter. Finally, a few Mascoutens were coerced into acting as guides, but their help was half-hearted at best, and they soon abandoned the expedition to its own devices.

Nearing the Wisconsin River at last, the Hurons

and Iroquois were struck by a blizzard that created giant drifts of snow. The flakes became stinging missiles as they were propelled by the howling wind. Fingers and toes froze and many of the warriors became discouraged and turned back to the winter camp at the Chicago portage. La Forest was not deterred. With the cream of his force still intact, forty hearty Hurons and thirty Iroquois, all equipped with snowshoes, he forged ahead to avenge his long dead brother.

Wolf and his two companions were moving to the southeast on snowshoes. Progress was slow due to the amount of snow that had fallen in the last two days. The wind had diminished, so although it was still snowing, it was falling in the form of gentle flakes. It was cold, but not as bad as it had been the day before. They had only been on the march for a very short while; in an hour or so, they would be warmed by their exertion. Wolf looked forward to the beaver hunt and had remembered to bring a long handled axe with which they could break into the beavers' stout lodges.

As they emerged from the woods onto a patch of prairie, Wolf spied some deer tracks leading east across the open ground. The food shortage in camp justified delaying the beaver hunt. Examination of the tracks led to the conclusion that they were very fresh. With luck they could bag this prize, bring the carcass to camp and resume their journey with only a negligible delay.

The three boys began to follow the tracks. As they passed the bed of a frozen stream, an arrow hissed by Wolf's face. He turned to the right and saw a dozen Hurons and Iroquois emerging from the depression where the frozen stream lay. He didn't have much time to look, but it seemed many more were still in the depression. His friends were in front of him, and had not yet seen the danger.

"Hurons! Iroquois! Hurry! We have to warn the village!"

The three boys turned and retraced their steps through the snow. They'd had little to eat in recent days, but their youth and fear for their families enabled them to overcame their fatigue, and the three were able to maintain a brisk pace back to camp.

The peaceful village was in sight very quickly. "To arms!" yelled the three boys as they neared the Fox lodges. "Huron and Iroqouis warriors are right behind us!"

Instantly, all was confusion. Mothers grabbed small children and sought what protection a lodge afforded. Warriors armed themselves as quickly as possible and set off toward the point of danger. Dogs barked, babies cried and young boys looked to their bows and arrows, anxious to aid the defense and thereby win the respect of their elders.

Kiala heard Wolf shout the alarm, and raced from his lodge, armed with musket and hatchet. The enemy was visible in the distance, no more than two hundred paces away. A few Fox warriors were a hundred paces closer to the Huron and Iroquois than Kiala, and these men began firing at the foe, seemingly with little effect. Kiala struggled through the snow to reach the front lines, realizing that he should have taken time to don snowshoes before leaving his lodge. He noticed that most of his men had similarly neglected their snowshoes, which severely hampered their mobility.

From what he could see, it appeared the Fox might

be slightly superior in numbers. Kiala knew, however, that many of his warriors were scarcely more than boys, like young Wolf and his friends. Of the remainder, not a few were well past their prime. But, thought the war chief, all of them were Fox, and that meant they would give their all in defense of their homes and families. The defenders had, for the most part, reached a clearing southeast of the village. The Fox warriors were firing ragged volleys of arrows and musket shots at the enemy. The Iroquois and Hurons were painted for war, but thus far had done little firing in return. The Iroquois who lived in the English colony of New York were friends to the Fox. Some of the Fox had even moved to the lands of the Seneca, westernmost of the Iroquois tribes. These Iroquois must be mission Indians from Montreal, concluded the Fox war chief, which would indicate that Onontio had lied when he promised at least a temporary peace. If it was to be war, thought Kiala, so be it.

The enemy moved closer, and Kiala noted that because of their snowshoes, they were a good deal more nimble than his men. Suddenly, the Hurons and Iroquois delivered a concentrated volley, reloaded, and fired again. Their marksmanship was very good; at least a score of the Fox defenders fell dead or wounded. The enemy warriors than dropped their muskets, pulled their hatchets, and bounded forward to the attack. The Fox eagerly closed with their foes.

Wolf remembered that he had the long handled axe strapped to his back that he had intended to use on the beaver hunt. He unslung the weapon, and found himself facing a Huron with long hair, the left side of whose face was painted yellow, and the right side red. The man was armed with hatchet and knife and he attempted to come to grips with Wolf, in order to negate the reach of his long handled weapon. Wolf blocked a downward stroke of the hatchet with his axe handle, jumped back to avoid a swipe of the knife, then stepped in and knocked his man down with a stroke of the axe handle to the face. The man was dazed, and this moment of inaction sealed his doom. Wolf finished him with a tremendous blow to the head, which clove him from crown to chin.

The lad looked around, and saw that his people were in trouble. Many of the warriors had eaten little or nothing for days, reserving what little food was available for the women, children or the elderly. Now the men were unable to match the vitality of their attackers. The Fox boys were eager for battle, but their skills were no match for the veteran warriors they faced. The older Fox warriors possessed the necessary skills, but lack of nourishment had eroded their strength, and they too were being overcome.

Kiala dispatched one of the Hurons with his hatchet, and had a moment to survey the field. He concluded that the day was lost, and the most that could be hoped for was to cover the retreat of their non-combatants.

"Fall back to the edge of the village! Hold there as long as possible, so our women and children can escape to the west."

The remaining Fox warriors attempted to defend their homes, but the defeat became a rout. Due to their greater mobility, a number of Hurons and Iroquois reached the town ahead of the Fox defenders. They began setting fire to the lodges, and killing anyone who tried to escape the flames, regardless of age or sex. Fox warriors tried to protect their families as they gathered a few meager possessions and hurried west into the wilderness, but the situation was soon completely out of hand. The majority of the defenders were already dead or dying. If they stayed longer, everyone would be exterminated.

"Leave the village!" ordered the war chief. "Take the people we have and head west. We can do no more for the rest."

Wolf made sure his mother was safely on her way, then resumed his place with the handful of remaining warriors guarding the rear of the column. Without food or adequate clothing, this remnant of the tribe headed toward the Mississippi, where several small bands of their countrymen resided. Hopefully the cold would not claim them all before they arrived.

Back at the smoldering Fox village, La Forest was pleased. One hundred and fifty Fox, including seventy warriors, were dead. He had captured more than one hundred and fifty more. All at the cost of only five of his men. The Fox were finished. He was sure of that. But a few had escaped, and he knew there were several small Fox villages along the Mississippi. He had a Fox chief whose right arm had been broken by a musket shot brought before him, along with six of the captured squaws. La Forest told them to find the Fox villages on the Mississippi and deliver the following message:

"Tell them the Hurons and Iroquois have just eaten up their chief village where they will remain for two days. If the Fox wish to follow us, they are free to do so, but as soon as we see them, we will begin breaking the heads of all their women and children. We will make a rampart of their dead bodies, and afterward will endeavor to pile the remainder of the nation on top of them."

The seven freed captives were found by Wolf and several other Fox scouts, and so were able to join the Foxes attempting to reach the villages on the Mississippi. Amazingly, these villages were providing shelter from the winter weather for several Frenchmen at the time Kiala and the other survivors arrived. When these Frenchmen heard what had happened, they assured Kiala that the attack on his village must have been planned in ignorance of the governor general's wishes. If the governor general had declared a truce until next summer, they were sure he would have kept his word.

Kiala wanted to believe these words were true. Otherwise, it appeared Onontio was determined to exterminate his people. Though he could have had them killed, the war chief did no harm to these Frenchmen in his power. He brought them back to his shattered village and recovered a hidden cache of furs. These furs represented all the remaining wealth of his decimated tribe. If they were to replenish stocks of weapons, tools and clothing, these furs were all they had to offer in exchange. Kiala gave these to one of the Frenchmen, a man named Dorval. Kiala asked Dorval to follow the victorious Hurons and Iroquois, and use the furs to ransom as many of the captives as possible. The man agreed, but when he caught up to the victors, he elected to keep the furs and leave the prisoners to their fate.

By the time the Hurons and Iroquois reached Detroit, they had already killed and scalped more than a third of their captives. A French officer at Detroit suggested that it would be dangerous to retain Fox prisoners, even as slaves. In response, most of the remaining prisoners were slaughtered, many of them burned to death after being subjected to the most hideous tortures. Governor General Beauharnois promoted the French officer, and personally hung medals bearing the likeness of King Louis around the necks of the chiefs who had led the winter campaign.

## CHAPTER 34

Darkness. Pain. Gradually, Jean Baptiste was able to recognize objects and people in the room. A musket hanging on the wall. On the opposite wall sunlight shone through a window. The sky was bright blue, with a few wispy white clouds. He tried to turn to the left to make himself more comfortable, but the resulting pain caused a groan to escape from his lips.

"Lad, you're awake! Thank God!" Jean Baptiste vaguely recognized Etienne Dufort's voice. "How do you feel?"

The cadet decided not to respond to that question. Other faces began to come into focus. He noticed that Maurice was holding his hand. Dominique was there as well, peering down at him with unmistakable concern on her face.

"Where am I?"

"In the commandant's house in Sorel," responded Maurice. "That was the nearest shelter from the spot where Etienne found you. He and two marines from the garrison built a rude sled and dragged you here from the woods. All of the family and many of our friends from the seigneury have been here to visit, but you have been unconscious the entire time until now. We thought for awhile that you were not going to make it."

"How long have I been here?"

"Twelve days," replied Dominique.

"And she has been here since the second day," said Maurice. "She would allow no one else to tend you. I readily endorsed the idea, knowing from first-hand experience that she is probably the best nurse on the continent."

"Thank you Dominique. It appears the Jouberts will always be in your debt."

"Your friend Etienne has scarcely left your side, even when I wished him to be gone," replied the beautiful woman. "It was as though he willed you to recover."

"I don't have very many friends," said Dufort. "I can't afford to lose two of them at the same time."

Something unpleasant had weighed on Jean Baptiste's mind since he regained consciousness, but he had been unable to focus on what it was. Dufort's words caused the horror to spring back into his mind. He sobbed.

"And what of Rene?" the cadet asked.

"We buried him at Hawk's Nest," responded Maurice. "Right next to all the family members."

"How are Jeanne and little Guy?"

"As well as can be expected," lied Maurice. In fact, La Pointe's death, occurring so soon after the death of her husband, had profoundly depressed their sister. All of the family members were worried about her. Guy was too young to really understand the implications of Rene's departure.

Jean Baptiste said nothing for a time as he solemnly reflected on the situation. Finally, he said he was tired, and drifted off to sleep.

When he awoke, Dominique and Etienne were in the room. The woman was dozing; Dufort was awake and looking at him as he opened his eyes.

"So, Etienne, did you have any trouble finding me in the woods?"

"You must be kidding. You left a trail of bodies that anyone could have followed. I counted fifteen while we were on your track, with a number of blood trails leading off to the east or west. Most of those died of their wounds or froze. I've never seen anything like it. When Sergeant Busquet and I found you, you were delirious, crawling on your belly south through the snow, mumbling about killing them all. You finally fainted from blood loss while we were bringing you back here."

"Did any of them get away?"

"Maybe a few. You made quite an impression on any survivors. After we brought you to Sorel, the sergeant and some of his men followed the blood trails of the wounded. Most were dead. They lost the tracks of a couple when a new storm began. They found one man you had disemboweled, sitting against a tree, dying and half covered with snow. He begged the marines not to let the devil get him. They asked whom he meant, and he said the man who could not be killed, the one who had destroyed them all single-handed. Never had he heard of such a thing. This could not be a man, he kept saying, but had to be some type of evil spirit."

"I guess I did go a little crazy. I don't really remember the details of what happened. Contrary to what that Mohawk thought, they were able to cause me injury. How badly am I hurt?"

"Considering the number of times you were shot, slashed and stabbed, you are in remarkable shape." This was from Dominique, who had awakened at the sound of their voices. "You lost a tremendous amount of blood, which I assume is why you were unconscious so long. You have three broken ribs, a broken left hand, a chunk of meat missing from your thigh, a musket shot in the shoulder and one in the side, and will survive with a collection of scars that any seasoned warrior would envy. But the key thing is that I believe you will survive. You have a long recovery period ahead, but when it is over, I think you will be mostly in working order."

Christmas and New Year's passed. Early in January 1732, after much urging on Jean Baptiste's part, Etienne dressed the convalescent warmly and he was placed on a dog sled. Dufort carefully packed a bearskin around his friend, thanked the marines from Sorel for their hospitality, and set off for Hawk's Nest. Jean Baptiste was completely covered except for his face, but it was exhilarating to feel the wind on his skin again. The dogs ran over the snow and ice, and Jean Baptiste looked up at the overcast sky. He was lying on his back on the sled, his head propped up, and as they sped along, he watched the flakes of snow that were falling shoot toward his face. The pain he felt when the sled hit rough patches was more than compensated for by the knowledge that he was going home.

When they arrived in mid afternoon, the Jouberts and their neighbors poured from their houses to greet him. Dufort maneuvered the sled near the front door of the main house. When the sled came to a halt, little Guy burst from the throng and put his arms around his injured uncle. They carried him into the house into a bedroom that had been prepared on the first floor.

"Let's eat!" said Jean Baptiste happily. "The marines at Sorel were most kind to me, but I needed to get back to mother's cooking. It will make me well in no time."

In the days that followed, Jean Baptiste did little except eat and sleep. When awake, members of the family took turns reading to him. Books on ancient history were his favorites, but he tended to request titles that covered Alexander the Great, the Persian or the Trojan Wars. He avoided anything that dealt with Hannibal, Carthage or the Punic Wars. He did not want to think about them, at least not yet.

On the northern outskirts of Albany, Thomas Blackthorne was helping to inventory the goods stored at his warehouse. He normally did not get involved in such menial tasks, but for the last several weeks he had slept little at night and had been unusually restless during the day. He had thought that a little physical labor might calm his nerves. He was honest enough to admit to himself that he was extremely nervous about the outcome of the attack on the Jouberts.

Ever since Jacob Cutler returned with his broken leg, Blackthorne had grave misgivings about the venture. Cutler's injury left that idiot Whittington in charge, a man only slightly more intelligent than the totally witless Tiny Mason. Adding to Blackthorne's worries was the lack of news. It had been weeks since Cutler returned to Albany. Since then, no word at all. Blackthorne was in the warehouse, repositioning several barrels of powder, when a shout from Cutler drove these somber thoughts from his mind.

"Someone is coming!" yelled Cutler.

Blackthorne emerged from the warehouse, along with two of his employees, and stared toward the north. Two men appeared to be dragging a third on a sled. As they got closer, Cutler recognized the men pulling the sled as two of the Mohawks who had gone on the expedition to Canada. One of the Indians had a heavily bandaged arm. Blackthorne motioned to the two men who had been helping him with the inventory, and they hurried to help with the sled.

The man lying on the sled was babbling incoherently as he was brought to the warehouse.

"It's Whittington," said Cutler.

"I can see that," replied Blackthorne testily. "See if you can get him to talk. Find out what happened."

Using crutches, Jacob Cutler moved closer to the sled. "Bob...Bob, it's me. Jacob. Bob, what happened to you?" Whittington looked like he was in very bad shape. Though the day was bitterly cold, the man was bathed in sweat. He had dark circles under his eyes, and kept uttering incomprehensible words and phrases. Finally, Cutler's words seemed to reach him and his eyes opened wide. At the same time he reached up and grabbed Cutler's arm.

"Jacob! Thank God you're here. Don't let him get me, Jacob. You know I've always been your friend. Just don't let him get me."

"I won't let him get you. Don't worry. Where are the rest of the men? Where's Tiny?"

"Dead. All of them are dead. Young Joubert killed them all."

"What is this nonsense?" interjected Blackthorne. "The youngest Joubert, what is his name?..."

"Jean Baptiste," said Cutler.

"Yes, Jean Baptiste. You've told me yourself. He's just a boy. How could he have killed Tiny and the others?"

"Bob, Bob! Talk to me. What happened?"

"He killed them all. Killed them all." All of a sudden the stricken man sat up, and they could see that much blood had soaked through a makeshift bandage on his back. He began deep, racking coughs. Blood then dripped from his mouth and he fell back on the sled, dead.

Cutler then questioned the two Mohawks, who were nearly as frightened as Whittington had been. The news was universally bad. The attack on the Jouberts had never occurred. The deaths of Guyotte and Strong Hand. The retreat with the lone relentless pursuer who would not die. As far as the Mohawks knew, they alone had survived.

"It's unbelievable," said Blackthorne. "The boy did all that damage?" Upon reflection, not all the news was bad. He was glad that Strong Hand was dead. That Indian was getting too unpredictable. He and Guyotte were both loose ends, people who could point to Blackthorne as the instigator of the recent trouble experienced by the Jouberts. It was better that both of them were silent. It might be better if these last two Mohawks were silent as well...

Before he could even complete the thought, that possibility was gone. Three Mohawks and two Oneidas called out as they approached the warehouse from the west. They brought beaver skins and wanted to trade for rum. The new arrivals saw the other Mohawks and an animated discussion ensued. Blackthorne cursed bad timing and ill luck under his breath. Maybe he should consider a shift of operations to a more temperate climate. Charleston perhaps.

As the weeks passed, Jean Baptiste grew stronger. Though still in pain, he forced himself to take walks, short at first, and then longer hikes through the woods. Etienne and Henri Gaultier were frequent companions on these excursions. Gradually, Jean Baptiste's stamina increased, and his muscles began functioning efficiently, though they protested the effort. Good food, plenty of rest and supportive friends and family members accomplished wonders.

Thus far, he and Jeanne had not discussed Rene. Then one day, when she was reading aloud to him about the Trojan hero Hector, he stopped her in mid-sentence.

"Jeanne," he said with tears in his eyes. "I can't tell you how sorry I am about Rene. Though my head tells me his death was not my fault, I know that there were things I could have done to prevent it. I knew how he was, reckless and without thought for his own safety. I should have thought about that and planned things differently. My concern with the sale of those furs to Jacques Delisle cost Rene his life."

"If you made a mistake brother, I know it was an honest one. You certainly wished Rene no harm. Life is hard here in Canada. In a short time, I lost my husband and another man I had also grown to love. I don't know if I want little Guy to grow up in this harsh land. If he stays, perhaps he won't live to grow up at all. Maybe we should move to France, near the Mediterranean where it is warm. Rene often spoke of the area around Marseilles. If I lived there, it would help me keep his memory alive."

"Please don't make any rash decisions. Your

family is here, and you know we all love both Guy and you. Hawk's Nest would not be the same without you."

Without further comment, Jeanne stood up and quietly exited the room.

Though the winter seemed endless that year, at last it began to loosen its grip on the St. Lawrence valley. The huge drifts of snow began to diminish under the strengthening sunlight. In places, patches of bare ground began to appear. The winds, though still strong, came from a warmer, more southerly direction. Trade goods had to be shipped to the interior posts, to be used to purchase the tribes' winter harvest of furs. Jean Baptiste decided to accompany one of the convoys to Michilimackinac.

"But you are not yet well," protested Dominique, who had delayed her move to Montreal so that she could continue as his nurse.

"I will be soon. This time I'll let Etienne do all the heavy work and I'll just relax in the canoe. Besides, my leave time is over. I have to report back."

No one in the family was enthusiastic about this decision, but Jean Baptiste felt it was his duty to return to the straits. Besides, he was confident the family business would now thrive. His father had concluded a financial arrangement with Henri that brought much needed capital into the operation. Maurice elected to work in the fur business full-time, and would run the Montreal office (conveniently located near Dominique's proposed dress shop). Louis, stationed in Montreal, vowed to devote more of his free time to the business as well.

One unusually warm morning, Daniel Joubert saw a canoe approach, as he worked near the bank of the St. Lawrence. It was an old (and probably his only) friend from Caughnawaga, Deer Hoof, along with his wife and two sons. The old man was a respected elder, and his wife was the clan mother of the Bear Clan. Daniel wondered what could have prompted this visit so early in the year, when ice was still present on the river.

"Welcome, Deer Hoof. I am pleased that you have survived another winter."

"Yes, Daniel, though I mark each passing year with less mobility and more pain."

"Come inside with your family. I'm sure we can provide some refreshment."

After a meal of smoked eel and brandy, the aged Mohawk broached the reason for his visit. "Daniel, I have heard amazing news from the south. Many wives and mothers mourn among the villages on the Mohawk. According to the tale, a single man, your son Jean Baptiste, killed many brave men with his own hand. Though many weapons were raised against him, none could do him harm. He avenged his fallen friend in a way that the Mohawks will always remember. Is this true? Those in the south now refer to your son as "the Deathless One."

"I'll let you see for yourself." Daniel found Jean Baptiste returning from a conditioning walk, accompanied by a tired Henri Gaultier.

Jean Baptiste entered the house and greeted Deer Hoof and his family.

"So it is true," remarked the aged Mohawk. "The son of Daniel still lives." The visitor seemed uneasy in the young Frenchman's presence, and soon made excuses that he and his family needed to return to Caughnawaga.

"Well," said Daniel, "it seems you will long be remembered by the Iroquois. I've never seen Deer Hoof act nervous before. I'm not sure if that's good or bad."

On a day in late April, Jean Baptiste and Etienne headed for the riverbank, to join the brigade of canoes that waited to take them to Michilimackinac. On the way, Jean Baptiste forced himself to stop at the family cemetery and say good-bye to Rene. He had avoided the spot since his friend's death, but he had already said good-bye to his living friends and family; it was only right to do the same to La Pointe. He and Dufort stood in silence for a few moments, then turned toward the waiting canoes.

Maurice was conversing with several of the voyageurs. When his brother and Dufort approached, he walked toward them and said, "I almost forgot, what do you plan to do about Hannibal's gold?"

"What can we do? Rene was the expert on the subject."

"Yes, but Rene told me that his brother Denis had a special interest in ancient geography, and his library in Marseilles had many volumes on the subject. Don't give up the search yet."

Jean Baptiste and Etienne looked at each other thoughtfully, chuckled, and headed for the canoes.

## CHAPTER 35

J ean Baptiste was happy to leave behind his sad memories, and embark on this return journey to the Great Lakes country. The days (and especially the nights) were for the most part still very cold, but the cadet was warmly dressed and as comfortable as the limited space on a canoe would allow. The bark vessels, bearing the hawk emblem of the Jouberts, made their way against the current of the St. Lawrence. When they finally emerged into Lake Ontario, they traveled along the north shore, avoiding close contact with the English at Oswego. In order to shorten the journey, the convoy utilized the Toronto carrying place that led to Georgian Bay. This route provided access to northern Lake Huron without the necessity of traversing Lake Erie. The only drawback from Jean Baptiste's perspective was that the shorter route by-passed the mighty falls at Niagara as well. Though requiring a strenuous portage, the sight of the falls would have been worth the effort.

Etienne worked hard to keep the mood light. At night he entertained the cadet and various of the voyageurs with tales of his amorous exploits. If you believed him, virtually every white woman on the continent and a sizable percentage of the Indian women as well had succumbed to his masculine charm at one time or another. He soon had Jean Baptiste and the others laughing uproariously at his stories of narrow escapes from jealous husbands and thwarted rivals. The crisp evenings passed quickly under the numberless stars. If only they did not have to eat so much pemmican.

During the first days of the trip, Jean Baptiste was little more than a spectator. Dominique had insisted that he was still far from recovered, and she made Etienne promise that the cadet would be allowed to do no hard work. As time passed, he became bored. He wanted to recover his strength as soon as possible, and he knew doing nothing would not accomplish that end.

The Toronto carrying place required an unusually long portage, and Jean Baptiste insisted that he participate. Etienne agreed, as long as the cadet carried only a single pack of trade goods and promised never to tell the formidable Dominique. Jean Baptiste found that he became easily winded and had to stop to rest more often than the others. Usually, unscheduled stops would be grounds for unmerciful derision from the hearty voyageurs, whether the target was a Joubert or not. However, these men knew of the injuries the lad had recently suffered, and appreciated his attempts to help. No catcalls were in evidence.

By the time the convoy reached the wooded shores of Georgian Bay, Jean Baptiste was still carrying a single pack during portage, but he rested no more than the others. He had also taken up a paddle for lengthy periods of time, and though the repetitive motion was painful, he felt that the exercise was benefitting his arms and shoulders. Of all his injuries, the musket shot in the left shoulder seemed the most troublesome. The first three days that he paddled extensively, it ached so fiercely afterward that he had difficulty sleeping despite his fatigue. Gradually, the injured area hurt less and grew stronger, until the only time he was reminded of it was when he lifted something awkwardly and he would experience a momentary flash of pain.

Jean Baptiste reflected on the history of the region south of Georgian Bay as they camped on the shore of that body of water. During the first half of the seventeenth century, those lands had belonged to the Huron, a numerous people who were allies of the French. The Huron had acted as middlemen in the fur trade between the French on the St. Lawrence and the Great Lakes tribes who trapped the beaver. The wealth they accumulated from this commerce attracted the jealousy of the Iroquois, who wished to play the role of middlemen themselves, and direct the trade through Albany rather than the French communities on the St. Lawrence.

By the 1640s, when the Hurons had been much weakened by exposure to smallpox, the Iroquois began a campaign of annihilation. For several years, large Iroquois war parties invaded the Huron homeland south of Georgian Bay, sparing neither the Hurons nor their Jesuit missionaries. Finally, the remnants of that once proud tribe had had enough. Some sought protection with the French at Quebec, and their descendants still lived at the Lorette mission. Others scattered to the west, some now living near the French settlement at Detroit. Their old homeland, once containing many thousands, now had few permanent residents. The only satisfaction Jean Baptiste got from this melancholy musing was the realization that the Iroquois, though victorious, had not accomplished their goal.  The Huron competition had been eliminated, but instead of the commerce falling into Iroquois hands on the way to Albany, most of the tribes continued to prefer to trade with the French.  The Ottawa and other tribes were able to assume the role of the departed Huron.  The Iroquois profited little.

The men of the convoy enjoyed a string of beautiful spring days as they paddled along the eastern, and then the northern shores of the bay.  The days were still cool in May, but they were favored by bright sunshine most of the time, and the blue sky was frequently filled with brilliant white clouds.  On several occasions, the sunsets were spectacular.  The sun changed from yellow to orange to red as it descended, suffusing the waters of the bay as well as the clouds with these various hues.  At night, they often camped on one of the numerous islands in the bay.  Late on one of those nights, as the fire burned low, Jean Baptiste began thinking like a marine cadet for the first time in many months.  Soon they would be back at the fort.  He wondered what had been happening over the winter.  Were the Fox still a menace, or had that problem been resolved?  He supposed that he would find out soon enough.

Fort Michilimackinac was in sight!  The convoy had followed the north shore of Lake Huron until they reached a spot due north of the fort.  They then headed south across the narrows.  This passage, at the point where Lake Huron met Lake Michigan, was more harrowing than they would have liked.  The narrows were somewhat more than a league wide.  It was mid-afternoon when they started across; the sky had been overcast all day, and a light rain was falling.  Then, when they were half way across, the wind picked up and it began to rain much harder.

"Brace yourself, lad," said Dufort to Jean Baptiste, who was sitting in front of him in the canoe. "The wind is up and the waves are building. The rest of the trip is going to be interesting."

As Dufort had predicted, the waves suddenly became mountainous, driven by a now howling wind from the west. The men in the convoy put every ounce of strength into their paddling. The wind and waves were pushing them off course, but they didn't care as long as they made it to shore somewhere. Jean Baptiste paddled as madly as the others. The canoe that he, Dufort and five other men occupied was last in line of the six vessels in the convoy. Though he had little opportunity to observe his surroundings, the cadet tried to keep track of the canoes ahead of them. Visibility through the wind and rain had become very poor, but Jean Baptiste was sure that two of the canoes had reached shore. Just as he was trying to locate the others, a monster wave broke over the right side of their canoe, spilling both men and cargo into the cold lake water.

Jean Baptiste was driven down deep by the force of the wave. He had had little time to prepare, not even enough to take a deep breath before the canoe capsized. He was held underwater for perhaps ten heartbeats; when he was able, he kicked to the surface, coughing out the water he had swallowed.

"Etienne!" the cadet shouted as he treaded water.

"I'm here lad," responded Dufort from behind Jean Baptiste. "I thought it might be a good idea to save the dispatch case you are supposed to give the captain."

"Did you find it?"

"Yeah, it came floating right past me.  It looks like it's all right."

They were perhaps three hundred paces from shore.  They swam slowly, conserving their energy, Jean Baptiste holding the dispatch case out of the water, and reached  the shallows without further incident.  One of the sentries at the fort had apparently seen their predicament and had sounded the alarm.  Men were running from the direction of the post.  Some of these men, along with voyageurs from the convoy who had already made shore, waded out to help Jean Baptiste and the others.

"Did everyone make it?" asked Jean Baptiste to one of the voyageurs.

"Only Adrien Demazure is missing.  The other six from your boat are safe.  The other canoes made shore safely."

As suddenly as it started, the storm began to abate.  Jean Baptiste and Etienne were among a half dozen men who took one of the Joubert canoes out to look for the missing man.  As they paddled back and forth through the still moderate rain, they recovered several bales of goods that were still afloat.  Then they found the corpse of the missing voyageur.  His neck was broken; a barrel or some other object had probably struck him when the canoe overturned.

The storm was over and small patches of clear sky were visible as they paddled toward the beach adjacent to the fort.  It was about an hour until dusk.  Jean Baptiste looked at the shore as they approached, and thought that two of the figures waiting for them looked familiar.  As they got closer he was sure of it.  Sergeant Jacques Fournier and Gaspard Roziere.

The sergeant greeted Jean Baptiste and Etienne warmly, but Gaspard nearly refractured the cadet's still tender ribs with his welcoming bear hug. Then Gaspard turned to Dufort.

"I hope you still have my sash, you old pirate."

"Safely packed away. Of course, our canoe was the one that capsized, but I'm pretty sure one of the items we recovered from the lake contains your precious sash."

The sergeant directed two of the Ojibwa from the nearby village to aid two fusiliers he sent east along the shore to see if any more cargo could be recovered. Jean Baptiste and Etienne changed into dry clothes, and the cadet brought the dispatch case to the commandant's residence. He was informed that Captain Montigny had been feeling poorly and was confined to his bed. Jean Baptiste left the dispatch case and joined his three friends at the trader's store next to the church. The three looked to be several brandies ahead by the time he arrived.

"Gaspard," said the cadet cheerfully, "It is good to see you well. Humming Bird is apparently an excellent nurse."

"She is at that. In fact, she made such a positive impression on me, that she is the new Madame Roziere."

"Congratulations."

From the look on his face, a thought seemed to be forming in Etienne's mind. "Does the new Madame Roziere know about the old Madame Roziere?"

"Quiet!" Roziere forcefully whispered. "Very bad things would happen to me if Humming Bird knew about that Illinois wench. If I were lucky, she'd make me a gelding. Swept up in the passion of the moment as I was, I may have forgotten to mention one or two trivial details about my past.  Better that she doesn't know anyway.  Why spoil her obvious bliss?  By the way, I don't see that human arsenal La Pointe anywhere.  Didn't he return with you fellows?"

The mention of their deceased friend's name cast a pall over Jean Baptiste and Etienne.  They briefly explained the circumstances of his death.

"What a loss," said Gaspard.  "He was little more than a lad, well educated, and brave as God makes them.  A toast to the departed Rene La Pointe.  May he sleep well."

Jean Baptiste and Etienne brought the others up to date on events in Montreal, including the activities of the late Gilles Guyotte.

"Do you think his brother Claude, the clerk here at Michilimackinac, was involved in any way?" asked the sergeant.

"I've thought about that, and I doubt it.  It seems that Gilles set the ambushes in motion personally.  The only time we had trouble far from Montreal was last spring when we tried to reach Sioux country, and as you'll recall, Gilles was here at Michilimackinac at that time.  Claude had many other opportunities to cause mischief if that was his aim, but I'm convinced he was loyal."

The four friends spent many hours drinking and telling tall tales.

"I think I want to spread the good news in the Ojibwa village, particularly among the young females, that Etienne Dufort has returned.  Would you gentlemen like to accompany me?  Jean Baptiste, I'm sure the comely Blue Otter has been pining for your embrace."

The sergeant declined the invitation, as did

Roziere, the latter due to Humming Bird's close proximity.

"I'll go with you," said the cadet. "I'd like to spend a little more time with Blue Otter. This time I'm sober enough that I think I'll remember the experience."

## CHAPTER 36

Blue Otter seemed genuinely pleased to see Jean Baptiste, and encouraged the immediate repetition of the physical aspect of their relationship. As the woman eagerly tore off his clothes, the cadet remembered that so far, sex had been the only aspect of their relationship. He supposed that they could talk later.

Though he had been drinking, he was sober enough to thoroughly enjoy the activity this time. He surmised that Blue Otter was about nineteen or twenty and that she had done this sort of thing a number of times before. She was momentarily taken aback by all the fresh scars on his body; then she kissed each of them, and a number of other places as well. After undressing him, she had him sit on a bearskin and watch while she slowly removed her buckskin top and skirt. Her expert use of hand and mouth kept him totally focused on the task until he completed it to her satisfaction. Then they did it twice more. When he awoke in the morning, he was holding the Ojibwa woman in his arms. He remained still so that she would not awaken.

Though probably not thought beautiful by most,

Blue Otter had very large dark brown eyes and long, lustrous black hair. She had a slightly stocky build with well formed, large breasts and a well- rounded behind. The cadet was able to confirm this analysis of her attributes when she awoke and began to prepare something for breakfast. She elected to remain naked while performing this task. She glanced at him slyly while he was admiring her backside, and as a result, the morning meal was delayed for an hour.

When he was able to take his leave from Blue Otter, Jean Baptiste returned to the commandant's quarters to see if the captain had returned to duty. The sentry said Captain Montigny had recovered enough to return to work this morning, and the cadet was admitted into the commandant's office. As usual, the old man was attired in full uniform, the only hint of informality that he had hung his blue and white justaucorps on the back of a chair. Working in his blue veste, he was addressing a large stack of paper in the center of his desk. It appeared he had reviewed about a third of it so far.

"Ah, young Joubert! Welcome. Please sit down."

As Jean Baptiste complied, he got a good look at the captain and noticed that the old officer had aged significantly since he had seen him last summer.

"I know. I look like hell." Jean Baptiste started to protest, but Captain Montigny cut him off with a wave of his hand. "I'm too old for flattery. I'm concerned with how things are, not how I'd like them to be.

"I think this past winter was my last in the wilderness. I just completed a letter to the governor general asking to be relieved of my command here. The cold, snow and isolation are getting too difficult to handle at my age. I want to spend the few years I have left with my good wife.

"Enough of that. I was able to read the dispatches you brought, though several were a bit damp."

"Sorry sir. My canoe capsized in the storm yesterday."

"It's all right. Everything was legible. You probably don't know this, but one of the letters you brought from the governor general concerned your activities over the winter. My God, you were going home to rest and wound up fighting a war single-handed! Governor General Beauharnois seems very favorably impressed. Your career is off to an excellent start."

"Thank you sir. And while I've been gone, what has been happening here in the west? Has there been any news of the Fox?"

"Yes, I've gotten several reports this spring that the remnants of the Fox were heavily attacked over the winter by Hurons from Detroit and Iroquois from the Lake of Two Mountains mission. Apparently, Fox losses were again severe. There can't be many of them left. In some of this correspondence, the governor general also mentioned that the Hurons and mission Iroquois had set out to strike the Fox. He really seems to want them eliminated."

"Yes, even though he supposedly granted mercy to the tribe last September when they sent envoys to Montreal."

"The Fox probably deserve ill fortune more than any other tribe I've dealt with over the last forty years. They've been a pain in the ass for a long time. They didn't live up to agreements they made, probably because no matter what the chiefs agreed to, the young warriors did as they pleased. They were constantly fighting with the Illinois, the Sioux and the Ojibwa, tribes with whom we were allied or wanted to be allied. And, they killed a lot of Frenchmen in the bargain, often at the instigation of the English who could provide them with little effective help. In the final analysis, they picked the wrong side, and are now reaping the consequences of that error. Still...."

"The governor general's blood lust seems to be excessive," interjected the cadet.

"Orders that originate at Versailles or Montreal are only ink scratches on paper to the men who make them. For those of us that execute them, these orders result in old men and women starving in the snow and babies with their heads bashed in."

"What can a soldier do to both perform his duty, and retain his honor?" asked the cadet.

"An excellent question," responded the captain. "I'm not sure how to answer you. A soldier cannot pick and choose which orders to obey and which to ignore. He is not in the business of setting policy. But, the soldier is often able to interpret the orders he receives."

"What do you mean?" asked Jean Baptiste.

"Let's use the Fox as an example. We both know that the governor general would be greatly pleased if every Fox man, woman and child were dead. At the same time, he is unlikely to commit such specific draconian instructions to paper, undoubtedly preferring that there be no evidence that he ordered mass murder should such a happy event occur. The orders received by the commander in the field would be more general in nature, and thus subject to interpretation. The governor general might hope that his officers in the field kill every Fox, regardless of age or sex, but based on the actual written orders they receive, those officers probably would be able to do their duty and defeat the enemy without besmirching their honor by slaughtering non-combatants. Still, it's a very difficult situation, particularly if some of your brother officers share the governor general's blood lust."

"Thank you for sharing your views. I know my brother Maurice was uncomfortable with what happened on the Illinois prairie two years ago, and I am beginning to feel the same way about our more recent dealings with the Fox. You've given me much to think about."

"Now I've got an assignment for you. I know that over the past several years you have made many friends among the Ottawas living nearby. I want you to go to their camp and spend a few weeks, praising the help they have given us over time, and giving gifts to the families of the two warriors lost last year. What were their names?"

"The Turtle and Sky Singer."

"Oh yes. I remember The Turtle. He acted as a guide for me on at least two occasions. A very competent fellow. Take what you think appropriate from the king's stores. Make a list of what you take and return the list to me."

"Yes sir. My father also sent gifts to the two families, as did the governor general, who donated two excellent muskets."

Etienne and Gaspard agreed to accompany Jean Baptiste to the Ottawa village, but they only planned to stay for a few days. Then they were going to return to the fort, fill their canoe with trade goods, and do some trading with the Ojibwas of Lake Superior. Gaspard seemed to truly love Humming Bird, but was happy to get away for awhile.

"I'd be the happiest man alive if only Humming Bird and I had traveled to Michilimackinac alone. Unfortunately, my bride insisted that her mother, two sisters and a worthless brother-in-law accompany us as well. Instead of enjoying a blissful honeymoon, I'm constantly working my fingers to the bone to supply this mob with everything they require. This little trip to the Ottawas and the longer one to Lake Superior are just what I need."

"Gaspard, you are a shell of your former self," said Dufort. "I blame myself. When you were hurt and needed nursing, I looked for the most attractive wench I could find. I should have checked her family background. Now you've gone and married her, which is something I never anticipated, and so are stuck with all her relations. As a result, your priorities have become confused. It's even difficult to persuade you to get drunk anymore. Things are in a sorry state."

The two voyageurs discussed the pluses and minuses of the institution of matrimony as the three friends paddled to the Ottawa village, which was located a short distance west of Michilimackinac. Dufort considered himself a confirmed bachelor. Though he consorted with women at every opportunity, he had never considered settling down with just one. And though Etienne continued to chastise his friend for surrendering so much of his freedom, Jean Baptiste thought he detected a note of jealousy. Gaspard may have relinquished unfettered carousing, but had gained much in return. Though Gaspard complained about his trials at the hands of his in-laws, Jean Baptiste saw that

Roziere had found his woman, and was content.

Late in the afternoon of that warm June day, they approached their destination. Many canoes were beached on the shore, and they could see some of the Ottawa lodges back among the trees. Several of the many dogs that invariably inhabited an Indian village began barking at their approach, and a number of Ottawas came down to the shore to greet the newcomers. The three Frenchmen immediately recognized their old scout, Raven Wing, who greeted them with enthusiasm.

The proprieties were observed. Jean Baptiste told the village chief that he represented Captain Montigny, and that the captain was well pleased with his Ottawa friends and allies. The captain had sent two kegs of brandy from distant Onontio in Montreal. Onontio, Captain Montigny and the Joubert family also had presents for the families of The Turtle and Sky Singer, brave warriors who had died in the service of France.

The old chief, Yellow Robe, was well pleased. "We accept these gifts from our French friends, and are gratified that the bearer of these gifts is he who is known as the Deathless One, terror of the Iroquois."

*So, news of my activities of last winter has penetrated even to this wilderness,* mused Jean Baptiste. *Well, this kind of notoriety is not all bad. To be respected as a warrior is highly prized among the tribes. At least these Ottawas seem willing to grant me this respect in considerable measure.*

The gifts were distributed, and Raven Wing invited his three old comrades to stay with his family. His mother set about roasting bear meat when they returned to the family lodge.

"I calculate those two kegs of brandy are just

about the right amount," said Etienne to his two companions when Raven Wing left momentarily to get some tobacco. "If they don't drink it too fast, and spread it out among everyone, it's enough to get everyone feeling mellow, but not enough for them to go so crazy that they start cutting each other up for sport. That Captain Montigny is definitely an experienced officer."

As Dufort had predicted, the evening was a success. At one point, two warriors in their cups started getting belligerent toward one another. They were on the edge of the encampment, and no one was paying them particular attention, so Gaspard and Etienne quieted them with blows from two stout cudgels before any serious damage was done. The warriors awoke hours later with no recollection of what had happened and began interacting like the friends they were.

Etienne had spent the bulk of his time that evening making new female friends, but Gaspard contented himself with a few cups of brandy. "Etienne and I will be leaving in the morning," the latter told Jean Baptiste. If we don't get moving, old Paul La Combe will have gotten all the best furs from the Ojibwa before we get to Lake Superior."

"That's fine, Gaspard. I'll be staying here for a few weeks, and will see you when you return to the fort."

"It's time you learned to make one of the things that we build," said Raven Wing to Jean Baptiste. "We use your guns and steel hatchets and iron kettles, but you Frenchmen use our canoes. The Ottawa are the greatest canoe men, and I will teach you, my friend, how they are made."

The next day, after Etienne and Gaspard departed, Raven Wing and Jean Baptiste entered the woods southeast of the village to gather some of the raw materials needed in canoe building. The Ottawa explained that he and his companions had obtained the sheets of birch bark that they needed earlier in the spring. Because the Ottawa had lived in the vicinity a long time, birch trees were becoming scarce. Finding large, straight trees with bark of sufficient thickness and few blemishes had been a time consuming task.

On this day, Raven Wing sought the cedar needed for the canoe's thwarts, gunwales, ribs and planks and the roots of the black spruce tree that served as the bindings for the vessel. They had some immediate luck, locating the latter in swampy ground about a league from the village. They gathered a goodly supply to bring back for processing.

The cedar took more time. Many of the trees they located had too many knots, or were not straight enough to be of use. It took several days, and the assistance of several of Raven Wing's friends, to obtain an adequate quantity.

Jean Baptiste became engrossed in the work. Indian canoes were lightweight, but at the same time strong and capable of carrying heavy cargoes. In the wilds of North America, where frequent portages were necessary, they were the ideal vessels for the fur trade. As he learned to boil and bend the ribs, form the gunwales and shape the outer skin, the cadet wondered if this knowledge might not become useful someday if he tired of being a soldier. Though normally women's work, he also learned how to lash together the inner and outer pieces of the gunwale and stitch the birch bark. He wanted to understand the whole process. Raven Wing and the other Ottawas encouraged him and were pleased with his rapid progress.

## CHAPTER 37
Spring, 1732

Kiala knew that he was running out of options. He had gathered the remnants of his tribe, less than one hundred fifty people of all ages, and they had returned to their ancestral home along the Wisconsin River. He realized that this move was no solution to the tribe's precarious situation. The war chief had about fifty warriors at his disposal, but some of these veterans were a little too seasoned, while others were mere boys.

While situated on the Wisconsin, the remaining Foxes were vulnerable to attack from several directions, and tribes fielding many more warriors than the Fox could mount these attacks. The various Illinois tribes as well as the Winnebagos were especially feared at the moment. Kiala realized that his tribe's arrogance and aggressiveness over a period of many years had earned the enmity of its neighbors, but nothing could be done to change the past. It was his responsibility to deal with the situation as it existed, and take whatever steps he could to save the tribe from destruction.

Yesterday, Eagle Claw had returned from imprisonment in Montreal. Onontio had released the crippled envoy in order to bring a message to the Fox.

Governor General Beauharnois wanted to assure Kiala that he had no hand in the attack by the Hurons and mission Iroquois last winter. On the other hand, since Kiala had not surrendered to French authorities as Onontio had demanded, the Fox should no longer rely on French protection from the other tribes.

Eagle Claw's body had suffered from the long winter of confinement in the cold, damp cell, but his mind was as active as ever. "I do not trust Onontio at all. When I was released, he tried to act like he was concerned about the supposedly unauthorized attack on us by the Hurons and the Iroquois. I don't believe it. Last fall when Kicking Bear and I met with him, he made no attempt to hide his true feelings. Over the years we have done much to upset his plans; he would like to see us all dead."

Whether the governor general had organized the attack or not, the assault had damaged Kiala's plans for alliance with other tribes. The belief was widely held that Onontio had in fact coordinated the attack. Tribes such as the Kickapoos and the Mascoutens, while still sympathetic to the Fox cause, were now afraid to do anything to antagonize the powerful French leader. The Fox, once thought nearly invincible, had been disastrously defeated on several occasions. Tribes too overtly friendly could suffer the same fate.

Kiala reflected on the loss of Onontio's "protection." He concluded that the Fox tribe had in fact lost nothing, because the governor general's word meant nothing. At least he now knew what to expect.

The war chief needed to move his people to a more defensible position. He had been thinking for hours on this subject, and he just remembered something. Years ago, he had gone hunting with a party of Mascoutens. They had been tracking a bear when Kiala came upon a large lake located a day's march northwest of the Chicago portage. A narrow spit of land between the lake and a marsh would provide an excellent site for a fortified camp. After various discussions, agreement was reached and Kiala instructed his people to get ready to move.

Nicholas-Antoine Coulon De Villiers was forty-nine years old and had been a lieutenant in the marines for nearly seventeen years. He felt he was capable of great things, but in peacetime, promotion was very slow and until recently, he'd had few opportunities to distinguish himself. That changed two years ago when a tired Mascouten runner arrived at Fort St. Joseph and told him that a large band of Foxes were trapped out on the Illinois prairie. His participation in that great victory had brought him to the attention of the governor general. Then, more luck. On two occasions, the Fox had chosen to negotiate with him, and he had even escorted two Fox envoys to Montreal where they begged for mercy from Onontio.

The governor general had rewarded Lieutenant Villiers by placing him in command at Fort La Baye on Green Bay. This was probably the most challenging of the frontier posts because it was the closest to the traditional Fox homeland. Beauharnois had said that he was confident the lieutenant would deal appropriately with the Fox threat, and had hinted that a promotion to captain was a distinct possibility.

Recently, a small party of destitute Fox tribesmen arrived at Green Bay and asked for his mercy. Mindful of Beauharnois' instructions, but unwilling to openly slaughter these helpless supplicants before the watching Menominees and Winnebagos, he gave them a non-committal response. Rightfully afraid for their lives, the Foxes hastily departed.

Soon after they left, Villiers began to worry. If word reached Montreal that these Foxes had been allowed to leave unmolested, what would the governor general think? He nearly had that captaincy, but it was still possible to throw it away through some mischance. Lieutenant Villiers vowed to himself to act more vigorously the next chance that he got.

About ten leagues northwest of the Chicago portage, Kiala's people were now well established. It was early autumn. In a few short months, his people had labored long and hard to construct a camp surrounded by an earthen wall and a palisade. Borrowing from French construction techniques, they had even erected a blockhouse inside the fortification that was both a defensive position and an observation point (Kiala's wife noted that they were becoming more French than the French themselves). The women and the young had planted small fields of corn and other vegetables, and also combed the area for edible nuts and wild berries. As they were too weak to do otherwise, the Fox had to remain vigilant and await developments.

They did not have long to wait. Their old nemesis La Forest, the Huron chief from Detroit, organized a war party to finish the work of annihilation he had started the previous winter. His recruits were mostly Hurons, with a few Ottawas and Potawatomis from the Detroit area. Additional allies were sought among the Mascoutens and the more distant Illinois confederacy, as well as the Potawatomis living near Fort St. Joseph.

The new recruits swelled the numbers of the attackers, but weakened their resolve. Many of the Ottawas, Potawatomis and Mascoutens who joined the expedition had little desire to punish the Fox again. The general feeling among many of the Great Lakes tribes was that the Fox had been guilty of many misdeeds, but that they had already paid for them in full.

Only La Forest's Hurons and the Illinois, the latter ancient enemies of the Fox, attacked the entrenched camp with enthusiasm. The Fox repulsed the assault and sortied from their fort, inflicting casualties particularly on the Hurons. It was now apparent to La Forest that his Ottawa, Mascouten and Potawatomi allies would provide little real assistance with the fighting.

Meguesiliguy was one of the Potawatomi chiefs who participated in the expedition. His brother in law was Kicking Bear, one of the Fox defenders, and since he loved his sister and her husband dearly, Meguesiliguy had little enthusiasm for this fight. He proposed to negotiate a truce with the Fox and since the Huron and Illinois leaders knew they could expect little help from their "allies," they agreed.

This end to the fighting was certainly welcomed by Kiala, even though one facet of the agreement called for him to settle his tribe near one of the French posts the following spring. His enemies returned to their homes, at least for the present. Another bright note: Meguesiliguy had confirmed Kiala's suspicion that many of the tribes in the region felt Onontio's treatment of the Fox was excessively harsh. They might not be willing to openly side with Kiala's people against the French, but neither would they whole heartedly help the French defeat the Fox.

After La Forest and his men withdrew, Kiala had much to think about. He realized that the Fox were fortunate to still exist. They had many enemies, any one of which outnumbered them. If several of their foes combined, as was likely, and attacked the Fox with vigor, the tribe was surely doomed.

As the air grew cooler and the days shorter, Kiala and his advisors met frequently to discuss the tribe's future. They soon agreed on one thing: If the tribe was to survive, they needed one or more strong allies. Though they all had recently fought against Wisaka's people, the Potawaomis, the Kickapoos, the Mascoutens and the Sacs were all considered potential friends. Many members of all of these tribes had intermarried with the Fox, and the bonds of kinship remained strong. Meguesiliguy the Potawatomi had shown himself to be a friend during the recent negotiations, but his village on the St. Joseph River was too open to attack by La Forest's Hurons at Detroit. The Kickapoos and Mascoutens had formerly been staunch allies of the Fox, but though they no longer wished the Fox harm, they seemed afraid of Onontio's long reach.

That left the Sacs. Two years before, during the debacle on the Illinois prairie, members of that tribe had gone out of their way to save a number of Fox children, even at the risk of incurring their allies' wrath. In addition, this tribe resided near the French post at Green Bay, which was commanded by Lieutenant Villiers. Kiala felt that officer would deal fairly with his people. Though Kiala had no faith in Onontio's word, he considered Villiers an honorable man and had his envoys deal with the lieutenant on a number of occasions. Kiala had committed to resettling his people near a French post, where Onontio's marines could watch them. Why not make it Lieutenant Villiers' post? After additional discussion, it was agreed that envoys would be sent to the Sac camp and to Lieutenant Nicholas-Antoine Coulon de Villiers asking for permission to settle at Green Bay.

Kiala was relieved now that the decision was made. When the two peoples were united, they would be able to put two hundred warriors in the field. Not an overwhelming force, but the Sacs were hardy warriors as well. A potential enemy would realize that he would have a real fight on his hands if he struck the consolidated tribes at Green Bay.

It was now November. Kiala was determined to enjoy what were undoubtedly his last few months of freedom. He had long delayed placing himself in the hands of the French, but he knew that if his people were to have any chance of a respite from the fighting, he had to do so when the tribe moved to Green Bay. He felt he would get fair treatment, at least as long as he was in the hands of Lieutenant Villiers. After that, he was much less certain.

Once the envoys to Green Bay had received their instructions and departed, Kiala felt a calm that he had not experienced in months. The decision had been made. All that he could do had been done.

He now had some time for himself. He had lived for forty-six summers, but his family was small. Only his wife Deer Horn, a young son and himself. Three other children had been born to them, but all were dead, two as a result of the white man's disease called smallpox, and the last, his son Black Duck, had been killed by the

Ojibwas seven years ago. But Deer Horn still remained and she had been a good wife. And the boy was one of the few joys in the war chief's life.

This winter he and Deer Horn would work to acquire as many beaver pelts as possible. The tribe needed almost all of the goods offered by the white men. They'd had  little access to blacksmiths recently, men who could have repaired their guns and their tools. Some of these things could be repaired next spring at Fort La Baye, but many new guns, axes and kettles were needed, along with powder, shot and clothing. In order to buy these things, many pelts were needed.

That night, after they made love, Kiala held Deer Horn tight for a long time. He had not told her that their days together were numbered.

## CHAPTER 38
Spring, 1733

J ean Baptiste had just returned to Fort Michilimackinac two days ago. He had spent the winter with Raven Wing and his family at their winter camp far south of the straits. The cadet was able to tighten his belt an extra notch after a hard winter in which the Ottawas experienced several periods of near starvation. In mid February, supplies of dried corn meal, squash, blueberries and gooseberries ran short after a bear broke into one of the family's underground caches of food and gorged himself on the contents. A real crisis was averted when Raven Wing and Jean Baptiste were able to track the intruder and bring his meat home to replace the stolen foodstuffs.

What the winter had lacked in sumptuous repasts, it made up for through knowledge acquired. The cadet learned much about winter hunting techniques, information that he would undoubtedly draw upon later in his career. Raven Wing was a master with traps and snares, and in a short while, Jean Baptiste became reasonably proficient. He also learned various ways that the Indians caught the precious beaver so coveted by the white men, ranging from setting sophisticated traps to bludgeoning holes in the beaver's dwelling and killing the beasts as they tried to flee.

Captain Montigny was still at the fort, a full year after he had hoped to be relieved. He would only remain at Michilimackinac a few more days, however. This morning a large convoy of voyageurs arrived at the water gate. Aside from food and trade goods, the canoes brought replacement marines. Among the replacements was Jean-Baptiste-Rene Legardeur de Repentigny, the new commander of Fort Michilimackinac. Captain Montigny would be leaving soon, after packing his things and briefing the new man on the situation.

The trouble with Corporal Charbonneau resumed as soon as the cadet returned to the post. Normally, Jean Baptiste had little difficulty co-existing with people, but Charbonneau had never been able to forget losing his sergeant's rating, and continued to take out his frustration on the cadet. Jean Baptiste had even fought the bigger man twice, man to man, without regard to rank. The cadet hoped that regardless of the outcome, these fights would clear the air. Each of them won once; after each fight, Charbonneau's antagonism abated for a time, but then returned.

"Joubert!" It was the corporal's now familiar bellow. "I've got three men heading southwest for firewood. I want you along as well. The others have assigned duties when all of you return with the logs. You, however, do not, so you can chop them into useable pieces and stack them next to the barracks."

"Yes, Corporal." *If nothing else, all the extra work I get from Charbonneau is making me much stronger. And my old wounds bother me very infrequently.*

Jean Baptiste headed for the barracks to change for this work detail. On the way he was intercepted by a marine in the full uniform the captain required of men on duty at headquarters. "Cadet St. Croix, Captain Montigny requires your presence."

Jean Baptiste followed the fusilier to the commandant's quarters, and entered the now familiar room where the captain transacted business.

"Captain Repentigny, I'd like you to meet Cadet St. Croix," said Captain Montigny as the cadet entered the room.

Captain Repentigny was a tall, thin officer whom the cadet guessed to be about forty years of age. He greeted young Joubert warmly. "So you are the man who handled the Iroquois so roughly two winters ago. That exploit is known throughout the service, but Captain Montigny tells me you are diligent as well as brave. According to him, the time you have spent cementing relations with the Ottawas will prove invaluable when next they are needed in time of war."

"Captain Montigny has been generous with his time and advice, giving me the benefit of his experience. Though I enjoy being with the Ottawas and would gladly spend time in their camps and villages anyway, the captain has always stressed the benefits we realize by keeping the tribes on friendly terms. As hunters in time of peace and scouts and warriors in time of war, their service to the king is invaluable."

"How old are you now, Jean Baptiste?" asked Captain Montigny.

"I will be twenty next month," replied the cadet.

"Your whole life ahead of you, and I must say, you've made a promising start. Captain Repentigny brought dispatches from Montreal when he arrived this morning. Much of it is undoubtedly the kind of routine paperwork that I've grown to detest over the years. Lists of supplies sent compared to lists of supplies requested, staffing authorizations compared to staffing requests and so forth.

"One document the good captain brought caught my attention immediately. Your exploits against the Fox and the Iroquois in 1731 brought you favorably to the attention of the governor general. Monsieur Beauharnois recommended your promotion last year, and he received word late last fall that his recommendation had been approved. Because of the winter, he was only able to forward the news now. When you arrived, I addressed you as Cadet St. Croix. That was an error. You are now Ensign Jean Baptiste Joubert, Sieur de St. Croix."

Jean Baptiste knew that his cheeks reddened as he stammered a response. Both captains shook his hand heartily. As he turned to leave, Captain Montigny called him back and said "Here, take this. I have an extra one."

The new ensign was in a daze as he left the commandant's quarters and headed back to the barracks. He had almost reached the entrance when he heard, "Joubert! You good for nothing slacker. I thought I told you to join the men cutting trees for firewood. They've been waiting by the land gate for a quarter hour. When you get back, you'll regret...."

Corporal Charbonneau's remarks were cut short when Jean Baptiste turned to face him. Around the young man's neck was the highly polished golden gorget of an officer.

Lieutenant Villiers couldn't be in a better mood if he'd just been awarded the Cross of the Order of St. Louis. After laboring in obscurity for many years, it seemed Villiers' luck had changed. A few weeks ago, Kiala and his entire band arrived outside Fort La Baye at Green Bay. They asked permission to settle among their kinsmen, the Sacs, and Kiala himself surrendered to Villiers to ensure the good conduct of his people.

What an opportunity to have his name linked to the final downfall of the Fox, a people who had been a major thorn in the side of the French for more than twenty years. It was decided that Kiala would be brought to Montreal and turned over to Governor General Beauharnois. How grateful would the governor general be to the man who brought in Kiala? Kiala had been the cause of many very unpleasant letters that Beauharnois had received from his superior, the Minister of Marine. At times, it had seemed that the governor general's position was in jeopardy because of the treachery and homicidal fury of these savages. Villiers assumed that the governor general would be very grateful to the man who delivered Kiala.

The lieutenant arranged for himself, five marines and four voyageurs to escort Kiala and three of his advisors east in four canoes. The brothers Kicking Bear and Eagle Claw, the envoys who had traveled to Montreal in 1731 to beg Onontio's mercy, were two of these advisors. In addition, Kiala's wife insisted on accompanying her husband to an uncertain fate. Villiers had been moved when Kiala surrendered and Deer Horn, his wife, refused to return to the safety of the Sac village.

"My place is with you; my family will care for our son." she had said simply, and none of Kiala's arguments had the slightest effect on her decision. Finally, the war chief assented to her wishes, though he was torn between happiness at not being alone and apprehension about his loyal wife's ultimate destiny.

This morning the convoy reached Michilimackinac, where Villiers wanted to make a short stop to pick up supplies. He had his men keep a close eye on the Fox prisoners so that they would come to no harm at the hands of the Ottawas or Ojibwas living nearby. Both of these tribes had fought the Fox even longer than had the French, and many of the local warriors had unpaid blood debts to collect.

News of Kiala's arrival soon spread throughout the fort, and Jean Baptiste hastened to see his old adversary. Kiala's party stood on shore near their canoes, closely guarded by Villiers' men from Green Bay. Based on the black looks directed toward the Foxes by a number of the Ojibwa and Ottawa warriors who had begun to collect on the beach, Jean Baptiste realized that Villiers' caution had been warranted. In fact, to ensure that the Fox had adequate protection, the ensign called to the guard at the water gate to send out four more marines to help.

At the sound of the young ensign's voice, Kiala looked his way. The war chief approached, followed closely by two marines.

"You are the youth who was involved in the ambush on the Wisconsin two years ago, are you not? And later that same year, one of the ones who captured a boy from my village?"

"Yes, I was present both times."

"I see the French have made you an officer, despite your youth. I have increased respect for them. Tell me something if you would. I have wondered about this for two years. The leader of your party on the Wisconsin warned you just before the ambush was sprung. How did he know something was wrong?"

"Our leader was my brother Maurice. Our Ottawa scout, the man you killed, should have left a sign letting us know no danger was near. There was no such sign."

"Your brother did well. The French should have made him a great chief."

"No, he was wounded in that fight and lost his arm. His days as a warrior are over."

"I am sorry, but I was repaid the next time we met. My shoulder still aches when the weather turns chill and damp."

Just then Lieutenant Villiers returned to the beach, and seeing the crowd of Ottawas and Ojibwas growing larger, he ordered his party back into the canoes. Two packs of pemmican were loaded from the storehouse at Michilimackinac, then the journey to Montreal was resumed.

When Villiers arrived in Montreal in late June, the reception he received from Governor General Beauharnois was all he had hoped for, and more. His superior was overjoyed to at last have the hated Fox chief in his power. Plans were made to send all the Fox prisoners except one to Quebec where they would be imprisoned prior to their being deported to the French West Indies. Once at that final destination, they would be sold into slavery.

Eagle Claw, the envoy who had been imprisoned in Montreal in 1731 and 1732, was to be returned to his people this time. He was to inform the Fox about the fate of those who opposed Onontio. His brother Kicking Bear would accompany Kiala to prison.

Villiers would bring Eagle Claw back to Green Bay, but now as a captain. Official notification of his promotion had been received at Montreal in April. Beauharnois had sent the news to Green Bay, but Villiers had left that post with Kiala before notice of his promotion arrived. How much better to have the governor general impart the happy tidings personally!

Before Captain Villiers departed Beauharnois' presence, the governor general took him aside for some private instructions.

"Captain, to be frank, I am not pleased that you allowed Kiala's people to settle among the Sacs. The Foxes are simply not to be trusted. They continued to be a pain in the ass even when they were whittled down to a handful. In league with the Sacs, their numbers are much more imposing.

"When you return to Fort La Baye, gather as many of the tribes friendly to us as you can. Go to the Sac village and demand that the remaining Foxes surrender. They are to be sent to Montreal as well, where they will be split into bands too small to be troublesome, and settled at the various missions. If they refuse, kill them all. Do you understand?"

"Yes sir. Do not be concerned. Your orders will be carried out to the letter. The Foxes are now few in number. They will not be a problem."

That evening, the governor general composed a long letter to the Minister of Marine, assuring him that the long standing Fox problem had been resolved at last.

**CHAPTER 39**
Late Summer, 1733

J ean Baptiste had misgivings about the present mission, and he was sure Captain Villiers, the commander of the force that had been assembled at Michilimackinac, felt the same. That officer, who Jean Baptiste had first seen at the governor general's residence at Montreal, had arrived at the fort by the straits in July, and had immediately gone into conference with Captain Repentigny. Villiers seemed to be an officer on the rise, especially since bringing Kiala to Montreal earlier in the year, and it was expected that momentous events would follow in his wake.

After several days of closed-door discussions, Captain Repentigny called a meeting of the fort's officers. Captain Villiers was the main speaker.

"Gentlemen, I've been given an assignment of the greatest importance by the governor general. As you know, the Fox leader Kiala has surrendered and been brought east. His tribe has been living among the Sacs at Green Bay. Governor General Beauharnois has charged me with the task of effecting the surrender of the remaining Fox tribesmen. They are to be sent east as well, where they will be split into small parties and distributed among the various missions. Their lot is hard, but keep in mind that they brought this on themselves.

"Captain Repentigny and I have been discussing the situation. He has graciously agreed to assist with this assignment. Though he has been a captain longer than I, I will be in charge since the governor general assigned the Fox relocation to me. In order to ensure that the Fox comply without resistance, we have decided to assemble a large force at Michilimackinac prior to making our demands on the Fox. If our strength is sufficient, even the Fox should realize that opposition is futile. We will recruit men among tribes not sympathetic to the Fox cause, mainly Ottawas, Ojibwas and Menominees. We plan to leave here at the beginning of September. By then many of the voyageurs will have returned to Michilimackinac from their summer trading. We will take as many of them as possible. Marines from Michilimackinac as well as my post at Green Bay will also be involved. Joining us will be several young officers from the Montreal garrison who arrived here with me and should benefit from this experience in the field." As the captain spoke these last words, he gestured toward five young officers standing to his left. All were smartly dressed in well-tailored blue and white uniforms. They seemed eager to get started.

"Captain Repentigny has told me that the contingent of marines from the straits will be under the command of Ensign St.Croix, who will also act as liaison to the Ottawa volunteers. Ensign St. Croix, you will be assisted by two of the officers from Montreal, Ensigns Hocquart and Lery. They will aid you in gathering the necessary supplies, canoes, bateaux, whatever is needed.

The other officers from Montreal will work with Captain Repentigny and myself as we gather Indian allies. Are there any questions, gentlemen?"

"Yes sir," said Jean Baptiste. "How do you think the Sacs will react to our demand that their kinsmen surrender?"

The captain looked uncomfortable and hesitated before he responded. "There is always the possibility that force will be necessary. We will be prepared for that eventuality. But I have dealt with the Fox for a long time, and have enjoyed some successes. I believe boldness will carry the day without any need to resort to arms."

Jean Baptiste did not believe him. If the captain really felt that the desired ends could be achieved without fighting, it is doubtful that the time and expense necessary to assemble a large force of Frenchmen and Indians would be expended, especially because once Indian allies are raised for war, they are not easy to control. The captain probably thought that significant coercion would be necessary, regardless of the wishful thinking he expressed to this group.

Jean Baptiste decided he would try to recruit Etienne and Gaspard for the expedition when they returned from their summer trading at Lake Superior. In the meanwhile, he had plenty to keep him busy. He selected Sergeant Fournier to gather the weapons, ammunition and food that would be needed. The sergeant picked six marines who would help with the preparations and accompany the expedition, including Jean Baptiste's old friend Corporal Charbonneau, who certainly had his shortcomings, but was literate and a hard worker.

Adrien Hocquart and Ignace Lery were both eighteen years of age and members of prominent families, the former from Quebec and the latter from Three Rivers. Adrien had probably been an excellent student; his reading, writing and arithmetic skills were excellent, and he proved a great help to Sergeant Fournier. Jean Baptiste took Ignace, the more athletic but less studious of his proteges, when he visited Raven Wing at the Ottawa encampment near the fort.

The captains had already visited the Ottawa camp, and many Ottawa warriors had decided to accompany the expedition. Naturally Raven Wing was at the top of the list; he still held grudges against the Fox for the deaths of his uncle, The Turtle and his friend Sky Singer. Raven Wing welcomed Ensign Lery and agreed to spend the month before the departure teaching the young man the Ottawa tongue. Ignace would then be able to help with the Ottawas when Jean Baptiste's duties called him elsewhere.

One day in mid-August, Jean Baptiste and Sergeant Fournier were discussing how many swivel guns to bring to Green Bay when a large pair of arms reached around the young ensign from behind and hoisted him in the air.

"Young sir, your most devoted helpers have come back home," boomed the familiar voice of Etienne Dufort. "Gaspard and I returned early from Lake Superior when we heard you boys were getting ready to tangle with the Fox again."

"Where did you hear that?"

"Among the Ojibwas on Lake Superior. Word traveled from the Ojibwas living here near the fort. You can bet that the Fox are aware of what is coming, because we saw a number of Sac traders from the Green Bay area dealing with the Ojibwas as well. I hope we're bringing a lot of men with us, because the Sacs fortify a camp as well as the Fox do, and they've had a lot of time to prepare."

"Captain Villiers told the officers that he does not expect a fight."

"He's dreaming," responded Gaspard while he shook the ensign's hand in greeting, as well as the sergeant's. "My wife's people are originally from Green Bay, though many of them have moved here where they can live from the sweat of my brow. At any rate, the Menominees still at Green Bay say that the Sacs and Foxes have bonded so that they are almost like one tribe. It is unlikely that the Sacs will stand by and do nothing while their brothers are rounded up and then scattered. Villiers is no fool and he's worked with those people a long time. He has to know that this is going to be trouble."

"Whatever he knows, or at least suspects, he's keeping to himself," said Jean Baptiste. It's my job to prepare the expedition, and I intend to prepare it like we're going to war. By the way, rumor has it that only about fifty Fox warriors remain. How many do the Sacs have?"

"More than one hundred and fifty," replied Roziere. "From what I've heard, the tribes being recruited are being told that if there is a fight, all they have to worry about are the handful of Fox remaining. Many of them don't know that the Sacs and the Foxes are living together in one village, and that instead of fifty warriors, they may have to face more than two hundred."

"Add those extra swivels to the list," Jean Baptiste instructed the sergeant.

The big day had arrived at last. Jean Baptiste and the other marines assigned to the expedition had worked far into the night loading bateaux with packs of pemmican, kegs of brandy and gunpowder, crates of extra muskets and all the other material needed by this little army. He and his men were exhausted, but the job had been well done. The young ensign had done his duty; the mission would not fail for want of supplies. Jean Baptiste was not, however, at all certain that he wished the mission to succeed.

Yesterday, Captain Villiers called a meeting for all the officers involved in the expedition to Green Bay. Plans for organization of the flotilla, where to assemble in case the vessels were scattered by a storm, the first night's campsite, and various other issues were addressed. As the assembly was ending Ensign Hocquart asked a question that was on the minds of many.

"Sir, you have told us that you do not expect the Fox to resist. If that assessment is incorrect and we have a fight on our hands, what are our objectives? Are we to attempt to capture as many of the Foxes as possible, so that they can be divided up among the mission tribes?"

Again Captain Villiers hesitated before he responded. Jean Baptiste was sure that the commander was about to impart unwelcome news, and the ensign was not wrong.

"The governor general gave me specific instructions in the event that the Fox resist deportation. We are to kill them all, without regard to sex or age. But I emphasize that I do not believe it will come to that. We have assembled our impressive armada specifically to demonstrate to the Fox that resistance would be futile. A brave front gentlemen, and we can realize our objective without bloodshed."

Jean Baptiste returned to his quarters sick at heart. Governor General Beauharnois was still determined to exterminate the Fox. Captain Villiers may have deluded himself into thinking the Fox would give up without a fight, but Jean Baptiste didn't believe that would happen, and he was sure the governor general didn't believe that either. He wanted the Fox to fight, so that they would all be killed.

Ensign St. Croix called his marines together, and got them started with the final loading of the bateaux. Before he joined them, he met with Etienne and Gaspard.

"Villiers actually said we are to kill them all if they fight?" asked Roziere. "In my opinion, the Fox will fight no matter what the odds. To surrender means the end of the Fox as a distinct tribe, and they will never agree to that. They will fight and fight hard. Though they undoubtedly don't know about Beauharnois' instructions, they have experienced his mercy on previous occasions, and will probably fight to the last. Be prepared, comrades. This encounter promises to be bloody."

The September morning of the departure was cool and bright, with a brisk breeze from the west. The Menominees had been assigned to be the lead contingent, and Gaspard left the shore near the watergate at the head of forty warriors, many of them his in-laws. Humming Bird stood solemnly near the gate as her husband pushed off in his canoe. Roziere was particularly resplendent now that he was wearing his orange, yellow and black sash again, which nicely complemented his tuque, which was liberally adorned with hawk feathers. Humming Bird had made him a beaded deerskin shirt, which he wore over a fine linen one she had purchased for him. His warriors had also taken pains with their appearances. Their faces and bodies were painted in a variety of red, yellow, green or black designs. Their hair, whether in scalplocks or worn long and straight, was carefully groomed with feathers, bells and various ornaments attached.

Next came the Ottawas, seventy in number. Ensign Lery rode in the first canoe with Raven Wing. Though not a scholar, he had learned the Ottawa language quickly, and he and Raven Wing had become friends in the last month, enjoying several hunting and fishing trips while they learned to communicate. Jean Baptiste rode in the last Ottawa canoe so that he could be near the supply bateaux that followed.

The French contingent was next, transporting all the necessary supplies and equipment. In addition to the two captains and most of the young officers from Montreal, this section included Sergeant Fournier's marines and about sixty voyageurs who had volunteered for the trip after returning from their summer trading.

The largest body of men formed the rear guard of the flotilla. The Ojibwas numbered more than one hundred in all. Etienne Dufort had been selected to act as liaison, due to his close association with many of the female members of that tribe. In fact, while Jean Baptiste and his marines worked through the night with the supplies and equipment, Etienne spent a long night cementing relations with several of the Ojibwa women. Like Jean Baptiste, he was tired, and also like his young friend, he felt the job was well done.

## CHAPTER 40

The expedition reached Green Bay without incident and joined forces with the garrison of Fort La Baye. Counting friendly warriors from the Green Bay region, Captain Villiers now had a force of over four hundred with which to confront the Fox. Four of the captain's sons served with him at the fort, and the eldest, Ensign Nicolas-Antoine Coulon de Villiers, Jr. gave the expedition's officers an update on the local situation.

"The Sac village, where the Fox are living, is located on the south bank of the Fox River where it runs into Green Bay. Since the Fox arrived, they have caused no trouble, and we have even done a brisk business with them. They apparently enjoyed excellent beaver hunting last winter, because they brought a lot of fur with them when they arrived.

"About six weeks ago, we noticed that the Sacs and their Fox guests began strengthening the palisade that surrounds the village. We did not have sufficient strength to intervene. Unfortunately, the defenses are now formidable, and include a strong earthen wall in addition to the original wooden palisade."

Jean Baptiste and the other junior officers were dismissed while Captain Villiers and Captain Repentigny deliberated. He returned to the section of Green Bay shoreline where the expedition had landed and gave orders for the unloading and storage of their supplies and equipment. As the work progressed, Etienne approached and the two friends walked off down the beach while Jean Baptiste told Dufort about the officers' meeting.

"Well, what do you think? Will the Fox fight or surrender?"

The portly voyageur thought for awhile before responding. "It's lucky for you that you're 'the Deathless One.' As for me, nothing is preventing me getting my butt shot off, and I'm certain there will be many opportunities for that to happen in the next few days. I think that we should start getting serious about finding Rene's brother and that Carthaginian gold before we test our luck one too many times."

As they talked, Corporal Charbonneau walked up to the pair, stood at attention, and announced that Captain Villiers was looking for Ensign St. Croix. Jean Baptiste returned and saw that the officers had reconvened.

"Gentlemen, Captain Repentigny and I have determined on a course of action. My eldest son will lead sixty voyageurs and Menominees around to the far side of the Sac village. They will choose a position upstream on the river from the village, dig in and ensure that the enemy cannot escape via this back door. The main force under Captain Repentigny will remain here under arms. I will approach the village with a handful of men and demand that the Fox surrender. Several of my sons and my son-in-law Francois Duplessis will accompany me. We are well known to both the Sacs and the Foxes, and I doubt they would fire on us. Ensign St. Croix, you will be in charge of a detail of six marines from Fort La Baye and will act as our escort."

Before departing with the blocking force, Ensign Villiers located the six marines Jean Baptiste was to command. Though all were privates, they had the look of men who had seen many years of service. All wore their blue vestes and fatigue caps, along with leather leggings and moccasins. Though the uniforms of several had obviously seen hard service, the weapons of all were clean and brightly shined. Each man carried a hatchet in place of the regulation bayonet. Jean Baptiste sent one of the men to Sergeant Fournier to obtain extra ammunition.

"Men, I'm not sure what to expect. We are to accompany Captain Villiers to the Sac camp, where he will demand the surrender of the Foxes living there. The captain expects no trouble, but we will assume the worst. I have sent for additional powder and shot. Reload your muskets; I don't want any misfires. We will be leaving soon. Good luck."

With Captain Villiers at its head, the small party of Frenchmen marched to the Sac village. As they approached, they saw a number of Sac chiefs including Tall Elk, waiting for them outside the palisade of the town.

"We have come to demand the surrender of the Foxes who reside inside your walls," said Villiers. "Onontio demands this, and I have come to do his bidding."

"Why does Onontio wish this?" asked Tall Elk. "Kiala has surrendered to you and his people live here in peace. You granted permission for them to live here yourself. Why do you now change your mind?"

"I allowed them to live here while I learned Onontio's wishes. Now I know. They must surrender and accompany us back to Montreal."

The Sac chiefs moved to the right about thirty paces to discuss the matter, but reached no decision on a course of action. Villiers told them that he had men stationed upstream on the Fox to block any escape, and that Captain Repentigny was nearby with a powerful force to ensure compliance with Onontio's demands.

"Return to your village and do as I have bid you, or I will go in there myself and get the Fox as Onontio commands."

Jean Baptiste listened to these negotiations with some amazement. The Sacs were a proud and undefeated people. He understood that Villiers' bold front was meant to intimidate them, but like most Indians, they possessed a large measure of pride, and the captain's disregard of normal etiquette might be pushing them too far.

Villiers approached him. "Ensign St. Croix, send a man to Captain Repentigny, and have the captain surround the village."

Jean Baptiste sent one of his fusiliers and then walked among the remaining men, talking to them quietly, trying to keep them calm in this decidedly nervous time. He gave permission to smoke, and he noticed that most of these men wore their pipe bowls hanging from a thong around their necks. The stems were attached after being retrieved from a waist pouch. It was strange to notice these details at such a time.

One other thing the ensign noticed was that a number of Sac warriors, perhaps thirty or more had gathered at the entrance to the village. They were well armed and began hurling insults at the French, as well as saying that they would never desert their kinsmen. No official reply was made to the French demands, and Villiers was growing impatient.

After additional delay, Captain Villiers decided that he had waited long enough. "Come on men," he called over his shoulder as he stepped purposefully toward the entrance to the village.

At the gate, the throng of menacing warriors had grown even larger. They cursed the captain, a man whom they had regarded as a friend, but a man who had gone back on his word. Tall Elk appeared and urged the French to withdraw. Jean Baptiste could see that the captain was becoming really agitated; the ensign moved his little party of fusiliers off to the left, where they had an unblocked view of the hostile crowd.

Finally, Villiers decided that the time for decisive action was at hand. He moved straight to the gate. Jean Baptiste ordered his men to prepare to fire, though the advance of Villiers, his sons and Duplessis blocked their clear field of fire. The captain and his sons tried to shoulder their way through the throng. Suddenly, several shots were fired and Pierre Coulon de Villiers fell dead right beside his father. The enraged captain fired his pistol into the face of a Sac who was aiming a blow with his hatchet. More shots were fired, one striking the captain in the chest.

Jean Baptiste could not order his men to fire, because the remaining Villiers men were in the way. He ordered his little band forward, and the six marines, swinging hatchets and musket butts, temporarily cleared the ground where their comrades had fallen. Jean Baptiste saw at once that the captain was dead. He had a hole the size of a small fist blown completely through his body.

"Grab the captain and Pierre and pull back!" As the corpses were dragged away by their arms, Jean Baptiste and two marines provided covering fire. One of the men, a fusilier named Roubeau, was shot in the leg and the wrist, but kept firing until they had withdrawn out of range.

Captain Repentigny had been overseeing the movement of the men as they surrounded the Sac town. When the firing started, he rushed to the sound of the guns, bringing several of the Montreal ensigns, twenty voyageurs and about fifty warriors from several tribes. The captain saw Jean Baptiste and his marines firing at the warriors near the gate, and brought his reinforcements at the run.

"My God, what have we done?" was all Repentigny could say when he saw the bodies of Captain Villiers and his son. He had no time for further reflection, for at that moment, more than a hundred Sacs and Foxes came boiling out of the gate and ran directly at the captain and his disorganized men. There was no time to prepare a proper defense. The captain drew his saber, fired his pistol at the oncoming horde, and then led the marines, voyageurs and Indian allies forward. The Sacs and Foxes fired a volley before the two sides came to grips; then a brief hand to hand combat ensued.

Jean Baptiste was reassured to see that Dufort and some of his Ojibwas were nearby. He had time for only a quick glance; he turned in time to see a Sac raise his war club for a fatal blow. He was able to block the stoke with his musket. The ensign then knocked his opponent to the ground with his musket butt, and crushed the Sac's skull with an additional blow. Individual combats surrounded him. Dufort was straddling a Fox while he strangled the man. A Sac nearly beheaded one of the Ojibwas with one swing of his hatchet. Captain Repentigny, his sword broken, wrestled on the ground with a burly Fox warrior. As the Fox held the captain still, two Sacs stabbed him repeatedly.

Then they were gone. The Sac and Fox warriors broke off the fight and retreated back to their fortified village. Their sortie had been a success. Captain Repentigny was dead, as was Ensign Adrien Hocquart and another of the young officers from Montreal whose name Jean Baptiste did not even know. Three of the voyageurs were dead and many others wounded. The Indian allies had suffered proportionately.

"Well, Sir," wheezed Etienne as he rose unsteadily to his feet, "What do we do now?"

"I believe that Ensign Villiers is the most senior officer remaining. He's with Gaspard at the blocking position upriver. Will you go and tell him what has happened, Etienne? I'll stay here and try to organize a defense."

When he heard about the deaths of his father and brother, Ensign Villiers abandoned his position on the river and rejoined the main body of the expeditionary force. Though casualties had been heavy, and the Indian allies, now completely aware that the Sacs would support the Fox to the end, were wavering in their enthusiasm, Villiers was determined to avenge his dead family members.

Inside the fortified village, the Sacs and Foxes were dismayed by their success. For years, Onontio had nurtured a great hatred of the Fox. Now, two of his fort commanders had been killed in a single battle. The governor general's anger would be multiplied many times, and he would never cease seeking their destruction. Now not only the Fox, but also their Sac allies would be marked for death. The remaining Fox leaders spoke far into the night with Tall Elk and the other Sac chiefs. All were in agreement that the combined tribes must go west and leave the lands where Onontio's traders and soldiers held sway.

Wolf, the young Fox warrior captured by Jean Baptiste years before, scouted upriver and found that the French had abandoned the position blocking their escape. He reported his discovery and that settled the matter. At the earliest possible moment the Sac and Fox tribes would move west of the Mississippi.

Three days after the battle, Raven Wing reported that the enemy village was empty. Before dawn, the enemy had fled upriver. Ensign Villiers was livid. He ordered an immediate pursuit, even though it was obvious that the Menominees and the Ojibwas in particular had lost their ardor for this particular fight.

Orders were orders, and after Etienne and Gaspard gave particularly impassioned pleas to their charges, the entire force broke camp and set out in pursuit. On the afternoon of the fourth day after the battle, the French and their allies caught up to their quarry. Or rather, their quarry allowed themselves to be caught. The Sac and Fox warriors were dug in along both banks of the river and waited for their pursuers while their families continued toward safety up the Fox.

Ensign Villiers led several costly assaults against the Sac and Fox positions. His remaining two brothers were wounded and two more of the young officers from Montreal were killed. Ignace Lery was grazed in the head by a musket ball, but Raven Wing and two other Ottawas dragged the unconscious officer to safety. Many were killed or wounded on both sides before Ensign Villiers called a halt to the fighting and the battered French force retreated to Green Bay.

## EPILOGUE

The deaths of Captains Villiers and Repentigny, along with those of the other officers, many of whom were members of prominent families, proved intensely embarrassing for Governor General Beauharnois. Onontio had been so indiscreet as to assure the court that the Fox threat was at an end. Now it was obvious not only that the Fox had survived, but that the French had to deal with the Sacs as well. Beauharnois was informed that Louis XV was displeased.

But the governor general was an experienced politician, as able to deflect blame as garner praise. He searched for someone to shoulder the burden, and found the ideal scapegoat —the late Captain Villiers. Beauharnois wrote that the recent calamity was caused by lack of caution on the captain's part, especially in view of the "gentle measures" that he, the governor general had instructed Villiers to adopt to achieve the subjugation of the tribe. He remained governor general another fourteen years.

Of course, someone had to pay for the disaster. Though the Fox continued to have trouble with the French on an intermittent basis, they were beyond Onontio's effective reach as long as they stayed west of the Mississippi.  But Beauharnois and the French court already had the ideal victim in hand.

Kiala and Kicking Bear had been imprisoned at Quebec before the battle at Green Bay.  Over the winter of 1733-34, both contracted serious illnesses in the cold prison cells.  Kicking Bear, the elder of the fearless brothers that Kiala employed as envoys, died.  As compensation for its dead officers, the French court considered executing Kiala, even though he had not been present when these Frenchmen were killed.  But cooler heads prevailed.  The Fox war chief's punishment would be more protracted.  Arrangements were made to have him sent to the West Indies where he would be sold into slavery.

The French population of Martinique was familiar with the background of this man.  The determined opposition of the Fox tribe to French influence over a period of many years had been well documented, as had Kiala's role in the struggle.  When he and his wife were placed on the auction block and bids for their purchase were entertained, none were forthcoming.

The wealthy planters on the island did not appreciate having the Canadians drop this problem in their laps.  Kiala had led his people with skill and daring in their war against the French.  He had no followers on Martinique, but his very presence was a reminder that resistance to French authority was possible.  The large landowners wanted him removed before he became the focus of a revolt by the substantial slave population.

The Governor of Martinique, the Marquis de Champigny, found himself unable even to give these troublesome slaves away.  Buckling to pressure, he at last decided that Kiala and Deer Horn should be abandoned on the inhospitable north coast of South America.

On a sultry afternoon in May 1735, Kiala and his wife were rowed ashore and dropped on the beach. They were near the mouth of the Orinoco River; dense jungle loomed nearby. The sailors left little in the way of food or equipment needed for survival. The two Foxes watched the long boat return to the French frigate; then they turned, entered the jungle and disappeared from history.

The great war chief's memory, however, lived on. In 1750, word reached the new Governor General of New France, the Marquis de La Jonquiere, that a new leader was also making his presence felt among the Fox. Though the tribe would never regain it's former power and influence, this young man was a living reminder of their past glory and will to survive. Raised by kinsmen because his parents were no more, he adopted his father's name as he neared maturity. He was called Kiala.